COME HERE, KITTEN

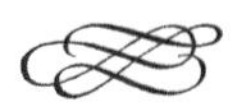

EMILIA ROSE

Emilia Rose

ISBN: 978-1-7346223-6-2

Cover by: The Book Brander

Editing by: Jovana Shirley, Unforeseen Editing, www.unforeseenediting.com

Proofreading by: Zainab M., Heart Full of Reads Editing Services and Kayla Lutz

Beta reading by: Zainab M., ErotiqueWrites, Allison Marie, J.M. Johnson, Leshaé Scheepers

Emilia Rose

emiliarosewriting@gmail.com

CHAPTER 1

AURORA

"Aurora!" Mom shouted from downstairs. "I don't want you sneaking out tonight while your father and I are gone."

I pulled Tony's *Sanguine Wilds* sweatshirt, which I'd stolen from him, over my head to mask my scent and opened my bedroom window. "I know!" I said.

She'd told me that every night this week, and I *definitely hadn't* left the house once—or so she thought. As far as she knew, I was the perfect little girl who she had been shaping for years to take her place when she stepped down as alpha; the girl who trained relentlessly during the day by herself because her mom didn't allow her to train with the bigger wolves; the girl who just sat in her room all night, studying textbook after textbook about the most successful alphas in history. Their strengths. Their weaknesses. Their every move.

"I'm being serious, A," she said, her voice stern and powerful. "Don't leave this house."

I gazed at my cat, Ruffles, who stopped mid-lick to give me a sassy eye roll from her side of my bed while I crawled out of the window, hanging on to the wooden windowsill with just my upper body. "I won't!"

Moonlight flooded in through my window, illuminating Ruffles's gray fur. I blew her a kiss and let go of the window, falling two stories to the ground. With a thud, I landed in a pile of blue blow-up rafts from the lake, which I'd strategically placed right under my window for this exact reason.

Mom knew I was training to become alpha, but she didn't know that a woman like me had needs. And those needs required me to be at the lake every night at eleven p.m. to meet Tony for our midnight *swim*.

I brushed off some dirt and lifted my nose to the air, inhaling a whiff of ash, charcoal, and marshmallows from the house next door. All I wanted to do was sink my teeth into a s'more and—

The front door of the pack house opened, and I ducked behind the bushes in the front yard.

Mom and Dad walked out of the house to attend some urgent meeting they were hosting with the other packs in the area. And apparently, I wasn't invited. I watched them impatiently, tugging some berries off the bush and popping them into my mouth.

With brows furrowed up in fear, Mom grasped Dad's hand tightly. "Ares is coming," she whispered.

I rolled my eyes.

Ares is coming. Ares is coming. Ares is coming. That was all they'd been whispering about the entire week.

The oh-so-great alpha of the east was burning up the lands, slaughtering the innocent, taking the weakest packs, and creating an empire for himself.

And we were next.

Supposedly.

Dad closed the front door. "What are you planning to do when he comes?" he asked.

I sighed to myself, wishing he'd grow a backbone. I loved Dad more than anything, but sometimes, he couldn't think for himself.

Since my brother Jeremy had died—I frowned at the mere thought of him—he hadn't been the same. He'd lost his purpose to lead this pack with Mom, and he let her run this pack however she wanted—even if her decisions weren't always the most informed.

If she listened to me, I'd tell her not to worry about anything. Alphas like Ares were easy to get rid of as long as we had the right resources—beautiful women, a night he wouldn't ever forget, and a few drinks spiked with wolfsbane.

"He's slaughtered every pack in his wake," Mom said, her voice hushed. "We're not as strong as we used to be, and"—she looked toward my window, and I ducked out of the way, so she wouldn't see me—"Aurora can't fight."

I broke a branch off the bush and clenched it in my fist, a wave of shame washing over me.

Aurora can't fight.

Her words hit me hard, struck me right through the damn heart.

Aurora can't fight.

I'd heard those words my entire life. Everyone in our pack had heard those words, too, and they all knew it to be true. A misfit like me couldn't fight, not after Jeremy had been murdered in cold blood by those feral rogues.

Aurora can't fight.

Dad hushed Mom and opened the door to their white sedan for her. After ushering her into the car, he backed out of the driveway and sped down the street. I stood back up, throwing the stick to the ground, and hurried through the lush green forest with my arms wrapped around myself.

Damn her. I tried so hard to make her happy, to be strong for our pack, to be someone they could be proud of, but … I would never live up to their reputation. I wouldn't be the first female alpha to grace these lands, like Mom was, and I didn't possess any of the qualities of the adored and honored warriors of Dad's family who had won the War of the Lycans centuries ago.

I was just Aurora, the nineteen-year-old girl sneaking out of her parents' pack house to fuck Tony at the lake.

Sanguine Wilds Forest stretched for thousands of miles across this continent. And while Mom only owned about twenty miles in each direction, warriors prowled through the thick brush for miles, looking for rogues. There were more guards in the forest compared to the last few nights, which meant one thing.

Mom expected Alpha Ares to be here soon.

I sighed and took the hidden route to the lake. I shimmied through a deserted cave, climbed down a slight cliff, and walked right off the property without anyone seeing.

Nobody knew about the secret pathway, except me.

After a few moments of surveying the area to make sure nobody was following me, I walked around one of the larger mountains that Jeremy used to always take me to and headed straight toward the lake. The air smelled fresh tonight, a sweet yet unfamiliar scent drifting through the woods.

My fingers brushed against the gnarled tree bark as I walked out from the forest and toward the small opening of the lake. The moon glimmered off the water, lightning bugs floating above it. I frowned. I guessed Tony was late.

I sat down on some rocks and dipped my feet into the water, splashing them around and creating ripples. All I had been craving for the past twenty-four hours was Tony playfully pushing me into the lake with all of my clothes still on, watching me get soaked through the tiny pink tank top that I had worn for him, pulling off his shirt and showing me all that thick muscle underneath.

My breathing hitched, and I closed my eyes, heat gathering in my core. Goddess, I couldn't wait for him to tug on my nipples. I drew a finger against them, making them hard. To pull my hair. I inhaled the sweet air and pushed my knees together. To thrust into me until I begged him to stop.

My phone buzzed in my pocket, and Tony's name flashed on the screen.

Tony: Sorry. Dad dragged me to the meeting with your parents tonight. Won't be able to make it until later.

I stared down at my phone, gripping it until my fingertips turned white. Why was he only telling me this now, and why the hell hadn't I been invited? It was almost as if he'd waited until now because he didn't want me to know about him attending the meeting without me—the soon-to-be alpha.

I hummed at the thought of Mom inviting Tony to this meeting instead of her own daughter. My phone buzzed again, and I knew it was Mom nagging me about something important. The mind link didn't work at this distance, and she never contacted me for just anything.

Mom: The Ironmane Pack was spotted ten miles away from our borders. You'd better be at home.

There it was again. The Ironmane Pack. Alpha Ares.

Get back home now, Aurora. You know you can't fight. They'll rip you in half, limb by limb. You'll die, like the way Jeremy did—in the hands of a monster.

I put my phone back into my pocket and stared out at the water. Not many people had ever seen Ares up close, and I couldn't find any pictures of him when I searched this morning. Legend was that he killed so many and so quickly that people didn't have a chance to even catch a glimpse of him. But the ones who had survived his brutality said he looked like a god with a back sculpted by the Moon Goddess herself, black tattoos that crawled up his forearms, and thick, tousled brown hair.

But I thought that was bullshit. No alpha ever looked that goo—

A twig snapped close behind me in the woods. I sat up taller and tensed. Someone had found my little hideout in the Sanguine Wilds, and I really didn't want to deal with whoever it was.

"Tony?" I asked, knowing for damn sure it wasn't him. I sniffed the air but couldn't catch any familiar scent anywhere. "I'm not in the mood for one of your games right now. You know I'm here for one thing," I said, standing up and trying to calm my racing heart.

It definitely wasn't Tony, but his name was the only damn thing that could calm my nerves right now. He might've been the most aggravating man sometimes, but at least he answered me when I called for him.

Almost instinctively, my eyes closed, and I breathed in the most captivating scent that I had ever smelled—hazelnut.

"And what are you here for?" someone asked in my ear, his voice impeccably smooth and deep.

I hopped up, my heart racing in my chest, and gazed at a naked man I had never seen before. The moonlight glistened off his rippling muscles, his hair was a wild mess on his head, and his deep brown eyes were nearly glowing when they gazed into mine.

Mate!

My wolf jumped around inside of me, doing flips in my stomach, acting giddy, like she did under every full moon. But I wasn't feeling giddy at all. From that small scar running diagonally through his left eyebrow to that captivating stare, I was terrified by how easily he had crept up on me.

"You're not Tony," I said, my voice smaller than I wanted it to be.

But of course, he wasn't Tony. Tony was off at the damn meeting and probably would be all night.

Something about him told me to run and to run fast, but an alpha didn't run from just anyone, especially when he wasn't a threat ... yet. He eyed me, his eyes flickering between his brown human color and his wolf's gold, canines lengthening from his mouth and then disappearing almost as quickly. A torn expression crossed his face, but then he clenched his jaw and stepped toward me.

"No, I'm not. But I'm curious why this *Tony* was planning to meet you here."

He took another step closer, and I sucked in a breath. His scent was driving my wolf wild. All she wanted to do was jump the man, get down on all fours, and let him take us, do whatever he asked.

He stood inches from me, and I scolded my wolf for all the dirty thoughts running through my mind because ... Goddess ... they were starting to drive me wild. I pressed my thighs together, so he couldn't smell me.

"Was Tony planning on taking what is *mine* tonight?" He towered over me, his large frame making mine feel so small, and then he grasped my chin between his fingers and forced me to gaze up into his dark eyes. His touch sent tingles throughout my entire body, making me feel things that I shouldn't feel for a stranger. "Because if he was, I'm going to have to take care of him. Aren't I?" he asked, fingers digging into my chin. So dominant, so chillingly dominant.

I gathered all my senses, cocked a brow, and pushed his hand away. "Aren't you what?" I asked, looking him up and down. "Going to act all ruthless and merciless just because I'm your mate and you're some"—*sexy*—"egotistical asshole who thinks he owns me?"

When he growled, his eyes flashing a breathtaking wolf gold, I forced myself to look away. Dad had told me never to settle for someone who thought they owned me. I had alpha blood and soon I would be *the* alpha of the Darkmoon Pack; I deserved more than that.

"Not interested," I said, but as soon as the words left my mouth, my heart started thrashing in my chest.

Maybe it was the way he stared at me, like he wanted to

devour me, or the way *I* wanted to let him, but he made me nervous. More nervous than I had ever been. My gaze landed on the lake again, and I tried to admire the rippling reflection of the moon.

He snatched my jaw in his hand this time and stepped closer until he pressed himself into my side. I could feel every muscle of his front. *Every* muscle. And I inhaled deeply, pushing my thighs closer together.

He caressed my cheek with his thumb. He was a daunting gentle, the kind that told me that though he wasn't thrusting himself upon me like any alpha would at the first sight of his mate he controlled this conversation, the kind that told me he could snap at any moment, the kind that made me wet.

"Cute," he said against my ear, voice husky. His hand slipped from my jaw to my throat. "Look at you …" He drew his nose up the side of my neck. "My mate acting like she hasn't been turned on since the moment she laid her eyes on me."

I gulped and stared up at him, my wolf purring at his touch. He lightly trailed his fingers down my forearm until he reached the front of my thighs. Heat warmed my core as they lingered right over the front of my pants.

He brushed his thumb over my pussy. "Acting like she's not wet for *me*," he said.

I clamped down harder and cursed the Moon Goddess for my innate attraction to him.

He pressed his hardness against my thigh and let me feel every inch of him. "Acting like my possessiveness isn't making her clench right now."

I gathered all the strength I had left in me and firmly pushed my hands into his taut chest. "You know what? I am horny. My pussy is wet. And your possessiveness is over-the-top aggressive alpha right now." I dug my fingers into his muscle, devouring his wolf's golden eyes with my own. Then, I tilted my head to the side and sneered at him. "But you're not going to do a damn thing about it."

He chuckled and grabbed my wrists, stepping closer, a strand of his dark hair curling onto his forehead. "Oh, I'm not?"

"No," I said, wrapping my fingers around his and inhaling the captivating scent of hazelnut, "you're not."

"Would you rather have Tony touch you like this then?" He released his grip on my wrists, dipped one hand between my legs, and rubbed his fingers against my pussy through my pants.

My eyes widened, my pussy aching.

When I didn't answer him, he clenched his jaw. "Huh? Is that what Tony is for? Making *my* mate come? Making *my* mate feel good?"

My heart pounded against my chest.

He stared down at me with golden embers in his brown eyes and ... laughed. I tensed and grabbed his wrist, my core pulsing.

Fuck. Fuck. Fuck. This wasn't what I was expecting.

"Go ahead, Kitten." He rubbed sweet, torturous circles around my clit through my pants. His canines brushed against my soft spot on my neck, and I nearly moaned. "Push me away," he mumbled against my ear. "I'll let you this time."

I squeezed his wrist in my hand, wanting to shove him back but not wanting him to stop. I really, really didn't want him to stop. Mom had been driving me crazy this past week, and all I wanted was a release.

"Stop me, or I'll really give you a reason to push me away."

I didn't know whether to moan, to nudge him away, or to do both. The pressure in my core rose with every moment. I needed something, anything. I stared him right in the eye, wanting to dare him. "What're you going to do? Throw me to the ground and tear me apart piece by piece," I said, sarcasm dripping from my voice. "Moon Goddess, I'm shaking in my bo— "

He growled lowly and plunged his hand into my underwear. Almost instantly, his fingers slipped into my wet pussy, thrusting in and out harshly. I gripped his broad shoulders, nails digging into the thick muscle.

Holy—

My pussy tightened on him, and I backed up until I hit the nearest tree, unable to hold myself together. The pressure in my core hadn't ever been this intense. He followed, never taking his fingers out of me once. The heel of his palm hit my sensitive clit over and over, sending a surge of pleasure through me.

"The things I want to do to you," he said into my ear, watching my body react to him. He curled a hand around my throat and squeezed lightly. "Bend you over my bed and fuck you until you can't stand. Push you to your knees and watch you suck my cock." He took my hand and placed it on his hardness. I clenched, slowly stroking it up and down. "Eat your wet pussy until you beg me to stop."

I drew my brows together, moaning softly. Another wave of ecstasy.

"I love the way your pussy pulses on my fingers," he said. "Imagine how tight you'd get with my cock inside of you. Thrusting in and out. Filling this tight … little … pussy."

My fucking Moon Goddess.

"Eyes on me," he said, tightening his grip on my throat. I gazed at him, breaths quickening. "Only me."

He brushed his thumb against my clit, and my legs shook as I released myself on him, not breaking eye contact once.

Wave after wave of satisfaction rolled through me. My entire body tingled. I closed my eyes and moaned, my hips moving back and forth on his fingers, riding out my orgasm. Hell, I had known my mate for two whole minutes, and I was a mess.

Coming on his fingers. Aching for more.

Tony never even fucked me this well.

He continued to thrust his fingers into me, not stopping.

I wrapped my hand around his wrist, trying to pull it off of me. "I-I came. You-you-you can st-stop" My eyes rolled back, and

I doubled over, resting my forehead on his bicep. Another surge of pleasure rushed through me.

"Is that what Tony does? Makes you come once and leaves?" He gave me an empty laugh. "I'm not finished with you. Not until you're begging."

I squeezed my eyes shut, the pressure in my core becoming harder to bear. My nails dug into his wrist, and I moaned out again as I released myself on him for the second time.

How was he even—

He smirked down at me. "How long do you think you'll last?" he asked. "Ten, fifteen times?"

My eyes widened, and I pushed his hand away. "Please, Moon Goddess, that was enough."

My mind was foggy with that hazelnut scent; my body was tingling in all the right places. He hadn't even touched the rest of me yet, but my body wanted more. My body was craving more.

CHAPTER 2

MARS

"Seventeen," I said, lying back in the grass next to the most beautiful woman I had ever seen. With brown locks that lay so perfectly down her back to the way the moonlight bounced off her pale skin, my mate was beautiful. "Not bad."

She lay next to me, her chest rising and falling with each heavy breath she took. The water from the lake just barely wet my heels. I watched her close her big blue eyes in utter bliss. She smelled so much like freshly picked lemons—my favorite—and it reminded me of Mom.

My fingers brushed against her bare hip bone in small, soothing circles. All I wanted was to bring her home with me, let her sleep in my bed, get her away from this Tony and his pungent scent, which was all over her.

"Alpha," my beta, Liam, said through our mind link. *"We have a problem."*

"Can't you handle it?" I asked, pressing my lips together. *"I'm busy."*

There was a pause on the other side of the mind link, and then Liam said, *"It's urgent."*

Though I wanted to bring her home, I couldn't. My pack

warriors had run to this part of Sanguine Wilds Forest for one reason and one reason only. The Malavite Stone. And we couldn't leave without it. We needed it more than we needed anything.

"I'll be there in fifteen minutes," I said, staring down at the rippling water.

My mate shifted next to me, curling her head into the crook of my neck, her breaths warming the spot on my skin where she'd mark one day.

"What's your name?" I asked, desperate to hear her speak again before I left her here alone for twenty minutes, at the most.

She opened her eyes and smiled up at me. "Aurora."

"Aurora," I whispered to myself so softly, like her name was meant to linger on my tongue for eternity—because it was.

I had heard Aurora's name spoken by some of my warriors before. Smart, sassy, and so damn sexy, she was the soon-to-be alpha of the Darkmoon Pack—the pack last known to have the Malavite Stone.

But what was the alpha-in-training doing outside her borders, unprotected and alone, meeting this man named Tony, who would definitely need to be taken care of? I might've known her name and title, but I didn't know the first thing about who she really was, and I definitely didn't know if she would like me when she found out who I was ... but I wouldn't let her go.

After everything Ares and I had been through, after all the shit we had done, the Moon Goddess still had blessed *us* with a strong mate. And I wouldn't take her for granted. She would be ours and ours only. For eternity.

Deep inside of me, I could feel a dark, sinister rage, my beast awakening. Clawing at our insides to see our mate for the first time, ripping me apart to touch her, growling at me not to leave her.

And I didn't want her to be afraid of him.

"What's yours?" she asked, her voice softer this time, her eyes closing.

"Mars," I said, brushing my fingers against hers.

I needed to get out of here sooner than I'd planned. I didn't want her to see that vicious side of me yet, but something told me that she'd find out who I was sooner rather than later.

Aurora's breathing evened out, and she curled into a ball next to me. I pushed a strand of her dark hair behind her ear and savored this moment with her. I didn't know when I'd get my next one.

"They call me Mars."

"Mars, like the planet?" she mumbled.

Something inside of me snapped, and I couldn't hold back the beast any longer. I possessively brushed my thumb across her jaw. Oh, my Kitten had a lot to learn, but she'd learn quickly.

"Like the god."

CHAPTER 3

AURORA

I grumbled to myself and rubbed my eyes, shifting on the grassy patch. The moon reflected off the still lake, and the forest was a jarring kind of silent. No yelling. No howling. No wolves. Mars and his sweet hazelnut scent were gone, leaving me to inhale the foul scent of Tony's thick navy sweatshirt.

My phone lay next to me, in the place Mars would've been, and I snatched it—3:03 a.m..

My eyes widened, and I shot up, some soreness lingering in my core. Mom was going to kill me. I dusted the sand off my back and hurried through the woods, not even bothering to look for *him*. It was apparent that all he'd wanted to do was fuck. Touch me in places that he shouldn't have and then leave.

Sure, there were plenty of wolves like that nowadays, but I hadn't expected my mate to be one. But who was I to talk? I was supposed to have met Tony at the damn lake to get off for the night.

I climbed the small cliff and shimmied back through the cave, sneaked right past Mom's warriors, and sighed in relief when I crawled through my window and an angry alpha mom wasn't waiting for me.

Ruffles glared at me when I turned the light on, blinding her. She gave me a hard *fuck you* meow and stuffed her face back into her paw. After tugging off my clothes and taking a quick shower, I lay in bed with her and stared up at the ceiling.

From my bed, I could hear Mom and Dad whispering in their room, about tonight's meeting, about Ares, about how they thought he would tear us down one by one, torture us until we gave him all our riches—not that we had much nowadays. And while Ares might be a threat, all I could think about was the man in the woods.

Mars.

I balled the thin purple sheet in my hand and yanked it up my body, so it covered my shoulders. I knew I should've stayed away from him. I knew I should've run when I had the chance—when he *gave* me the chance. But I hadn't wanted to run. My wolf wanted to stay with him.

I guessed he hadn't wanted to stay with me.

But who was he? Possibly a scout from a nearby pack ... but how would that explain all those scars? Maybe he was a warrior from Alpha Ares's Ironmane Pack. Mom would have my head if he was.

After sulking for a few more moments, I shook the thought away. It didn't matter anyway. He had left me alone in the middle of the damn woods after giving me the hottest night of my entire life. If he didn't need me, I sure as hell didn't need him.

I was soon-to-be alpha of the Darkmoon Pack, and not even my mate would get in my way of trying as hard as I could to be the leader that Jeremy would've wanted me to be.

There was some rustling by my bedroom window that I'd left slightly ajar. Ruffles lifted her nose and glanced at it, her eyes narrowed in a *leave me alone, I'm trying to fucking sleep* expression. A tree branch brushed across the glass, the wind picking up outside and drifting into the room. I inhaled softly and swore I smelled hazelnut. But after a few moments, it was gone.

Just the damn wind taunting me.

I squeezed my eyes shut and growled. Fuck Mars for leaving me. Fuck Mars for touching me. Fuck Mars for being the egotistical asshole that I had known he was.

Moon Goddess, I wanted to fuck Mars.

CHAPTER 4

ARES

"*No killing,*" I said through the mind link to my warriors, hopping out of the narrow cave and onto Darkmoon's property.

One by one, my warriors walked out and stood behind me in their wolf form, eyes trained on the patrol guards in the forest a mile away.

The early morning sun filed in around the monstrous trees, hit the forest floor, and created grotesque shadows. These lush greens would turn into a fucking bloodbath soon because I wasn't leaving until I found that damn stone.

I'd search for it even if it was the end of me. All these packs in Sanguine Wilds played games, taunted me about it, plotted ways to rid me of something so precious.

But I was done with that shit.

I needed the stone, and I needed it now.

Liam stood next to me with his head held high, saliva dripping from his canines.

I growled to silence all my warriors. "*We take the stone and then take Alpha Theia's daughter.*"

Aurora. Her name was Aurora.

But I didn't want anyone to know her name yet. She was mine. All mine.

She was the goddess with the brown hair and eyes as bright as the dawn. An alpha wolf who would rule by my side—whether she wanted to or not. I had waited to find my mate for years, always wanted her to be a strong warrior who could run with me.

She didn't know me yet. She only knew Mars. She'd lain with him. She'd touched him. She'd begged for him. Then, she'd disappeared in the middle of the night after I had to head back to camp to deal with pack drama.

I had traced her scent through the entire forest and used—what seemed to be—her own secret little passage until I found her pack house. Part of me wanted to tear right through her home to find her, scold her for not staying, but it was my fault. I'd left her vulnerable.

But nothing would stop me from having her this time.

Now, I stood inside of her borders with the need for her growing stronger every moment. She might not know I was here for her, but when we attacked, when she smelled the fear of her own people, she'd know.

"We run."

I sprinted ahead, the wind rushing through in my fur, rage in my blood, fresh air in my lungs. Our paws hit the ground in a thunderous roar, and I let out a ferocious growl to let the Darkmoon Pack know who had arrived while they slept so innocently in their beds.

As if they were waiting for an attack, enemy warriors ran at us with their teeth bared.

"No killing," I repeated through the mind link.

There would be blood but no deaths. I only did that shit to hounds—those vicious rogues who lingered near my property.

Claws on fur. Flesh tearing. Blood splattering. We clashed.

Searching for her, my gaze traveled across the herd of werewolves running at me. As she was the next alpha, I expected her to be here, but I couldn't smell her scent on any of these wolves. I smelled Tony. I smelled that rotten stench, same as the dirty, used sweatshirt Aurora had worn last night.

Black fur. Blacker eyes. Teeth dripping with blood.

He sprinted at me with so much ferocity that, if I didn't know better, I would've thought he was the next in line to be alpha. I stepped out of his way, let him fall flat on his face behind me, and growled.

They knew what I wanted. They knew all they had to do was hand the stone over, give me any information on its whereabouts. That was all I fucking wanted. And if the stone really wasn't here, I'd still come out of this battle victorious because I'd take my mate, Aurora, back home with me.

I didn't care if she pleaded, screamed, hit, or flat-out refused. She would be mine.

CHAPTER 5

AURORA

Sunlight flooded into my room, creating cute patterns from the shadow of the cherry tree outside my window. Ruffles lay on my chest and licked my face, her breath smelling suspiciously like potato chips. I sank into my sheets and sighed.

Stupid Mars. Stupid Aurora for giving in to Mars so easily. Stupid feelings for my stupid mate.

I shifted in the bed, let Ruffles hop off, and sat up. What was wrong with me? Why was I letting this get to me? Maybe it was because when I had been growing up, I'd watched Jeremy and his mate sneak away at night to spend the night together. I had seen those stolen glances and smiles, those lovely words of affection they shared.

Now that Jeremy was gone and all I heard from Mom were lies about how strong and great she thought I was, I wanted to find my mate more than anything. But, Goddess, not a mate who didn't seem to care about me at all, not a mate who had left me alone in the forest after getting me off.

My wolf whimpered, and I knew she still wanted him and his wolf.

They were fated mates after all.

In the distance, growling erupted through the woods. I yawned and opened the window wider, breathing in the crisp morning air. Practice didn't start for another hour. What—

A patrol guard scurried through the woods toward the direction of the pack hospital, a trail of blood following him. My eyes widened. We were being attacked.

I threw on a pair of clothes as quickly as I could.

"Mom?" I asked, running through the house.

Everything was silent, and my heart dropped in my chest. I tried the mind link and didn't get a response from anyone, which made me think the worst. Mom must've been right; Alpha Ares was here sooner rather than later. I could just feel it.

"Mom!"

I raced through the woods, making sure to stay hidden in the trees. Mom had known that he was here, but she hadn't even bothered waking me up, so I could help fight.

My body ached with shame at the mere thought of her shaking her head at Dad and saying, *He'll take her first. She's the weakest link.*

After a few miles of sprinting in my human form, I stopped. Wave after wave of iron and blood hit me, and I crouched behind a tree, scrunching my nose. Through the woods, I watched the warriors fight. Wolf on wolf. Teeth on teeth. Claws on claws. Flesh and fur being torn off. Blood spewing everywhere. My pack howling for Mom to do something.

And there he was.

Alpha Ares.

Standing in the center of the two enemy packs, he circled Mom like she was some sort of prey. He stood taller and larger than the rest of the wolves, his thick midnight fur glistening under the sunlight.

There was no doubt in my mind that he would kill her.

Dad stood a few feet away, holding up a fight against a wolf large enough to be a beta. My heart raced, and I tried to think up a good plan within the next few moments. But Ares moved so fast that I barely had time to think of anything other than a surprise attack. I'd leap at him when he was about to clamp down on Mom's neck, just when he thought he had conquered another pack.

It would ruin him. I would ruin him. And maybe it'd prove something to Mom too.

After sneaking closer to the fight, I tried to analyze his movements. I needed an opening, some type of distraction to get into the center so I could save her. But Mom ruined my entire plan when she suddenly shifted into her human.

"Stop," she said to her warriors and to Ares. "We have a proposition. One that you won't pass up."

Alpha Ares growled, his teeth dripping with sanguine-colored saliva. His warriors stopped their attacks and bowed their heads to him so quickly and so effortlessly that it scared me how much power that man had over feral animals. Ares scanned Mom's warrior wolves as if he was searching for someone, and then he shifted to his human.

My eyes widened. Mars—Ares, whoever he goddamn was—stood in front of Mom, his taut chest smeared with blood, his eyes as golden as the sun.

"Where is she?" Ares said through clenched teeth. "Where is Aurora?"

I froze behind the tree, my entire body tense. Anger and betrayal and so much hurt rushed through me. He must've followed my scent back through the forest, using my secret route. It was the only way he could've gotten on our property and caused this much damage this quickly.

He'd *used* me last night to get what he wanted—an unguarded entrance to my pack, an easy way to get past the warriors on patrol, for me to trust him. With that stupid-ass smirk and those stupid-ass eyes and that stupid-ass scent of hazelnut, he had manipulated me, and I'd let him.

He let out another guttural growl and stepped closer to Mom. "I'm not going to ask again."

I dug my fingers into the hard tree bark, peering from behind it and at my mate. Moon Goddess, even when he was angry he was ho—

I shook my head. *Stop it, Aurora. That man is a violent, vicious animal.*

He stepped even closer, and Tony moved in front of Mom to protect her. Ares let out a lifeless chuckle, lip curling into a snarl, and then grabbed Tony by the throat, his entire hand wrapping around Tony's fragile neck.

"Release him," Mom commanded, acting like Ares's threats didn't intimidate her. But she glanced nervously at Tony and then at Dad. And I knew she was afraid of losing the next beta of this pack. "And we can talk."

Ares turned around with Tony in his hold, gazing through the forest. "Come out, Aurora. I know you're watching." He inhaled, and I swore his features softened for just a moment. "I have your *precious* Tony."

I ground my teeth together and walked through the forest to the fight. I might not be good at fighting, but I cared about my pack. They would do anything to protect each other, and I would do anything to protect them.

When Mom saw me, she growled like she always did when she didn't want me to listen in on her shitty alpha decisions. "Aurora, get back in the pack house."

"Put him down," I demanded, meeting Ares's glowing golden gaze. "Now."

Mars—Ares's eyes danced with excitement as he glanced at Mom. "If you don't have the stone and have absolutely no information on its whereabouts, there's only one deal that I would ever accept."

Mom stepped forward, regaining her composure, and tried to posture over him. "What?"

"Aurora."

My eyes widened as a rush of adrenaline ran through my veins. "No. Absolutely not." I shook my head, ignoring the pleas from my wolf. "I told you yesterday that I'm not interested."

"You saw him yesterday?" Mom asked, brow cocked at me. "I *told* you not to go out."

Ares chuckled. "She doesn't listen," he said, a smirk stretching across his face. "But I can fix that."

His eyes were burning into mine, and my heart was racing even harder in my chest. It was an unspoken promise, a promise to bend me over his bed and fuck me until I listened to every word he said.

He thought he had control over me, but I knew how to put him in his place. I walked right up to him, standing in a puddle of wolf blood, and stared him right in those golden eyes. "If what you plan to do is anything like your performance last night, you'd never put me in my place."

A growl ripped from his throat, and he tightened his grip on Tony's neck. Tony grasped his wrists, his cheeks flushing red, but Ares didn't even flinch.

"I was going easy on you last night, *pup*." He turned to Mom, rage emanating off of him. "Aurora or your pack, Alpha. One way, I take Aurora and leave, never coming back to hurt your people. The other way, I kill everyone here and still take your daughter. Your choice."

I crossed my arms over my chest and scowled at him. Who did he think he was, demanding an alpha as his own, personal war prize? Nobody in this pack would ever let that happen.

Dad looked at Mom, not saying a single word, and Mom refused to make eye contact with me.

Instead, she pushed back her shoulders and nodded her head. "Fine."

My eyes widened, and I dropped my arms. *Fine?* What the hell did she mean by fine? She thought that this was fine? She was going to just give me away to my psychotic alpha mate?

I glared at her, about to call her every possible name in the book, but I held myself back. Now that Jeremy was gone, I was her only heir, and she was giving me away like I was nothing to her. My heart hurt, and I wanted to refuse to go with him, but by the look in her eye, I knew she wouldn't budge. She'd tell me that this was best for the pack, that we couldn't afford another loss.

Before his pack of bloodthirsty warriors, Ares stood like he was a fucking king, praised by every one of them. Then, he smirked, cocked a finger in my direction, and said, "Come here, Kitten."

The words sounded so disgraceful. Disgraceful to my whole legacy. To my father, who claimed to have come from the strongest warrior family in all of the nations. To my mother, the first female alpha. To me, Ares's stupid fucking mate.

My gaze shifted from Mom to Dad to Tony, who looked so desperate in Ares's arms. He dangled there with Ares's claws in his neck, his eyes on me and me only. He looked so pitiful. He looked less than a beta and more like a sorry-ass rogue, begging for forgiveness.

I didn't know if I was angry with Mom for handing over the only heir to her pack, with Ares for using me last night, or with myself for actually believing that his name was Mars. I was such a damn fool.

But for my pack, I clenched my teeth together and stormed to Ares, ripping Tony from him. "You're a monster."

He chuckled lowly, drew his fingers up the side of my neck, and grasped my chin in his hand like he had done last night, making me look into those golden eyes. "And you're mine, Kitten." He roughly brushed his thumb over my bottom lip. "All mine."

CHAPTER 6

AURORA

I clenched my teeth together and ripped myself out of his grip. "Don't you dare touch me like that again." I crossed my arms. "Let's get one thing straight. Just because I'm going with you doesn't mean that you own me. And it sure as hell doesn't mean that you"—I gazed around at his pack, who were all staring at me intently—"or any of you will disrespect me."

Gasping for air and clutching his neck, Tony stepped forward, as if he wanted another chance at fighting Ares.

I turned on my heel to face him and pointed a sharp finger at him. "No," I said, my voice coming out stronger than I'd expected it to with all the pent-up anger I was holding back. "War with Ares is over, just like our *alpha*"—I gave Mom the most bitter side-eye I could muster—"wanted it to be. Go get Ares clothes, so he doesn't have to walk around here half-naked with his ugly ass."

Without another word, I stormed to the pack house, tracking someone's blood throughout the entire forest. Ares growled behind me, and I growled back.

Hit a nerve, did I?

I'd hit a damn big nerve. Ares wasn't ugly, but his heart and his soul were.

"Aurora," Mom called, following after me.

I rolled my eyes and walked faster until I reached the pack house. I slammed the large wooden front door as hard as I could and hoped it hit her right in the face. It was childish, but at least I hadn't sold her out to Ares just because I was afraid of him and at least I'd shouted for her before I went out to fight our enemy.

After kicking off my bloody sneakers, I stormed up the stairs and threw my bedroom door open. Ruffles stared at me with wide eyes from my desk, gnawing on the plastic of a potato chip bag. I opened my closet door, threw my suitcase onto my bed, and angrily unzipped it.

Stupid. This is so stupid.

She sold me out. Fucking sold me out.

To Ares. To Mars. To whoever the fuck he is.

I bet she did it because she doesn't think I'm fit to become alpha.

My bedroom door opened, and Mom walked into the room.

"Aurora," she said softly, rubbing her palms together and acting as if she were really sorry for doing what she had done. But she wasn't.

"*Alpha*," I said, hurling my clothes into my suitcase. "Excuse my language, but I'm fucking busy, packing my fucking bags to leave this fucking pack."

She growled at me and snatched my arm, claws digging into my skin. "Do not speak to me like that. This was our only choice. He had us cornered. He would've killed everyone here without a second thought."

"There's never only one choice," I said, staring her right in the eye. "There's always another way. You taught me that, but you seem to have forgotten about that since you got Jeremy killed."

She glared at me with glowing gold eyes and slapped me hard right across the face. I clutched my stinging cheek, my eyes wide. She'd just … she'd just—

"Do not bring Jeremy up. This has nothing to do with him."

I was done with backing down from her. I was done with being treated like garbage.

I stepped toward her. "It has everything to do with him, and you know it. Ever since that day, you've been terrified of losing your pack members. Ever since that day, you've lost your spark, you've lost your edge, you've been scared of being an alpha."

"He was your brother," she said harshly. "Don't talk to me like you know anything about losing a child or like you know anything about leading a pack. I've been preparing you for years to become an alpha like Jeremy was going to be, and you—" She stopped herself before she could finish the sentence.

My heart raced. Shame. All I felt was shame. "What, Mom? What did I do?"

She pursed her lips together and turned away. "Forget it, Aurora."

"No," I said, heart tightening. "Tell me ... tell me how I will never fill his shoes. Tell me how you've trained me for years, yet I'm still not good enough for you. Tell me that you've never thought that I'd be strong enough to lead this pack."

"Aurora, stop."

Tears filled my eyes to the brim, but I refused to let them fall. "Tell me, Mom."

Her chin quivered. "I never meant to make you feel that way."

"Well, you did." I turned back to my suitcase and stared down at the contents from the past nineteen years.

All the memories of Jeremy's death flooded my mind, and I bit back the cries. Ever since that day, our family hadn't been the same. We didn't go out together, didn't eat together, and didn't fight together anymore. We were broken, and she was the one who had broken us.

"Aurora," she said softly. She placed her hand on my shoulder, but I pulled away from her. "You can't even shift into your wolf."

"I can shift," I whispered.

My wolf whimpered inside of me, feeling defeated. She knew she couldn't shift like we used to. She knew she was a disappointment to Mom and to this whole pack. If anyone found out, we'd be an easy target.

"When are you going to admit it to yourself, Aurora?" she asked. "It takes you ten minutes to shift sometimes. Ten minutes, and all I hear is your wolf whimpering the entire time."

I stared down at my clothes, curling one of Jeremy's old high school football jerseys in my fist. It was true. I hadn't been able to shift easily since those hounds attacked us and my spine broke into a hundred pieces. "It's not my fault," I said, my voice raspy.

I wanted her to admit that this was her blunder, that she was the reason I couldn't shift, that she had made the senseless decision to fight a group of hounds, knowing we wouldn't win. Not me. It was a surprise attack, yes. But we could've easily retreated to the pack house, made sure all the pups were safe, and come up with a damn plan before we attacked them back.

But Mom never took the blame.

She shook her head. "You can't lead this pack the way that we need to be led," she said with so much finality that I almost believed it.

My heart hurt, and all I could feel was pain. Pain from all the years I'd tried to suppress thoughts of Jeremy's death.

She stared at me with the blankest expression. "And I'm not letting anyone else in this pack die."

"So, you decide to never see your daughter, just like you won't ever see your son again?" I asked, my voice cracking.

Hold back the tears, Aurora. Don't let her see how weak she's made you.

She snatched my chin in her hand, squeezing it roughly. Though she had grabbed me in the same place Ares had, her touch felt nothing like his. It felt so … mean. "Sacrifices need to be made to ensure this pack's survival. Don't make me feel bad for this decision, Aurora. If I thought he would hurt you, I wouldn't have agreed to it." Lie. "From his possessiveness, the second he laid eyes on you, I knew that you were his mate. With him, you'll at least be safe. He's one of the strongest alphas around."

I glared at her through teary eyes. "Leave."

She pressed her lips together, turned on her heel, and walked right out of the room, shutting the door behind her. I growled and let one single tear fall. Then, I sucked it up and continued packing for hell because nobody would save me from this. Dad was too much of a wimp to stop her. Tony wasn't strong enough. And the rest of the pack ... some of them refused to even talk to me anymore when I trained with them.

I grasped Jeremy's shirt in my hands. Jeremy's jersey, stained with dirt from his high school football days, had been the only thing getting me through these past few years. I wanted to double over it and scream at the top of my lungs for him to come back, so all of this would be better, but I'd learned to hide that weak side of me.

A few moments later, my door reopened, but I didn't bother turning around.

"Leave me alone," I said, continuing to place my clothes into my suitcase.

Mom had pissed me off one too many times. I couldn't handle another minute of listening to her bullshit. I couldn't do anything about being weak or not being able to shift easily. If it wasn't for—

I shook my head and refused to even think about that day or the harrowing days that followed.

The door closed, and I inhaled a whiff of Ruffles's cat litter mixed with—

I turned around, nostrils flaring. Ares stood by the door, gaze traveling around the room so slowly. He had found some clothes that looked like Tony's, yet they were a size too small for him. They hugged his tanned biceps, his shoulders, his chest.

Moon Goddess, why have you given me such a delicious asshole of a mate?

When his gaze met mine, he gave me an adorably crooked smile, his lip curling a bit wider to the right than the left. It made him look real, like he wasn't just a divine creature created by the Moon Goddess herself.

"Not what I was expecting."

"You think I was expecting for my mate to show up at my pack as the alpha who's been murdering everyone in this part of Sanguine Wilds?"

"Someone's cranky." He walked into my room, glancing around at all the photos of my *picture-perfect* family. We hadn't taken any new ones since Jeremy died.

"Don't talk to me like we're friends," I said, turning back around but watching him intently out of the corner of my eye, just to make sure he didn't touch anything that he wasn't supposed to. Definitely not because he was leaving his sweet hazelnut scent all over the room and it was driving me wild. "Because we're not."

He walked back around my bed toward me and stepped close. Though he wasn't touching me, I felt his body heat against my backside. Teasing me. Taunting me even. "How do you want me to talk to you?" He brushed his nose against my hair and inhaled deeply. "As the woman that I'm going to take to my bed and devour until she's trembling in my hands tonight or as the pitiful alpha traded by her mother?"

"If you think I'm going to sleep with you, you're crazy."

"I am?" he whispered into my ear, fingertips lightly brushing against my hips.

"Yes," I said, tingles running up and down my sides. My wolf purred. "You are."

One of his hands trailed down the side of my body, and he grasped my chin in his other. "I'm not crazy, Kitten." He brushed his thumb against my bottom lip, and I parted them slightly. "Unless you want me to be."

When his fingers barely grazed against the front of my pants, I shuddered against him. My pussy tightened, and I tried to calm my wolf, who was raging inside of me, who wanted nothing more than to let him be *crazy* with me.

Bend me over the bed and take me right there. Force my legs apart and press his tongue against my clit as I squirmed against him. Whisper all those dirty, filthy words into my ear, making me wetter for him. Hell, I wanted to plunge *my* hand through his hair and tug on it so roughly until *he* knew he was mine.

Control yourself, Aurora. Don't give in to him that easily.

I shook my head and stepped away from him. "I hardly know you." But I wanted to know him.

Ruffles hopped onto the bed and jumped into my suitcase, snuggling in all of my clothes and making sure her fur was on each piece. I opened my drawer and pulled out my more personal items, watching the smirk on Ares's face widen.

"You can get to know me," he said, reaching out to brush his fingers against mine. "Fire off the questions, Kitten."

I arched a brow. Questions, questions, questions. I had so many questions for Ares. But I had one dire inquiry that I needed the answer to now. "What should I call you—Ares, Mars, or Asshole?"

He chuckled. "Anything you'd like when we're out in public." He stepped closer to me, mere inches away, pushed a strand of hair behind my ear, and leaned down. "But when we're alone, you can call me Alpha."

My breath caught in the back of my throat, and I clenched. Wetness pooled between my legs. His fingers dipped between my thighs, and he rubbed my clit gently. I opened my mouth to speak, to tell him to get away from me, to tell him to fuck off, but I couldn't form any words.

Someone knocked on the door.

"Ares, we need to talk about our agreement," Mom said.

I pressed my lips together and growled under my breath at her for ruining the moment and my life.

"We'll finish this conversation later," Ares said. He pulled away from me and walked to the door. Before he opened it, he glanced back at me. "Call me what you want, Kitten, but I'd prefer you call me Mars."

CHAPTER 7

AURORA

When I turned back to my suitcase, Ruffles had one leg up in the air, her toes stretched out, as she licked her belly. She looked up at me briefly and narrowed her eyes.

"Don't look at me like that, Ruffles," I said, trying to calm myself down. "My wolf can't help it."

She meowed and glanced past me, her pupils dilating. Someone cleared their throat. Goddess, why couldn't I be left alone for one damn moment? All I needed was time to clear my head and to figure out how I would survive living with Ares for the rest of my life.

Tony closed my bedroom door, rubbing the claw marks on his neck. His dirty-blond hair was a disheveled mess with streaks of red blood in it. He cautiously stepped into the room. "Aurora."

"What, Tony?" I asked, seething.

"Come on, A. Don't do that." He took my hand.

His woodsy scent, which used to be so comforting, suddenly made me shiver in disgust and step back.

"Don't do what?"

He brushed a piece of hair from my face and frowned. "Act all

... distant."

"My mother just sold me out to the alpha that she's been terrified of for years." I growled, realization finally setting in. She'd really traded me, really gotten rid of me like I was nothing. "I can be distant if I want to."

He intertwined my fingers with his, brushing his thumb over my knuckles. "You don't have to be distant with me."

"Well, seeing as I'm going to live with Ares, we're about to be quite distant," I said, stepping away from him.

"We can still meet at the lake every night to spend time together."

Tony stepped closer to me, and I pursed my lips.

"You know the only reason she sold me out was so you could lead," I said.

Tony was beta, second-in-command, the strongest person to lead if there was no successor. There was no other reason and could be no other reason. I was weak in her eyes. So fucking weak.

After brushing a strand of hair out of my face, he frowned. "That's not true." He gave me a small, supportive smile. "She's been shaping you to be alpha since Jeremy died."

"She didn't ask me to go to the meeting that you attended with the other alphas. She didn't wake me when Ares was attacking. She sold me out without a second thought." My heart ached. What had I done to deserve this?

He tilted his head to the side and lightly seized my hips. I could feel his breath on my lips, could smell the sweet scent of his mint gum. He brushed his nose against mine, and for a moment, I closed my eyes and enjoyed it.

Then, I turned my head away. "I can't, Tony."

"Aurora," he said, lips brushing against my ear. He pushed his hips further against me, letting me feel his hardness pressed against the front of his pants. "Just one last time before you leave me."

"No, Tony, I—"

He glided a finger across my chin and forced his lips onto mine. Hard.

I shoved him back, adrenaline pumping through me. "I said, no."

He grabbed my hands and held them to his chest. "Aurora, look at me," he said.

I clenched my jaw and gazed over at him.

"I'm sorry. What do you want me to say? I can't make it better. It's not my decision. I never thought that your mother would ever actually go through with the—"

Before he could continue, he stopped himself. My eyes widened. All I felt was anger and rage, a need to hurt someone because Mom had hurt me long enough.

"This was her ... plan, her proposition?"

"No. This was the worst-case scenario." He glanced over at my closed bedroom door, pulled me closer to him, and lowered his voice. "Let Ares take you. I'll ascend as alpha. We'll buy ourselves time to form a plan and an army to destroy him. And when we do, I'll take you back, and you'll become my luna."

Ascend as alpha? Become his luna?

I'd bet this was his stupid fucking plan all along. He wanted my place, and he wanted me to be his little plaything.

"Oh," I said, nodding as if this all made perfect sense. "What a great plan!" Have a beta who knew nothing about the threats this family had faced and about the stone in my spine, which had helped fix me, become the alpha of this pack and lead us straight into ruins.

My nails lengthened into claws behind my back. Damn her. Was she stupid? Did she not understand that trading me to Ares wouldn't stop the hounds from attacking our pack? Could she even comprehend that she'd lose another child?

Tony smiled at me, nose grazing against mine. "I won't let him hurt you, I promise."

And then as if kissing me would make up for everything, he pressed his lips to mine, grabbing me harshly and pulling me to him. I pushed him away again, harder this time, my mind all over the place.

Just as I was about to sink my claws into his neck and tell him to never touch me like that again, he was ripped from me and thrown against the wall. He hit it with a thud and fell right onto Ruffles. Ruffles hissed and swatted at his face, scratching him across the cheek and immediately drawing blood.

Ares stood in front of me, back muscles rippling against his shirt, staring at the man who had touched his mate. He scooped him up by his neck, thrust him against the wall again, and held him there. This time, he held nothing back. His claws pierced his skin, and blood ran down Tony's neck and stained his white shirt.

I narrowed my eyes at Tony and watched him squirm in Ares's death grip, trying so desperately to breathe and to get out of his hold, but he was too weak.

And Mom wanted him as the next alpha.

Pinning him to the wall, Ares stepped closer, his lips next to Tony's ear. "What did I fucking tell you?" he asked, voice impeccably calm.

Tony didn't say anything.

"I told you not to touch my fucking mate again, didn't I?"

Tony grasped his wrists, but Ares just tightened his grip. His biceps flexed hard, and his canines lengthened past his lips.

"Didn't I?"

When Tony still didn't say anything, Ares squeezed his neck harder.

I yanked his arm away. "Ares, stop." But he didn't. "Ares."

His eyes were gold. Pure wolfish gold. I didn't know what to do to get him to calm down. I wanted to punish Tony for touching me, but I didn't want him to die. He would be the next alpha of our pack whether I liked it or not.

"Mars," I said, hoping to the Goddess that he'd stop. Ares's eyes softened at the mention of his name. "Let him go."

"So you can let him fuck you?" Ares growled.

"No, so I can kick him out of my room," I said. "Now, stop it."

Ares glared at Tony, whose cheeks had turned purple. "Pathetic." He gave him one last shove against the wall. "Next time you *think* about touching my mate, I will snap your fucking neck."

Ares stepped back, and Tony fell to the ground again. Ruffles hissed at him, narrowing her eyes and lengthening her claws. She went to smack at him again, but he shuffled out of the room, holding his neck and slamming the door shut.

"I could've handled that myself," I said through clenched teeth. Why did all of the damn men in my life want to be saviors? I swore they all had damn problems, called being an alpha-hole.

"Get your things," he said through his teeth. "We leave in ten minutes."

Before he walked out of the room, I grabbed his arm. "You said you wouldn't hurt anyone in my pack if I went with you."

He growled lowly, baring his canines at me, his mate. "I also said that I was going to have to take care of Tony, didn't I?" He stepped closer to me, towering over me and making me feel terrifyingly small. But something about his possessiveness made me weak for him. "I gave him a chance. If he hadn't come into your room, touched you, flirted with you, *kissed you*, maybe I wouldn't have."

"You're over the top and out of *fucking* control."

"Out of control?" He stepped toward me again, a sinister look in his eye.

I never thought I would see it, but it was there. The look of a god, the look of war, the look of utter chaos. I sucked in a breath, never having been turned on at the sight of such a man.

He snatched my jaw and gently caressed my cheek with his thumb. "Aurora, you have not seen me out of control." He was deathly calm, and it scared me more than it should have. "If I were out of control, you would be on your knees with my cock down this throat of yours"—he trailed his fingers down the column of my throat—"until you were gasping for breath."

My wolf purred at the thought, but I didn't want her to feel anything toward such a violent, savage creature even if he could make us feel so much while barely touching us.

"If you are anything like the man you were earlier when you had Tony's throat in your hands, I'm sure I'd be highly disappointed. That wasn't dominance; that was called being fucked u—"

He snatched my throat in his hand, squeezing lightly. "You want to see me out of control, Aurora?" he asked, lips grazing against mine. As his hardness pressed against my stomach, I clenched. "Get on your knees."

My breath caught in my throat, and I parted my lips to speak. But I couldn't say a word. Goddess, I wanted this more than anything. He pushed me away slightly, his eyes a mix of gold and brown.

"Knees," he said. "Before I have to push you down onto them."

I boldly brushed my fingers against the front of his pants and swore to myself at how big he felt inside of them. All I could picture was him inside of me, thrusting in and out until I could barely stand.

He suddenly lowered his hand, and I stumbled down onto my knees, my face close to his crotch. This was wrong. So wrong. But damn, did it make me feel good to be with someone who knew exactly what I wanted.

"Unzip my pants."

My heart was racing, and I didn't know what to say. All I knew was that my pussy was pulsing and that heat was crawling up my body until I felt like I was on fire. I willingly unzipped his black jeans and stared at his hard cock through a pair of gray briefs.

I didn't care how long I'd known him or how much I hated him at that moment. I couldn't think about anything other than the ache growing between my legs, the heat festering inside of me, my wolf begging me to please our mate like he had pleased us last night.

He pulled down his briefs, his cock springing out of them.

My pussy tightened at the sight. "Out of control," I said, sneering up at him. I wanted him to get angry, wanted him to show me what he looked like when he was out of control.

"This is out of control, Aurora." He grabbed his cock and rubbed it against my lips, and then he snatched my chin and the top of my head and pulled me toward him, making me take his length in my mouth.

He pushed himself into me ruthlessly, immediately hitting the back of my throat. I pushed my hands against his thighs, gagging.

But he refused to move, just stayed there and said, "All the way down."

I furrowed my brows together and pushed more of him down my throat until my lips were at the base of his cock.

"Fuck," he said under his breath. "Just like that."

He pushed his hips closer to my lips and thrust in and out of my mouth. I dug my nails into his thighs, my core warming. Goddess, nothing had ever felt so good. All I wanted was for him to touch me and my pussy again, rub it until I screamed.

With every thrust, he became rougher, and he tightened his hand around my neck. "Fuck, my cock feels so good down your throat." He took my hand and placed it against my throat, holding his hand over it and making me feel him inside.

I moaned on his cock, a wave of pleasure rolling through me. I pressed my thighs together and moved my hips side to side, trying to ease the throbbing between them.

He pushed himself all the way down my throat and stilled. "Let me see your eyes."

I gazed up at him through teary eyes and pushed a hand into my pants.

His eyes flashed gold, and he pulled his cock out of me. "Look at you. Loved it so much, you can't even resist touching yourself for me." He swept his thumb against my bottom lip. "You want more, don't you, Kitten?" he asked.

I growled under my breath—my wolf taking control—and rubbed my clit in quick, rough circles.

"What do you say?"

"Fuck you," I said, spit dripping down my chin. My nipples were pressing hard against my bra, and all I wanted was for him to reach down and tug on them. Touch me in any way he wanted.

"You say, *Yes, Alpha*." He grabbed my chin harsher in his hand. He shoved himself down my throat, and I clenched. "Let's try it again."

"Ares," someone said from outside the door.

Ares curled his fingers in my hair, gently tugging on it. He stared down at me, jaw tight, ignoring the man. My eyes watered when I looked up at him. Moon Goddess, I fucking loved this.

"Ares," the man said again.

Ares pulled his cock out of my mouth, and I gasped for breath. I posted my hands on the ground and looked down, chest rising and falling. He brushed a finger under my chin and lifted until I was gazing up into his bold brown eyes.

Why did I feel so good?

"What, Liam?" he asked harshly.

There was a pause.

"Charolette's on the phone, says she needs to talk to you."

His eyes immediately softened.

Charolette? Who was Charolette? And why was she calling my mate?

He released my chin from his hand, redid his pants, and walked to the door. Leaving me kneeling on my bedroom floor for *him*.

Ruffles walked over and rubbed herself against me, purring.

"Ten minutes," he said, pulling the door open and gazing back at Ruffles and not me. "And no cat."

CHAPTER 8

ARES

"When will you be home?" Charolette asked over the phone.

I blew a breath through my nose, hearing her soothing voice, and leaned against the car that the Darkmoon Pack had graciously *lent* me to bring Aurora home. Tony stood at the edge of the forest, arms crossed over his chest, talking to Aurora's parents. I let out a growl directed at him. Goddess, he was lucky I hadn't ripped him piece by piece.

I'd promised Mars I'd take it slow with Aurora. But when I had seen Tony kissing her, I hadn't given a fuck about promises anymore. He had been kissing what was and what would stay mine.

"Hello?" Charolette said again.

There was some rustling in the background, and then she yelled to Marcel—my warrior in charge of guarding her and training the pack—to shut up.

"Soon," I said.

"When you get home, come over. I have something for you."

Aurora's mother approached me, arms crossed over her chest.

I glanced up at the sky and suppressed another growl. "I have to go, Charolette. I'll see you soon."

She hummed. And before I hung up the phone, she mumbled a sweet, "I love you."

It was enough to calm me down for now, but I knew it wouldn't last. All I could smell was lemon drifting through the air from Aurora's bedroom window, driving my wolf crazy. He wanted to run back up the stairs to show her what a true alpha male felt like, to prove to her that Tony was less than nothing, to make her obedient.

The mere thought of turning such a strong woman into a puddle for me ...

I clenched my jaw and held back a groan, composing myself as Alpha Theia started talking my fucking ear off about this agreement.

It was all nonsense I didn't listen to because I wasn't going to let her tell me how to treat my mate.

All I needed was the answer to one question and one question only. "Why wasn't Aurora on the battlefield this morning?"

Alpha Theia and her mate, Theron, glanced at each other. An eerie silence erupted throughout the entire forest, and some of the wolves from her pack stared over at us, waiting for her response.

My gaze drifted from Theia to Theron. Though Theron was from one of the greatest warrior families, he looked so weak, so exhausted after a short battle. Letting his mate do all the talking. Having no say in any decisions she made. It was pitiful.

Theia stepped forward and pressed her lips together, dark hair blowing in the breeze, showing me all the scars on her neck and shoulders from years of fighting. "We wanted to protect her from you," she said strongly, but her gaze faltered.

Shame.

Written on her face. Etched into every one of her wrinkles. Shown in her slouched shoulders. Yet she tried to hide it behind her commanding alpha tone, behind her strong eyes. It was pathetic how disgraceful she was, how she could barter a smart and fierce alpha without a second thought.

"Then, why'd you trade her to me so willingly?" I asked. When neither she nor her mate answered, I growled. "Why'd you not wake her when the battle began? Why didn't you tell her she would be your pawn? She's a warrior and an alpha. She should've known everything going on in this pack, not just the things you want her to know."

I didn't know how Aurora was treated here, but things were about to change for her. And I'd be the one to change them.

CHAPTER 9

AURORA

I hurled my backpack over my shoulder, rolled two suitcases to my bedroom door, and frowned at the hot-pink pillow that Ruffles always slept on. She never lay anywhere else at night, except on my chest. It was full of fur, old, and raggedy, but it was hers. So, I grabbed it, wanting nothing more than to keep it forever and ever.

The suitcases were stuffed full of my clothes and essentials, the zippers stretching so much that they were bound to rip at any moment. I picked them up, one in each hand, and walked down the stairs, following Ares's stupid fucking voice.

When he saw me, he grabbed the bags from my hands, his biceps flexing, and carried them the rest of the way to the car that he had bullied Mom into giving him since his pack had run here.

"I could've done that myself," I said, gently setting my backpack down in the backseat and unzipping it a few inches.

"I know," he said, shoving the bags into the trunk. "Is this all your stuff?"

I pressed my lips together, glancing up at my window, where Ruffles usually sat, and frowned. "Yes."

I pushed past him to the passenger seat, but he caught my wrist. My skin tingled, my heart racing faster than I wanted it to. And I cursed the Moon Goddess. Ares didn't deserve how my wolf felt toward him. He was a no-good, psychotic alpha who had been destroying the lands for a stone he knew nothing about.

"And the cat?"

I growled and snatched my hand away. "She's sitting on my bed, wondering why my asshole of a mate isn't letting me take her."

Mom walked toward me, stretching out her arms to hug me. I glared at her and walked to Dad instead, enveloping him in a halfhearted hug. After Jeremy had died, he had been the only one to give me a chance, letting me read his books about the War of the Lycans, where a vicious group of hounds were defeated by our warrior family—but that defeat didn't last long as the hounds have started to torment these lands once again.

Dad rested his chin on my head, caressing my hair with his hand. "Don't hate your mother. She's ... doing what she thinks is best," he said.

But even his plea didn't change my mind. What kind of person traded their daughter to someone known for his blatant destruction, for his vicious killings, for evil? A bad mother and an even worse alpha.

I rested my head on his chest and expected Ares to break us up, to tell me that it was enough and we had to go, but he waited patiently by the passenger door.

Dad kissed my forehead. "Stay strong, A," he said, and somehow, I felt even worse.

What kind of warrior would let his mate trade his only daughter? Not any kind of warrior he used to tell me stories about when I was just a pup.

"I'll take care of Ruffles for you," Dad said in my ear before pulling away.

I forced a smile and bit back the angry tears. "You don't have to." I walked to Ares, brushing right past Mom and Tony, who was glaring at my mate.

"Aurora," Tony said.

"Don't," Ares snapped.

He pushed me into the car and slammed the door, a growl ripping from his throat the moment he turned back to Tony. They exchanged a few harsh words, and I stared at them through the car window, not listening to a word they said.

So much testosterone. I could only imagine what it was going to be like at Ares's pack. All the rumors had told me that Ares's pack was just like him—ruthless, cruel, and heartless. The Moon Goddess and I both knew that I wouldn't be able to handle everyone thinking with their instincts rather than their brains.

I blew out a deep breath and tapped my fingers on my knee. Who knew how many hours of hell I'd be in the car with the god of war? It was going to be a fucking nightmare. Ignoring him the whole time, listening to his breathing, smelling that damn good scent of hazelnut.

Ares walked to his door and scooted into his seat. Then, without turning back, he started the car and drove out of the driveway and off of my property. I watched my pack disappear in the rearview mirror and didn't see an ounce of guilt on Mom's face.

Trees whizzed past us, their leaves rustling together in the wind. I frowned, wanting nothing more than to run through that forest again, to let my wolf free the way I used to before I was hurt, to feel the wind in my fur, to be happy with Jeremy.

Miles ahead, the clouds turned from cotton white to an ominous gray, looming over Sanguine Wilds. I wondered how Jeremy was as he ran with the wolves up in the clouds. He'd always loved the thunderous storms, rain beating down on the leaves, watching the lightning strike trees from our hideout cave deep in the forest.

Was he happy? Would he have exchanged me for his pack?

Tears welled up in my eyes, yet I didn't let them fall. Jeremy would never have done that. He'd have stood up and fought or traded his life for mine. I balled my hands into fists. Goddess, I missed him.

Ares turned to me, one hand on the steering wheel, the other inching closer and closer to my thigh.

"Don't even think about it," I said through clenched teeth.

We came to a stop sign, the road splitting off into two directions. Ares turned right into the fog. Tilted slightly and adorned with large bite marks, a silver stake was stuck into the ground to my right with a sign attached to it, labeled *Hound Territory*. I tensed and sat up in my seat, gaze flickering across the forest to catch any signs of rogues.

"Talk to me," Ares said.

"No," I said, keeping my eyes focused on the windshield.

Leaves blew wildly around us, and little droplets of rain started hitting against the glass. Out of all the ways Ares could go to get back to his property, why'd he take the rogue route?

"Kitten ..."

"What?" I snapped, fear and fury rushing through me. "What do you want me to say to you? That you're a dick for making me leave my family? That I think you're a complete idiot for destroying packs just for power? That I would rather be at home, continuing my comfortable life without you?"

Okay, that last one was a bit harsh and totally untrue. After last night and earlier in my bedroom, I was more than glad that I had met him. My wolf hadn't been this excited since Jeremy was alive. She was doing flips in my stomach, jumping up and down, running around in circles, like his scent was some kind of wolf-nip.

She was happy, but part of me wished he weren't my mate. He was an aggressive asshole who killed people for power, and I didn't want to lead that kind of life. But now that I was being thrust into that lifestyle of pure violence, I had no other choice.

He growled, his knuckles whitening on the steering wheel. "You know nothing about me," he said. "Nothing about the reasons I do what I do."

"I know that you plucked me right out of my home because you wanted me for yourself. I know that you used me to gain access to my pack. I know that you—"

Someone ran right out into the deserted street, and Ares slammed on the brakes, sending me forward. My seat belt cut into my collarbone, and I groaned.

"I know that you're completely senseless," I said under my breath.

He gazed at me for a moment, looking me up and down, and then turned back to the woman in front of us. She knelt in the middle of the street, clutching her neck. Blood seeped through her fingers and drenched her raggedy red hair. The woman glanced up through the fog lights at me, and I immediately recognized her as a rogue. Her hair was wild, her stench putrid, her skin cut up with scars only a rogue would have.

Ares parked the car, and my eyes widened.

"What are you doing?" I asked, clutching my seat belt.

Nobody should ever stop in Hound Territory, not even for an easy-to-kill rogue. Hounds used rogues as bait. Though a type of rogue themselves, hounds were more vicious, stronger, and so much more violent. They didn't give a damn about anyone.

Ares opened his door. "Stay here."

I undid my seat belt. "Are you crazy?" I asked, grabbing his forearm. "This is Hound Territory, and you want to go out there to help a rogue you know nothing about. Hounds could be chasing her for all you know."

"Are you afraid of the hounds?" he asked me, lips curling into the smallest of smirks.

I growled and released his wrist. Fine, if he wanted to go out there and lose his shifting abilities like I'd lost mine to the hounds, I would get a front row seat. I didn't care anymore. I'd drive off as soon as they attacked him.

"Stay here," Ares said sternly, a bloodthirsty look crossing his face. There it was again—that look of a god.

He closed the door and approached the woman, saying something to her that I couldn't quite hear. She shook her head and wiped tears from her cheeks with the back of her hand. She motioned to the forest and crouched down, grasping her stomach. Moon Goddess, this was going to take longer than I wanted.

What was supposed to be a few hours' drive was going to turn into an even longer one.

After glancing around the forest once more to make sure it was clear, I grabbed my backpack from the backseat and unzipped it. Inside, two black eyes gazed up at me, and it meowed. I smiled and pulled Ruffles out along with a bag of Ruffles chips.

She rubbed against me, like she always did when she wanted food or knew I was worried.

"Sorry, girl."

I tore open the chips, and she stuffed her head in the bag, munching on one. Her cute little crunches made me smile and relax back into the seat.

"My mate didn't want me to bring you ... but I wouldn't leave you behind."

She hopped onto the driver's seat, placed her two paws on the steering wheel, and stared at the scene in front of us with a single chip in her mouth.

My gaze fell on Ares, who was walking into the woods *alone* while the woman just stood on the two yellow lines in the middle of the road. I wiped my sweaty palms on my jeans. Moon Goddess, he shouldn't be going out there. He should be in here, with me, where he would be safe.

After a few minutes, Ares emerged with a young pup on his

hip. The pup was crying, his hair disheveled. The woman fell to her knees and reached up for the boy, unable to hold back her emotions. Ares placed the boy in her arms.

Ruffles glanced over at me and meowed.

Ares gave the woman a breathtaking smile and handed her the child.

My eyes widened slightly, and I nodded my head to Ruffles. "I know, girl. I know."

She meowed again and swatted my knee. I looked down at her to see her staring at my passenger window. And just as I looked over, something smashed into the side of the car, the glass shattering all over my lap.

I screamed and scurried away from the window, my heart hammering inside my chest. Two black eyes of a hound stared right at me as it sprinted straight for the passenger door again.

A vicious growl exited Ares's throat and echoed throughout the entire forest. He shifted midair into his wolf and sprinted toward the car like his life depended on it. The hound hit the side of the car again, blood-colored foam oozing from his mouth. He thrust his snout into the broken window, trying to latch his teeth into my shoulder.

More hounds appeared through the forest, trapping Ares. My heart pounded in my chest, and I threw myself over Ruffles to save her life, like I wish I had done with Jeremy. But Ruffles had other plans.

She hissed, jumped on my shoulder, and swatted at the hound with both paws, tearing into his skin. It wasn't hard but was enough to be annoying. Her tail stood straight up, and she caught him in the eye. Thrashing back and forth, the hound howled.

Goddess, I wished I could shift, so I could kill him instantly. The rogue shoved himself further into the car, saliva dripping from every one of his teeth. I glanced back at Ares, hoping that he, the woman, and her son were okay. But what I saw instead were two hounds lying dead in the middle of the street and Ares surrounded by four more.

Rain beat down diagonally around him, fog sitting heavily in the air.

Damn it. Damn it. Damn it.

I felt useless. Completely useless. My mate was fighting the monsters—the same ones I had dedicated my life to finding a way to eradicate—while I just sat in the car, trying to protect myself and Ruffles from being ripped to shreds.

This was how Jeremy had been murdered. Surrounded by four wolves. In the pouring rain. Unable to escape. Torn to shreds. The leader of that hound group had killed him almost instantly with a look of pleasure on his face.

I tossed Ruffles to the driver's seat and scooted into the seat myself, kicking the wolf's snout with my heel. He sunk his canines into my foot. I fumbled with my backpack, grabbed the silver knife inside the bag—because silver was the Achilles heel for wolves, and shoved it right into his mouth.

The blade sliced through the back of his neck, and he released my foot, shaking his head from side to side. I kicked him again, crawled over to my seat, wrapped my hand around his neck, and snapped it.

When I looked back at Ares, he was pulling a hound's throat from his neck, and the other three were lying dead on the cement with their comrades. Ares's teeth dripped with blood. He gazed over at me with the darkest golden eyes that I had ever seen and growled lowly.

I lured Ruffles back into my backpack with the bag of chips before he had a chance to notice her and cursed to myself for ever coming with Ares. We hadn't even made it a couple hours before shit happened.

Ares gazed around the forest twice and shifted into his human. Blood gushed out of a bite mark in his chest. He hurried over to the car, opened his door, pulled out a phone that he had gotten from somewhere, and glared at *me*.

"Liam. Hounds. North Sanguine Wilds. Get here now." He threw his phone onto the seat and growled at me. "What was that?"

My eyes widened, and I pushed my backpack into the backseat. "What do you mean?"

"He attacked you."

"Yeah, and they attacked you." I pressed my lips together, unable to hold back my rage. "Why the fuck are you angry with me for your stupid-ass decisions? I told you not to go out there."

"You didn't shift." He clenched the door handle in his fist, muscles flexing. Beads of blood rolled down his naked and tensed abdomen. "You could've gotten killed because you didn't shift, Aurora."

I wanted to argue with him, but nothing came out. How was I supposed to tell my mate—one of the strongest alphas of our time—that I couldn't shift? That I wasn't the alpha he thought I was. That I was useless to Mom and that I'd be useless to him too.

My wolf whimpered at the thought. *Mate won't want us if we tell him. Nobody will want us. We can barely even protect ourselves.*

She disappeared in the back of my mind, and I wrapped my arms around myself. Ruffles would want us. She would always want us. But my mate might not.

I'd become a lone wolf. Maybe he'd feed me to the hounds himself when he found out. The horror stories of him told me that he would do such a thing. And then we'd cease to exist together.

"It was one hound," I said, brushing it off as if it were nothing, but my voice wavered.

Ares continued to glare at me with eyes so rageful and so hateful that I thought he would kick me out of the car right then and there for not protecting myself. And I didn't know how to feel about that. Part of me thought that it would be great. I could go back to my pack—my pack that didn't want me. The other part of me dreaded the mere thought of being without my mate, without Mars or Ares or whoever the hell he really was.

After a few moments, he gestured to the mother and child. "Get out of the car, so I can watch you."

"I can watch myself."

He clenched his jaw. "Now, get out of the fucking car. I'm not going to say it again."

I grumbled to myself, trying not to touch the shattered glass sprinkled along the seat, and stepped out of the car. Some had cut into my leg, but I hid it well with my dark jeans. It didn't need to be treated now. I'd deal with it later.

After Ares found a spare pair of pants in the back of the car, we approached the woman.

She turned to Ares, tears streaming down her face. "How can I repay you? I-I don't have anything of value."

"With information and by accepting membership into my pack, so we can keep you safe."

My eyes widened. He was going to let her into his pack just like that? While I had sympathy for her and her son, she was still a rogue, and rogues were known for betraying, slaying, and murdering innocent wolves.

She fell to her knees. "Yes, of course. You're my savior today. What kind of information do you need?"

"The Malavite Stone. Tell me all you know about it."

I stiffened. I should've known he'd ask about that.

The Malavite Stone.

The stone he tore apart packs to find. The stone that could really make him a god with all its power.

The stone that I had inside of me.

After the hounds had attacked my pack, it had been used to heal me. Half of it was inside my back, keeping me alive. And the other half was with the hounds—lost forever.

The stone had powers that not many knew about. Healing

properties. Strength properties. Power properties. Properties that hadn't even been unlocked yet. It was the rarest gem in the entire world. Every alpha wanted to get their hands on it, but nobody knew where it was. Except Elijah—one of my closest allies —and me.

"I don't have any information about the Malavite Stone," the woman said, blood draining from her face. "As far as I know, it's not even around here."

"Don't lie to me," Ares said in his alpha tone, so frighteningly deep and stern.

My wolf purred, heat warming my core at how powerful he sounded. Damn mating bond.

She stepped back toward the woods. "I-I don't know anything about it." She snatched her son's hand, tongue clicking against her teeth.

Her gaze was fixed on the ground, and I knew she was lying. Ares knew it too.

He snatched her chin hard. "Tell me," he demanded. His voice was deadly quiet. "What do you know?" When she didn't say anything, Ares gripped her chin tighter. "Tell me now before I have to make you."

After parting her lips a few times and squeezing her son's hand, she nodded. "Okay," she said quietly. "I … the hounds have the stone … a man with a large scar down the side of his face rules over them. That's as much as I know."

He glared at her for a few minutes and then shoved her back and released her chin. *Wow, what a total bipolar—*

Ares's beta and a few other warriors pulled behind our car. They sniffed out the forest around us, looking for other hounds but found none. When they returned, Ares instructed them to take the woman and her pup back to his pack and get them food, water, and shelter.

But something wasn't sitting easy with me. This wasn't the

Ares I knew. All of the stories I had heard of Ares were about him being ruthless and cutthroat, killing anyone and everyone in his path without a care in the world. This was different, and I didn't know how I felt.

Because Ares didn't save people from disaster. He caused it.

CHAPTER 10

AURORA

Ares grabbed my hand and led me to Liam's car, tossing my bags in the trunk. Liam and the others disappeared through the forest. And instead of asking Ares why they hadn't just come with us, I pressed my lips together.

I didn't want to speak to him and his annoying ass. He had gotten us into this mess by stopping in Hound Territory. All I wanted was to get away from here and go somewhere I could rest with Ruffles on my chest. Somewhere without interruption, without a mate claiming me, without feeling like shit because I'd almost gotten myself killed by not shifting.

Ares slid behind the wheel, started the car, and said, "I need to clean off."

"Can't you wait until we get to your pack house?"

"I'm covered in blood, and my property is hours away by car."

I turned toward the window, hoping he wouldn't suggest running back to his pack, and stared out at the darkness that suddenly engulfed the forest, swallowing the trees, refusing to let the moonlight hit the ground. It was eerie and terrifying, just like the night before the hound attack that had killed Jeremy.

"Well, whose fault is that?" I asked.

He growled lowly and continued driving until we finally made it out of Hound Territory. The first dirt road he found, he drove down, tapping his fingers against the steering wheel.

"Great," I said sarcastically. "Turn down a dark dirt road. What a good choice."

"You always have something to say, don't you?" he asked, jaw tight.

"Yes, I do." I pressed my lips together and glared over at him, trying to suppress the growing urge my wolf had to rip his clothes off right then and there. Moonlight flickered in through the windshield, hitting his perfectly sculpted face, his brown eyes looking hard yet utterly sensual. I swallowed and turned my head away from him, so I wouldn't stare anymore. "Especially when people make stupid decisions."

He parked the car, cut the headlights, and stepped out without saying a word. After a few moments of complete silence, he disappeared into the woods. I glanced around at the darkness. We weren't in Hound Territory anymore, but we were close. So, I followed after him. Definitely *not* because I was scared at all. I just wanted to give him a piece of my mind.

"You know what else too?" I asked, following his hazelnut scent.

In the near distance, water splashed gently against a shore. We walked into a clearing, and moonlight glimmered against a lake.

Ares peeled off his shirt, throwing me a cheeky look. "What?"

I gulped and tore my gaze away from his muscular back. Last night, I had seen him without his shirt, but I hadn't known it was Ares. All I could think was how true the rumors were. Ares looked to be sculpted by the Moon Goddess herself, muscles swollen under the light, scars decorating his back.

Don't think about it, Aurora. He's a dick. Remember that.

"You're disgusting."

He shimmied out of his jeans *and* underwear. I forced myself to stare at anything but his back, his flexed triceps, and that ass. It all meant nothing if he was always such a dick.

After giving me a hard look, he stepped into the water. "What did I do that disgusted you so much?"

"Wanting that stone."

"You don't know what people would do to have that stone, what people have to give up for it."

He submerged himself all the way in the water, and I cursed myself for even being here with him. I shouldn't have left the car because my wolf wouldn't stop going crazy.

While I hadn't shifted into my wolf in almost two months, she was still as loud and excited as she always had been, maybe even more so now. Since she couldn't get her energy out in the form of running, she made sure she got it out in other ways, like this.

When he came back up, he shook out his wet hair, letting it fall into his face. Beads of water rolled down his taut chest. And all I could imagine were my hands gliding over his biceps and the way his fingers would dance alongside my hips if I were in the water with him.

"Not everyone is who you think they are, Aurora." He glanced over at me. "Not even me."

My wolf purred, just watching him in that water, all alone. She wanted to get in there with him. She wanted *him*. *Now*. And no matter how hard I tried, I couldn't control myself around him.

I dipped my toes into the water. "Then, show me who you are, *Alpha*."

Waist deep in the lake, he grazed a hand down his abdomen, and my gaze followed. "Show you who I am?"

Maybe I'd gotten ahead of myself. That *was* a big statement for someone who was supposed to hate him at that moment, for someone who was supposed to not want anything to do with him at all.

He raked his golden wolfish eyes down my body and smirked.

"Take off your clothes and come to me, Kitten. I'll show you who I really am."

My heart pounded in my chest. *Moon Goddess, help me.*

"Don't make me say it again."

"And if I want to make you say it again?" I whispered.

He chuckled, beads of water running down that taut chest of his. All I wanted was his hand around my throat, his fingers inside my pussy, his lips devouring mine like I was his to claim.

"Try me," he said, stalking closer and closer to me, the water rippling around him.

Damn it. What the hell was wrong with me?

I forced myself to turn around. If I looked at him for another second, I would jump right into that lake with him and have no regrets. I would do anything that he told me to without thinking it through. I would forget that *I* was an alpha, too, and alphas didn't react so rashly ... unless they went by the name of Ares, the god of war.

The water stayed silent behind me, and my heart pounded against my chest.

It was too quiet. Too fucking quiet.

Suddenly, Ares snaked his hand around my neck from behind and pulled me toward him. "Take off your clothes," he said against my ear, raking his fingers over my breast.

I shivered at his touch, my nipples immediately hardening against my bra.

"Now."

Fuck acting cautiously.

Turning around, I curled my fingers under the hem of my shirt and tugged it over my head. My wolf stirred inside of me, willing to do anything that her mate asked her to do, betraying me and all my deepest, darkest wishes.

"Good girl." Ares lightly his lips against my neck. He looped a finger in my bra cup, tugging on it. "Now, this."

I unclipped my bra from behind me, remembering how his

hands had felt on my body last night. He had made us feel better than anyone ever had. My wolf purred, wanting that again. Goddess, she wanted him to devour us like he had promised he would earlier.

Ares tore it off of me and groped my breast firmly in his hand. He ran his palm over my nipple, and I clenched.

Mate. Mate. Mate. Mate. Claim us.

He plunged a hand into my jeans and rubbed my swollen clit through my panties. "You're always so wet for me, Kitten."

Sucking my bottom lip between my teeth, I brushed my fingers against his hard cock. "Let me finish what I started before," I said. I couldn't take this anymore, hadn't really stopped thinking about earlier since we left the pack house.

"Needy, are we?" He chuckled against my skin and rubbed me harder. "Take off your panties. It's my turn."

My eyes widened, and I grasped his cock, stroking it slowly. "Your turn?"

He pressed his lips against mine and stared down at me, knowing that he had full control over my every move. It was like he had some divine aura or power to him. One way or another, this man had been fated to destroy me.

"Take them off and hand them to me."

My pussy pulsed wildly. I just wanted him inside of me, thrusting his huge cock into my tight pussy, over and over until I was begging for him to stop. I kicked off my pants and slowly stepped out of my underwear. He held out his hand, and I placed them in it.

After tossing my thong toward the pile of his clothes, he pushed two fingers against my clit, rubbing gently. "Tell me how bad you want it, Kitten. Tell me how much you wish my face were between your legs, my tongue on your sensitive little clit, my fingers inside of you."

He slid them down my folds to my opening, and I suppressed a moan.

"Come on, Kitten. Don't be shy."

"Ares," I said softly, eyes closing. I gripped his wrist. Moon Goddess …

"What do you want?" He pressed his fingers against my core, teasing me. "Tell me."

I furrowed my brows together, watching his fingers rub against my folds. "You," I said under my breath. "I want you."

He growled lowly, picking me up and placing me down on the grassy patch by the lake. He spread my legs apart, and almost immediately, his breath was on my pussy. He inhaled. "Fuck." He pushed a finger inside of me. "I've been waiting for this all fucking day." He pressed his lips to my folds, his tongue massaging my swollen clit.

I moaned and arched my back into the grass, thrusting a hand through his hair. Holy—

"You taste so good." He gently sucked my clit between his lips.

My toes curled, and I tried to stop my legs from trembling. Yet all I could imagine was how the great and powerful Ares couldn't get me off his mind all day, how he'd wanted to taste me, how *I* had the power. His tongue was driving me wild, sending pleasure through my body, making me crave more.

"Say my name," he murmured against me. "I want to hear my name on your lips."

Such a vicious creature, *begging* me to say his name.

"Ares …" I dug my nails into his shoulders, trying to displace the pressure rising in my core with each thrust. "Moon Goddess, you're so fucking good at that."

"If we were home"—he flicked my clit with his tongue—"I would eat your pussy all night."

He tugged on my nipple, and my body jerked into the air. My claws dug into his shoulders, my lips parted in pure bliss, my entire body shook with ecstasy.

I moaned loudly as my body tingled with delight. Wave after

wave of pleasure rolled out of me. I took a deep breath and relaxed against the grass, my chest rising and falling raggedly.

He gazed up at me with a mischievous glint in his eye. "I'm not finished with you yet."

"I can't do what we did last night, Ares. My pussy is so—"

Instead of going in for seconds, he picked me up off the grass, threw me over his shoulder, and walked toward the water. My eyes widened, and I struggled in his hold, arms and legs flailing everywhere.

"Oh no, no, no, no, no, no."

"Yes." He wrapped his arms tightly around my torso, holding me to his chest as he submerged us into the water.

"Ares!" I shouted, my nipples hardening from the coldness of the water. "It's freezing!"

He pressed his body against mine, and his arm wrapped around my waist under the water. He pulled me in closer, lips curling into a smile, and rested his forehead against mine. "Call me Mars, Aurora, please."

"Why?" I ran my fingers over his muscles, loving how smooth and big they felt under the water.

He was so close, but I wanted him closer.

"Please," he said so desperately. "Mars."

"Mars."

After burying his face into my neck and pushing a lock of my wet hair behind my shoulder, he inhaled my scent. Though the water was cold, being close to him made it bearable. I relaxed under his touch and kicked my legs back and forth under the water.

I had barely known Mars for an entire day, yet I had learned more about him than any rumor or *Lunar Daily Newspaper* article could tell me. Though an asshole, he was a fun asshole, a cute asshole, and a somewhat sweet asshole. Helping that rogue when she shouldn't have been helped. Pulling me into his chest when I hadn't wanted to be close to him, when I hadn't wanted to feel these feelings for him. It was ... refreshing.

I wondered how many other girls had fallen under this spell so easily.

My wolf growled at the thought, and I soothed her by clutching him closer. "Why do you really want that stone?"

The sudden, playful Mars was gone, and that godly look crossed his face. "Not now." Even his voice was tense.

"I just want to know," I whispered because I had half the stone inside of my body and didn't want him ripping it out because he had this insatiable thirst for power.

I couldn't allow myself to fall for him and let my guard down, only to die by the hands of my mate. When he found out that I couldn't shift or fight easily, I would become useless to him.

If Mom thought I was worthless, a god like Ares would really have no use for a cripple like me.

My entire body tensed, and I pulled away from him. I couldn't get close. I had to put space between us. I had to forget about whatever kind of goodness I had seen in him today. Because Alpha Ares wasn't good; he was cruel. And when he found out I had the stone, he would tear me apart, just as he had done to so many packs before me.

CHAPTER 11

ARES

After driving the rest of the way in silence, I placed Aurora's sleeping body down on my bed, rested her head against the gray pillows, and draped the blankets over her shoulders. Moonlight flooded in through my window, bouncing off her perfect fucking face.

It had been less than a day, and I had lied to her already.

Yet I couldn't help myself. It happened so naturally now, like a fucking protective mechanism or some shit.

The way she had said my name in the water, the way the moonlight had made her face glow like a goddess's, everything about her … and I'd had to lie. I peeled off my shirt, hurled it into the hamper, and picked up Aurora's backpack.

Little whimpers had been coming from it all day. And when I opened it, two big black eyes stared up at me. I reached in, pulled out Aurora's cat, and held back a sneeze. "Moon Goddess …" I walked with the cat and Aurora's backpack to the spare bedroom across from mine and set her on the ground. "I can't believe she left you in there all day."

She walked to the other side of the room, her little butt swaying from side to side, just like Aurora's did, jumped onto a high dresser, and glared down at me. I shut the door behind us and searched through Aurora's things, looking for her food.

Laptop. Chips. Pencil. Notes. Chips. Bloody silver knife that smelled like that hound. Chips. Chips. More chips.

I stared down at the five small bags of Ruffles chips and glanced up at the gray cat. She licked her lips, stared lovingly at the plastic bags. I picked one up, opened it, and pulled out a chip, moving it from side to side in front of her face. Her gaze followed my fingers.

After sneezing, I stuck the chip right in my mouth. The cat leaped right off of the dresser, wrapped her arms around my neck, and swatted the chip right out of my mouth. When it fell onto the floor, she hopped down and snatched it between her teeth.

I waved my hand in the air, trying to get rid of all the cat fur before I started sneezing and couldn't stop.

My first lie was that I hadn't wanted the fucking cat. I didn't care that she had it. I just ... couldn't take all this ... fucking shedding of fur. It drifted in the air and caused me to sneeze again. I took a step toward the door and cursed.

Damn, I wished that this were my only lie.

After opening a couple of bags of chips and setting out a box —we'd have to get litter tomorrow—I left the cat in the room and walked to my dimly lit office. It was two in the morning, and Liam was sitting in one of the chairs in front of my desk, glancing through a file.

"How is the rogue and her son?" I asked.

He tossed the file onto my desk and stood. "Living with one of the elders. Told him to keep an eye on her for tonight. I'll watch her until she gives us something about the stone. She knows more than she's saying."

I ran a hand over my face. Hunting for this damn thing was so tiring. I just needed the search to be over. We didn't have time to sit around and wait anymore.

"Did you find any information regarding the stone at Aurora's pack?"

"No," he said. "We need more time."

I growled, nails lengthening into claws. "We don't fucking have time."

Time was running out quicker than I wanted. We needed the stone, and we needed the stone now. I'd destroy the whole fucking world to find it. Packs. People. I didn't care who or what got in my way.

"I know," Liam said.

I snatched his throat, shoved him against the wall, and growled. "No, you don't." I pressed my lips together. *Think of Aurora. Aurora. Aurora.* My grip loosened on his neck, and I released him, turning my back. "You know how hopeless this all is without that stone."

He rubbed his neck slightly and snarled. "Don't think I don't know the consequences of not getting that stone. Her life will turn to shit without it. She'll just get worse." Liam looked away and into the moonlight out the window.

What most people outside my pack didn't know was that I didn't want that stone for power or strength. I didn't even want that stone to rule the lands. I wanted that stone for her, for Charolette. The one woman that I cared for the most, the one woman who had gotten me through every hardship, the one woman who I'd sworn to protect from anything—even my mate, if it came to it.

Telling Aurora that I wanted power … that was me—Ares—lying to her.

"I know," I said under my breath. I glared around my office, looking at the leather couches, at the oak desk, and even at the moonflower in a bright yellow flowerpot Charolette had brought over this morning for me. Everything I'd worked so hard to achieve for this pack would all be for nothing without a miracle.

I needed to clear my mind. Every day that Charolette was sick only stressed me out more. I loved her with everything I had, and I needed her with me. After Mom … I couldn't let anyone else close to me die.

"I need to run."

Before I could leave the room, Liam caught my shoulder and tugged me back. "We have other problems."

"What?" I asked, shrugging him off me.

"Your mate."

I clenched my jaw, narrowed my eyes, and snarled. "What about Aurora?"

"One, everyone is too excited to meet her tomorrow. Especially Marcel."

My wolf growled at the mention of Marcel. That asshole was the best warrior I had but also notorious for flirting with mated women. He didn't give a shit who he got with or what he said to anyone.

"I'll handle Marcel," I said through clenched teeth. "What else?"

"Two, I believe the hounds are tracking Aurora down. The rogue woman said that there was a bounty on Aurora's head and that the hounds want her dead. Nobody knows why."

My wolf growled again, this time aching for blood. "Then, we'll kill them. One by one." I wouldn't let anyone even *think* about hurting my mate. I'd rip them limb by limb before they had the chance to touch her.

"Three"—Liam smiled—"I can't wait for her to get on your nerves." He walked to the door and pulled it open. "Finally, someone able to test you, Ares. I don't think you're ready for it."

Oh, I was ready.

I was ready for anything she could throw at me, for any lie she could tell, for any fight she tried to start with me. Mars and I wanted it all from our alpha mate. We already loved when she back-talked, when she got all up in our face, thinking that she was the toughest wolf we'd ever come across. Our mate was the one thing we could agree upon, the one thing we didn't fight about … but I knew this calmness between us wouldn't last for long. Mars probably thought that if she spent enough time with me, she'd start to hate me too.

It wasn't always this way with Mars and me. We hadn't always been two different people trapped in the same body, but after what had happened with Mom, I needed to protect him. The world might've been fucked up back then—hell, it still was now—but if it hadn't happened, I never would have met Aurora, only Mars would've.

No matter who we were to her, neither of us could wait to see her wolf, to run with her up to Caraco Mountain and decide which group of rogues we would hunt that day. I'd bet her fur was soft, just like her hair, her scent even more tantalizing than her human, her strength nearly matching mine.

I had waited for this moment for twenty-four years, and I'd almost screwed it up already.

CHAPTER 12

AURORA

I snapped my eyes open when I heard Ruffles meow. Sunlight flooded in through the dark curtains, giving —I was assuming—Ares's room a slight morning glow. I still didn't know what to call him. Was he that godlike alpha or that man I'd met at the lake a couple nights ago? Maybe he was both.

Monstrously dark and sleek, the room had an oddly homely feel to it with a couple pictures on the walls and—*wait a damn second.* I squinted my eyes at a picture of him and a young woman across from me. Frizzy blonde hair, piercing blue eyes, lips the color of cherries, she was beautiful.

They stared happily ahead, his head on her shoulder, giving the camera the biggest grin I had ever seen. Nothing like Alpha Ares, the notoriously powerful alpha from the Sanguine Wilds.

My wolf growled, jealousy creeping into my veins. Who was she, and why did she have her arms around my mate like that? Why'd they look so happy and youthful, like they were ready to take on the world together?

Ruffles meowed again. I gazed around the room and sat up almost immediately. I'd find out who she was later. Now, I had to find Ruffles before he found her and threw her out into the hound-infested forest.

Ares lay in the bed next to me, one arm draped around my waist, pulling me closer. "Kitten, lie back down with me. You smell so good."

"No," I said. "I need to go—"

He easily curled me to him, making me fall back onto the bed "That was an order." He pressed himself closer to me, lips brushing against my ear, making me shiver. "Things are going to be different here than they were at your old pack."

"You mean, my home," I said, wanting to keep him talking so he didn't hear Ruffles meow. Moon Goddess, what was she getting into?

He growled lowly in my ear, canines brushing against my neck. "This is your home, Aurora, and you'll soon find out that this pack is run differently than your mother's." His hand slipped under the hem of my shirt, fingers rubbing soothing circles on my stomach. "For instance, you're not going to disobey me when I give you an order."

I snorted and sat back up. "Yeah, okay," I said sarcastically. "I'll obey your every command, sit at your feet, worship you to—"

He snaked a hand around my neck, yanking me back down next to him. "Another rule … you don't leave my bed in the morning until I've eaten."

"Moon Goddess, Ares, you expect me to wait until you're finish—"

"Yes." He placed lingering kisses down my neck, disappeared under the blankets, and yanked down my underwear, staring up at me from between my legs. "Every morning, you wait until I'm satisfied."

My eyes widened. Oh … he meant … "But you just did it last n—"

He pulled my folds apart with his fingers and placed his lips on my clit. "I did, and I'm going to do it again." Ares spread my legs and flicked my clit with his tongue. Holding my trembling legs as far apart as they would go, he gazed up at me and said, "Fuck, Kitten ... I can't wait to be inside of you tonight."

Tonight? Oh, no, no, no, no, no, no. Not tonight. We couldn't do it tonight.

I wasn't ready for him like that. We had to keep as much space between us as possible. I was not falling in love with an asshole after some good sex and then getting my heart ripped out of my damn dead body.

Yes, we are, my wolf purred in the back of my mind.

I tensed and let him touch me because it felt damn good, but I didn't want to be another one of his whores. According to the rumors, this man had a thing for anyone with a pair of tits. And while I didn't care that he'd had sex before me, he was still my mate. I was allowed to be a tad bit jealous over any other woman who'd had her paws all over him.

"Does my mate have a problem with that?" he mumbled against me, golden eyes of his wolf staring up at me. He sucked my clit between his lips, pushed a finger inside of me, and hummed against my pussy.

I furrowed my brows together and clenched, hating how much I loved this.

"I asked you a question," he said, voice hard and utterly demanding.

"Y-yes." I clutched the sheets in my fists, arching my back as heat warmed my core.

I wanted more. I always wanted more of him, more of this. He was too good at it.

He pushed another finger inside of me, moving them dreadfully slow. "Does she have a problem with me thrusting my cock into what's *mine,* or does she have a problem with how much she is aching for it?"

When he added another finger and stilled, I tightened around him. I'd spent the last two lousy years sleeping with Tony, and he couldn't even compare to *this*. Call me greedy, call me a whore, call me every name in the book, but I refused to let Ares stop now. I moved my hips back and forth slightly, needing some friction.

"So desperate for it," he said, closing his eyes and inhaling. "So desperate for me."

Wetness pooled between my legs.

"Show me how you want me to fuck you."

"Wh-what?" My heart raced.

"Show me how you want me to fuck you. Move your hips on me. Use my fingers to make yourself come. I want to watch this pretty little body of yours tremble."

My eyes widened for a brief moment. So damn confident in himself. So damn sexy. So damn … I grabbed his wrist, thrusting it closer to my pussy … so damn big. His fingers slid into me with ease. I pulled them out and then rammed them back into me again, moaning.

"Faster," Ares said.

I moved his hand faster, pounding his fingers into me as far as they would go.

"Come on, Kitten. Is that all you have?" he asked, shaking his head in disapproval. "Let me show you how it's done."

One arm curled around my waist. He thrust his fingers hard and deep into my pussy, the pressure almost becoming unbearable. I grasped on to his shoulders, digging my nails into his skin, and pushed myself back. Needing to create space between us. Needing to breathe for a second.

But, Moon Goddess, he didn't stop.

No matter how much distance I tried to put between us, he followed me. Curling his arm tighter around my waist and thrusting his fingers up into my pussy until I was plastered against his headboard, my feet on his thighs, my legs shaking uncontrollably.

Someone knocked on the door, and my eyes widened.

"Ares," Liam said from the hall.

"Come back later, Liam." Ares kept his gaze on me.

"But there—"

"I said, come back later," Ares said, growling.

A wave of pleasure rolled through my body. I was so close to coming, so close to releasing myself for him, so close to feeling my body tingle with excitement.

He placed his lips on my stomach, looked up at me, fingers still thrusting wildly, and said, "Come for me, baby."

I parted my lips, slapped a hand over my mouth, and moaned into it, coming almost instantly. Dear Moon Goddess. He continued to thrust his fingers into me, slowing down only slightly.

"Charolette wants to see you," Liam said again.

Charolette?

Ares tensed and then slowed his fingers. "Tell her that I will see her during the party," he said. He knelt next to me, sliding his fingers out of my aching pussy and sucking them into his mouth.

Was that who the woman in the picture was? He seemed to respond to her name like he would a mate, always there when she called, alert to her whenever and wherever she was.

After a few moments, he stood and nodded toward the door. "Come on, Kitten. It's time for you to meet the pack."

My wolf growled, and I pulled down my shirt to cover my bare pussy, suddenly feeling so … so … distant. I didn't want to think the worst, but Mom had beaten it into my head that Ares was a no-good, lying, whore-loving man.

What was the point of me even being here, of me enjoying this, if one day, I'd be less than nothing to him too?

"I'll be down in five minutes." I pulled the blankets up to shield myself from him.

If Ares found Ruffles before I did, he'd probably rip her to pieces and serve her tiny little body to me for breakfast.

Ares pulled on a pair of shorts. "Five minutes. If you're not downstairs by then, I'll come and get you. And you don't want me to come back up here, angry, Kitten."

Yes, we do.

My wolf purred, and I swore at her in hopes to suppress her goddamn hormones.

I gazed at the door, blinking as I waited for him to leave. "Okay, well … bye."

He paused for a few moments, eyeing me, and then left the room. As soon as the door closed, I sprinted to my purple backpack, which sat just below his dresser. It was unzipped, and Ruffles was gone.

Fuck.

Where the hell did she go? And how did she get out? Where are all her damn chips?

She meowed again, and I followed the noise out into the hallway. Since Ares had disappeared into the house, I tiptoed around and peeked my head into each room, noticing how everything seemed so divine.

Large drapes. Shiny oak floors. Grand hallways.

Though I used to live in a pack house, it didn't compare to *this*. Everything here seemed livelier and richer, mighty and strong, celestial almost. And I wondered how Ares, such a bloodthirsty beast, could sustain such a lavish life. Had he stolen these things from other packs, or had his pack always been this wealthy?

After creeping down the hallway and finding only spare rooms and a bathroom, I opened the door to a smaller room with yellow curtains and three empty bags of chips lying on the floor. I cocked an eyebrow and entered the room, closing the door behind me.

Ruffles lay on the bed, on her back. Eyes closed in pure delight. Whiskers coated in chip dust. Tail curled.

"Ruffles!" I whisper-yelled at her.

She opened one eye, annoyed that I'd woken her up, and

meowed.

"What're you doing in here? And how'd you open all of those bags of chips?" I picked up the bags and threw them in the garbage. "What if Ares had found you?"

She meowed again.

I plucked her off of the bed. "Don't give me that."

Breath smelling of salt, she didn't even protest when I moved her. I hurried down the hall to Ares's bedroom. It wasn't safe to keep her in the bedroom in case he found out about her, but at least I would know where she was.

Moon Goddess only knew what kind of contraptions and people roamed around Ares's pack house. I expected to run into a couple torture devices and a few warriors who liked to inflict pain on others.

When I walked into the room, someone shouted from downstairs for me.

Damn it. Damn it. Damn it. I told Ruffles not to escape again and that I'd find her a better place to sleep tonight. Then, I slammed the door, leaving her inside the room.

I hurried down the hall, expecting to see Ares waiting for me, but Liam stood at the foot of the stairs. Instead of saying anything, he just nodded his head and turned toward the back door. After taking a deep breath and preparing myself for the worst, I followed him outside.

The sun blazed overhead, making me break out into a sweat. We walked through the forest until we reached a small lake. People were gathered around, talking to each other and grilling hot dogs on a wild and blazing fire.

In the midst of the pack, I stopped and glanced around, trying to figure out how so many people lived here. There must've been thousands of people in Ares's pack, all under his rule and control. I pressed my lips together. And they didn't even seem like they had such a bad life.

I'd assumed he treated his people like shit, forced them to do his dirty work. I'd expected cruelty, pain, fear from his pack members. Not ... this. Yet no matter how friendly they looked, nobody dared to start a conversation with me. It seemed like they didn't like outsiders that much.

When I turned to ask Liam where Ares was, I found Liam had disappeared through the crowd. I raised a brow and walked around by myself, listening to people whisper about me, about why an alpha had been traded in war. Some smirked, and others laughed. I ignored them all and continued toward the lake.

A group of men—warriors—gazed over at me from the rocks near the lake. When I looked at them, they just kept staring like I was the most fascinating thing they had ever seen. While some looked vaguely familiar, I didn't recognize the one staring at me with such ferocity.

"Can I help you?" I asked.

With long, wavy silver locks and scars all over his body, the young man stepped forward. "Just admiring the latest trophy Alpha Ares has brought home," he said. "An alpha this time."

The guy next to him chuckled. "He always likes to go bigger and better."

"At least this one's hotter than the last few," one of the older men said.

I flared my nostrils and growled. No disrespect—that was my only demand I'd had. If one more word came out of their mouths, I was going to—

The silver-haired asshole stepped closer to me and drew his finger up the column of my neck. "A feisty one, isn't she?"

Before he touched my face, I grabbed his finger and bent it backward until it broke. "I don't care who you are, but you don't touch me like that."

He chuckled lower, as if his finger didn't even hurt. "Trophies from war are everyone's property, darling, not just the alpha's."

"Well, I'm not a trophy of war," I said through clenched teeth. My wolf wanted me to tell him that I was his new luna, that whether he liked it or not, he would have to respect me, but something held me back.

If we weren't here, I would've already snapped this guy's neck. But since this was my first meeting with the pack, I wanted to make a good impression and stay under the radar, blend in as much as possible, try to hide the fact that an alpha like me couldn't shift easily.

These fools were fiends for power. If one of them questioned my abilities and challenged me to a fight—because I'd heard more than enough stories about Ares's pack staging battles for fun—and I couldn't shift ... if someone looked into me and my history and found out that I had part of the stone, they would try to kill me.

And if they succeeded, Ruffles would die here alone.

Not going to happen.

"Really?" he asked condescendingly.

He glanced into the woods, and I followed his gaze. Through the embers and smoke from the fire, Ares walked toward us with that same blonde girl from the picture in his room. She had her arm looped around his as she grinned up at him, her bright blue eyes sparkling.

I glared at the two in shock and disgust.

After she grasped his jaw and placed a kiss on his cheek, he stared down at her with so much love. My hands clenched into fists, claws ripping the skin on my palms. Jealousy and anger bubbled inside me. Moon Goddess, I was seconds away from ripping them both apart.

For someone who always thought things through before I acted, I couldn't hold my wolf back from growling. Last night, he had brought me home, laid me in his bed, kissed my forehead, and begged me to call him Mars.

Not the fierce Alpha Ares who took whores from packs.

Mars.

The silver-haired asshole nudged my shoulder. "Didn't think

you were his one and only, did you?"

I should've known that it was all too good to be true. I should've thought with my head instead of my heart. I shouldn't have trusted a man who had used me to get into my pack and taken me.

He chuckled under his breath, threw an arm around my shoulders, and pulled me in close, his striking silver hair brushing against the side of my face. "You're just an alpha, here as a trophy to add to his growing collection of whores."

CHAPTER 13

AURORA

"Don't fucking touch me." I ripped myself out of his grip and let out a guttural growl from deep in my throat.

Without looking back at him, I stormed in Ares's direction. Some people looked over, whispering, but I didn't care.

Who did that man think he was, calling me a whore in front of everyone? And who did Ares think he was—bringing me home, letting me sleep in his bed, acting as if he wanted a mate when he clearly had a relationship with a pretty blonde already?

Was I arm candy? Another one of his trophies?

My wolf whimpered. *That's all we will be, especially when he finds out that—*

Shut up. I was tired of letting my shifting abilities command my fucking life. Whether I could shift or not, it didn't matter. I wouldn't spend the rest of my life at the hands of a controlling man who had an insatiable thirst for war.

Ares would never find out that I had the Malavite Stone because I would never tell him.

The only other people who knew about it were Alpha Elijah and his doctor—the men who had found me and performed the surgery that saved me.

Hell, at that time, I hadn't even known if I would live ... but now that life was certain, I wasn't about to spend it like this. In the arms of a man who obviously had no respect for the mate bond. In a sea of thousands of blood-hungry warrior wolves. Inside a pack that would eventually become my own personal prison.

I had kept it a secret over the past decade, even from Mom and my pack. I didn't put it past her *or* Tony to take the stone from me, leaving me permanently disabled, just to absorb its power themselves. They'd say that if I wasn't healed completely, then I wasn't using it right or that the Moon Goddess didn't want me to have it.

Ares gazed over at me, that fucking smile falling from his face. He dropped that bitch's arm and walked toward me. "Kitten, what's wro—"

I slammed my finger into his chest, seething. "Don't *Kitten* me. I need to talk to you." I stormed right past him, not daring to look at his side piece, who had the most innocent fucking expression on her face.

Pushing past people, I continued deeper into the lush green forest, not stopping when he shouted my name and asked me what had happened or when he growled as viciously as he had yesterday morning when he was holding Tony by his throat and calling for me to come out of hiding.

When we were out of earshot from the rest of the pack, I stopped and glared at him. He walked toward me, eyes a fiery gold.

"What do you think you're doing?" he asked.

"What do I think I'm doing?" I stepped closer to him, canines emerging under my lips, ready to kill him. "What the fuck are *you* doing? Taking me as a fucking trophy, bringing me to a fucking party, parading other women around after you say that you care *oh-so much* for me—your mate?" I said through gritted teeth.

My wolf begged me to release her, so we could run through

the forest, away from him, away from here. But she and I both knew that I couldn't do that. Shifting was a big, fat *no*.

He pressed his lips together, jaw twitching, and crossed his huge arms over his chest. "What are you talking about?"

"Your warriors, Ares."

"Stop calling me that," he said, growling under his breath.

"That's who you are." I moved closer until I stood inches from him and glared up into his godlike eyes. "Alpha Ares. A god of war. An expert at deceiving others, even your own mate. A—"

He grabbed my jaw harshly in his hand and pushed me against the nearest tree. His eyes became a dark, murky gold. "I am all those things, Aurora. I have deceived others for control. I have slaughtered entire packs for power. I have taken *warriors* as trophies."

I slammed my hands into his chest, but he didn't move. Not an inch.

"But have I done any of those things to you?" he asked with such fury.

"Take your hands off of me, Ares."

He growled, an untamed divine vibe radiating from it. "I do what I want with what's mine. And that's not my name." The last few words came out harsher than the others.

The mere sentence made me clench, yet my anger didn't dissipate. Two could play at this fucking game.

I tightened my fist and grabbed his jaw in my other hand. "I guess that's why you let that whore kiss you, isn't it? Is she another one of your trophies too?" I asked. All I could think about was how hurt I was.

Every day, I felt so fucking useless. Now, I had to deal with this shit.

He shoved me against the tree harder and shook his head. "What whore are you talking about?"

"The blonde. Charolette. Who knows if you have more of them?"

His eyes faded back to their normal deep brown color. That expression of wild ferocity turned into a soft smile, light eyes, and a laugh that I would've thought was breathtaking if it were at any moment other than this. He released my chin and chuckled.

"You're psychotic," I said. I pressed my lips together and stared at him.

Why the hell was he laughing? What was so funny about this? He surely hadn't been laughing when Tony was coming on to me. Why was he laughing when she came on to him?

"Crazy, just like the rumors say."

He placed his hands on his hips, chuckled slowing, and stepped closer to me. "Kitten," he said, head tilted to the side and a smirk on his face, "Charolette, that blonde that I was with, is my sister."

His sister?

My eyes widened.

Fuck, he had to be lying. But the lighthearted expression on his face told me that this was the truth, that though he was great at deceiving, this wasn't a lie. Charolette was his sister. I'd gotten fired up for no reason at all, shown him that I actually cared about him like that.

I fanned my burning cheeks, staring down at my shoes in embarrassment. I could hear Jeremy's voice in the back of my mind, telling me that assuming always made an ass out of people and that I was the biggest ass here. In that big-brother kind of way.

Mars stepped closer to me, one foot between mine, hips pressing into my side. He dipped his head, resting his forehead against mine, and drew a finger up the column of my neck to my chin. "I never thought you'd be so influenced by those rumors. From what I've heard, Alpha Aurora always thinks through everything before she acts," he whispered.

There was a sudden ease between us.

He gently brushed his thumb against my jaw. "Tell me, Kitten, was that little outburst of yours a subtle plea for me to mark you? So everyone knows that you're mine?" He brushed his nose up the side of my neck, and I shivered. "Or maybe you want to mark me? So everyone knows I'm yours?"

I paused.

"Yours, Kitten." Mars tilted his head to the side, baring his neck and giving me permission to sink my canines into it and claim him as my mate.

My wolf went wild, clawing at my insides to let her out, to claim our mate, to make him ours. But I couldn't … I … not when I was hiding the biggest secret of the century from him.

All I could do was stare at it, my heart racing fast, my canines lengthening just slightly. Aching to mark him. Desperate to connect to someone, deeper than I ever had with Tony. I just wanted someone to love me for me.

He grabbed my hand and placed it right on his neck. His pulse raced, and my wolf purred. She wanted all of the wolves here to know that he was hers. Nobody else's.

Mine.

"This is all yours," he murmured, moving my hand down his shoulder, down his taut chest, down his abdomen to the front of his pants. "Every part of me. The good, the bad, *the big*."

I stifled a laugh and nearly cracked a smile. Moon Goddess, I didn't know how I'd survive here. One moment, he was fury; the next, he was peace. One moment, the infamous Alpha Ares. The next, Mars, the man I'd met at the lake. It was like a switch that he could turn on and off when he wanted, when his wolf craved violence or when his wolf craved me.

"Mark me, Kitten," he said boldly, but there was desperation in his voice.

The same type of desperation I'd felt every day in my pack, when I needed to prove myself, when I needed someone's reassurance that I was good enough.

As quickly as I'd heard his desperation, it was gone. And for a moment, I wondered if I'd ever heard it at all because the Mars *and* Ares I'd seen so far didn't need any type of reassurance. He was a self-serving asshole who did what he wanted for power, for land, for women, and for himself.

He dug his nose into my hair and inhaled. "Sink those small canines into my flesh, let your claws dig into my back, purr for me." He brushed his fingers down the sides of my body, hovering them over the front of my pants.

I swallowed, trying hard to control my wolf. Marking his neck looked too inviting to pass up. But I couldn't give in to him. Not yet. Not until I knew the real reason he needed that stone. I wasn't going to be deceived, nor was I going to be used.

My lips grazed against his ear, and it took everything inside of me to hold myself back. "Maybe tonight. Depends if you're a good boy or not."

He growled lowly, digging a single finger into my abdomen and drawing it all the way up my body until he reached my chin. "Kitten, you don't like good boys." He smirked down at me, his golden eyes as bright as the sun. "You like them rough and dirty and bad, just for you."

We hadn't even known each other but for three days, and he already knew me so fucking well. I didn't know how long I'd be able to hide all my secrets from him. A few days? Weeks? Was that how much longer I had to live?

After gathering up all the strength that I had left, I pushed him off of me. "That's what you think." I shrugged my shoulders and began walking back through the woods toward the pack house. Green brush grazed against my shins. I stepped over a couple tree branches, looking around the forest and trying to get used to my surroundings.

Mars chuckled and grabbed my shoulder. "Wrong way." After turning me around and leading me in the opposite direction, he gripped my shoulder tightly. "Now ..." he started, any softness in

Mars's voice disappearing. And suddenly, the enraged Ares returned. "Who told you that I brought you home as a trophy?"

"Some guy with long silver hair."

He growled, the guttural sound echoing through the forest. "What did he say to you?"

"That I was a trophy to you."

His eyes clouded with gold, his jaw twitched violently. "And?"

In the distance, the forest cleared, and I could see the silver-haired man with that arrogantly youthful look stretched across his face. I parted my lips and then smacked them shut. I could handle that asshole myself and didn't need Ares blowing this up. I didn't need to be treated like a baby, and I didn't need more attention put on me.

I'd handled things by myself back home; I'd handle them here.

"Now, Aurora." His voice was stiff, as if he wasn't going to let this go anytime soon.

After sighing deeply, I dismissively waved my hand. "He just said that you do this all the time, that I was another one of your trophies to add to your collection of whores ..."

I gazed around the party, locking eyes with the silver-haired freak. He had the damn audacity to wink at me.

And when he did, I said, *Fuck it.*

"He even told me that your sister was one of them."

Visibly shaking with fury in his eyes, Ares released my shoulder, stormed right up to the man, and grabbed him by the throat. "This silver-haired asshole, Aurora?" Ares asked, his voice eerily calm.

A deafening silence fell upon the forest. Nobody said a word. Nobody laughed. Even the pups stopped playing. Everyone stared at the three of us, even Charolette.

I parted my lips, adrenaline pumping through my veins. "Yes."

Ares growled viciously at the man and hurled him across the yard so hard that when the man hit a tree, the tree itself cracked.

Before he had a chance to move, Ares grabbed him by the throat yet again. "You're lucky I don't kill you right here."

Eyes overtaken by darkness, the vein pulsing violently in his neck, large canines glistening with saliva, Ares gazed around his pack. "Let him be a fucking example to everyone here. I don't care who you are. I don't care how high you rank in my pack. If you don't respect your luna, I'll hang you by your fucking toes, latch my fingers into your pathetic throat, and watch the blood pool out of you, ounce by fucking ounce until you're lying in my prison. Dead."

My eyes widened. Oh dear Moon Goddess.

"Does everyone understand?"

"Yes, Alpha," his pack said in complete unison.

Ares glared at Mr. Silver Hair, held the man by his throat, and squeezed tighter. "Now, apologize to my *mate,* Marcel."

Marcel grabbed Ares's hand, desperately trying to claw his way out of the grip of a god, and looked at me, face reddening by the second. He parted his lips, but no words came out.

"Say it." Ares tossed him to the ground like he was a piece of trash. "Or I will kill you right now."

Marcel rolled onto his hands and knees, staring at the dirt and gasping for breath. "I'm sorry, Luna."

Ares growled again. "Look at her when you apologize. She's your luna, and she's an alpha. Respect her like you respect me."

Respect me? My eyes widened even more, and I gulped. Never in a million years had I expected Ares to tell everyone that I wasn't just his mate, but that I was also his equal—that my alpha abilities weren't to be ignored just because we were fated to be together—or to demand respect for me.

I stared at him, my heart racing. Yes, he was crazy. Yes, he was even fucking psychotic at times. But he was nothing like any man before. Nothing like Tony, who had known about Mom's plan to sell me out and gone along with it because he couldn't become an alpha any other way. Nothing like the guys back home.

Ares was a whole new level of man. Ares was a god.

Marcel gazed up at me, looking me dead in the eye, jaw clenched. “I’m sorry, Luna.”

“I’m done with this shit. Party’s over.” Ares snatched my hand and tugged me toward the pack house. “If you wish to meet my mate, you can come to the pack house tomorrow.”

CHAPTER 14

AURORA

After two hours of letting Ares calm down in the pack house, I hopped off of the bed and grabbed my backpack. Inside, Ruffles munched happily on her last bag of chips. I needed to get her cat litter, cat treats, cat toys, and more chips—a growing list to keep this cat happy and quiet.

"You're not leaving me, are you?" Ares asked when I walked past his office.

I peeked my head into the room. "No, not yet." I threw him a smirk, listened to him growl, and hurried down the grand hall. "I'm going to the store. Why don't you go talk about the next pack that you're going to try to take or that stone that you're looking for while I'm out? I know you've been aching to talk to your beta about it since this morning."

He walked to the door, arching a brow at my departing figure. "The next pack is the Firegazers. Four days. And that stone … we're going to find that stone."

"And if you do, then what?" I asked quietly, turning around to face him.

Instead of answering me, he just chuckled and shook his head.

"Go shopping. I'll be waiting for you to return. I have a surprise for you tonight."

A surprise? My stomach filled with annoying little butterflies. I hadn't felt this way in so long, and I knew I shouldn't feel excited … I knew I shouldn't get close.

But the god of war had a surprise for me.

"I'll ask Charolette to accompany you," he said, and my stomach tightened.

After my possessive outburst this morning, it'd be a good idea to talk to her. But I couldn't wait for her to come here. I needed to put space between me and him now, and I had to get Ruffles her litter and food as soon as possible.

"No," I said. "I'll go alone."

He paused. "Go then," he urged, a breathtaking smile tugging on his lips.

I waved awkwardly in his direction, trying to brush off the sinful look he was giving me, and walked out the door. After receiving some *gracious* help from some pack members who looked beyond scared to talk to me, I stepped into Mad Moon Grocery and opened my backpack.

Ruffles popped her head out and gave me a loud, drawn-out meow.

"Yeah, yeah, I know. We're out of chips," I said.

She mewed again, climbing up onto my shoulder and licking the back of my neck.

"Girl, I'm getting you some now. Settle down."

I pushed a cart down the aisle and stared amazingly at how big this place was. It looked like an indoor football stadium with about fifty aisles, food stocked on every shelf, and it was crowded beyond belief. Some people smiled at me, and others stepped out of my way and avoided me like wolfsbane, eyeing the cat on my shoulder.

When I finally made it to the chips, Ruffles sighed in my ear. I needed to stop feeding her addiction. It was quite unhealthy. I glanced around at the large variety. Ruffles Flamin' Hot. Ruffles Double Crunch Hot Wings. Ruffles Loaded Chili and Cheese. My gaze landed on the Ruffles Reduced Fat, and I smiled. This one would do.

Ruffles hissed when I placed the bag in the cart.

"Ruffles, come on. You can't eat the fatty stuff all the time."

She swatted my chin with her paw.

"Ruffles ..."

"*Meow.*"

I rolled my eyes and put the Reduced Fat chips back on the shelf, getting her favorite original Ruffles chips instead. She purred delightfully, rubbing her face against mine. This girl was more addicted to chips than Ares was to war.

"Now, get back into the backpack," I said.

She hopped into the backpack, her purrs vibrating through it. Tapping my fingers against the cart, I hummed and continued walking, my thoughts consumed by my mate. Ares and Mars were the same person but so entirely different. I didn't really understand it.

It was like he had a dual personality or something—with Mars being so soft and gentle, and Ares being so incredibly savage and ruthless and ... sexy.

I blinked a few times, trying to get him out of my head. What was I even thinking? I didn't like Ares. He was too pushy, too arrogant, too fucking dominant and tempting. Why was I so addicted to such a monster?

Someone bumped into my cart as I turned the corner.

"I'm sorry!" Charolette said, running her hand over her pin-straight hair. Her pink lips softened into a smile. "Oh, it's you."

My cheeks flushed. I still couldn't believe that she was his sister. Not his lover. Not his trophy. His sister. Stupid, jealous me had made a fool out of myself earlier. I'd let my guard down and acted as if I cared about Ares in the slightest.

She stuck out her hand. "By the way, I'm Charolette!" she said.

I took her hand in mine and inhaled the scent of roses.

"Sorry about earlier. If I had known that Mars hadn't told you about me, I wouldn't have been so close to him."

I shook my head, my cheeks flushing even more. "No, it's my fault. Don't apologize. My wolf … I …" I gave her a smile. "I let Marcel talk me into getting jealous." Because *I* wasn't jealous. Nope, not at all. I didn't like Ares. I *couldn't* like Ares.

She rolled her eyes and walked down the aisle with me, a shopping basket hanging off her arm. "Moon Goddess, Marcel. Don't listen to a word he says unless it has to do with fighting. He's a major player, and he will probably try to get into your pants more than once. Just avoid him at all costs, trust me."

"I'm sure Ares will make sure of that."

She giggled, picked up some Fruit Loops, and put them into her basket. "I'm glad Mars found you. You're going to be good for his crazy ass. Ares can be hella hard to tame."

I let out a laugh, trying to figure out if Ares or Mars was just a nickname for him, and smiled at her. Charolette seemed fun, like she'd be a good friend. And damn, did I need a friend to talk to after what had just happened. Besides Tony and Elijah, I didn't have any friends back home.

"Amen to that," I said, glancing at the ground. "I just don't know if he's going to be good for me."

"He'll drive you insane, but"—she quieted down—"it's because he cares about you. It can be hard to deal with both of them, but it'll be worth it. They love hard."

"Both of them?" I asked, hoping to get some more information about his two polar opposite personalities.

"Mars and Ares," she clarified. "He has dissociative identity disorder. We met Ares over a decade ago. We rarely see Mars anymore. It was a hard transition for my dad and me, but it was even harder for Mars. He … hurt himself over it and some other stuff." The last words came in a whisper.

"Dissociative identity disorder," I whispered to myself.

My mate had two personalities, and I had already seen both of them despite Charolette saying that Mars wasn't as *active* anymore, if that was even the right way of saying that.

It made so much more sense now, but why'd Ares suddenly appear? Did something happen to him?

Just as I was about to ask, Charolette gazed in my cart—which was full of cat litter, cat treats, cat toys, and chips—and steered the conversation elsewhere. "You know, I didn't think he'd ever find someone he liked enough to let her bring a cat into his house."

And so I dropped my question, deciding that it was too personal right now.

"Why's that?" I asked.

"He didn't tell you?" she asked, brow arched. "He's allergic."

"Allergic?" I asked, my heart clenching.

He hadn't wanted me to bring Ruffles because he was allergic to cats, and I'd brought her anyway. I'd thought he was just being heartless and cruel.

I needed to find another place to keep her. I thought about asking Charolette to watch her until I got things sorted out ... but Ruffles would never forgive me for it. I hadn't spent more than a day without her since she stumbled into my life after Jeremy died, and it was way too soon to ask strangers for favors.

Maybe I could store her away in one of the spare rooms that he never went into, play with her when he was taking over some pack and trying to find that stone, feed her early in the morning when he was still sleeping. I didn't want him to—

Suddenly, a window near the front of the store shattered into a million pieces. Mothers pulled their pups to their chests, leaving their carts and hurrying to the back exit. People started yelling and screaming in panic, sprinting down the aisles toward us.

A vicious growl echoed throughout the store, and I froze. That wasn't the growl of an average wolf ... that was the sound of a hound. I clutched my backpack and Charolette's hand and ran toward the rear exit.

Hundreds of people crowded around the door and tried to squeeze out of it. I swung my backpack over my shoulder, grabbed the silver knife from the side pocket, and told Charolette to guard Ruffles with her life.

"What are you doing?" she asked, shaking her head. "We need to get out of here. Ares will be here to stop—"

Another growl ripped through the room, and a hound turned down our aisle. He stared at me, ignoring all other wolves around him, and sprinted in my direction. Bloodied saliva dripped from his sharp canines, his piercing yellow eyes fixed on me.

I clutched the knife until my knuckles turned white. There was no escaping these monstrosities. For years, I had tried to hide from them ... but they always seemed to find me.

With terrifying yellow eyes, the hound rushed down the aisle, springing himself forward on his two hind legs. Foam oozing from his mouth, teeth dripping with blood, he was coming for *me*. They always came for me.

I stepped in front of Charolette and Ruffles, determined to protect them with my life. The silver knife burned my palm, but the pain was never as bad as the pain of watching a loved one being torn apart by ruthless animals.

When he leaped into the air, all I could see was Jeremy. Being severed to pieces. His limbs being ripped off. The hounds devouring his flesh. The images were forever lodged into my memory. Never to leave.

"Aurora!" Charolette screamed.

The hound dug his claws into my arm, and I howled out in pain. Moon Goddess, I wanted to shift. I wanted to kill him with my teeth. I wanted him to pay for everything that his kind had done to me. But I hated that I couldn't shift and despised myself for it.

I clutched the knife harder, pretended that the gash in my arm wasn't bleeding profusely, and hopped out of the way before he could hurt me again. I sprinted down the aisle to get him away from the others and stood between the chips and my cart of cat litter.

Just as I'd hoped, he turned on his paw, wildly shook his head, and stalked toward me once more. I would kill this piece of shit before he could hurt anyone ever again.

In the distance, I heard Ares growl, claws tearing into fur, and the whimpers of the hounds. My wolf called out to our mate, and I forced her to shut up. I could handle this beast myself.

Coming at me faster this time, the hound sprinted down the aisle. When he leaped at me, I crouched down, stepped out of the way, and stabbed the damn thing right in his neck. The monster growled in pain and fell to the ground on his back.

I crawled on top of the animal, straddling his waist to keep him in place, and stabbed him over and over, right into the jugular. This was for everything that had happened to me. This was for my inability to shift. This was for Jeremy.

Blood sprayed onto my face and gushed out of the open wound in my arm. Tears welled up in my eyes. But I didn't stop. I hated them so much. Thoughts of them tortured me every single fucking day.

"Aurora," Charolette called.

The hound lay limply under me, yet I took the blade, cut right through the few threads of skin left holding the hound's head in place, and ripped off the skin to make sure this fucker didn't come back.

I saw red.

Figuratively and literally.

"Aurora!" she shouted again.

Suddenly, someone scooped me into their strong arms and picked me up off the hound. My silver dagger slipped out of my hand, and the scent of hazelnut engulfed me. My body relaxed in Ares's arms, but all *I* wanted to do was continue to make the hound hurt, displace all this pain I'd been carrying around for the past ten years.

Blood dripped from Ares's canines. His chest was stained red. All I could see was wrath in his eyes. I squirmed in his hold, yet he didn't let me down. The hound was lying dead in the middle of the store, and I could only imagine that there were others dead in the forest. Ares pulled me closer to him, letting me feel his raging heartbeat.

I took a deep breath, breathing with the rhythm. *Calm, Aurora. Calm.*

He walked to Charolette, placed me onto the ground, and looked at Marcel, who was drenched in blood from head to toe next to her. "Double security around the borders. Nobody comes onto the property, and nobody leaves the property without me knowing. Kill anyone who disobeys."

Marcel nodded, glanced quickly at me, his lips curling into a smirk, and handed me my silver knife. I growled and snatched it from him, wanting to cut all of his locks of stupid silver hair and keep *it* as a trophy.

When Marcel left, Ares examined Charolette to make sure she was okay, and then he snatched my wrist and dragged me toward the exit of the store. "We're leaving, Aurora."

I pulled myself away and glared back. My mind was reeling. Anger. Violence. Pure adrenaline. But I wasn't about to leave Ruffles without her proper necessities. I didn't care what anyone said. She would always come first. She had found me when Jeremy died and stayed with me ever since.

"I came here for *things*, and I don't plan on leaving without them."

He growled under his breath, jaw twitching violently. "You just got attacked by a fucking hound. These *things* can wait."

I flared my nostrils. "No, they can't. Now, you're going to wait while I get them."

"Get what you need to get, but you're not leaving my sight," he said through clenched teeth.

After a few moments, I decided that he wasn't kidding. "Fine."

I frowned at my backpack that Charolette was clutching to her chest. Ruffles deserved more than to have no place to poop or pee. If I didn't buy some litter soon for her, she'd start peeing all over Ares's clothes, and then he'd have an allergy attack.

I swallowed hard. "Just ... give me a second."

I walked toward Charolette, holding my arm to stop the blood, but Ares followed. "And stay here, or you won't be getting any *breakfast* tomorrow," I said.

That'd teach him.

When I reached Charolette, she handed me my backpack. "Are you okay? I can take care of my brother for you, if you need me to. All he needs is a good kick in the ass when he gets too protective."

"No," I said, glancing back at him.

Ares raised a brow at me, a scowl set deeply on his face, and I pulled Charolette even closer.

"Ares doesn't know about Ruffles. I thought he was just being an asshole when he told me not to bring her. Now, I have to hide her. I was going to hide her in one of his spare rooms and buy her litter, but he won't let me out of his sight. Could you get some for me? I know this is a huge favor to ask of you."

She smiled widely at me. "Ooh, I like you already." She grabbed my hand, her manicured pink fingernails lightly digging into my palm. "He doesn't usually go into the spare room, three doors down from his bedroom, the one with the yellow curtains. I'll bring some litter and a litter box over and leave it in there tonight." She grabbed my bag back from me. "I'll bring Ruffles too. Spare room. Yellow curtains. She'll be in there."

I pulled her into a hug, squeezing her tight. "Thank you so much. I owe you my life."

CHAPTER 15

MARS

When I'd found Aurora in her human form with a deep gash down the side of her arm, straddling the rogue and stabbing him relentlessly in his neck, all I could feel was an intense fear. She shouldn't be here. She shouldn't have done that. I didn't want her to become like Ares.

From the doorway, I crossed my arms over my chest and watched the doctor clean her arm with alcohol. Two times. We had been attacked by hounds two times since I had been with her, and she hadn't shifted once. If I'd lost her today—before I even had a chance to get to know her—because she didn't shift, I would've lost it.

Ares would've taken full control, slaughtered every single hound in that goddamn forest, slaughtered innocent people, slaughtered our own people. We couldn't lose Aurora to hounds, especially not after we had lost Mom.

After the doctor wrapped some gauze around Aurora's arm to stop the bleeding, I grabbed her hand and pulled her out of the grocery store. Stars danced against the dark night sky, and all I wanted was to enjoy this night with her. Take her out to the lake, show her the waterfall, pull her under the water with me, and admire her smile. Run free with her wolf.

I was even going to let her mark me tonight.

When I'd mentioned it earlier and her small little body got all tense, I could barely contain myself. I wanted her to accept me and Ares, accept that we were two crazy pieces of one man who'd do anything for her. I wanted to show her that I was more than that ghoulish monster all the rumors had made me out to be.

But that couldn't happen. These hounds had been out of control these past few days … maybe even after her, like Liam had said. It was hard to believe that my mate had so much history with the hounds that they wanted her dead.

On our walk back to the pack house, she snatched her arm away from me, but I grabbed her hand back and held it close to me, as if I'd lose her if I didn't.

"Why are the hounds after you?"

Aurora tensed and glanced at her feet. "They're not after me," she said a bit too quickly. "They were never this violent before I met you."

"Well, they never attacked *my* pack before I met *you*." I opened the pack house door for her and followed her up the stairs, watching her ass sway back and forth.

Mad Moon Grocery was on the edge of our property; they had to have had a good reason to kill two guards at the borders to get Aurora.

Ever since I had taken over as alpha, hounds hadn't dared to step on my property. They knew to stay away.

She pushed our bedroom door open. "That's not my fault, *Ares.*"

I growled at the name, feeling him slowly awaken inside of me. I thought I had suppressed Ares earlier, but he had just been waiting to take control, to scream at her for not shifting, for not protecting herself the way she should have.

"Tomorrow, you start training," I said. "With Marcel."

She turned on her heel, blue eyes wide. "What! Are you serious?"

"Yes, Marcel will train you to react with your wolf in that kind of situation."

"But you hate him. *I* hate him!"

It was true. I hated his guts. But I couldn't let Aurora get hurt. I wouldn't be able to handle Charolette's death if it happened, and I really wouldn't be able to handle Aurora's too. Marcel could make her stronger. He was my best warrior and the greatest trainer in the pack. He had pushed me to be better than I'd thought I could be, had trained Ares relentlessly to make him unstoppable. But I wouldn't let her ever be alone with that asshole.

She stared up at me with a blazing fire in her blue eyes and crossed her arms over her chest. "I don't need training. If you haven't noticed, I've killed two hounds within the last two days. I think I know how to defend myself."

I growled, feeling Ares stir inside of me, and stepped toward her. "Then, why didn't you shift, Aurora, huh?"

Moon Goddess, did she not know how? How was it that she hadn't shifted once when there was a threat? Did her wolf not sense it? Or maybe she just didn't think she had to. Whatever the reason, it was unacceptable. This wasn't a game of strength or pride.

"Those hounds will kill you. If more than one were coming at you, you wouldn't be strong enough to defeat them without your wolf."

"Not strong enough?" She growled and met my glare with an intense one.

All I wanted to do was shove her against the wall and take her right there. Those wide eyes. The pure heat radiating off of her. Her strength. It was everything that I had ever dreamed of having in a mate.

"I am strong enough to defeat them."

I snatched her chin in my hand, squeezing roughly. "If you're strong enough, then push me away," I said.

She shoved her hands right into my chest, but I didn't move.

I stepped closer to her, growling. "Do it, Aurora."

She shoved her hands right into me again, harder but not hard enough.

"What're you waiting for?" I stepped closer, pinning her to the wall with just my hand. "Shove me away."

She struggled, and Ares took complete control from me.

ARES

"Ares"—she seethed—"let me go. I don't have to prove shit to you."

My hand slipped around her pretty little throat, thumb brushing roughly against her jaw. I pushed her head to the side and stepped closer to my mate. "Yes, you do."

I breathed in her rich lemon scent and felt her pulse. Such a fast beat. Such a beautiful fucking neck that I could claim.

"You're *mine*, and it's my job to make sure nobody tries to take what's mine from me." I chuckled lowly in her ear, making her shiver. "You're oh-so pretty, Kitten. And there are far too many people who will try to take you away from me."

She clenched her jaw and shoved her hands back into my chest, but instead of pulling them away, she curled her fingers into my skin. Claws in my flesh. Canines emerging under those plump lips. Her wolf and mine.

"And I will kill them," she said.

"Then, fucking prove it to me, Aurora."

My hand tightened around her throat, and all I could see was black. Pure black. The hounds could've killed her today. They could've taken her away from me. They could've brought her back to their hideout, ripped off her clothes, and taken her dignity.

"Prove to me that you wouldn't have let them pin you against the wall." I pushed her further into the wall, letting her squirm. "Prove to me that you wouldn't have let them press their lips to your throat." I inhaled deeply, her scent becoming overwhelming, and kissed the spot I would mark soon. "Prove to me that you wouldn't let them touch you like I do." I pushed my hand into her pants, drew a single finger down her folds, and relished in how wet she was for me.

It hadn't even been three fucking days yet, and here she was, making me feel things that I had never felt before. An innate need to make her mine. A thirst to thrust myself inside of her—and only her—for the rest of my life. A hunger to show everyone how fucking strong my mate was, to make every other alpha jealous, to make her my fucking goddess among such peasants.

She gulped, her breath in my ear. "What if I don't want to prove it to you?"

I tensed when I smelled her arousal. She wanted the same, and it freaked me the fuck out. How could she want a monster like me, someone so menacingly vicious, someone so brutal?

"What if I want you to take me, Ares?" she whispered, trying to taunt me.

I growled and pressed my hard cock against her stomach, letting her feel where I would be later. That deep inside of her. Tearing up her tight little pussy.

"You want all of me, Kitten?" I asked against her ear. "Because I'll give you all of me."

CHAPTER 16

AURORA

Moon Goddess, I didn't know what was wrong with me, but damn, I wanted Ares so fucking bad. The way he had torn me off that rogue earlier, that desperate look full of want and need in his eyes, the pure dominance dripping off of every inch of him.

I drew my fingers up the front of his pants and inhaled his hazelnut scent. He could do whatever he wanted with me, and I would let him.

"Does my Kitten want to play?" he asked, curling a finger around a lock of my hair.

I wanted him so bad that it scared me. He was already angry because I hadn't shifted during a fight. How would he feel when I told him that I couldn't shift as easily or as quickly as normal wolves do? Would he feel any sort of pain for me, his mate and his pack's luna? Or would he kill me without hesitation, tell me that I was useless to him, mate with another woman so much stronger than me?

Everything he had said about me was true. I was weak. Mom thought it. Tony thought it. I thought it.

My gaze dropped, and I immediately regretted everything I'd

said to him. I shouldn't have told him that I wanted him so soon. When he found out about me, he wouldn't want me. He'd take what he needed and toss me out.

Part of me wanted to tell him about the stone so bad, to just get the hurt over with sooner rather than later, but I couldn't get the words out. My mouth was dry, my throat closed up.

"I want you," I whispered, feeling him press himself harder into me. I wanted every single inch of him, could only imagine him just sliding into me until his hips bucked against mine. It was all that I had been able to think about these past few days, and I both loved it and hated it.

Catching him in a moment of weakness, I pushed my hands into his chest and shoved him away. "But not now. I'm too dirty."

He grabbed my wrist and pulled me closer. "I like dirty."

After glaring into his eyes the hardest that I could, I opened the bathroom door. "Well, I don't."

Walls made of white marble, a glass shower door, and a tub big enough for two perched in front of a grand window, the bathroom was bigger than my room back home. I fumbled with the shower and turned it on.

Ares leaned against the counter and smirked. "Clean yourself then, Kitten. I can wait."

I arched a brow at him, letting the steam from the shower fog up the door. "Okay, well, can you"—I nodded toward the bedroom—"leave?"

He crossed his arms over his chest, eyes turning playful. "No." He tilted his head. "I told you that you weren't leaving my sight. Now, can you undress yourself, or do you need my help?"

I gnawed on the inside of my cheek, my heart racing. It was just a shower. It wasn't like he'd get inside with me and thrust me against the wall, the water dripping down his bare chest, his canines ...

"I can do it myself," I said.

After turning toward the shower, I took a deep breath, fully aware that he was watching my every move, and lifted my shirt over my head. I tossed it in his direction, hoping it would smack him right in the face and hinder his eyesight while I stripped my pants and hopped into the shower.

The water seared my skin, and I stumbled back out. "Goddamn it!" I covered my chest with my hands, stood outside of the shower, and lowered the temperature of the water.

Goddess, what was wrong with me? I should be angry with him. I should hate him. I should not want him in any sort of way … yet I couldn't stop.

As the water cooled off, he stared right at me, his eyes dancing with excitement. Hair tousled, arms crossed over his chest, shirt *suddenly* off. My wolf purred for him, wanting him to touch us the same way he was staring at us. Passionately.

I narrowed my eyes and stepped back into the shower, letting the water run down my body and slowly—very slowly—peeling my arms away from my chest. I grabbed the bar of soap and the loofah hanging from the shower caddy.

It smelled like him.

Call me nasty, but I wanted to drag it all over my body. I wanted his scent on me, to soak into my skin, to become a part of me. I lathered the loofah in soap and rubbed it against my chest, scrubbing off the blood and letting the soap drip between my breasts. I brushed it over my shoulders and down my stomach and up my thighs.

Staring at me from the sink, Ares growled and rested a hand against the front of his pants, stroking his hard cock through them. I let the soap run down my abdomen and dip between my hips, roll down my legs.

Without any shame, he pushed his hand into his pants, touched himself, and groaned while he watched me. I clenched, my cheeks flushing and my pussy throbbing, and furrowed my brows together.

I wanted him in here with me.

I pushed a hand between my legs, touching my folds, and slowly rubbed my clit for him.

This was so wrong, but it felt so right.

Pleasure surged throughout my body. He pushed down his pants, his hard cock springing out of them, and walked toward the shower. Opening the door, he stepped under the water and shoved me against the wall.

With his hand around his cock, he stroked it back and forth, making me tighten. It was so fucking big, so thick. I placed both of my hands on his abdomen, unable to wait for him to be inside of me.

It was more than want or desire. It was need. Pure, innate need.

"I didn't tell you to stop touching yourself," he said, placing my hand back on my clit. "Rub your pussy until you come for me."

My pussy clenched. "Ares," I breathed out, closing my eyes.

He snatched my chin in his rough hand and growled. "Your eyes should be on me, Kitten. You will come, staring at *me*. Thinking about *me*. Feeling *me*."

Heat rushed to my core. The tension was building so quickly. I rubbed my fingers against my swollen clit and whimpered, "Ares, please."

"Faster."

My fingers moved faster, the pressure rising still. He rested his forehead on mine, beads of water dripping from his dark hair, and stroked himself. It was so close to my entrance, so close to just slipping inside of me and filling me completely.

I reached for his dick with my other hand, needing to feel it, but he pinned my wrist to the wall.

"Please, let me touch it," I begged.

"Not until you come." He sucked my bottom lip between his teeth, trailed his hand down my arm to my chest, and cupped one of my breasts. "After you come, I want you on your knees for me, taking my cock down your throat." He groped my breast harder, rolling my nipple against his palm. "Do you understand?"

"No," I panted.

I was so close. So fucking close.

"No?" he asked, eyes glowing gold. He slipped a hand under my thigh, lifted one of my knees into the air, and pulled it against his hip. After he stepped closer, his cock grazed against my entrance.

"I want you inside of me," I begged.

He tensed, jerking his cock faster. "Fuck, Kitten," he groaned.

I rubbed my pussy harder for him, the tension too intense. He tugged on one of my nipples with his fingers, and I screamed out his name. My leg trembling in his hand, my whole body tingling from him. Wave after wave of pleasure pumped out of me.

"Look at that pussy quiver." He tugged my hips closer and pressed his cock against my entrance. "I can't wait to feel it pulse around *me* like that."

I hazily nodded my head and relaxed against the wall.

Moon Goddess, I wanted more. More of him. More of this.

"Is this what you want?" he asked me, pushing his cock against me, almost inside, just one more inch. The head of it glistened with my juices, and my pussy clenched harder, needing to wrap around him. "I won't ask again, Kitten." He snatched my chin in his hand and forced me to look into his darkening eyes. "I'm about one second away from thrusting myself into your pussy and ruining you."

I took a deep breath, my mind foggy. "Then, ruin me, *Ares*."

"Don't take your eyes off of me." Ares curled one arm under my leg, hiked it further up his hip, and pressed the head of his cock against my entrance. With his other hand, he gripped my chin and held me in place, staring so deep into my eyes that I couldn't look away even if I tried.

My pussy tightened, and I sucked in a breath. This was happening. This was really happening.

When he slid himself inside of me, I clenched harder around his cock until every single inch filled me. Water beat down on his back, wetting his hair and making drops roll down his chest. I curled my fingers into the taut muscle and moved my hips back and forth, meeting him halfway.

Steam clouded the glass door, and I laid my hand against it, trying to keep myself steady.

He grabbed a handful of my ass and squeezed, growling lowly in my ear. "Wrap your legs around me."

Without hesitation, I curled my legs around his waist and pulled him closer to me. With one arm around my waist and the other around my throat, he pumped in and out of my pussy, his fingers gently stroking my jaw.

He started slow and passionately, taking his time with my body as I reacted so naturally to him. Every time he pressed himself all the way inside me, my hips bucked, my nails dug into his back, and I couldn't stop moaning his name.

And then faster and faster and faster until he pinned me to the shower wall with one hand and pounded so savagely into me. He glided his lips against my neck and sucked on my sensitive skin until he left a mark.

Eyes flashing gold, he let his canines lengthen until they peeked out from behind his lips, taunting me. All I could imagine was him burying them deep inside of me, claiming me, taking me as his and nobody else's.

"My Kitten likes that, doesn't she?"

I clenched even harder on him. "Harder, *Ares*."

He dipped his head and sucked my nipple into his mouth, biting down. "Alpha," he corrected.

I moaned and grasped on to him for dear life, pleasure ripping through my entire body.

Goddess, this was exactly what I wanted.

Him to be inside of me. Him to fill me. Him to claim me.

"Are you going to come for me already?" He smirked down at

me with golden lust in his eyes. "I haven't even started with you yet."

I curled my toes, my body unable to hold back the rippling orgasm I was having just from him being inside of me, and hugged him to my chest. Wave after wave of ecstasy rolled through my body. My legs tingled. My mind became foggy.

All I could feel was him. All I *wanted* to feel was him.

After turning off the water, he walked out of the shower and placed me on my trembling legs so we were both facing the mirror. "You've had your fun, Aurora. Now, you're going to watch me fuck you for real this time." He swiped his palm across the steamy bathroom mirror, giving me a clear view of our naked bodies. "Watch how easily my cock slides into your tight, wet pussy."

He wrapped his arms under my legs from behind, picked me up, and pressed the head of his glistening cock against my entrance. I furrowed my brows together, relaxing against his chest as he held me with ease, and clenched.

Goddess, this was more than I'd asked for, yet I didn't want it to stop. My wolf wanted more. I knew it was wrong. I knew I shouldn't be getting close. But I … I couldn't help it. My mate bond drew my wolf to him, but something else made *me* want to stay.

When he pushed the head of his cock into me and stilled, I whimpered and stared at him through the mirror. My fingernails dug into his forearms, my pussy pulsing around his cock. "More."

"Is my little Kitten begging for it?" he mumbled against my ear, never taking his eyes off of me.

He pushed another inch inside and then pulled out, teasing me. I cried out again, my pussy desperate to hold on to him.

"I want to hear you beg for me, Aurora."

"Please," I said breathlessly.

He pushed his head back into me.

"More."

Another inch.

"Goddess, please, Ares."

"Alpha," he corrected me for a second time.

"Alpha," I whispered, and he granted me another inch. "Oh, fuck me already," I begged. "I can't handle—"

He thrust himself all the way inside of me and pushed himself as deep as he could. I clenched hard on him, watching his lips part and eyes close in the mirror. He was big, bigger than Tony, bigger than any toy I had used, stretching me out, filling me up.

"More. I want more."

After opening his eyes, he slowly thrust up into me, watching my breasts bounce through the mirror. He brushed his fingers against my bare clit and then slapped it hard. My body jerked in his arms, my pussy tightening.

"You like that, Kitten?"

A wave of heat warmed my core. He slapped my pussy once more, and I cried out. My body trembled in his hands, the pressure rising in my core. Heat from the bathroom started to fog up the edges of the mirror again, but I couldn't take my eyes off him.

Holding me in his arms. Thrusting himself up into me. Slapping my aching, bare red pussy. Ares refused to stop until he knew I was teetering on another body-shaking orgasm. One last time, he slapped my pussy hard, buried himself deep inside of me, and stilled.

I moaned out his name. My head felt light and full with ecstasy. Tingles shot through my body. I moved my hips back and forth on him, trying to ride out my orgasm for as long as I could.

When I finally came down from my second orgasm, I relaxed in his arms. He held me on his cock, and I tightened my pussy around him. I wanted him to come too, wanted it more than anything.

He took a deep, shaky breath. "Fuck, do that again, baby."

I tightened myself around him, squeezing his cock as hard as I could.

"You're going to make me come," he murmured against my ear.

I moaned and tightened myself on him over and over, watching him furrow his brows in the mirror.

"Fuck, I'm ... gonna ... come."

He shuddered against my body, his cock pulsing inside of me, his lips parted in delight, and that savage, stormy look on his face relaxed into one of pure ecstasy. Canines brushing against my neck, he breathed in my scent and pulled out of me.

Creamed with his cum, my pussy glistened in the mirror. He spread my legs a bit wider and let it drip out of me and onto the bathroom floor.

But instead of putting me down, he reached between my legs and rubbed my clit in quick, rough circles. "Come on, Kitten. Come for me one last time."

Tingles ran up and down my body from my last orgasm, and I didn't know if I'd be able to handle another one after—

My pussy tightened almost immediately. It was as if he didn't even have to try or he was just so good at this or maybe my body just couldn't resist him.

I parted my lips, grasping on to his hand and trying to ride out the high as pleasure pumped through my body. I screamed out his name, on the verge of tears from the intensity of my third orgasm of the night.

Each time my pussy pulsed, more cum dripped out of me. Ares just stood there and watched it with a satisfied smirk on his face, golden eyes devouring the entire scene—my body in his hands, my eyes flickering gold, his cum inside of me.

"Mine," he said, teeth brushing against the side of my throat. "You're mine, Kitten. Let me mark what's mine."

CHAPTER 17

AURORA

The belligerent and notorious Alpha Ares wanted to mark *me* … an alpha who could barely shift, an alpha who was weaker than he thought, an alpha he'd rip piece by piece when he discovered my secret.

Though my heart raced in excitement at the thought, I couldn't let him do it.

I placed my hands on his chest, gathered all my strength, and pushed him away. "No."

He tensed, his brown eyes fighting to stay their natural human color but eventually surrendering to their wolfish golden suns. "No? You don't want me to mark you?" There was the usual mix of shock and fury in his voice, as if after everything, he'd thought I'd submit to him.

It should've been an easy decision. I should've pushed him back further, thrown his savage smirk right back at him, and told him he'd never mark me. At least, that way wouldn't end in my heartbreak. But instead of doing any of that, all I said was, "No, not yet."

After the words left my mouth, Ares slumped his shoulders

forward slightly and frowned, golden eyes still intense but filled with anguish, almost as if he were a whole new person.

"Do you want to mark me?" he asked softly, taking my hands in his larger ones.

"Ares—"

"Mars," he said. "I'm Mars now."

"Mars," I whispered, correcting myself. It was going to be difficult, separating the man from the monster, but they were both my mate, and part of me wanted to tame each of them.

"I want you to mark me. I want to be yours," Mars said.

Mine.

The god of war wanted to be mine without knowing that I was the woman who had the one thing he'd killed hundreds of werewolves to find.

"Not yet." I brushed my fingers against his stubble. Lips curled down in a frown, he looked ashamed that I'd refused to mark him. A wave of guilt washed over me, and I grasped his hands. "I want to get to know you, and I *need* you to know me."

It wasn't a lie, but it was an excuse to stall. Stall because I wasn't strong enough to tell him the truth. And I hated myself for it. But I didn't know how to control that more demonic, hellish side of him yet. I didn't know if I'd ever be able to control Ares. All I knew was that he'd kill for the stone.

After giving me his best half-smile, he grabbed a towel and wrapped it around my body. Although we were still soaking wet and dressed only in our towels, he led me to the kitchen and sat me on the counter.

"I wanted to run with you tonight. Your wolf and mine in our forest, but after the hound attacks, I don't want to risk it. So"—he opened the pantry, which must've had ten bags of Ruffles chips inside of it, all different kinds—"I'm going to make you dinner."

My eyes widened. "Why are there so many bags of chips in your pantry?"

He gave me a prideful grin. "I saw that you had them in your backpack, and I wanted to have a snack that you enjoyed here."

I pressed my lips together to try to suppress a grin, but I couldn't help the warmth I felt in my heart because of his thoughtfulness. If he only knew that it wasn't me who enjoyed those chips, but Ruffles. That cat would find all those bags and eat them within the next week if he didn't hide them well. She had a nose stronger than a werewolf's sometimes. She'd catch a whiff of them, find a way out of her room, and chew right through the plastic.

"So," I said, kicking my legs back and forth, "what're you going to cook for me?"

He shut the pantry door and opened the freezer, which was packed with so much food that I swore it could feed about twenty growing pups. "What're you feeling?" He pulled out a sirloin steak and a box of frozen pretzels. "Steak or pretzels with cheese?"

"You're going to cook me pretzels with cheese for our first meal together?" I asked, arching a brow and smiling.

His cheeks flushed the lightest shade of pink, and my heart warmed.

I never thought I'd see the god of war blush.

"Let's have the pretzels," I said.

"We can have the steak if you want. I'm just—"

"No." I hopped off of the counter, tightened my towel around my body, and grabbed the black box from him. "I want the pretzels, but on one condition." I poked a finger into his bare chest and stared up into his soft, inviting eyes. "You promise not to lick the cheese off of me when we're finished."

"Oh, Kitten, you've got some pretty weird kinks there." He smirked. "But I can't keep that promise to you. I'd lick anything off your body, sprinkle some salt on you." He grabbed the box and gazed at the directions to cook the pretzels. "Bake you at four hundred twenty-five degrees until you're golden brown."

I playfully shoved my shoulder into his, letting tingles rush through my body. Why hadn't anyone told me about this side of him? The gentler side, playful side, the side that might or might not have a pretzel kink.

Maybe I had just been too blinded by hateful rumors to notice.

"I'll be waiting in your bedroom for our five-star meal."

Before I could leave the kitchen, he said, "Aurora, don't leave this house."

"You sound like my mom." I hurried down the hall, wanting to set up Ruffles's bedroom before she got home and before Mars could ask what I was up to. I wanted her to be comfortable, which meant making the bed smell like me and bringing her favorite pillow so she could lie on it.

"If you leave, I'll hunt your cute little ass down and—"

"I'm not going anywhere, Mars."

Not yet.

I grabbed the pillow from my suitcase, dressed myself in one of Mars's shirts, and walked into Ruffles's new room. Perched on a heap of Mars's clothes, which were lying on the bed, Ruffles sat and smiled at me like she was a queen.

I shut the door behind me, eyes wide. "Ruffles! Charolette brought you home already?"

Oh Goddess, Charolette probably heard us in his bedroom.

Ruffles's litter box was set in the corner of the room, and there were three different toys on the ground. A ball with a bell inside of it, a stuffed wolf that Ruffles had nearly torn through already with her teeth, and a laser pointer. A food bowl was filled on the ground near the door.

Ruffles stood up and arched her back to stretch, her little booty in the air. "*Meow.*" She walked over to me and brushed her small, fluffy body against my leg.

I knelt down and frowned at her, petting her head just where she liked it. She rubbed her face against mine and purred some more.

"I'm glad you're okay too, girl. That hound was scary, but you did so good."

When I stopped petting her, she bit my finger and sashayed back over to Mars's clothes to lie on them.

I placed her pillow on the center of the bed and plopped her right onto it, but almost immediately, she stood back up and walked to his clothes.

"Ruffles, I know that he smells good, but he's allergic to you."

I put her on the pillow again, and she did the exact same thing —but this time, she bit the pillow, took it in her mouth, and dragged it to Mars's clothes, laying it right on top, hopping onto it, and plopping right down.

"Kitten," Mars called.

I gazed at the door and crouched down to Ruffles's level. "This isn't over. I'm taking his clothes away from you tomorrow," I said.

She closed her eyes with her *fuck you* attitude and turned her head toward the dark glass window.

"Coming!" I shouted.

I shut her door behind me and hurried to his bedroom.

Lying on the bed in a pair of gray sweatpants with a plate of warm pretzels and hot cheese on his lap, Mars stared at me with a soft smile. I crawled onto the bed with him and grabbed a pretzel.

"Five-star worthy?" he asked, brow furrowed in an attempt to look smooth … but I could see the worry and anticipation in his eyes.

"Hmm …" I dipped the pretzel into the cheese and stuffed it into my mouth. "I give it a four-point-five."

"Four-point-five?" He sat up and grabbed another one. "What if I feed it to you?"

I almost snorted. "Are you going to say choo-choo when you feed it to me too—"

He stuffed it into my mouth and pressed my lips together. "Choo-choo, Kitten."

I chewed and playfully slapped his chest. "What's wrong with you?"

"A lot of things." He cracked a smile, placed the pretzels between us, and turned onto his side to face me. Unlike earlier, when he had torn through the entire pack of hounds in the woods with the vicious look in his eyes, he looked so boyish and innocent. And all I wanted to do was protect him with everything I had. "Which do you want to hear about first?"

My wolf purred for him, wanting him, needing him.

"Tell me about all of it, Mars." I rested my head on his pillow, pushed a strand of hair from his face, and smiled at him. Moonlight flooded in through the windows, hitting his face, sculpted perfectly by our Goddess. "What goes on in that head of yours?"

"Bad things, Aurora. Bad ... bad things."

"Am I one of them?" I asked teasingly.

He brushed a finger under my chin, lifted my face to meet his, and cracked a smirk. "You're all of them."

CHAPTER 18

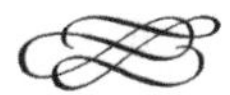

MARS

Aurora lay in my arms, one leg sprawled over my thighs, her head on my chest, sleeping. I closed my eyes and stroked her hair, letting myself get lost in her lemony scent. From a distance, I heard Ruffles meow, and I smiled.

Never had I thought that I'd have a cat in my pack house or a strong alpha mate in my bed. The Moon Goddess had blessed me, yet I didn't think I deserved Aurora. She was one of the smartest wolves in all of Sanguine Wilds—that was what my scouts had said about her after infiltrating her surrounding packs to gather information about that stone.

Someone knocked on my bedroom door. "Ares?"

I growled at the name. If it wasn't for Ares, maybe Aurora would've let me mark her tonight, or maybe she'd have wanted to mark me. But she was terrified of him, and I couldn't blame her.

Using blood as cologne, collecting canines as trophies, leaving packs in ruins, Ares was a ruthless, savage, and feral animal who lived up to his reputation.

At least, that was what he wanted people to believe.

Whenever he took control of me, I couldn't stop him, couldn't talk him down, couldn't tame him. Only Aurora had been able to so far. And maybe, one day, she would, but until then, I'd use him as a shield to protect her from the hounds and to hide us both from my past.

Liam knocked again. "Ares."

"What?" I asked through clenched teeth.

The door opened, and he peered into the room. I pulled the blankets over Aurora's body and tugged her closer to my chest. He glanced at her for a moment and then back at me when I growled at him for ogling my mate.

"I have information."

I waited for him to continue, not wanting to leave my mate and feeling Ares stir inside of me ... but I didn't want to give up control to him again. He took too much energy out of me, made me feel so weak some days. Sometimes, it wasn't even physical, just mental.

Liam leaned against the doorframe. "The rogue doesn't know anything. No names, just that a wolf with a scar down the side of his face had the Malavite Stone at some point," he said.

My entire body tensed. She had told me the same thing the other day, but I'd brushed it off because I didn't want to believe that *he* was back. Hell, I didn't even know if it was *him*. It could be someone different.

"Do you think it's *him*?" I asked.

"Him, as in the hound who rap—"

I let out a low growl. "Don't finish that sentence." After taking a deep breath, I nodded. "But, yes, him."

"Thought he had two scars crossing in the middle of his face?"

"He does," I said. I just couldn't have him around now, especially since I had Aurora with me.

Liam pushed himself off the doorframe. "I'll ask around, see if anyone else knows a wolf with that scar, and get back to you tomorrow."

He shut the door, and I stared up at the ceiling with wide eyes, nerves racing through my body.

I prayed to the Moon Goddess that it wasn't him, but with the two hound attacks in the past few days ... I didn't think she'd answer my prayers. Something in my gut told me that the man in my nightmares was back, but this time, he was coming for my mate.

CHAPTER 19

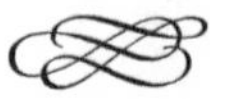

AURORA

The morning sun beat down on me as I stared out at the open training field. Hundreds of warriors sparred on the grass, throwing punches, dodging kicks, doing takedowns and judo throws. I watched Marcel jog over to Ares and me, a Dri-FIT navy-blue shirt plastered to his body.

Last night, we'd stayed up until the wee hours of the morning, talking about how he always wanted a strong female mate, one who could put any other she-wolf to shame, one like me.

But he didn't know me.

I shouldn't keep the stone a secret or lead him on. I should've told him about it last night. Hell, I'd *tried* to tell him last night. I really had. But ... with the way he'd kept smiling at me with so much love, I hadn't wanted to ruin the moment.

Whatever was happening between us was happening faster than I wanted it to. Ares and Mars were different people ... and part of me was falling for both of them already. It scared the living hell out of me how I just wanted him to be happy for a little bit, how I wanted to clear his head of all his insecurities, how I wanted to feel wanted—not by my parents, not by Tony, but by Ares or Mars.

But my wolf wouldn't let me tell him anyway.

"There she is," Marcel said, his silver hair blowing in the early morning breeze. "Has Princess decided that she wants to join us warriors for practice?"

"Don't push it," Ares said. He tore off his shirt and threw it to the side. "Train her like you train Charolette. They should both be training harder than any of the other she-wolves here."

After Marcel fake-saluted Ares, I watched Ares jog toward the other warrior wolves to start training.

Marcel turned to me with a smug smirk on his face, eyes twinkling a psychotic blue. "Long night last night? I'm sure Ares kept you up."

I narrowed my eyes at him. "What's your problem?"

He stalked around me, looking me up and down. "Not getting enough sleep weakens your reflexes."

"My reflexes are fine," I said.

He lunged at me, and I easily stepped out of the way and slammed my fist into his ribs.

"Like I said, my reflexes are fine."

He stumbled back and chuckled. "Feisty."

"Yeah, well, she's about to be intrusive, too, when she puts her fist up your ass, especially if you keep messing with her," Charolette said, throwing her gym bag down on the ground next to me, bumping her hip against mine. "Hey, girl."

Marcel clenched his jaw. "Charolette, what are you doing here?"

"Keeping Aurora away from your disgusting, flirtatious remarks."

The expression on Marcel's face changed from playful to annoyed in less than a second. Nostrils flared, he gave her a pointed stare. "If you're staying, you're training."

She crossed her arms over her chest and raised a brow at him. I could just feel the tension between them, and I didn't know if they had been together before or were itching to sleep with each other.

"Well, big shot, show me what you got against an alpha like Aurora," he said to her.

She *humphed* in his direction and pulled me onto some softer grass, so we could fight. Though she was small, she was fierce. Running at me, almost faster than I could react. Landing punch after punch on my abdomen. Taking me down once.

I let her.

I let her because I didn't know how much she could take and because I didn't want to give away that while my abilities far surpassed hers, they weren't available in my wolf form. Only my human. If I showed off too much, they might expect more of me. But if I didn't show off enough, they'd know something was up.

After fifteen minutes of Marcel critiquing our forms and giving me tips that I'd already known, he crossed his arms over his chest. "Okay, let's run."

Heaving to catch her breath, Charolette disappeared behind a tree and returned as a petite wolf. Unlike her blonde hair, her fur was a deep brown, similar to Ares. I looked at her, then at him, and then at Ares watching me from across the field.

Liam whispered something into his ear, and Ares let out a ferocious growl. Thick muscles glistening with sweat, he stormed toward me. I turned away from him and back toward Marcel.

Marcel cleared his throat. "Aurora, shift."

I glanced back at Marcel, an uneasy feeling building in the pit of my stomach. Thank the Goddess that Ares was about to blow up about something because I wasn't about to shift just to run.

"We have insight on the stone," Ares said to Marcel but didn't take his gaze off of me.

I parted my lips. *Oh Goddess, please don't tell me that he knows about me already.* I hadn't been here for a few days yet.

"Alpha Elijah had half of it."

Shit.

Shit.

Shit.

He stared at me with eyes so golden that I thought they'd burn right through me. "Did you know about this?" he asked, jaw clenched. "The Darkmoon Pack's closest ally is Elijah and his pack."

My heart pounded in my ears, my chest tightening. Someone had found out about the stone, about the doctor from Elijah's pack who had put it inside of me, and now, someone would die in Ares's hands for it.

And that someone would be me.

I tried to think of the best-case scenario when Ares found out about the stone, my back, and my inability to shift easily into my wolf. I tried to remember how much love he had shown me last night, when we had a stupid-cute dinner in bed. Pretzels and cheese. His smile lighting up the whole damn room. Those beautiful, soft eyes.

"Aurora," Ares said my name. Not Kitten. Not mate. *Aurora* with distaste.

"Ares, I-I didn't know." My fingers shook.

This was my mate ... but this was not the gentle Mars that I had seen last night. This was the terrifying side of my mate. Ares. The side that would kill for power and for that stone.

He growled, his jaw twitching violently. "I will tear whoever has that fucking stone piece by fucking piece, rip it right out of their power-hungry body, and take it for myself."

My eyes widened, and I wrapped my arms around myself.

Oh, Moon Goddess, no.

No. No. No. No. No.

This was what I never wanted to happen. This was why I'd told him not to mark me. I had hoped—prayed—that he wouldn't do that to me ... but deep down, I had known he would. The stone had given me a second chance, and now, it was about to destroy me.

"Ready the warriors," Ares said. "We run to Elijah's tonight."

I swallowed hard and tried not to look so guilty. *Someone, save me, please.*

This man was a god with an insatiable hunger for violence, for war, for fury, and for rage. When I'd told him to ruin me, I hadn't meant like this.

CHAPTER 20

ARES

Aurora had a fucking secret.

Something she obviously didn't want me to know about.

From the second I'd mentioned Elijah's name, she had gone white. Numerous scout reports and just common knowledge had told me all I needed to know about the Darkmoon Pack's relationship with Alpha Elijah. They worked closely together, trained together, fought together.

Too fucking close.

"Elijah?" I asked through clenched teeth.

Aurora sucked in her cheek and gazed at the ground, unable to look me in the fucking eyes. "I already told you. I-I don't know, Ares," she said, voice strong … but I didn't miss the way she'd stuttered.

I should've marked her right then and there. I should've shown her that she was mine and only mine. I should've taken her so mercilessly that she knew not to play with me like this.

But instead, I balled my hands into fists and let out a murderous growl.

I wouldn't be surprised if Aurora and Elijah had fucked.

What wolf would be able to keep his paws off of Aurora? She was a fucking goddess.

But she was mine now.

"Anything you want to tell me about?" I asked, pushing her to admit it. I'd let him off easier ... I wouldn't hurt him that bad ... but if she wanted to keep it a big secret from me, then I'd let him have it.

She covered her neck with her hand. Nervous. My mate was nervous because she was hiding it ... and she thought I wouldn't notice.

I had already taken care of Tony.

Elijah was next.

CHAPTER 21

AURORA

I excused myself from the conversation, speed-walked back to the pack house to find my phone, and dialed Elijah's number. It was saved under my Emergency Contacts, like Jeremy had instructed me to do years ago before he was killed by that scar-faced monster.

Ares wouldn't even give me a few moments to myself, so I had to make this quick. I hid myself in Ruffles's room and bounced on my toes, listening to the ring.

"Aurora?"

"I can't talk for long. Ares is going to attack your pack tonight. Be prepared," I said.

There was some shuffling in the house, and I glanced at the door. Ares was here, trying to find me, because I wasn't supposed to leave his damn sight and I had.

A breeze gently blew the yellow curtains against the bed.

"What do you mean? Why?"

"He's looking for the stone."

Elijah became deathly quiet, as if Ares were there with *him* and he were trying not to say a single word. "Aurora, you didn't tell him, did you?"

"No," I said, grasping the phone tighter.

The shuffling outside became louder. I plastered myself to the wall and scooted down it. Ruffles walked over to me, brushing herself against my legs and showing me her butt.

"But Ares knows. Someone must've found out somehow. Did you tell anyone? Anyone at all?"

"I haven't spoken a word about it. I'll ask the doctor who performed the operation—"

"Aurora!" Ares shouted from somewhere in the house, his voice booming.

I ushered Ruffles into the closet and shut the door in case he decided to come into the room. If he found out about the stone *and* about Ruffles, Moon Goddess … he'd do more than just kill me.

"Are you with Ares?" Elijah asked.

"Yes," I whispered.

More footsteps.

"Listen to me carefully." He took a deep breath, and all I could imagine was him running a hand through his thick hair in an attempt to think quick. "Don't tell him about your stone. I don't care what he tries to do to me, but if he finds out that you have it, he will hurt you. He's been looking for that fucking thing for years. He has killed so many people for it, and he will not have a problem doing that to you."

I gulped and squeezed my eyes shut, inhaling Ares's strong hazelnut scent. He had to be right outside the damn door.

"Okay," I whispered. "I have to go." I pressed my finger on the End Call button and stood up, my heart pounding. There were so many thoughts rushing through my head that I couldn't keep them straight.

Ares's scent was strong, but I couldn't hear a single sound. And I'd bet this was what it was like to be hunted by him. Not knowing where in the damn world he was, but knowing that he was close and that he was coming for you.

I hurried to the door to get out of Ruffles's room before he had a chance to find her. My fingers trembled as I tried to delete Elijah's call as quickly as I could, but Ares stood outside the door with his arms crossed over his chest and a wrathful look on his face.

"I told you not to leave my fucking sight," he said.

I fumbled with my phone, trying to stuff it into my pocket. *Think positive, Aurora. Think about last night when you were sharing pretzels and cheese, when you were up until four a.m., talking about life, when he told you that he wanted you forever.*

Ares glanced at my pocket. "Who were you talking to?"

I brushed past him and walked to our bedroom. Oh Goddess, I was calling it ours now.

"Nobody," I said.

He clenched his jaw and followed me. "Who, Aurora? Who'd you tell that I was going to attack their pack tonight?" He waited as if he *wanted* me to admit it.

My eyes widened slightly, but I continued walking. He had heard me from all the way downstairs? I'd tried to keep myself quiet, and he'd still fucking heard me.

"Nobody." I stepped into the room and headed right for the bathroom to take a long shower, so I could wash away all the dirt and sweat and lies.

But before I could pull the door open, he placed his hand on it, snapped it closed, and spun me around to face him. "Give me your phone." His eyes were a dangerous kind of gold, the kind that I had only seen before—when he was about to rip out Marcel's throat the other day for disrespecting me.

"Why?" He had to know who I called. Maybe he just wanted to see it for himself.

"I will *not* ask again."

"No."

He reached for the pocket in my leggings, and I grasped his wrist to try to stop him. But after we fumbled with each other for a few moments, he snatched the phone from me. I grabbed for it, clawed for it, hoping that it had magically deleted the call history itself, but he lifted my phone out of my reach.

I crossed my arms over my chest. "I can't have even one bit of privacy with you. You won't let me shower alone, you won't let me out of your sight, and now, you want to look at my damn phone?"

He growled, reading the names in my Recents.

"You're cra—"

"Don't finish your fucking sentence." He turned around to face me, eyes blazing. "Don't tell me I'm fucking crazy when you were talking to Elijah. Elijah out of all fucking people." He threw the phone to the ground and stepped closer to me.

Instead of screaming at me, he became silent. Deathly silent.

He didn't say anything for one, two, three long moments, and I was scared.

Fucking terrified.

Ares closed his eyes, and I had the urge to jump out the second-story window and run away from him this very second. But he looked so peaceful with his eyes closed and his entire face relaxed completely.

"I am enough for you, Kitten, aren't I?" he asked calmly.

For a moment, I thought Mars was back, that I could talk some sense into him, that he wasn't about to explode on me. But when he opened his eyes, their wrath golden flares seemed to burn right through me.

My heart pounded in my chest, and I stepped back. I didn't know what to do anymore. Should I tell him about the stone? Yes, but not when he was looking at me like this, not when he was angry because it'd make him even angrier.

"Yes," I whispered. "You are enough."

He placed his hand on my chest, right over my heart, his claws softly digging into my flesh. He could rip it right out; I knew he was strong enough to do it.

"Your heart's beating awfully fast. Are you lying to me, Aurora?"

Help me, Goddess. Help me, please.

"No, you *are* enough for me." I held my breath, hoping that it'd still my racing heart, hoping that something would calm me down because his godly stare was too intense.

He paused for a long moment, tilting his head, clenching his jaw, and touching my chest like he owned the heart inside. "You *are* lying to me."

It wasn't a question this time. It was a statement.

His voice was laced with disappointment and sorrow, yet I could feel his wolf under his skin about to come out to claim what *was* his. Because Ares didn't ask for permission; he took everything and dealt with no consequences.

"I'm not lying, Mars," I said, using the name he'd asked me to use to try to soothe him.

Another growl ripped from his throat. He stepped even closer to me and shoved me against the wall. Then, he grasped my chin and held it tightly in his hand. All I could see was brutality and barbarity in his eyes—a worshipped leader who had seen war after war, curse after curse, violent past after violent past; a man who had been trapped in a god's body for centuries upon centuries; a boy who had been wronged one too many times.

"You didn't want me to mark you. You didn't want to mark me. You were talking to the man who knows exactly where to find the stone and warning him that I'm coming to find it," he said, jaw twitching. Like a spear, every word Ares said hit hard and deep in places that I knew were hurting him just as much as they were hurting me.

"I shouldn't have warned him." I placed my hands on his chest. *Calm down, Ares. Please calm down.* "I'm sorry he knows that you're coming for him now. It won't happen again."

Stepping even closer to me, he pressed his body against mine. "Let me be clear, Aurora. I don't give a fuck that he knows I'm coming for the stone. He could prepare for war for months, and I'd still run on his pack, rip each one of his warriors piece by piece, and take what is mine." He pushed a strand of hair behind my ear in a domineering manner. "I'm angry that *you* went behind my back to warn him."

All I wanted to do was to scream at him that it was *me* who wasn't enough for *him*, not the other way around. I wanted to tell him everything that had happened to me and hoped that he wouldn't kill me, but I couldn't open my mouth. My wolf whimpered, and I was getting so tired of hearing her whine about her mate not wanting her, but I felt her pain.

We felt this kind of heartbreak every fucking day, and it took a damn toll on us.

He growled, his canines emerging from under his lips. Moments ... he was mere moments from marking me and making himself enough for me. "Tell me how I am not enough, so I can make sure I am."

I parted my lips and then closed them. *What do I say to that?*

He slid his hand down my throat, pushed my head to the side, and grazed his canines against my neck. I shuddered against him, the feeling of his teeth on my skin making my entire body react so submissively and so innately to him.

"Will this prove it to you?" he asked, canines just barely pricking my flesh.

Heat rushed to my core, my wolf purring softly.

No, no ... I couldn't let this happen. I couldn't ...

"Maybe this?" He pushed two fingers against my clit and rubbed gently. "Does this make me enough for you?" He moved his fingers in small, torturous circles.

I grabbed on to his wrist, my knees close to buckling already.

"Or is it this?" He grasped my hand and placed it right on the front of his pants, letting me feel how hard he was for me.

Goddess, I just wanted a nice, relaxing day. Not this. Definitely ... not ... this ...

"Answer me, Aurora." He skimmed his lips against my ear, his breath warming my neck. "If you don't"—he chuckled lowly, and I shivered—"I'll keep you in this bedroom until I prove to you that I am everything you've ever been searching for and everything you'll ever need."

When I didn't answer Ares, he snatched my chin and forced me to look up at him. There it was again ... that same look I had only heard rumors about. Glowering with valor and strength, vengeance and cruelty, he curled his lip into an ugly smirk. And I thought it was the end for me. I thought he knew my secret. I thought he'd kill me.

"Take off your clothes."

My eyes widened. "Ares, I—"

"It wasn't a request." He released my chin and stepped back, watching me. "It was a command. You can follow commands, can't you, Kitten?"

I gulped and glanced at my feet. Well, okay, not exactly what I'd thought was going to happen. I took a deep breath and tried hard to ignore the pressure building in my core already. What the hell was wrong with me?

He crossed his big arms over his chest. "Look at me."

Moon Goddess. My pussy was pulsing, and he hadn't even touched me. I was supposed to be afraid of him; I was supposed to be thinking of a way to stop him from going to Elijah's and killing him. Not this.

Before he could ask again, I found myself tearing off my shirt and pushing my leggings to the ground. My nipples were pressed hard against my cupless sports bra, and the breeze from the window didn't make it any better.

"All of it," Ares said.

My wolf purred inside of me, loving the attention from our mate. It didn't make me feel any better that *my* wolf couldn't make up her damn mind about him. One minute, she didn't want him to know our secret. The next, she was willing to let him have us like he had last night.

Anything for his acceptance.

Anything to feel loved again.

I tugged off my bra and underwear, standing naked in front of him. He glanced down at my body, taking in all of me, and then stepped toward me, fingers hovering above my clit but not touching me yet.

"I bet you're clenching for me right now, aren't you?" he asked, staring into my eyes. "Thinking about my cock thrusting into your pussy, about your mate filling you with his cum again, about him making sure you know that you're his and his only."

A wave of pleasure coursed through my body. I seized his wrist and tried so desperately to pull it toward me.

"Kitten, is that enough for you already?" he asked in such a degrading manner that it actually turned me on even more. "I haven't even started." With his other hand, he drew his fingernails up the center of my chest and over my nipple.

I cried out and stared up at him, begging with my eyes for him to touch me more.

"You know, Kitten, I think a lot about claiming you … about taking you in the forest in the middle of the day and letting everyone within miles listen to you moan because of me. About taking you here, in the pack house, when everyone is downstairs and listening to you try to muffle those precious little whimpers of yours so nobody can hear you."

My pussy clenched hard. "Ares, please."

"I think about ruining you for anyone else, about you kneeling for me when I come home from war …" He grabbed my hand and placed it on his cock. "About you taking my cock all the way down your throat again, about throat-fucking you until I finally make you my perfect little Kitten."

I gulped and grasped him through his shorts, aching for him to be inside of me.

He held me by a fistful of my hair and pulled me toward him. "Tell me, Aurora, do you need more than that?"

To hold in my moans, I pressed my lips together. All I wanted was for him to plunge himself inside of me like he had last night, but I didn't foresee that happening anytime soon. Ares wanted to punish me for calling Elijah, and I didn't blame him.

And because I wanted him to prove to me that he wouldn't hurt me, that despite me going behind his back, he would love me for me and he wouldn't hate me for my secret, I said, "That's not enough."

He growled, picked me up, and tossed me onto the bed with ease. Crawling up with me and pushing me to the headboard, he grabbed my thighs and spread them, so every fold of my pussy was bare and on full display to him. Before I could even react, he pressed his tongue against my clit, making my body jerk.

I drew my knees together to ease the tension, but he forced my legs apart again and slapped my pussy hard.

"Mine."

He rested my thighs on his shoulders and stuck a finger inside of me, thrusting in and out as he ate me. I squirmed in his hold, trying to pull my knees together again, but he refused to let me go and hit my clit again.

"Mine."

Fingers thrusting in and out. Tongue flicking against my sensitive clit. Stubble tickling my inner thighs. A wave of heat warmed my core and made me tighten on him.

"Ares ..."

"Alpha," he corrected.

It was one simple word but was nothing more than a statement of dominance. He slid his hand around my throat and squeezed lightly, and I knew I was moments away from releasing on him.

"Say it, Aurora." He moved his fingers faster inside of me, hitting my G-spot every single time.

So close … I was so close. All he had to do was—

"Now."

He tightened his hand around my throat, his tongue hitting my clit just where I liked it.

"Alpha!" I screamed it for him, my back arching hard, my fingers grasping the bedsheets. Wave after wave of pleasure was pumping through me, making me feel so good, so wanted, so needed that I never wanted to come down from this high.

Ares slid his fingers out of me and slapped my pussy again. "Good girl."

I drew my legs together, unable to take any more pressure, and whined, "Ares, please."

He pinned them against the mattress and buried his face back between my legs. "Tell me what I want to hear, Aurora."

"Oh, Moon Goddess … Ares, you're enough for me." My toes curled, and I waited for him to flick his tongue against my clit, so I could unravel under him yet again, but he pulled himself away from me, his breath warming my pussy.

"I don't believe you." He slowed his fingers and tightened his grip around my neck. "Convince me, Kitten. Beg for me. Beg me to eat your tight, wet pussy. Beg me to thrust my fingers in and out of it. Beg me to make you come over and over and over until you're trembling in my bed and *begging* me to stop."

I raised my hips, scrambling and shuffling around to try to get him to touch me again. I was so close, so fucking close to just coming on command for him. "Please, Ares."

He slapped my pussy hard. "I said, beg."

"Please," I whimpered, brows furrowing.

"Louder," he said, fingers pressing against my entrance but not into me.

"Please." I sounded desperate, and I was.

"I want everyone in this fucking pack to hear it."

He pinched my nipple between two of his fingers, and my body jerked up.

"Please, Ares!" I cried.

He shoved his fingers inside of me, thrusting them wildly and sending me into a heaven of bliss. Tingles shot up and down my arms. Heat rushed to my core. I tightened on him, riding out my orgasm.

So many feelings raced through me. Rapture. Ecstasy. A want to submit.

After a few moments, I lay back against the pillows and sank into the sheets. My pussy was hurting—with both pleasure and pain. I could still feel his hand smacking down on my swollen clit. Time after time after time.

I expected Ares to storm out of the room, to slam the door so hard that it fell off its hinges, to lock himself in his office to cool down, but he rested his head on my bare chest.

For a moment, I thought he'd change back into Mars. But Mars would've drawn his fingers in circles on my hip bone. Ares just pressed them into my side, as if he were holding on for dear life.

"I shouldn't have been rough with you, but I'm not going to apologize for it. I can't control myself since I got to taste you last night."

Last night when he'd claimed my body.

"I want to mark you."

Ares had been close to doing it, not once, but twice now. He could have sunk his teeth into my neck and claimed me or ruined me far worse than he had already. But he'd controlled himself, which surprised me.

He continued to surprise me.

A part of me believed that if I told him about my stone, he wouldn't hurt me. Mars would hold Ares back from destroying every inch of my body to find it. But ... I needed to be sure. I couldn't just tell him without preparing for the worst.

"And what does Mars want?" I asked, running my fingers through his hair.

"Mars wants you to be happy." His voice was quiet. "He wants you to feel safe. He doesn't like that you … called Elijah, but he knows that you were only contacting him because it is your job as an alpha to protect your allies."

I sighed deeply. "I'm not an alpha anymore. Thanks to you."

It was supposed to have come out lighthearted, but instead, it had come out harsh. It was a cruel reality for me though. Mom and Tony had just thrown me to the most vicious pack without caring that I had been training to be an alpha since Jeremy died. Everything had been taken away from me in a fraction of a second because of the hounds and then again because of Ares.

He pressed his lips to my chest. "You're still an alpha, Aurora." Pressed them to my neck. "You're still strong." Pressed them to my jaw. "And you're still going to lead with me." Pressed them right against my lips. "Because you're mine."

I grasped the sides of his head, breathing deeply, and brushed my fingers against his cheekbones. His beautiful eyes seemed to lead right into his soul, and I was taken aback. On the verge of tears. The emotions were almost too much.

"Ares," I whispered, "would you ever hurt me?"

Ares—the man who'd do anything for that stone—looked me right in the eye with so much sincerity that I was tricked into believing anything that came out of his mouth. "No."

No.

No, he wouldn't hurt me now. Because he thought that I was innocent. Because he thought that I didn't know where the stone was. Because he didn't know that I had it.

I took a deep breath and hugged his head to my chest, unable to even look him in the eyes anymore.

I needed to be honest with him.

"I didn't shift either times the rogues attacked because I'm terrified of them," I said honestly. "They killed my brother."

It was so hard to admit this to him. I had never said it aloud before. Not to Mom, especially after Jeremy's death, because I wanted her to trust that I could handle them. Not to Jeremy's gravestone because I didn't want to seem like a weak alpha. Not to myself because I was ashamed.

When Ares turned to look up at me, I held him in place and squeezed my eyes shut. "Let me continue." I gnawed on the inside of my lip. "I didn't shift because my wolf—"

Someone banged on the door, and Ares ignored it, still pressing his fingers into my hip bone. The knock came again. When Ares didn't even move for it, Liam peeked his head into the room.

Ares growled and pulled the blankets up my body. "What're you doing, Liam?"

"The warriors are ready. If we want to get there before nightfall, for an attack at midnight, then we must leave now."

Ares growled. "Leave us. I'll be there in a moment."

When Liam shut the door, Ares stood up from the bed and grasped my face in his hands. "You and your wolf are safe with me. The hounds won't hurt you. Your wolf doesn't have to be scared of anything." He kissed me. "Tell her that when we get back, my wolf and she will run freely through the woods together under the moon. I'll make sure to have the forest guarded."

My heart hurt. I should've told him.

"I can't wait to meet her." He handed me some clothes from the dressers that he must've put away for me because I surely hadn't planned on unpacking and staying here with him.

I pulled on the T-shirt and pants that he had given me and jumped off the bed, trying not to make eye contact with him.

It was getting harder and harder to tell him my secret. Every time that it came up, I either chickened out or was interrupted. Maybe it was the Moon Goddess telling me that now wasn't the right time, that I should wait, that I should *run* when he tried to find that damn stone. It would be my only chance.

"Come here, Kitten." Ares opened the door and held out his hand.

I wanted an us ... but this secret was too big. And though he'd said he wouldn't hurt me, I didn't believe him. Not when the universe was set on me not telling him. Not when I knew he could destroy me in seconds. Not when I didn't trust myself to stop him from ruining me.

"Ares, that's not what I—"

"Ares," Liam said from down the hall, hands stuffed into his pockets. "Marcel wants to know which group he's commanding."

Ares took my hand and walked with me to the front door.

Standing outside, Marcel was leaning against a running SUV with his arms crossed over his chest, smirking at a furious Charolette. "That's not my fault, Princess."

"It's always your fault, Marcel."

"Says the woman who—"

Ares growled, and they stopped bickering. He stepped forward and handed Marcel the keys to the car. "You'll be escorting Charolette and Aurora."

My eyes widened. So, now, I was going with them to watch Elijah get tortured to fucking death, ruining my chances of ever escaping? This wasn't what I had planned. I was meant to—

"Again?" Marcel said with an overexaggerated sigh. "I did it last time."

"Oh, come on!" Charolette said. "You're going to make me sit in the car with that asshole again? I can't stand another second of—"

"Ares, I can't go with them. I thought you said you wouldn't let me out of your sight."

"Enough," Ares said.

We all fell silent, and I cursed myself for what I had said. All I wanted was to get out of his sight for a few moments, so I could think about all of this logically. Figure out my best course of action when Ares found out about me. Maybe decide who would get Ruffles once I was dead.

"You're all going. You"—he looked at Charolette—"nor you"—

he looked at me—"are staying here alone, where I can't get to you within a minute. And you're definitely not running through Hound Territory with us. Marcel will drive you to Elijah's and then will drive you back once he has given us what we need."

Liam stepped forward, jaw clenched, and glared at Marcel. "You fucking touch her, and I will kill you."

"Ooh, boyfriend is mad." Marcel waved his hands in the air, acting scared. Then, he hopped into the car and slammed the door shut.

He watched through the window with an ugly scowl as Liam hugged Charolette to his chest and placed a kiss on her forehead. Charolette slid into the car.

"You'll be safe with him," Ares said to me one last time. "The only reason that you're going with him is because I don't leave Charolette—or you—here when I hunt. And"—he brushed his fingers up the side of my neck, making me shiver—"this pretty little neck of yours doesn't have my mark. I'm not going to risk someone trying to take you while I'm gone."

CHAPTER 22

AURORA

About halfway to Elijah's pack, I had neither convinced them to turn back nor spoken a word. I didn't want to convince anyone. I didn't want to run away from Ares. He was so excited to see my wolf, yet I didn't have the courage to tell him that my wolf didn't come out that often, that we wouldn't be able to run free together.

"Can you turn the AC down? It's freezing." Charolette reached for the middle console.

Marcel pushed her hand away and clenched his jaw. "Touch the damn thing one more time, Charolette, and see what happens."

She scoffed, "What're you going to do? Hit me?"

"I don't hit women who don't know how to fight."

"Well then, you should have no problem hitting me."

"You don't know the first thing about—"

"Why does Ares want that stone so bad?" I asked, unable to hold the question in any longer and hoping that this wasn't all just for power. Maybe there was a good side of Ares.

The two suddenly became quieter than they had been this entire car ride. Marcel glanced at Charolette, and Charolette glanced at him and then at her lap. She parted her lips, briefly looking up at the windshield, and screamed. Marcel hit the brakes, and I flew forward in the car, the seat belt digging into my neck.

Tony stood in the middle of the street, naked and sweaty. I blinked my eyes a few times to make sure that I wasn't seeing things.

What the hell was he doing here? In Hound Territory? Out in the open? By himself? Was he stupid, or was he fucking stupid? A stupid alpha to lead Mom's stupid pack when she retired.

Marcel took his foot off the brakes, his hand tight on the steering wheel, immediately shifting into warrior mode. "I'm going to drive past him. Leave him for the hounds."

I clenched my jaw. "No. Stop the car." I hated the guy, but I didn't want him dead. Yet.

Charolette stared at Tony with wide eyes and then at Marcel.

Marcel gazed at me through the rearview mirror with hatred in his eyes. "Ares will not like us stopping, especially in Hound Territory."

"Now, Marcel."

"Ares is going to have my fucking ass for this." He sighed deeply through his nose and put the car in park. "Don't get out of the car, Charolette."

I hopped out of the car and walked right up to Tony. "What the hell are you doing here?" I lowered my voice and looked around the dark, grotesque forest. Trees loomed over us like hellish monsters, ready to attack at any moment. "We're in Hound Territory."

Tony stepped toward me, and I noticed some of the other warrior wolves from Mom's pack behind him. "I'm bringing you home."

Bringing me home? I wasn't going anywhere with the one man who had willingly stolen my place as alpha. I wanted to run from Ares, but I wasn't going to run into the arms of a weak man like Tony. And plus, this seemed all too convenient for him to show up on the exact route we were taking to Elijah's.

"You're not safe with Ares," Tony said.

From behind me, Marcel jutted his chin and tilted his head, as if he was about to kill Tony if he got too close.

I furrowed my brows at him, trying to figure out why he was here. How could he have known we'd be here?

"Let's go." Tony grasped my wrist and pulled me in the other direction.

I yanked myself away from him and glared. "I asked why you were here."

He clenched his jaw and stepped closer to me. "Because I know about the stone," he said under his breath.

My heart stopped, a lump forming in my throat. Tony knew about the stone? No … he was just bluffing. He didn't know anything about it.

"I know why you can't shift," he said even quieter. "I know that the stone has been inside of you since your brother passed."

"How?" I shook my head in disbelief. Nobody knew. How did he? "Wait, you knew and you still told Ares that Elijah had it?!"

Fury raced through my veins. Ares was about to rip Elijah to shreds because of this piece-of-shit alpha wannabe. Everything had been going just fine until this happened. I could've hidden it from Ares longer, but Tony had had to ruin it for me, just like he'd ruined my chances of becoming alpha.

Wrapping my hands around his throat, I squeezed as tightly as I could. "Fuck you for everything that you've ever done to me. Jeremy wouldn't have wanted this. You know what Elijah meant to him. Even when he's dead, you continue to disrespect my brother."

What was this all for? Why did Tony want me back? He had everything he could ever want, everything he'd been lusting after since Jeremy left—a pack to call his own.

Tony grasped my hands and tried to pull them away. "I'm

doing this to protect you. You think that the rogue and her kid just ran out in front of your car when you were leaving with Ares just because? I'd hired her to tell him what I knew, so he'd run off, power hungry, to Elijah's, and then I could get you back."

"No," I said, refusing to believe anything that came out of his mouth and squeezing his neck even tighter. "You're doing this to have me, to own me, so I am always in your debt." And I was done being his little puppet. I pulled him close, so my lips met his ear. "Leave now, and I won't tell Ares to snap your neck. I would do it myself, but Ares would relish in how good it felt."

And plus, I couldn't kill him, no matter how hard I tried. I didn't want to see Mom's pack—my old pack—go up in flames. I still cared about them. I still wished the best for all the pups. I wanted them to thrive too. I just wished it could've been me leading them.

When I walked back to the car, Marcel raised his brows at me. "Actually have some fight in you."

I slammed the car door shut and clenched my teeth together, staring at Tony as he disappeared back into the woods with his posse.

Marcel got into the car and gazed at Charolette and then at me. "What was that about?"

"Drive, Marcel. Just drive."

After ten more minutes of complete silence from Marcel and Charolette, I sat in the backseat, nearly shaking. What was Tony's problem? Why did he always think that I needed saving? The only one I wanted to save me was Ruffles. Only Ruffles. I didn't need any alpha-holes thinking that they owned me.

Deafening victory howls sounded through the forest. I gazed out the car window in the direction of the wolves, my heart dropping. About a quarter mile east, warrior wolves were gathered around a man—a god—Ares, who stood naked on two feet with blood dripping down his chin to his chest, holding a beaten Elijah by the throat.

Ares was seconds away from ripping Elijah's throat right out of his neck, punishing him—for something that was *my* fault. He would kill him, and I would be that weak alpha Mom had always said I was for letting it happen. My heart tightened until I could barely breathe.

"Stop the car," I said to Marcel.

Charolette gazed at me with wide eyes and shook her head. "Ares never lets him stop the car while he's hunting."

"Stop the damn car, Marcel, or I'm jumping out."

From here, all I could see was how utterly cruel Ares was treating Elijah. Throwing him around like he was a rag doll. Punishing him like he deserved it. But it wasn't Elijah who deserved anything. It was me. I deserved this all. I deserved to be punished for this. For being an alpha who could barely shift, who couldn't protect, who had made her entire family and pack so ashamed that they traded her.

Marcel pressed onto the gas and drove us further into Elijah's property. "No."

When he didn't stop the car, I opened the goddamn door—because I had to do *everything* myself—and jumped out. Not caring if it would hurt me because watching Ares torture Elijah hurt more.

I somersaulted three times and landed hard on the cement, leaving my whole body aching badly. My wolf howled inside of me from the impact, but I tensed and took it like any alpha would.

Marcel hit the brakes, and the car screeched against the pavement. Everyone in the forest looked over at it, except me. I hopped right off of the ground, dusted myself off like it was nobody's business, and stormed to Ares, who still had that sinister look in his eyes.

"Put him down!" I shouted, my whole body trembling in both rage and heartache.

If Jeremy were alive ... Jeremy wasn't alive, so I had to keep Elijah safe or at least look out for him.

Elijah was more than just an alpha. He led a pack with intelligence instead of violence, had the best doctors and smartest wolves in the entire world, and had found love with my brother. They'd spent hours together every single night, and he was the first person I had seen Jeremy truly happy with. He was family even if Mom didn't approve of him.

Ares's large hands were around Elijah's neck, squeezing and squeezing and squeezing until Elijah's cheeks turned purple. Elijah—already broken in three places and bruised all over the left side of his face—lay helplessly in his arms. I needed to protect him. Not only because he had made Jeremy happy, not only because he'd saved me, but also because it was the right thing to do.

I dug my claws into Ares's forearms and pulled with all of my might. "Let go of him now, Ares!" I screamed, except he didn't budge.

I didn't think that he even knew I was there. His eyes were pure gold calamity, focused on his prey with vengeance and valor, arrogance and superiority.

"Ares. *Now*," I commanded in my alpha tone.

Ares spared me a single glance, pressed his lips together, and growled viciously. "What the hell are you doing here, Aurora? You're supposed to be with Marcel. Somewhere safe."

"Well, you're not supposed to be killing Elijah. Now, are you?" I gave him a pointed stare and yanked on his arms one more time. "Think for one fucking second. *You need him.* You need Elijah because he's the only person who knows how to surgically place the stone into someone's body. If you want all the fucking power in the world, you need him."

I grasped on to anything to buy Elijah a few more moments. I wouldn't let him die, but I needed time. Time to get us all back to Ares's pack house, so I could say good-bye to Ruffles forever.

Simmering, Ares threw Elijah to his warriors, as if he were throwing a spear into someone's heart. "Take him back home. Lock him in the prison. Capture any of his warriors who try to protest." Then, he stormed through the forest, heading back toward Hound Territory.

But I wouldn't let him get away with hurting someone I loved. I rushed after him, running as fast as I could to catch him before he shifted, and snatched his arm. "So, what? You're just going to throw him in a cage and torture him until he gives you an answer?"

"If that's what I have to do, Aurora, then that's what I'm going to do."

I clenched my jaw, angry yet terrified. "Well … what if he gives you an answer that you don't like? What if he tells you where the stone is … but you don't … *accept* it?"

He let out a long and tense sigh and dragged me back to the road by my wrist, where Marcel waited in the car. "Let's be clear, *Kitten*. There will be no answer that I won't accept. I will have that stone even if it kills me. I will trek to the ends of the earth, walk through fucking hell to get it. Hurt anyone and everyone I need for it to be mine."

Every word tore into me like claws, digging deeper and deeper until my heart nearly stopped.

I wanted to ask him again if he'd hurt me, but I was afraid of the answer. Ares looked ready to kill me now for jumping out of the car and onto his battlefield. Before, Ares had been calm when I asked him; now, he was the man the rumors loved.

Marcel tapped his foot on the ground, arms crossed over his chest.

Ares thrust me to him, and I hit his hard chest. "I told you to watch her."

"You didn't tell me that she would jump out of the fucking car." Marcel shoved me into the backseat, where Charolette now sat.

Instead of protesting, I wrapped my arms around myself and refused to look at Charolette, or I would cry.

Ares ... Ares was ... more frightening than anyone gave him credit for.

Ares slammed the door in my face, and I stared at the seat in front of me. He was either going to kill Elijah or he was going to kill me. It wasn't in my blood to have someone hurt for my short-comings. I was a damn alpha.

An alpha who couldn't shift when she needed to. An alpha who couldn't protect the people she loved. An alpha whose mate wouldn't want her after he found out her secret—that she was useless, just like her mother thought.

It took thirty minutes to get back to Ares's pack house, and the whole car ride, Charolette tried to soothe me, but there was no soothing something so deep, something that would ruin everything, something that would shatter her brother, who would then shatter me into a hundred thousand little pieces.

When we reached the pack house, Marcel escorted me up the stairs to the yellow-curtained bedroom and stood outside the door, guarding me from leaving. After hugging Ruffles to my chest and telling her that she was the only one I'd ever loved—dramatic much, but she deserved all the dramatics—I threw open the window and climbed out of it, hitting the ground with a thud.

I followed Elijah's trail of blood to the prison. There were seven guards in the front of the main and only entrance. They all tried to stop me, but I did whatever I had to do to get past each one—punching, kicking, *biting.*

Elijah would not die.

When I made it inside, I shut and locked the door, taking out the key from the knob and putting it into my pocket. This way, nobody would be able to get in to stop me from doing whatever I had to do to get Elijah out of the dungeon.

I walked down the cold stone steps and into the dimly lit, rusty cells. It reeked of blood and rotting corpses and—I scrunched up my nose—shit. And while the smell was overwhelming, I followed Elijah's scent.

In the back of the prison, Ares stood menacingly over Elijah's body, blood dripping from his fingers. When I saw the silver chains clasped around Elijah's wrist and neck, both of his eyes swollen shut, blood spewing from open wounds on his abdomen, I screamed for my life, for Elijah, for Jeremy.

Ares didn't flinch, didn't move, didn't even react to my shouting, so I tried to find the one person who would.

"Mars," I whispered.

Ares gazed at me, eyes widening in fury, and tried to grab my wrist, but I pushed him away and collapsed onto the ground with Elijah.

"What—what did you do to him?" I took Elijah's head in my lap, brushing the hair out of his face. I could barely recognize him. "Wh—"

"Mars is gone, Kitten." He grabbed my wrist and pulled me off the ground, holding me there like he was about to clasp a silver chain on me too.

I tried not to be intimidated by him. Mars was in there somewhere. He needed to be. He needed to see me, to see how much of a mess I was, to love me for my secret.

"You will stop this now, Mars," I said. "Let me clean Elijah up. I can talk to him about the stone. I can see if he knows where it is."

"No." Ares curled a hand around my throat and forced me to look up at him. "Why do you want to protect him? What is your fascination with a man who isn't your mate?"

"Ares ..." I gently grasped his wrist, hoping that it would calm him down.

When I told him about the stone, I didn't want him to be angry. Maybe I could talk some sense into him and convince him not to hurt me. His mate. His only mate.

"Answer me, Aurora!" He seethed, eyes blazing gold.

"He-he—"

"Do you like him?" he asked. "Does my mate like another wolf and not me?"

"Ares, what are you—"

"It's a simple yes or no answer. Don't complicate it."

"Don't talk down to me," I said, pushing him away.

He stumbled back for the briefest moment, and I took the chance to fall back onto the ground with Elijah and cradle him in my arms. No, I didn't like Elijah or Tony or any other guy for that matter.

For some stupid, crazy reason, I liked Ares and Mars ... but ... they wouldn't like me.

Ares growled, gazing down at Elijah's head in my lap, and yanked me up again. This time, harder. He wrapped a hand around my throat and pushed me all the way to the cold cement wall. "You're mine, Aurora."

I squirmed against him, trying to push him away, but he held me tighter to him, his hand closing around my throat.

"Only mine," he said with more authority.

My heart raced in my chest as I watched his canines lengthen from under his lips.

"And you'll always be mine."

Then, he pushed my head to the side and sank his canines deep into my neck.

CHAPTER 23

AURORA

My whole body shook with pleasure, my eyes rolling back in my head. I could feel his canines inside of me, sliding deeper and deeper into my flesh as he claimed me as his mate. My wolf let out a lascivious purr, and I dug my fingers into his shoulders.

He had marked me. My mate had just marked me.

Though my wolf loved every single second of it, I didn't. Mars wasn't the one to mark me like he'd wanted to, like he had told me the other night. Ares had marked me out of pure possessiveness and jealousy. Taking everything away from Mars.

I slammed my hands into his chest, but my fingers curled into his muscles instead of pushing him away from me. He relaxed under my touch, his whole body slouching forward. A satisfied moan escaped his mouth, his breath warming my neck.

When he pulled his teeth out of me, he was back as Mars. Not angry Ares. Not that terrifying god of war. Just plain old Mars. My Mars.

He gazed longingly at me and then at my neck, and his eyes widened. "Oh my Goddess." He gently held my face, staring at my mark as if he had no recollection of actually doing it. "You're marked. I ... Ares marked you."

Just like that, Ares was gone. But I knew that with one wrong move, Ares would appear again, and this time, since he had claimed me, he'd think that I would willingly submit to him.

Mars's lips quivered, and I swore that if he wasn't holding my face, he would've fallen to the ground. "I-I'm sorry. I'm so sorry," he said as if he was lost for words.

He searched my face for something, and I tried to hold back the tears.

Tears that Ares had taken my moment from me. Tears that Ares was going to kill me.

Elijah grunted and turned onto his side on the cold cement.

Mars's eyes flashed gold. "I'm so s-s—" He grasped my face harder, shaking his head and trying to stay in control of Ares. "I didn't me-me-mean to," he stuttered.

Though he had just marked me, my heart hurt for him. Mars was fighting that innate evil inside of him. He was fighting a demon that he would lose against time and time again. He was fighting Ares—the man who never apologized, the man who didn't give in until he finished the job.

He shook his head again, his eyes glowing brown for a long time, and then squeezed his eyes closed. "I-I—" he said. His eyes snapped open. That lovely, luscious brown had turned into a burning gold.

Mars was gone.

My mark tingled, and my wolf purred at the mere sight of Ares.

"We're not sorry," Ares said, moving closer to me.

I stepped back, heart pounding wildly again.

"We should complete our bond, thrust you against the wall in front of Elijah, take you so you know never to think of another man again."

Elijah grunted once more, and Ares snapped his head in his direction.

"But I haven't been this close to the stone ever, and I'm going to find it." Ares stormed back to Elijah and snatched him by the neck, his claws sinking into his flesh.

"Stop, Ares." I grabbed his bicep, trying to pull him away from Elijah.

"Aurora, stop," Elijah said, voice barely audible. Brows furrowed together, eyes barely open, Elijah begged me to leave. "Go before you watch your mate kill me and see the side of him that you don't ever want to see."

My fingers were shaking, trembling. All of my fears, all of my insecurities boiled down to this moment, and I didn't even know if I was strong enough to walk out of this cell and never turn back.

Ares's mark was burning my skin, searing it, connecting me to him. And I hated it. I wished that he had never done it because now ... now, I didn't want to go. That was exactly what he had wanted too. He didn't want me to leave him.

"Ares, stop, please."

Tears welled up in my eyes at the sight of Ares doing this to him, of Ares the monster. He pushed Elijah further against the wall and held him there by the throat. The silver chains dug into his skin, blistering it. Elijah tensed, trying not to cry out and show Ares that this was killing him from the inside out, but Ares didn't need to hear it to know that Elijah was breaking.

He just didn't know that I was breaking too.

"I'll tell you where it is, Ares! I know where the stone is!" I shouted at him.

Ares shifted his head toward me, eyes flickering gold. "You fucking know? Or are you lying to protect him?"

"I know," I whispered. "I really know."

Elijah shook his head. "Don't, Aurora." He seized the silver chain in his palms, burning the skin right off of them. "Please, don't. I promised your brother that I would take care of you. I can't protect you if you tell him."

Ares shook with anger. "Aurora, I swear to the Moon Goddess that if you don't tell me where it is, I will snap Elijah's neck."

"Please," Elijah pleaded with me.

I gazed back and forth between the two of them, my chest tightening by the second. It was now or never. Now or fucking never. I parted my lips to say something, to say anything, but my wolf wouldn't let me speak.

"If you don't want to fucking tell me …" Ares grabbed my wrist and jerked me toward him. He placed my hand on Elijah's throat, his hand over my hand, making me grip his neck in my hand. "You'll fucking do it."

Though I always thought that Elijah was strong, his throat felt so fragile against my palm. Like … if I squeezed any harder, it'd snap. I would snap it. Jeremy would hate me. I couldn't form coherent words. Tears streamed down my face. Why was he doing this to me?

"I don't know what the fuck is going on between you two, but one of you will break and tell me where that fucking stone is," Ares said.

Moon Goddess, Ares really was crazy. He'd snap my throat in a second … but I would rather be dead than kill the only man who had helped me survive that hound attack.

"Do it," Elijah said, his face turning a deeper shade of purple. "Do it, so I can see your brother again."

My heart ached. "Ares, don't make me, please."

Don't make me say it. Don't make me make you hate me. Don't make me tell you exactly what you want to hear.

I couldn't handle this. I felt like I was falling apart. I shouldn't have kept this secret to myself, but I wanted to tell him when I was ready. Not like this.

He would hate me. Just like Mom. Just like I hated myself.

"Now, Aurora," he said through clenched teeth. "Every fucking minute that you waste is another minute—"

"Another minute what?" I asked, desperately trying to buy myself time to think of a plan.

"Another minute that your precious Elijah gets tortured by *your* hand."

A blood vessel broke in Elijah's eye, making it red with blood. Another tear slipped down my cheek. He parted his lips to say something else, but Ares just tightened our hands around his throat.

Ten more seconds. He had ten fucking seconds. I could feel it.

When Elijah's eyes slowly closed, I screamed, "Okay! Okay! Just stop!"

Ares let go of my hand, and Elijah's body smacked against the concrete floor.

Elijah rolled onto his hands and knees, gasping for breath. "Aurora … don't," he pleaded.

I gazed up at an angry Ares, fear running through my veins.

"Now, Aurora," he said, "tell me."

I glanced at the cell door and inched my way closer. Once I told him, I would make a run for it. I wouldn't get far, but it was my only option. I gulped nervously and faced all of my fears.

"It's me," I said quietly. "It's me. I have the stone."

CHAPTER 24

AURORA

As soon as the words left my mouth, I sprinted out of the cell, slammed the silver bars to buy myself some much-needed time, and ran out of the underground prison like my life depended on it … because it did. Ares growled viciously, the sound echoing deep into the night and sending shivers down my spine.

After pushing through all the guards who were rushing down the stairs to help their alpha, I bolted through the woods. Running. Running fast. Running as fast as I could. Needing to get away from him and go somewhere my mate would never find me.

But where could I go?

Mom wouldn't have me … and even if she would, Ares would rip her to pieces to get to me. Elijah's pack would be too obvious. Maybe I could go to Hound Territory. After I'd told him I was scared of them, he wouldn't even think I'd go there.

In the night, the trees looked like soaring soot-colored monsters, looming over me and waiting to attack, their branches jutting out at all different angles like deformed limbs against the moonlight. I blindly rushed forward through the thick fog and prayed to the Moon Goddess to help me move move swiftly.

I must've been three miles from Ares's property when I heard another one of his growls rip through the forest, warning me to keep running. *To run faster.* Because he was coming. For me. For his mate.

My human legs wouldn't take me all the way to Hound Territory that quickly. And it would take a good ten minutes to even shift into my wolf, especially since I hadn't done it for a while. I knew I had to be smart, but so many distracting and vile thoughts rushed through my mind that I couldn't think straight.

"Get back here, Aurora," Ares said roughly through the mind link, which had formed the second he marked me.

My heart raced quicker than it ever had. My lungs felt so dry that I could barely breathe. I hid behind a tree, knowing that I could never outrun him like this. And even in dire situations, even when my life depended on it, I couldn't shift as quickly as I needed to shift.

I held a hand to my mouth, trying to muffle my ragged breathing and my cries. My mate was going to kill me, just like the hounds had killed my brother. He'd rip me piece by piece by piece until only the stone was left for him to have, like the fucking king he was.

Twigs snapped around me. The forest was so quiet that the smallest sounds were deafening. Sweat rolled down my chest, and my heart raced so fast that I could hear it in my ears. I curled my arms around my body and willed myself not to make a sound unless I *wanted* Ares to find me.

About twenty yards away, I listened to him shift into his human form, his thick bones loudly snapping back into place. He walked around the woods, crunching leaves and breaking twigs. Every step he took closer to me made it harder and harder for me to breathe.

This couldn't be happening. Goddess, I should've just gone

with Tony. Maybe I'd have been able to use him as a human shield or something. Keep Ares distracted instead of focused on killing me. His mate. His only mate.

I held my knees to my chest and stopped breathing, my body trembling.

"Come here, Kitten," he said, his voice low and daunting. Yet I could hear the excitement in it. This wasn't the Ares that I had lain with earlier, nor the Mars who had promised me that he'd never hurt me.

This was terror.

Complete and utter terror.

I squeezed my eyes closed and shook my head. No. No. No. No. No. No. No. I didn't want my life to end like this. I'd thought I'd die on the battlefield as a respected alpha, not as a fragile young woman.

One moment passed.

Two moments.

Three.

"If you want to make this a game, I'm happy to play with you."

He walked closer to me, and I thought about Ruffles, the only one who had ever loved me. What would he do to her? Would he kill her too? Maybe he'd make me watch him kill her. Or even worse, make me do it. Tears threatened to spill from my eyes. She didn't deserve to die. And neither did I.

Another branch broke.

"Purr for me, Aurora."

I held my hand over my mouth.

This was all a game to him. All a fucking game.

He dropped down onto all fours and shifted again, his bones cracking. No matter how dirty I was from running in the mud and forest, Ares's wolf would be able to smell me. I had to run. I had no other choice.

Forcing me onto all fours, my wolf wanted me to shift more than anything to get away from the man hunting her, who was really supposed to love her. All my wolf felt was pain and betrayal. She just wanted to be happy with her only mate.

I let out an ear-splitting scream as my bones broke, yet I didn't transform into a normal werewolf. Instead, my bones snapped back and forth, my vision intensified and dulled, my jaw lengthened and shortened, all in a painful attempt to shift from human to werewolf. Every part of my body ached, and when I heard Ares growl, my heart broke.

This was it. This was how my life was going to end.

I turned onto my back to find Ares's huge black wolf standing over me. I stared up into his big, vicious eyes and scurried away from him on my hands and heels. Tears streamed down my face. All I could feel was pain.

"Please don't kill me, Ares. Please. Please. I'll do anything," I pleaded.

I backed up until I hit a tree. I parted my lips, a frail cry escaping them. This was who I was. An embarrassing alpha. A weak alpha. A powerless woman who was about to be killed by her mate.

He stalked forward with his head held low and his eyes fixed on me. My fingers trembled so hard that I had to dig my claws into my palms to stop them from shaking.

I parted my lips, feeling my salty tears on them, pulled my hair behind my shoulders, and bared my neck to him. "Please, if you're going to kill me, make it easy. The stone is in my spine, at the base of my neck. C7."

Stepping closer to me, he pushed his snout against my neck and let his teeth graze against the back of it. I curled my arms around my body, sticking my face into my knees and shielding myself from him, waiting for my mate to kill me.

"Pl-please don't tear me limb from limb. I don't want to end up like Jeremy."

CHAPTER 25

ARES

"If you care about me ... if you even"—she hiccuped—"respected me at all, please don't tear me to pieces." She cowered under me, shielding her face from me, hiding her mark, showing me the back of her neck and nothing else.

Mate is upset.

My mate was hurt. Aurora was hurt. *I* had hurt her.

I could feel every ounce of her pain, could feel how much it hurt her to think that I—her own mate—would be the one to kill her. She was terrified of me, of Ares *and* Mars. We had become one monster to her, and that hurt us too.

After staring down at our mate for another moment, I lay on my stomach and just watched her body heave up and down. We both wanted to soothe her but knew that we had broken her trust. She would run away from us for good.

We would lose her, like we would lose Charolette soon.

Her breathing was jagged and uneven. Her heart was racing. She gazed up at me through terrified, teary eyes without raising her head. I waved my tail back and forth, hoping that it'd soother her enough so she'd show me her face, her beautiful face.

Instead of looking back up, she sat there and held herself, as if she'd fall apart if she didn't. A light breeze blew, making her soft brown hair drift against her moonlit face.

Mate is hurting because of us.

I closed my eyes, trying to calm down my wolf.

The strangled sound of hounds howling deep in the forest echoed through the woods, and Aurora tensed. We were close to Hound Territory, which meant I needed to calm Aurora down enough to get us to safety before they could smell us.

Standing on all four legs, I stepped closer to her. She pulled her legs to her body, curling herself into a ball and tensing even more from me than she had from the hounds. My heart shattered into a million pieces as I watched my mate—the strong alpha woman I had brought home—look so broken *because of me*. It had never been my intention …

But the stone.

Why did she have the stone? She wasn't using it for power; she was fierce enough. She wasn't using it for wealth; all she needed was Ruffles to keep her happy. She wasn't using it for her health … she seemed perfectly healthy.

"Aurora," I said through the mind link, hoping that she'd answer.

Complete silence.

I stepped toward her again. *"Aurora ... Kitten."*

She turned away from me at the sound of my nickname for her, and I frowned. She didn't want to be called Kitten anymore? Or maybe she just didn't like the way that I had said it.

Mate doesn't want us. Mate doesn't like our nickname anymore. Mate wants to reject us, leave us. But we don't want her to leave. We love her.

As my wolf spoke to me, I stopped walking toward her and rested my snout at her feet. She raised her head to gaze at me and frowned. Tears slid down her cheeks, and all I wanted to do was brush them away and hold her to my chest. But … she wouldn't want that.

All of the cries she tried to suppress finally slipped out of her mouth. She sobbed loudly, her howls echoing through the silent forest. Pain. So much pain. Her body shook back and forth, and she tried so hard to hush herself, but she couldn't.

"I'm not going to hurt you," I said.

But it only made her cry more.

Mate is crying. Help her. We need to help her.

"I ..." Her voice was quiet. "I'm so weak, Ares. Just take the stone out of me. Elijah's doctors can do it for you. You don't want someone like me. An alpha who can't even ..." she whimpered. "Who can't even ..."

My heart clenched, chest tightening. Just hearing her degrading words made me shift into my human and grabbed her hand. "Aurora, I would never leave you. Don't think that for even a second."

She gazed up at me. "Mars might not, but ... Ares will."

Every single part of my body hurt. "I would not do that. I would never think about leaving you, whether you have the stone or not. I love you so fucking much." I paused for a moment. "But ... why do you have the stone? What do you need it for?"

"I can't shift," she whispered, the words so soft that I almost couldn't hear them. She tried to pull her hand away, to shield her tears from me, but I held it tighter. "Without it ... I wouldn't be able to move."

I parted my lips to say something, but nothing would come out, except, "What do you mean?"

I didn't understand it. My mate couldn't shift? She couldn't shift into her wolf? We wouldn't be able to run together through the woods. I would never get to see her wolf in all of her glory, couldn't play with her, couldn't run with her, couldn't be with her. Ever.

"On a bad day, it takes ten minutes for me to shift to minimize the pain. It hurts so bad every single time." She shook her head, brushing some tears away. "You should reject me. You deserve a strong luna who can lead with you. You need someone who can run in the forest with you and someone you can be happy with and someone—"

I grasped her face in my hands and kissed her hard on the lips. Nothing she said or could say would ever make me want to reject her. She was a force despite all of this. My mate couldn't shift, but she had killed two rogues in her human form, she had stopped me from shamelessly killing and torturing another alpha, and she had survived the harsh words of countless people who had put her down for this ... this disability.

It was me who was fucking weak. The alpha who terrorized every other pack just to find the stone so he could save his sister. The alpha who couldn't control himself. The alpha who hid behind the horrendous rumors so he wouldn't be seen as a soft man—because soft men always got hurt in the end.

All I wanted to do was lay her on the ground and worship every inch of her body until she knew that I wasn't going anywhere, but she let go of my hand and shoved it away.

I pushed away her tears with my thumbs. "Aurora, I don't want the stone for power. I never wanted that stone for power."

She hiccuped against my chest, her body jerking in my arms. "Yes, you do." She stood up and stepped away from me. "All it seems you want is power. You nearly killed Elijah for it. *You nearly killed him,* Ares." She crossed her arms over her chest. "If you had, I would've never forgiven you."

Never would've forgiven me ...

The words sank deep. If I had killed him, Aurora would've left me.

In that moment, I made a promise to myself not to ever kill Elijah or anyone Aurora cared about.

I stood up next to her and pleaded, "Don't leave me, Aurora."

I loved her with everything I'd ever had. She was one of the only people Mars felt comfortable around anymore, and she was the only damn person who could calm me down.

"Please, stay."

After giving me a long, bruising glance, she walked away from the conversation and toward my property. I stood there and stared at her departing figure with a frown. I had so much shit to make up for, so many truths to tell her. I didn't know where to start or if she'd believe me, but … I needed her to stay with me.

I'd do anything for her to stay.

Hell, I'd do anything to make her fucking happy.

CHAPTER 26

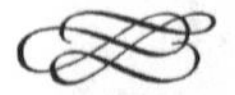

AURORA

"Aurora," Ares shouted as he jogged after me.

I hurried through the dark woods, not because I was angry, not because I was childish, but because I was … unsure of his motives and confused about my feelings toward him.

So many rumors that ex-pack members had beaten into my head about him all seemed to be damn paradoxes. He'd sprinted after me in a rage, like I was his sworn enemy and he was a war god. Yet he hadn't touched me and hadn't hurt me, and I would go so far as to say that he *wanted* me for what I was—weak.

I just didn't know if this was all to fuck with my head or if he was being truthful.

Did he truly want me? Would he really pick me over the stone, or was this all some elaborate scheme to get me to trust him, so he could slowly kill me? The god of war always had something up his sleeve. But the Moon Goddess wouldn't have chosen him as my mate if the mate bond didn't mean something to both of us.

Maybe it was because of his mark on my neck, or maybe it was because I had seen another side of him these past couple of days, but I wanted to trust him so badly. I wanted to be his. I wanted to be wanted for once.

Continuing to walk through the forest, I tried to ignore the growls from hounds in the distance. We were too close to Hound Territory, but I couldn't gather enough strength to think clearly. All my mind wanted to think about was my mate.

"Please, talk to me, Aurora," Ares begged, taking long strides to keep up with me.

Never in a million years had I thought that I'd ever hear the feared alpha beg for anything, let alone beg me to not only talk to him, but to also stay.

"I will do anything to get you to trust me again. Just tell me what you need me to do."

When he grabbed my hand, familiar tingles shot up and down my arm and made everything even more difficult for me. I pulled away, not trusting my wolf around him, and a look of deep anguish crossed his face.

After walking in silence for another five minutes through the eerie forest, Ares suddenly stopped and tensed, his pitiful eyes hardening into an intense, divine gaze. "Aurora, don't move."

I stopped and gazed back at him, listening to the snarling hounds surrounding us. They sprinted through the forest in all directions. Branches snapped, thunder suddenly started rumbling overhead, and lightning flashed through the fog. First, one hound. Then, two more. Then, five more. Until we were surrounded by eight hungry beasts.

Ares pushed me behind him, shifting into his wolf and preparing to attack. But he couldn't take on all eight alone and protect me at the same time, like I knew he wanted to.

He paused, looked around at them, and growled, *"Go for the two north. The one with the shorter tail, the other with the one eye. I know that you can hold them off or kill them. And if you can't, run."*

He leaped forward into the herd of six hounds, his razor-sharp teeth latching into their fur and his claws tearing through their flesh. I swallowed hard, trying to think of anything that I could use to help me fight them. Every other time I had come across hounds, I'd been armed with the silver dagger that Jeremy had given me. But now, I was defenseless.

So, I did the only thing that I thought I could do. I sprinted toward the one with a single eye, leaped into the air when he bolted toward me, and landed on his back with a thump, grasping on to his raggedy fur to stay on top of him. Then, in Ruffles's honor, I dug my claws into his eye so hard until I could feel it pop out of his head and fall into my palm.

The wolf under me howled to the Moon Goddess and jerked his body side to side, trying to throw me off of him. I clutched on to his fur harder, desperate to stay on his back. The hound with the short tail bared his teeth at me and lowered his head, trying to figure out how to attack me without hurting his comrade.

I kicked my hound hard in the ass with my heel, making him leap forward and straight into Short Tail. Feeling flesh, No Eyes bit Short Tail's neck and took a whole chunk of muscle out. My eyes widened, and I took this as an opportunity to hop off of his back and snap the other's throat.

No Eyes wandered around aimlessly, growling and baring his teeth. I slammed my foot into his underbelly, snatched his neck, and pushed my thumbs so deep into him until I broke through his skin and could tear out his insides.

Ares had killed four of the six hounds and was working on the last two. While I didn't have a chance at killing either of them, as they seemed stronger than the last two I'd killed, I would help him as best as I could.

But just as I was about to jog over, another hound leaped into the air from behind me, knocked me to the ground, and towered over me—one paw on either side of my neck, salivating all over me. I desperately wriggled onto my back and stared up at the deadly beast above me.

My eyes widened. It wasn't just any hound. It was the hound

who I'd remember forever. Hollow black eyes. Two scars forming an X across his face. The pungent scent of cornfields and better days, staying out late with my only brother, but never getting a chance to spend the rest of my life with him, of happiness that had been torn away, of the hound that had murdered Jeremy.

Now, he would kill me too.

Two wolves howled in the distance, and I watched Ares rip their throats right out of their bodies, one by one, with his teeth.

"Ares!" I screamed.

He turned his head, eyes a vicious black, and raced in my direction.

But before he could get the hound off of me, another sprinted out from the woods, latched his teeth into the other hound's neck, and ripped him off of me. I stared at the two hounds with wide eyes, never having seen two fight against each other before, and the image of Jeremy flashed into my mind.

Of his last moments breathing—when he had gazed over at me and reached out his hand for me to take but Mom pulled me away too quickly for me to help him, when his lips had curled into the smallest of smiles and he mouthed the words *I love you*, when his eyes had become two dull and soulless orbs.

Ares stood in front of me and growled harshly. Jeremy's killer sprinted into the woods. The other wolf paused for the briefest moment, tilting his head to the side to look at me. I sucked in a sharp breath, recognizing something so eerily familiar about him, and grasped on to Ares's paw.

The wolf ran into the forest, following Jeremy's killer, and disappeared.

"Let me kill him," Ares said.

"No," I said through the mind link. *"Let him go. Take me home. I don't want to be left here alone."*

Ares shifted and stood up with me. I swallowed hard. So many thoughts, questions, and uncertainties were rushing through my mind. Part of me couldn't believe what I had just witnessed. No hound had ever hurt another before—at least, to my knowledge.

"Do you think it's because of the stone?" Ares asked on our walk home. He breathed deeply through his nose, his bloodied, brawn chest heaving up and down. "Do you think that's why they keep attacking you?"

I pressed my lips together, struggling to keep eye contact with him. "I'm not sure."

The fog cleared, and I could see the grayish-white clouds breaking just enough to let the dawn sunlight filter out over the trees. Some of Ares's warriors watched us walk back to the pack house through the forest. I ignored them and continued, my thoughts becoming fuzzy with Ares again.

Ares had marked me out of pure rage and jealousy.

Ares had chased me through the forest with his teeth bared.

Ares had terrorized me.

Yet ... he loved me. He had said it in the woods, and he had proven it in the woods. He had told me that being unable to shift wouldn't make him leave me. But I didn't quite believe that fully. He needed the stone for some reason. And though he'd said it wasn't for power, he hadn't told me why.

How could I live with someone who made me so anxious, with someone who couldn't control his wolf, with someone who terrified me?

Before we reached the pack house, Ares grasped my hand. "Aurora, I want to tell you why I need that stone, but I can't," he said, reading my thoughts.

Stupid mate bond.

I pressed my lips together and pulled my hand away from him. "Why not? If you want to gain my trust again, you have to give me something—*anything*—that I can believe."

It wasn't enough to tell me he couldn't; I needed answers.

A conflicted look crossed his face, and he pushed a hand into his hair, avoiding all eye contact with me. I stared at his face, searching it for any sort of reasoning, any sort of *something* that I could latch on to. I wanted him to reassure me that though Ares needed that stone, he wouldn't tear it out of me while I was asleep—when he couldn't see my terror, when he couldn't feel my hurt.

He sighed deeply through his nose and rubbed his face. "It's not my place to tell you. You have to talk to Charolette."

"Charolette?" I asked, brows furrowed together. "Why do I need to talk to her?"

More pain crossed his face, and he suddenly got quiet. "You just have to. I can't tell you."

I wanted to be so angry with him; I wanted to hurt him like he had hurt me; I wanted to make him feel all the pain that I had … but I could feel the agony festering inside of *him*.

From the moment I'd met *Ares*, I had felt it, but I always thought it was just his immense anger. But this was killing him slowly on the inside, tearing him down, making him hurt just as badly as I always did.

"I will talk to Charolette later. I need to go help Elijah. Don't follow me, and make sure none of your guards get in my way, or I'll lock them inside one of those cages and do to them what *you* did to Elijah." I turned on my heel and stepped away.

He grasped my wrist. "Promise me that you won't leave me, Aurora, please. Promise me that if you leave this property, you'll come back to me."

I swallowed hard and stared at my feet. Then, I placed my hand on top of his and pushed him away. I needed to find Elijah. "I'll see you tonight."

CHAPTER 27

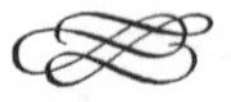

AURORA

Elijah sat against the stony cell wall, his head tilted back. The pungent stench of the prison's rusty metal bars and plaster nearly made me gag.

When I saw him, I burst into the room, knelt by his side, and gently grasped his swollen face. "I'm sorry. This is my fault. This is all my fault."

Blood soaked through his Sanguine Wilds T-shirt. I peeled it off of him, careful not to hurt him more than Ares already had, and cleaned out his wounds with some supplies I'd picked up from the pharmacy next to Mad Moon Grocery. It took nearly an hour to wipe off the blood, stitch him up, and bandage his stomach. But by the early afternoon, he stood in fresh clothing in the prison bathroom.

"Goddess, Aurora, I thought he'd killed you," he said, his teary eyes still swollen but not nearly as bad as Ares had left them. "The way he'd marked you. The way he had run after you. The look of pure malice and terror in his eyes. It was nothing that I had ever seen before, not even during hound attacks." He blew a deep breath out his nose. "Whatever you decide to do with him, please be careful."

From the moment I had come here, I had known I needed to be careful around Ares. He was a loose cannon and could snap at any moment. But what he had done—or rather *hadn't* done—in the woods was the polar opposite of his rumored bloodthirsty ways.

"Can you get my glasses?" Elijah asked, using the wall to guide him back toward the cell. He squinted his eyes and tilted his head in the direction of the wall. "I think they fell over there."

Splattered with blood and with both lenses cracked, his glasses sat in the corner of the room. I wiped off as much blood as carefully as I could and handed them to him. Though he could barely see out of them, he put them on and leaned against the wall.

"Why did you tell him about the stone?" he asked.

"I'd rather he kill me for the stone than kill you for protecting me."

"If he had killed you ..." He took a deep breath, pulled off his glasses, and tossed them to the side. "I don't know what I would've done. Jeremy would've never forgiven me, and neither would ..." His eyes went wide. "Never mind."

"Neither would who?" I asked, brows furrowed together. "Who were you going to say?"

A look of fear crossed his face for a brief moment, and then he cursed. "I'm not supposed to tell you or anyone, but during the hound attack that killed Jeremy, a veiled woman in green gave me half the stone and told me to save you. She visits me every now and then, asking how you are."

"Veiled woman?" My eyes widened slightly. "Who is she? Where is she from?"

He shrugged. "She's never told me, and I've never asked. I'm just grateful."

Instead of asking Elijah more questions that he probably didn't have the answers to, I grabbed his glasses and deposited them into my pocket. "I'm going to get you a new pair, and then I'll have someone take you home."

We walked around the property, trying to find somewhere to get new glasses. Since I had only been here a few days, I hadn't really had the chance to check out everything yet.

After walking around aimlessly for a good fifteen minutes, I retraced my steps to the pharmacy, faintly remembering that I'd passed some reading glasses inside. Maybe they'd have something for distance.

At two p.m., the store was relatively empty. There was a small optic center within the pharmacy near the back, which seemed to close at 1:59:59 p.m. on the dot for a late lunch. I gazed over the counter at the doctor who wore a pair of thick bifocals and was gathering his things for his break.

"Excuse me," I said.

Deep creases in his forehead and a full head of graying brown hair, the man glanced over at me. "Aurora," he said, surprised, holding out a strong hand. "It's great to finally meet you."

I hesitantly placed my hand in his. "I'm sorry. What's your name?"

"I'm Mars's father. You can call me Mr. Barrett or Steve. Actually, Steve works better."

He chuckled, and I grasped his hand tighter.

This warm, calm man was Ares's father?

"What can I do for you?" he asked.

"You're a doctor?" I asked.

He cracked one of Ares's infamous teasing smirks. "Picked it up as a hobby when Ares took the pack from me." He gazed behind me and winced when he saw Elijah. "Ahh, Alpha Elijah." He leaned closer to me. "Did Ares ..."

"Yes," I said.

"I'm fine," Elijah said curtly before Mr. Barrett could apologize. "I just need a pair of glasses."

"Give me a second. Let me see what I can do." He grabbed Elijah's broken glasses and disappeared into the back.

"I wanted to talk to you about the stone ..." Elijah said while he was gone. He glanced around at the other people in the pharmacy and lowered his voice. "I'm working on finding the other half."

"The other half?" I whispered.

The other half could do so much for me. After all these years, I might be able to shift completely and without pain.

"I think I have a lead, but I need to double-check first. And ... I can't tell you in public, especially not here."

Within a few moments, Mr. Barrett came back out with a pair of prescription glasses in his hand and gave them to Elijah. "This is what I can do for now. Free of charge," he said.

Elijah put the glasses on and thanked him.

Mr. Barrett hiked his briefcase back up onto his shoulder and walked out from behind the counter. "Let me know if there's anything else you need, Aurora. You can find me and Charolette just down the street from the pack house. Second house on the left, bright blue shutters. You can't miss it."

Before Mr. Barrett left the pharmacy, he leaned closer to me. "And, Aurora, Ares is ... harsh at times, I know. He just loves too much. And ..." He paused. "Look, all I'm trying to say is ... give him a chance. He's had it rough after his mother passed."

I watched as he walked out the door and frowned at him. Something had sounded so sad in his voice, and I thought about how much I'd hurt after Jeremy was murdered.

Elijah placed a hand on my shoulder. "Well, I should get going too."

"I'm going to find someone to drive you," I said.

Ares would flip again if I left without warning. So, I looked around, found Marcel standing under the blue Pick-Up sign at the pharmacy counter, and walked his way.

When he saw me, he leaned against the counter, raised a

single brow, and crossed his arms over his chest. "What do you want?"

"You are going to give Elijah a ride back to his pack."

"Does it look like I'm a servant?" Marcel asked, his bright silver locks in his face.

"I don't care what you are. You're going to take Elijah home because I told you to."

Elijah tugged on my shoulder. "I can get home myself, Roar."

"Roar? Is that your little nickname?" Marcel taunted and tugged on a strand of my brown hair. "Do you *roar* for Ares instead of purring like he wants you to?"

Feeling all the rage, turmoil, hurt, and betrayal from the last twenty-four hours inside of me, I punched Marcel right in the nose and watched the blood spurt out of it. "Do you bleed out of your nose, or do you bleed out of your nose, asshole? Take him home."

A pharmacist walked up to the counter, scanned an item, and handed it to Marcel. "Pickup for Charolette Barrett."

Marcel snatched the prescription from her and stuffed it into his pocket. "Come on, Elijah," he said and then glanced at me. "And don't fucking tell anyone about"—he nodded toward the counter with a clenched jaw—"this."

After Marcel stormed out of the pharmacy, Elijah and I followed him to his parked car down the road. Elijah pulled me into a hug, thanked me out loud, and whispered that we would chat soon about the stone.

I watched them speed away and walked back to Ares's pack house. All I could think about the whole way home was what I would say to Ares when I saw him. Though Elijah's scars would heal within a couple days because he was an alpha, my scars would take longer.

Marking me without my consent, charging after me, standing over me with such cruelty—it wasn't something that I could get past just because Ares was damaged.

CHAPTER 28

AURORA

When I finally made it to the pack house, I braced myself for Ares and opened the front door. But I couldn't find him. He wasn't in our bedroom, wasn't in the kitchen, and wasn't even in his office. I walked around aimlessly, trying to listen for his breathing.

I wanted to love him. I really did, but what had happened between us made it so much harder.

On the bright side, he hadn't belittled me like I'd thought he would. He hadn't ripped me piece by piece. He hadn't even acted like everyone else did when they heard I couldn't shift. He'd treated me like an equal when the hounds attacked. He'd treated me like I had wanted so many people to treat me.

The door to Ruffles's room was ajar, and my eyes widened. Goddess, this cat. If she had gotten out and was walking all over his clothes—

I peeked my head inside to see Mars lying on the bed and staring up at the ceiling, stroking Ruffles's fur. I could tell it was him by the way he was gentle with her, not aggressive and daunting. She lay across his body, purring loudly. Ruffles meowed in response and head-butted his palm with her head.

"Do you think she will forgive me?" Mars softly asked from inside the room.

My heart softened when I saw them together. Had he known about Ruffles the whole time? Wasn't he—

Mars sneezed, his whole body jerking in the air. Ruffles curled her claws into his chest and clung to him, as if he was the most magical man in the world. And then he continued to pet her.

"Do you think she hates me?" he asked.

"Meow."

"Have you seen her wolf before?"

"Meow."

"Is she beautiful?"

"Meow."

"Did she—" He tensed sharply. "Did you just fart?" He scrunched his nose. "We need to get you off of those chips. Damn."

"Meow."

I stifled a laugh and smiled, my heart warming. These two would be the death of me.

I opened the door wider and leaned against the doorframe with my arms crossed over my chest. Mars gazed over with wide eyes and scooted up the bed until he was resting against the headboard. And Ruffles ... well, she sank her claws into his chest and moved with him, gazing over at me with that smug smirk on her face that said, *He's mine*.

"You've known about Ruffles the entire time, haven't you?" I asked.

Mars parted his lips to say something but then cracked a smile and brushed his palm against her back, making her fur wiggle. "Yeah." His face scrunched together, and he sneezed again.

I grabbed Ruffles off of his chest and let her rest her head on my shoulder. She growled in my ear but relaxed after I scratched her head. "Why didn't you just tell me that you're allergic?" I asked.

With his shoulders slumped forward, he gazed down at the yellow blankets. "Because I wanted you to be happy."

"But you're allergic to her."

"Yeah, but ... I can deal with it. I couldn't deal with not having you around, Aurora."

A deep guilt washed over me for blindly believing all those rumors about him. Some of them were true, but I'd *never* heard about this softer side to him. I didn't know how to feel. My wolf and I were both hesitant to trust him, but hearing my real name roll off of his tongue instead of his nickname for me hurt ... a bit.

I needed to talk to Charolette about why Ares and Mars wanted the stone, but it was night now, and I didn't want to disturb her or Mr. Barrett. So, I placed Ruffles down on Mars's shirt that she had claimed with all of her fur and nodded to the forest. "You promised me that we'd go running in the forest when we got back." I tugged my hair into a high ponytail and let Mars see Ares's mark on my neck. "Have you changed your mind?"

He furrowed his brows. "But ... I thought you couldn't shift."

"That doesn't mean I can't run." I started toward the door and threw him a small smile. "Have your guards in the forest. Let them watch me kick your ass, even in human form."

Staying here would mean that he would want to talk about my shifting abilities, and I was fine with talking about it, but I needed to show him. Seeing it up close was different than just *talking* about it. Seeing it was real. Hearing it was real. Experiencing it was real.

We could talk about it all he wanted, but once he saw me try to shift ... that was when I would know if what we had was genuine. If he could stay with me and still want me after that, then I could start to trust him.

And if he went batshit crazy on me, I could actually run away from him.

Mars broke out into a grin, his eyes lighting up with excitement. He followed me out the back door, humming and smiling to himself like a love-drunk idiot. We started through the forest in our human forms, and I tried to pump myself up for what I was about to do in front of him—shift.

For years, I hadn't shifted in front of anyone. I would always go behind some trees or shift deep in the woods and try to hide myself. I didn't want anyone to see how weak I truly was, but I needed Ares and Mars to see.

My wolf stirred inside of me, not wanting to even think about shifting. It hurt her worse than it hurt me.

While we ran much slower in our human forms compared to our wolf forms, he didn't say a word about it. He continued to run next to me, his forearm brushing against mine every so often. I jumped over some twigs and ran around some other trees, and then I finally slowed when we approached a lake.

"Do you want to run in your wolf?" I asked, gnawing on the inside of my lip.

"No," he said almost immediately. "This is fine."

I grabbed the bottom of my shirt and tugged it over my head. Half of me felt like I had to show him how vulnerable my wolf truly was, but the other half really *wanted* to show him. I wanted to run with his wolf. I wanted him to see me for who I was. Nobody had accepted me like he had, especially not Mom and Dad.

Mars stayed quiet, watching me strip my pants. My breathing hitched, and I willed myself to gather all the strength I had. Fear ran through my veins.

"We are going to run in our wolves," I said.

Eyes widening and flashing gold, Ares was slowly awakening. "No, Aurora ... we can't."

"Don't you want to see my wolf?" I asked.

He ran a hand through his hair. "Goddess, more than anything."

"Then, I will shift."

He clenched his jaw and growled. "Aurora, it will hurt you. I hurt you too much last night. I don't want you to go through any more discomfort for me. Hell, you don't ever have to shift again, if you don't want to." He tugged on my wrist. "Let's continue running. There is a waterfall about a mile further into the forest."

I pulled my hand away from his and rested it on his chest. "I have to show you this, Ares," I said, hoping that if I said his name, he would awaken fully and take control. "I need you to see me for who I am."

The moonlight bounced off the lake and onto his golden eyes. After searching my face for any hint of regret or resistance, he furrowed his brows. "Okay," he said. "But if you need or want to stop, stop"—he grasped my hand so tightly—"please."

I slid my bra straps down my shoulders and stared right at him. "You have to promise me that you'll stay here and watch the whole time. Don't leave me here. Don't look away. Promise me you will stay, no matter how long it takes, no matter how loud I scream, no matter how much pain I am in."

Again, he nodded. "I'm never going to leave you."

After placing my clothes in a pile near Mars, I called my wolf, dropped down onto all four, and took a deep breath. *Dear Moon Goddess, please make this quick. Please don't make this hurt as much as it did last time because my mate won't be able to handle it.*

Won't work. Can't shift. Mate ... My wolf gazed at a patient-looking Mars. *Mate won't love us once he sees.*

She howled inside of me, cramps erupting all over my body. I clenched my jaw. We hadn't even started, yet it was like I could already feel the pain creeping into my veins, pumping through my entire being.

It had been exactly fifty-four days since we last shifted. My wolf had always been terrified but not like this. Not only did we have to worry about the shift itself, but this time, we also had the added pressure of feeling our mate's distress while it happened.

Mate will hate us.

"We don't know unless we try," I whispered to myself.

Mom hates us.

I frowned, tears filling my eyes from all of her harsh words. I remembered the first time I'd tried shifting after the attack and the look of pure disgust on Mom's face—that *you're not my daughter, this isn't my daughter* look.

Mom hates us so much for it. We are nothing to her. She traded us to have a prosperous pack. Ares will try to trade us back. He will call us cripple, worthless, incompetent too.

"Please," I whispered again.

If he rejects us—she paused for a long time—*don't blame me. I tried to warn you.*

A sharp ache split through my side, and I dug my fingers into the dirt. I clenched my jaw to try to keep my whimpers to myself. My skin suddenly stretched further than it should have. Instead of turning into fur, it continued to stretch, and so did my muscles. I could hear my bones snapping and joining back together in a terrorizing symphony.

Time passed, and I stopped counting the minutes until I shifted. Instead, I thought about each bone in my spine morphing into one of a wolf, breaking and bending at familiar angles. I needed to get through this.

My thoracic spine cracked, and I let out a piercing scream, feeling nothing but debilitating throbbing.

"Aurora"—Mars knelt down in front of me, placing his hands on the ground and scooting down to my level—"you don't have to do this."

I growled at him and then cried out to the Moon Goddess. Larger than human canines ripped through my gums, making them bleed. The blood slowly dripped out of my mouth, rolled down my neck, and fell on the dirt beneath me.

My lumbar spine cracked next, contorting into a shape that I hadn't felt in a couple of months. The snap was worse than my thoracic, but the worst was when my cervical spine cracked, right above the stone.

Sweat dripped down my neck, and I tried so hard to shift. I tried so fucking hard. But the tenderness at my joints was unbearable. My bones continued to crack, every muscle in my spine seemed to be reverberating, tears streamed down my cheeks, and I couldn't even quiet my cries.

We can't. We can't do it. Too much pain.

I furrowed my brows together and wildly shook my head back and forth. We had to.

We can't.

My body suddenly felt weak, and my head was cloudy, the soreness so raw. I couldn't do this. My wolf was right. All we were was weak. I slouched forward, trying to take some pressure off of my back. The stone was burning into my muscles and vertebrae so intensely that I felt like I was in flames.

Mars approached me, and I was about to scream at him to leave me alone. But then I saw his wolf standing over me.

He shoved his face into the crook of my neck and licked his mark. *"You can do it, Kitten. You can do it."*

My heart clenched, and I used all the strength I had left. I pushed through all the hurt that I had ever felt. And I let the last part of my body—the vertebrae right near the stone—crack, so I could shift.

CHAPTER 29

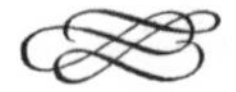

MARS

I had absolutely no words for it.

Aurora had gone through hell, had been screaming, crying, and hurting for nearly ten minutes before she completed her shift while Ares and I looked on helplessly. And it was all to show us who she was, but it wasn't what either of us had expected.

I'd watched her spine bend at three different angles and her bones break and fuse so many times that I lost count. My entire body ached, just from seeing it. I couldn't even process how much pain and suffering she must have felt every time she shifted.

Nearly as big as us, she stood in her brown wolf with those piercing blue eyes. The mere size of her wolf made the shift almost unbearable for her, and I just knew that a shift like this would have killed her if she hadn't had the stone.

My gaze slowly traveled down her body as I tried to remember every inch of her like this because I didn't know when I would see something so beautiful again.

"Ares," she said through the mind link, calling out to us.

While it usually bothered me when she called me that name, I didn't mind right now. We were both here with her, and she needed the reassurance that Ares wouldn't hurt her after what he had done earlier.

I wanted Aurora to be able to shift with ease. I didn't like that she was in pain. She said that only half the stone was inside her, which meant the other half was still out there, carrying powerful healing properties. I wanted to find it for her, but I needed it for Charolette, so she could get better. Charolette might've hated Ares for half the stuff he did for her, but if we didn't get it for her so she could live, we would regret it every single fucking day. Just like how I regretted not doing as much as I could for Mom before she died.

Aurora gazed at me, the moonlight bouncing off her fur. *"Say something, please,"* she said, voice so fragile and so desperate in my mind.

All I wanted was to kill everyone who had made her feel as if she wasn't enough because of this disability.

I walked over and brushed my snout against hers. I never expected that this would be the first moment that I saw her wolf, but I wouldn't change a thing about it. My mate was strong.

When I curled my neck around hers and licked her mark, she relaxed. She lifted her snout to the moon and let out a harmonic howl, one that I already loved.

Then, she turned to me and ... smiled. *"Run with me,* Alpha."

She turned on her heel and started through the forest, her tail swaying back and forth. Pushing herself hard, she disappeared behind the trees. I lifted my nose to the air, howling deep into the night, and followed her lemony scent through the forest.

Aurora was mine, and she wasn't going anywhere.

"So, Aurora can outrun the great and powerful Alpha Ares?" she taunted through our mind link. She knew that name both infuriated me and awoken the beast, yet she called for him anyway.

I couldn't see her, but her perfume was smothering me. Ares stirred inside me, wanting to run faster, to chase our mate, to put her in her place—right by our side. But … I hadn't given him complete control since he ran after her.

After he had marked her in the prison and chased her, I'd reined him in. Never letting him control me like that again—at least, not around Aurora. He wanted her so bad, it hurt, but when she finally found out what he was truly capable of … I didn't know if she would run away from us for good.

The rumors that he'd killed entire packs, burned anything to the ground, slaughtered for power were all true, and those tales didn't even do him justice. Everyone feared Ares, but they didn't know that his want for power was because he never wanted me to feel helpless again.

I pushed myself harder, seeing her tail wagging only a few yards ahead of me. Her scent intensified, and her kittenish threats were riling Ares up.

"Alpha Ares," she said. *"So strong, so powerful, so* slow."

He growled inside of me and made me run faster toward our mate. I caught her tail between my teeth, tugged on it ever so gently, and leaped on her. We tumbled on the ground, somersaulting a few times over the pine-covered forest floor.

She struggled under me, playfully swatting me with her paw. I pinned her to the ground, her body easy to control … but I knew she wanted it that way. If she were really fighting back, I was sure she'd have had me on my ass by now.

I stuck my nose into the crook of her neck—right where Ares's mark was—and brushed my canines against the spot, pressing them into her, just not enough to break through her flesh. For a moment, she tensed and then shuddered in delight. She stopped struggling under me and sighed deeply through her nose. Her eyes glistened under the moonlight, like two stars under a new moon.

Gazing down at Ares's mark, I saw that while she had been terrified of Ares earlier, she wasn't afraid anymore. She trusted us not to hurt her, and we would never hurt her again. I would make sure of it.

She howled to the sky, and I smiled down at my mate. This was the moment I had dreamed of since I was a child. All I wanted was my mate, to play with her, to laugh with her, to tease her … but I didn't know when I would ever get to experience this again.

Earlier today, she had bared her entire soul to me, shown me all of her insecurities, let me feel how she did during her shifts so I could understand her. And now, it had to be my turn. I had to show her mine.

Sooner or later, she'd find out about all of the secrets that I had been hiding from the world. Secrets about Mom. Secrets about Charolette. Secrets about—I gazed down at my scarred front legs—myself.

All I wanted was to be enough for her before I told her. I wanted to make sure she knew how much she really meant to me. I hoped that I could show her that because … I didn't want this feeling to ever go away. I felt like I was walking on the clouds with the Moon Goddess herself, staring down at utter perfection.

She caught me in a moment of adoration and turned us over, pinning me to the ground. She stared down at my neck, her hungry eyes taking in the spot that she would mark.

I turned my head to the side, giving her permission. *"Do it, Aurora."*

I closed my eyes and smiled. I wanted to be hers.

White teeth glistening, she drew her tongue against them. All I could imagine was her claiming me, reassuring me that I would never be alone, that she would never leave me, that I was hers and only hers.

One second passed, then two, and then her teeth were brushing against my neck.

Goddess, I was ready to be hers.

Suddenly, she pulled away from me, blue and gold specks

shimmering in her eyes, and stood up. After a bit of watching her fight with her wolf, she turned back to me, lifted her snout to the moon, and said, "*Shift*," through our mind link.

It wasn't a question. It was a command. Her alpha command.

I shifted into my human form and watched as she struggled to shift back into hers. It didn't look as painful as the shift to werewolf, but she still endured it for several minutes. I leaned back against my forearms and watched her.

Though I was disappointed that she hadn't marked me, I knew that she was still wary and needed to keep her guard up. She wanted to be certain.

When she shifted completely, I went to stand, but she just pushed me onto my back, in the middle of the forest, and crawled on top of me. Cracking a smile, she straddled my waist and let me feel her wet pussy glide against my cock. "You've had your fun with me." She grabbed my cock in her hand and rubbed my head against her wetness. "Now, it's my turn."

Curling her fingers into my chest, she let the head of my cock slip into her sopping wet pussy and then sat all the way down on it. She stared down at me with that same look she had given me the first night I met her—the look of passion and need for *me*.

I rested my hands on her hips.

She was a goddess. She was *my* goddess.

CHAPTER 30

AURORA

Every part of my body tingled. I couldn't get enough of him.

Standing by my side. Urging me to shift. Believing in me.

It was enough to prove to me that Ares and Mars wanted me and that they loved me. I wasn't going to be one of those girls who didn't see a man's effort until he was on his knees, begging.

Ares might've screwed up, but if he hadn't, I might not have told him yet. I would've put it off, drowning in all of my fears that he would reject me, that he would call me names, and that he would ultimately kill me.

But here I was, in this forest with him. Naked, weak, and so damn turned on by his loyalty. Maybe it was the mark on my neck talking, but I *really* wanted to mark him. I wanted to complete our bond, for him to be mine.

By the way his eyes tinted the lightest shade of gold and his grasp tightened on my hips, I could tell that Mars was gone, and Ares was back, ready to prove that he would stay through anything with me. He slowly moved his hips up and down to thrust into me.

I peeled his hands away from me, pinned them beside his

head, and leaned over him. "I said, no. Now, it's *my* turn to have *you*."

After placing my hands on his taut abdomen, I moved my hips up and down on his cock—slowly, so he could feel me squeeze every inch of him. Then, when I couldn't handle it any longer, I moved my hips faster and faster, the tension rising in my core. His gaze traveled from my eyes to my lips to my tits as they bounced softly.

"Touch me, Ares," I said.

He drew his fingers over my nipples and groped my breasts.

I curled my fingers into his chest and arched my back. "Harder."

He pinched my nipples between his fingers and tugged on them. The pressure rose in my core, shooting through me so intensely that I was about to orgasm already. I rode him for a few more minutes until I came and my pussy was aching.

I rested my chest against his, trailed my lips up the side of his neck, and smirked against his jaw. "Are you hungry, *Alpha*?"

After growling into my ear, he rolled us over and pulled himself out of me. His eyes became golden suns, and he kissed all the way down my body to my pussy. I rested my thighs on his shoulders and let him bury his face deep between my legs. My fingers snaked into his thick brown hair, and I pulled his lips against my pussy and held him there.

He smirked against my folds, his tongue slowly massaging my clit. "Your pussy is so wet for me, Kitten," he murmured.

I clenched, my core warming. He pushed two fingers between my folds and continued to play with my clit with his tongue until my legs trembled.

I didn't care that we were so deep on Ares's territory that everyone around could hear us. I didn't care that there were guards out here, protecting the borders. I moaned his name so loudly, letting it roll off of my tongue like it was meant to be there.

"Louder," he mumbled against me. "Say my name louder."

I thrust my hand into his hair and held him closer to me, the pleasure shooting through my entire body. His fingers continued to move in and out in a rough, quick rhythm as my pussy pulsed on him.

"Ares," I whispered. "Ares … oh Goddess … I'm going to …"

Just as I was about to come, he pulled his fingers out of me and stopped. My body teetered on the edge as I waited for him to thrust them back into me and help me feel good. But instead, he chuckled against me and let his fingers linger millimeters away.

I squirmed under him and lifted my hips, trying to get him to touch me again. "Ares, let me come."

He glanced up at me and smirked devilishly. "You're not going to come unless it's on my cock, Aurora," he said.

I grasped his hair tighter, trying so desperately to pull him back onto me, but he pinned my wrist to the ground beside me, knelt between my legs, and brushed his thumb across my lower lip.

"Oh, Aurora … you're so precious." He dragged his thumb down the center of my body to my clit and rubbed small circles around it. "Trying to dominate me like this. It's … cute."

I squeezed my eyes closed, the tension starting to build up again.

"Tugging on my hair, squirming under me"—he pushed a single finger inside of me, and I clenched—"it only turns me on more, Kitten."

Moaning softly, I tried to control my trembling legs. My pussy was tight around him as he pumped his fingers in and out of me, bringing me so close to the edge again.

"Do you want me to fill your tight little cunt up like I did the other night?" he asked, eyes a deathly gold. I tensed hard around his fingers, my heart racing, and he gazed down at my pussy, cracking another smirk. "Feels like you do."

I furrowed my eyebrows and whimpered for my mate, all

sense of control gone. All Mars had to do was surrender to Ares, and I submitted to his every touch. It was so dangerous but so thrilling.

"I bet you've been thinking about me filling you up with my cum and letting it drip out of you when we're finished." He kissed just below my ear. "Or maybe ... thrusting it deeper inside of you and making you bear our pups."

Something about the power he had over me made me feel so fucking good. No, I didn't want pups right now, but just the mere thought of it made my wolf crave him. My pussy pulsed even more intensely on his fingers as I just waited for him to fill me up, for him to make me come over and over, like he had the other night.

I hadn't gotten over the feeling of him being inside of me. I didn't think I ever would.

"Does my Kitten want that?" he asked, fingers pushing into me and pulling back out, so agonizingly slow. I nodded at him, my head in such a daze, as the pleasure coursed through my entire body. "Use your words."

"Yes, Ares."

He growled lowly, crawled next to me, and pushed me onto my side, my back against his chest. He brushed his lips against my ear from behind and lifted one of my legs into the air, positioning the head of his cock right at my entrance. He spread my legs wider, his hand slipping down my thigh to rub my clit. "Beg," he whispered in my ear. "I love it when you beg for me, Kitten."

My mark burned with pleasure every time he pressed against my wetness. "Please, Ares," I begged.

He pushed himself harder against my core.

"Oh Goddess, please, I need it."

After slipping his arm underneath my neck and cradling my head, he brushed his fingers against my lips. "Please what?"

"Put your cock inside of me."

Without speaking another word, he drew me closer to him,

kissed my mark, and plunged himself inside of me. My whole body jerked up, but Ares held me to him.

"I love the way your pussy wraps around my cock." He rubbed my clit harsher, pumping in and out of me. "The way your tits bounce every time I thrust into you."

Pleasure rushed through my body.

"Your purrs," he whispered in my ear. "Goddess, I love the way you purr for me, Kitten."

My pussy clenched harder on his cock, and I moaned out his name, unable to hold myself back. All I could feel was him pulsing inside of me and the surge of delight I felt from it. I arched my back and came hard.

Wave after wave of ecstasy rushed through my body, making it tingle with delight. He slowed his pace, came inside of me, and groaned deeply into my ear. I could already feel his cum coating my pussy lips.

After he pulled himself out, I rolled onto my back and stared over at him, my breathing heavy. The moonlight bounced off his sculpted face so perfectly, and my heart warmed. So many things had happened since the last night we had been together, yet I felt even closer to him.

We stayed quiet for a few moments, and then he pushed a strand of my hair behind my ear. "My dad invited us to dinner tomorrow night. Do you want to go?" he asked nervously.

While I hadn't had one simple night here to relax, I wanted to meet his family. It would be a good time to figure out who Ares really was, what had happened to his mother, and why Charolette was the only one I could ask about the stone.

"Only if you take me back to the pack house and feed me some more of those pretzels with cheese tonight," I said, giving him the best proposition he'd ever get from me.

He chuckled against my lips, picked me up right off of the ground, and carried me home. "Anything for you, Kitten."

CHAPTER 31

AURORA

I dumped my gym bag onto the ground at the edge of the training field and tugged my hair into a high ponytail, so everyone could see Ares's mark on my neck. Though he had marked me less than two days ago, his teeth had sunk so deep into me that my mark was still red and swollen. People from his pack gazed over at me, eyes lingering longer than they usually did.

The warriors and members in his pack weren't the most personal people, but they were getting used to me. Some even smiled at me this morning. But since I'd been here, they all seemed like something was haunting and hurting each one of their hearts.

At the front of the pack, Ares stood with Marcel and sneaked a gaze at me when Marcel instructed the pack through warm-ups. Marcel was definitely the biggest asshole I knew, but he was one of the strongest wolves in this pack. It was just weird that he never went on hunts with Ares and just kind of … *babysat* Charolette.

Charolette bounced on her toes next to me, smiling wide. "Morning."

After fiddling with my fingers a few times, I mustered up my best smile. All night, I had stayed up, trying to think about how I was going to ask her why Ares needed the stone. The last time I had asked her and Marcel, she had been so hesitant to say anything. And I had a bad feeling that Ares needed the stone because something had happened with her.

"Three-mile run around the property. Take our usual route," Marcel said.

Everyone shifted into their wolves, except Ares, Marcel, Charolette, and me.

Marcel cocked a brow at us. "Even you two."

"I'm not running in my wolf," I said with confidence, so nobody would suspect a thing.

Ares was the only person here who knew about me not being able to shift easily, and I wanted to keep it that way until I was comfortable.

He would protect me any way he could, but he couldn't stop the way people would look at me. They'd judge me for being an alpha and their luna who couldn't shift. How could I be the god of war's mate? How would they respect me once they found out?

I could snap any one of their necks in my human form, yes ... but I wouldn't do that just because they judged me for it. I didn't want to lead by fear. I wanted them to respect me for me, and I had to earn that respect, even as an alpha.

"She'll run in her human form." Ares nodded to the woods. "I'll run with her."

Marcel grunted. "No. She needs to run, and so do you." He stepped closer to Ares, lowering his voice. "You need to be strong for when we find that fucking stone."

Charolette looked between us and stepped forward. "I'll run with Aurora."

Marcel shook his head. "You run with me."

Ares growled. "She will run with Aurora for today. They need to talk."

I straightened my posture and clenched my jaw. "Go," I said, not wanting to draw attention to myself.

After a couple of curse words from Marcel, they shifted and disappeared through the woods.

Charolette and I jogged in our human forms on the same sunny path.

We got about a half-mile into the woods when she asked, "Why don't you shift?"

My eyes widened, and I slowed down just a bit. This was not how I'd wanted or expected this conversation with her to start. I'd wanted to figure out about the stone and Ares's need for it before I told her anything.

"Um ..." I hopped over some branches. Birds chirped softly above us, flying low overhead. "I just ... don't like to shift."

She furrowed her brows, her breaths becoming uneven, as if she were almost out of breath already. "I can see if you don't like it when we practice—because shifting takes so much energy—but ... you don't even shift when there's danger."

I parted my lips and swallowed hard. *Shit. Shit. Shit.* Had Ares said something to her? Had he told her that I couldn't shift? Had he told anyone else that I couldn't shift? If he had ... Goddess, there would be so many people who might try to challenge me for my place as luna. Though challenging an alpha or luna for leadership didn't happen often and I didn't think that Ares would allow it, that didn't mean I could just walk around his pack and think I was safe.

There was a hierarchy. Only the strong survived. And I was weak.

"Come on," Charolette said. "You can tell me."

I parted my lips. "If I tell you the truth, will you tell me something?"

A smile broke out on her flushed face. "Anything."

After hoping that I could trust her, I slowed to a walk and

rubbed my hands together. Charolette stopped, still breathing heavy.

"I …" I started, fumbling with the ends of my dry-fit shirt. "My pack was attacked by hounds a long time ago. My brother died during an attack, and I was paralyzed from my neck down, so it's difficult for me to shift."

Almost immediately, her eyes filled with tears. "But … how? Why? Wh—how are you still walking? How can you be walking?"

I gnawed on the inside of my cheek to hold the tears back. It had been bad enough, telling Ares about this last night. It would hurt me so much more, trying to tell someone else about how shitty my life had been since Jeremy passed.

But the truth felt so freeing sometimes. I wanted Charolette to accept me the way that Ares had. I didn't want her to judge me or try to make my life easier because of this disability. She was my only friend here.

"Half of the Malavite Stone is in my back," I whispered.

"You have the stone inside of you?" she asked in disbelief. An expression that I couldn't quite decipher crossed her face. She grabbed my hands and pulled me to the side of the path. "You can't tell Ares about it. He … he'll hurt you. He's been searching for that stone for years. He'll do anything for it."

"He already knows."

"He knows?" She frowned at me and let a tear fall down her cheek. Then, she threw her arms around me and pulled me into a tight hug. "He's hurt so many people, trying to find the stone. I'm honestly … so happy that he hasn't hurt you too. I'm so … so … happy for you—that you get to live your life to the fullest and aren't paralyzed anymore. Ares needs a strong woman in his life." She pulled away. "After Mom and now me"—tears rushed down her cheeks—"I think he might start to hurt himself ag—"

I furrowed my brows. "What do you mean, you?" I asked.

Ares's mother had died, but Charolette was healthy.

She stepped away from me and swallowed hard. "Aurora …"

Her eyes widened. "Wait … Ares still hasn't told you why he wants the stone?" She placed a hand over her heart. "Oh Goddess, what's wrong with him?"

"What's wrong? What's going on?" I asked quietly. My stomach tightened, and I wrapped my hand around the front of my neck.

What could be so terrible?

I thought back to all the times I had spent around her and the pack. She fatigued during our run. Marcel got her some kind of medication. Ares was so protective over her …

"Aurora …" Her fingers trembled. "I have cancer."

My eyes widened, and I shook my head. No. No, she couldn't. She was so healthy. She was so fucking healthy, so happy, so …

More tears streamed down her face, and she let out another cry.

"No," I said, not wanting to believe it. "No, you can't—"

"Leukemia." She gripped my hand harder. "I've had it for a few years, have been through chemo … and …" She squeezed her eyes shut.

This couldn't be true. I barely knew her, but she had quickly become one of my only true friends.

"It's not working," she finally said, wiping the tears from her cheeks. "It's hard for me to do so many things that I used to be able to do. I can barely run. I can barely fight. I'm just trying to live my last few days happy."

This was why Ares hadn't wanted to tell me. He was in too much pain over Charolette. First, his mother had died, and now, Charolette might die too.

She frowned and watched the warriors gather in the field through the trees. "My wolf's fur is becoming thinner every day, and I've lost the hair on my head. That's why I don't shift in front of people. I don't want them to see me without my wig … I always loved how I looked … and now … now, I'm nothing. I'm nothing," she repeated, voice cracking.

I pulled her into a hug and let her rest her head on my shoulders. She grasped on to me tightly, curling her fingers into my back.

"It's okay, Charolette." I gently rubbed her back, trying to be strong for her.

But it wasn't okay. None of this was okay, and it never would be.

"Ares thinks that if he finds the stone … he'll be able to fix me …" She shook her head. "But … I don't believe it. Nothing has been able to fix this, and nothing will ever be able to fix me. I'm broken."

CHAPTER 32

AURORA

Ever since Charolette had told me she had cancer this morning, I couldn't stop thinking about it. The word had been on my mind for hours, terrorizing me in the worst ways possible. Charolette was Ares's only sibling, just like Jeremy had been mine. And I knew the pain and heartbreak he was feeling, knowing ahead of time that he'd lose her one day if he didn't find the stone.

We skipped the rest of practice—despite Marcel telling her she needed to train to be strong—and got ice cream at Pandora's Parlor. She told me that doctors were giving up on her, that the money Ares had poured into chemo was for nothing, and that they thought she only had a few months left at best unless the Moon Goddess presented her with a miracle.

When I got home, I locked myself in Ruffles's bedroom and cried for the first time today. Ruffles hopped up onto my lap and rubbed her face against my cheek, knowing that something was wrong. I hugged her to my chest, my entire body shaking.

We needed to find the other half of the stone as soon as possible. But even that was iffy. If we found it, could only half the stone treat her cancer and keep her alive? What if it didn't?

I brushed my fingers across the slightly raised skin on my back, feeling the stone's power vibrating through them.

If half the stone didn't work, then I would give her my half too. I had to; I didn't have any other choice. I would not let Ares or Mars experience what I had when Jeremy died—the anguish, the heartbreak, the feeling of *you could've done more to save him, but you just didn't try hard enough*. If I had to spend the rest of my life unable to walk or to shift, then I would do that for Charolette. Though I didn't know her as much as I wished I did, she had helped me so much already—even if it was just hiding Ruffles for me.

But until then, I would try my hardest to find the stone.

I opened a bag of chips to distract Ruffles, picked up the phone as I listened to her little crunches, and dialed Elijah's number. While I didn't think he had any new information about the stone yet, I needed to talk to him because his doctor had put the stone in my back. Maybe I could convince him to put the other stone into Charolette once we found it. And if my stone was attracting the hounds like Ares thought, maybe we could somehow find the other half of the stone using this one.

Something.

Anything.

Elijah didn't answer, so I called him again. The second call went straight to voice mail.

"Elijah, please answer. I need to talk to you about the second half of the stone. We need to find it now. Call me back."

Mars knocked on the door and peeked his head into the room. Dressed in a short-sleeved pink button-up that hugged his biceps perfectly and a pair of fitted white jeans, he smiled. "Are you ready? My dad wants us over at six."

I gazed at the clock, which read five fifty p.m. in glowing green numbers, and hurried to his bedroom, throwing on a baby-blue summer dress and a pair of red sandals. Mars snatched up my hand and led me out of the pack house and down the street.

He stayed quieter than usual as we walked down the white-paved sidewalk.

I crossed the middle of the street when I saw Mr. Barrett's bright blue shutters and said, "Your sister is sick," before I could stop myself.

Stopping on the cracked pavement, Mars looked over, his eyes soft. "You talked to her?"

"Yes …" Guilt hit me like a fucking train. I had judged him for something I knew nothing about just because Mom had told me. "I'm sorry for getting angry with you and for calling you power hungry. I'm sorry for … for what's happening. I didn't know, but"—I grasped his hand tighter and tried to smile up at him—"I am willing to do everything to find the other half of the stone. And if we can't find it in time, then I'm going to give her the stone inside of me."

All that softness in his brown eyes disappeared and was replaced with a hard, intense stare. "No." He pulled me toward his dad's house. "I won't let you."

I yanked my hand out of his. "I'm not asking for your permission."

Mars let out a menacing growl and glared down at me. "You're not going to give your life for hers. I appreciate your offer, but Charolette nor I will accept you doing that."

"If it's life or death, Mars?" I shook my head. "I am going to do it."

Wind shook the trees above us, and a strand of Mars's hair blew into his face. "I'm not going to fight with you about this. You will not risk your life. You're the luna of this pack. You need to be strong and to stay strong for me, for when shit hits the fucking fan and I spiral out of fucking control …" He swallowed hard, eyes filling with terror that I hadn't seen before. "You will need to lead this pack."

"Well, you need to understand that—"

"Aurora!" Mr. Barrett smiled from the front door and held it open for us. "Mars! You're here! Come on in."

Mars grabbed my hand and pulled me to the house, staying deathly quiet. When we walked in, Charolette was already sitting at the table with Liam, kicking her legs back and forth with a giant smile on her face.

"Hi, A!" She smiled widely at me with a twinkle in her eye that had disappeared this morning. Mars nodded at her, and she scrunched up her nose. "I was talking to Aurora, not you."

Mars pulled out a chair for me. He sat next to me, his sharp jaw clenched hard, staring from me to his sister and back. I smiled at her and pressed my lips together, not wanting to say anything that would cause Mars to lose control. If we were back home, I would. I would fight him on this. But we were eating with his family for the first time, and I wanted to make a good impression.

While Mr. Barrett disappeared into the kitchen to finish cooking, I gazed around at the cozy interior. A fireplace in the living room, moonflowers in a flowerpot on the table, and family pictures hanging on the walls. Gaze drifting from picture to picture, I stopped and stared at one of their entire family.

It looked as if it had been taken years ago—when Mars appeared to be in his early teens. Mrs. Barrett stood behind him, her arms around his shoulders, her chin resting on top of his head. Mars had this huge boyish grin on his face, his eyes closed in utter delight. I had never seen him look so happy.

After following my gaze, Mars frowned at the picture, placed a tense hand on my inner thigh, and squeezed lightly. I could feel all of his hurt. The pain in his veins. The ache in his bones. The spears jutting right through his heart. I wasn't sure he'd even tell me what had happened to her if I asked.

Mr. Barrett placed a heaping bowl of mashed potatoes in the center of the table and sat across from Mars. And before I knew it, they fell into an easy conversation with each other.

Though Mars and Ares were nearly a spitting image of their

father, Ares didn't act anything like him. Always stone-faced, tense, guarded even. Mars acted almost exactly like him. But still I frowned and wondered what had hurt Ares so bad to have him change from that smiling boy to the distant and domineering man he was today.

All I wanted was to see him happy like that again, all the time.

"Has Mars cooked for you yet, Aurora?" Mr. Barrett asked.

I raised a brow at Mars. "He knows how to cook?"

Mr. Barrett gave him a pointed stare. "You haven't made your mate dinner?"

"He's made me pretzels and cheese," I said, playfully elbowing Mars.

Mr. Barrett's stare softened, and he chuckled. "Mars and his mother always used to make those together. That was their go-to midnight snack, wasn't it?"

Though I could tell that he was still a bit annoyed, he smiled tenderly and nodded. I placed my hand on his thigh and grasped lightly. My heart warmed at the thought of him being so comfortable with me that he'd let me in on the nightly tradition he used to have with his mother.

All those rumors about Alpha Ares slowly started to fade into an abyss. Ares wasn't heartless; he was heartbroken.

When dinner was over, Mars took my hand and led me down a hallway decorated with pictures of his mother and him. He pushed open a door and walked into a room that looked to be the remnants of a playroom. Football posters and crayon drawings hung from the brightly colored walls, blocks were stacked almost a foot in the air near the teal leather couch, and a wooden toy box, which had a pink teddy bear and a family picture on it, sat in the corner of the room.

"When the pack house got too hectic, my family came here." Mars closed the door behind us and pulled back the curtains to stare out into the woods. "My mom used to bring Charolette and me here to play."

I walked to the picture and smiled, grasping it in my hands. Something about it was so terribly sad, yet I didn't know what it was. I gazed down at the picture, feeling Mars's fingers glide across my waist from behind me. He rested his head on my shoulder, pulled me closer to him, and smiled.

"I wish that you could've met her. She would've loved you," he whispered in my ear.

After a few moments of debating on whether or not I should ask him, I placed the frame down and parted my lips. "Mars, wh—"

He gently placed one arm over my shoulder and drew his fingers down my lips, his other hand wandering to my breast. I gently shoved him away.

"What are you doing?" I asked, but I knew exactly what he was doing.

He didn't want to talk about what had happened, and this was his attempt to change the subject.

And, Goddess, was it going to work.

"You're more amazing than I ever imagined my mate being." He trailed his nose up the side of my neck, making me shiver and lean into him. "All I want to do is worship you, Kitten, all the fucking time."

I swallowed, my pussy warming, and playfully pushed him away. "Well, not here. We're at your father's house." I hurried to the door and pulled it open to escape, thinking I still had a chance.

Mars placed his palm against the door and shut it before I had time to slip out of the room. He turned me around, curled a hand around my throat, and pulled me closer to him. "I didn't dismiss you."

"You don't have to dismiss me," I said, staring up into his lovely gold wolf eyes.

With his hand still around my neck, he pinned me to the door.

"You're right, but I don't let my mate leave me when I can smell how wet I'm making her."

"You're not making me wet."

He tightened his grip on my neck, yanked up the front of my dress, pushed down my panties, and drew two fingers over my slit. After sliding them inside of me, he pulled them out and brushed his wet fingers against my lips. "This isn't wet to you?"

My pussy pulsed, and I swallowed hard, my heart pounding in my chest. He smirked and trailed his fingers back down my body to my pussy again, thrusting them inside of me. I clenched and let out a soft whimper.

"We're at your father's house," I whispered.

He grazed his canines against the bare side of my neck and growled lowly in my ear. "And my mate is wet."

"Mars ..."

Grabbing my hand, he placed it right over the bulge in his white jeans, making me feel just how hard he was for me. I bit my lip and found myself slowly stroking him. Goddess, this was not the place for this. His whole family was sitting in the other room, probably wondering why the hell we were taking so long to come back out for dessert.

His fingers moved around in circles, massaging my G-spot. I stroked him faster, unable to control myself, and pressed my lips together, so I wouldn't moan out loud. He felt so fucking big inside his jeans, and all I could imagine was him inside of *me* again.

That was all I seemed to want lately. My wolf was desperate for him, especially after he had accepted us. She was horny all the time, and I was not complaining about it. Ares and Mars knew how to fuck so good that I had to beg them to stop.

My wolf howled inside of me, wanting Mars to mark me and wanting to mark him.

"Take them off of me," he said into my ear.

I fumbled with his button, pulled down his zipper, and

wrapped my hand around his cock. With one hand, he held me against the door by my throat, and with the other, he grabbed my leg, hiked it into the air, and rested my thigh in the crook of his elbow. He positioned the head of his cock against my glistening pussy.

He slapped a hand over my mouth. "Don't make a sound, Kitten," he said into my ear.

My brows furrowed together, and I whimpered when he plunged himself into me.

He sucked on the skin just below my ear. "I said not to make a sound. You don't want my family to hear you, do you?"

I arched my back, my pussy aching. Every inch of him slid inside of me with ease, and he began pumping himself in and out.

"Tug on your nipples for me," he said.

My pussy clenched on his cock, and I groped my breasts through my dress to pinch my already-hard nipples.

"Fuck," he groaned, staring at my tits through the dress. "Just like that. Make your tight little pussy clench on my cock."

"Aurora! Mars!" Charolette called down the hallway.

My eyes widened, and I pulled his hand away from my mouth. *Stop,* I mouthed.

"I didn't tell you to stop touching yourself, did I? Continue," he said. I parted my lips to protest when he tightened his grip around my throat. "Don't make me tell you again."

Hesitantly, I placed my hands back on my breasts and tugged on my nipples through the dress. Mars continued to pound into me, his thrusts becoming faster and rougher.

"You guys are going to miss dessert!" she shouted.

"We'll be out in a minute, Charolette." He gazed down at my breasts. "Harder," he said quietly to me. "Tug on them harder."

I tugged on my nipples harder, my pussy pulsing on his cock. He slammed himself deep inside of me, his teeth grazing against my neck, and my body trembled back and forth. I slapped a hand over my mouth and squeezed my eyes closed.

Holy ... fuck.

Wave after wave of pleasure rushed through me. I leaned my head against the door and cursed under my breath, opening my eyes to see his brows furrowed together and lips parted slightly. He stilled inside of me, filling me with his cum.

"Your pussy's so tight."

When he pulled out, my pussy lips were coated in a thick layer of his cum. Some slid down my inner thighs.

Mars grabbed my underwear and pulled them up my legs, ruining them. "We'll get you others," he said, lips curling into a smirk. "Don't worry about that, Kitten."

"I'm not worried about that." I stepped away from him and smoothed my dress out. "I'm worried about how you're going to be able to control yourself, knowing that your mate is filled with all your cum at the dinner table and that when we get home, your mate's going to let you fuck her again ..." I brushed my lips against his ear, fingers drawing up his tense abdomen. "Or that your mate can't wait to plunge her teeth into your neck and claim you."

He growled under his breath, and I pulled the door open and walked out of the room. His dark golden eyes flickered down my body, and he followed after me, his fingers never leaving my hips.

Charolette and Liam sat at the dining table.

"Did Mars show you our old toy room?"

I nodded my head and smiled back at her, trying to hide my flushed cheeks. My phone buzzed on the table, and Elijah's name popped up on the screen.

Elijah, *finally!*

"I have to take this," I said to them, excusing myself from the room. "Elijah! Did you get my message?"

"Do you have time to talk?" he asked.

"Yes." I walked back down the hallway. "Do you have any idea who might know where the stone is?"

He sighed deeply through his nose and then said, "I do, but

you're not going to like it."

"Who?" I asked, heart racing.

"Tony."

"You're fucking kidding me," I gritted out through my teeth, gripping the phone so tightly that my fingers hurt.

Tony?

All this fucking time, Tony had fucking known where the other half of the stone was. I could've been able to shift; I could've become the alpha that Mom always wanted me to be; I could've been happy.

But instead, that little shit had hidden this from me.

Mars stared at me from down the hall, his voice ringing through the mind link, asking me if everything was okay. I gave him a curt nod and stepped back into his old playroom, shutting the door behind me.

"I don't think he has it," Elijah said as I walked toward the window. "But since he told Ares I knew where the stone was, I have had warriors watching him."

Balling my hand into a fist, I stared out into the night. Moonlight flooded in through the window and shimmered against Mr. Barrett's pool, the water rippling in the wind. I rested my forehead against the window and growled. My wolf wanted to run right on Mom's pack and kill Tony herself.

Why had he caused all this trouble? What was the point? To drive Ares insane? Maybe it wasn't his plan at all, but Mom's. Tony might've been strong like all *alphas* had to be, but that boy was stupid with a capital S.

"What makes you think he knows where it is?"

"He met with a hound."

My chest tightened. A hound? Tony had met with the fucking hounds who had been trying to kill me for years since Jeremy's death? The same hounds who had ripped him piece by fucking piece? I balled my hand tighter and let my claws cut through the skin on my palms.

"Have you seen him before?" I asked. "Was it the one from the attack that killed Jeremy?"

"My warriors didn't get a good look." Elijah paused. "Ares isn't listening in, is he?"

I glanced back at the closed door, unable to think clearly. "No."

"Meet me at Pink Moon Tavern, near the cave you and Jeremy used to run to when you were kids. I can tell you more there. Come without Ares. He thinks with his emotions too much. I need you to help me come up with a solid plan."

"I'll be there in twenty." I ended the call and dialed Marcel's number.

The Pink Moon Tavern was near Hound Territory, and I knew that Ares wouldn't let me go alone. Hell, it'd be difficult to persuade him to let me go without him, but I needed to because Elijah was right. As soon as he heard that Tony might have the stone, he'd run on Mom's pack without a clear thought in his mind. He'd go there for blood, and he'd get it, but he wouldn't find the stone that way.

Marcel answered on the third ring. "What?"

"Marcel, I need you—"

"You're not the only one who needs me at the moment, Princess."

I heard a woman moan in the background and scrunched up my nose. "Are you fucking someone right now?" I shook my head. "Forget it. You need to pick me up outside Mr. Barrett's house in two minutes."

"I'm busy."

"Two minutes, Marcel."

After I hung up and shoved my phone into my dress pocket, I walked back down the hall to the dining table. I looked at Mars, who had a slice of some very delicious cheesecake in front of him, and nodded to the other room.

Brows furrowed together, hands holding my hips, he followed me. "What's wrong, Kitten?"

I placed my hand on his chest, hoping to calm him down before he even got riled up. "I need to go meet with Elijah. It's important ... like stone-related important."

Eyes darkening, I saw Ares for a moment. "He knows where it is, doesn't he?" He dug his fingers into my hip bone. "I should've kept him here, should've gotten as much as I could out of him."

I grasped his chin in my hand and forced him to look at me. "Settle down, please, Mars." Before Ares appeared and decided things for himself. "I have to go. I promise that when I come home tonight, I will tell you everything that I know."

"You can't go alone. It's not safe."

"Marcel is going with me."

"You asked Marcel to go?" he asked, canines emerging from under his lips. All I could see was hurt on his face.

I glanced out the window to see a car pull up to the side of the road.

"Why didn't you ask me?"

"Because you make irrational decisions sometimes." I took a deep breath and hardened my stare. Nearly killing Elijah, chasing me out into the forest, the list went on and on and on, but I didn't want to bring any specific instance up. I didn't want him to feel bad for wanting to protect his sister because if I had another chance ... I'd do anything to protect Jeremy.

After taking his face in my hands and bringing it down to mine, I placed a kiss right on his lips. "I love you," I whispered before I could stop myself.

My eyes widened.

Love? I loved Mars?

I hadn't even known that I had fallen so hard for such a vicious, daunting man. Yet here I was, telling him that I loved him and watching his beautiful golden wolf eyes shift through a thousand shades until they melted into his chocolate browns.

Love, he mouthed. He grabbed my hands, held them to his chest, and grinned down at me with the same boyish smile I had seen in that picture he had taken with his mother.

"I have to go, Mars." I kissed him again, my eyes closing softly, and smiled. "I'll be back in an hour. If you need me, text me."

Mars nodded his head, eyes in a daze, as if he was still thinking about how I loved him, how I wanted to be with him forever, how I never wanted to let him go, and how he'd always be mine.

I gazed over his shoulder, smiling at Mr. Barrett and Charolette. "I have to go," I said to them. "Thank you so much for dinner. Hopefully, next time, I can stay for dessert."

Someone laid on the car horn outside, and Charolette got up from her seat.

"That's Marcel, isn't it? Goddess, it sounds like that car is shrieking." She hooked her arm in mine. "I'll walk you out."

After saying my good-byes, she pulled me down the stairs. I glanced back at Mars, who had sat down at the table and was grinning down at his cheesecake. And in that moment, I knew that I really was in love with that man.

It hadn't just been said in the heat of the moment. It was real.

Stupid, young love. *Real* stupid, young love.

Charolette pulled me outside and gave Marcel the finger from the door. I hurried to his car and hopped into it, my mind still buzzing with thoughts of my Mars and how three silly little words meant the world to him.

Marcel stared at me and then at Charolette and clenched his jaw. "You had dinner with them?" He pressed on the gas, and the car lurched forward. "Liam is there, isn't he?" he asked, gripping the steering wheel until his knuckles turned white. "Fucking idiot," Marcel said under his breath and then stepped on the gas harder, heading toward the pack exit.

It seemed like someone was jealous. And this time, it wasn't Ares.

CHAPTER 33

AURORA

The Pink Moon Tavern was relatively empty tonight, only a few high schoolers sipping on milkshakes out front. Elijah sat in a turquoise booth in the back, drinking a Moscow mule. While his eyes were still bruised, the swelling had disappeared completely, and most of his wounds had healed already.

Gaze traveling from me to Marcel, Elijah raised a brow at me in question.

"It was the only way Ares would let me come," I said, sliding into the booth. "What did the hound look like?" I asked, fore-going the chitchat. Elijah's gaze lingered on Marcel for a moment longer, and I waved a hand to dismiss Marcel. "Don't worry about him."

Elijah turned back to me. "Black hair and broad."

"Black hair? He was in his human form?" I asked, eyes widening.

It was a known fact that hounds didn't—or couldn't—shift from werewolf to human. They were thought to be stuck as animals forever, which made them extremely dangerous.

"Yes," Elijah said. "My warrior heard Tony and the hound mention the stone several times."

Marcel slammed his hand against the wooden table. "That fucking prick knows where the stone is?" he asked.

Elijah's mule sloshed over the side of his cup and spilled.

So much for emotionless reactions. I wiped a napkin over the spilled drink.

Elijah shook his head. "I don't know if he knows where it is, but he has information. My warrior said they seemed friendly."

"How could Tony do this? He knew exactly how Ares would react to you having information on the stone." I pressed my lips together and shook my head in disbelief.

Tony and I had spent so many nights together, and he'd never acted like this … but maybe he was always an asshole, always out to hurt, always out for power.

"We need a plan," Elijah said.

"A plan?" Marcel growled. "Why don't we go to your fucking mother's house and torture the son-of-a-bitch until he tells us where that stone is?"

I gnawed on the inside of my cheek, feeling as I thought Ares would in this situation. Cruel, violent, and bloodthirsty as the darkness begged for me to let it in. Mars wanted the stone, but Ares … he wanted the person who had it to hurt.

Once he found out that Tony had information on it, he would do exactly as Marcel had suggested—run on Mom's pack, capture Tony, and torture him.

No. Questions. Asked.

The thought should've terrified me, but it didn't. If Tony had any sort of information on the stone and hadn't told me—after watching me grow up in pain—he deserved to get punched more than a few times. And as for my asshole mother, who had traded me—her only heir—because she didn't think I was good enough while the strongest alpha in the world did, I didn't care what happened to her either. If she didn't care about me, why should I care about her?

Elijah sipped his drink. "Tony would rather die than tell Ares anything."

It was true. Tony had a tolerance for pain, both physical and emotional. Every time I had seen him fight—besides the time Ares had raided our pack—he was terrifying. During the first hound attack when we had still been young wolves, he had torn out so many throats and then swallowed them like a fucking psychopath. I didn't put it past him to have something up his sleeve, so he could kill Ares and be claimed the most ruthless man alive.

"I will tell Ares tonight," I said to Elijah. "We will run on my mother's pack early tomorrow morning. I will talk to Tony despite Ares demanding me not to speak a single word to him. I have to try to talk some sense into—"

Marcel's phone buzzed on the table, and he sat up tall, his pupils dilating. "I have to go." He tossed me the keys to his car. "Bring it back."

"You're going to run home?" I asked, brows furrowing.

"It's not like you can," he said. The words came out light-hearted and shouldn't have hurt as much as they did.

I'd told Ares and Charolette to keep this a secret because I wasn't ready for the entire pack to know just yet. I still felt like I needed to prove myself.

Marcel furrowed his brows, as if he didn't know why I was frowning at him. "Ares would have my ass if I let you run out in Hound Territory."

I plastered a smile on my face and nodded in agreement. Okay, good, nobody had told him yet. Marcel was just terrified of Ares, as he should be.

Marcel left the tavern and disappeared into the woods in wolf form, carrying his clothes and phone in his mouth.

I turned back to Elijah and grabbed his hand. "What will you do?"

"What my pack does best," he said. "Find information. Study Tony. Figure out who has the stone." He grasped my hand tighter in his, smiling over at me. "Ares is taking good care of you?"

I nodded my head, thinking about earlier at his father's house when I'd told him that I loved him. The words had come out so quickly yet so naturally. I barely knew the man, but I already knew that I couldn't wait to spend my entire life with him.

"You have that spark in your eye," he said, lips curling into a smirk. "The same one that Jeremy always used to have with me." He paused for a moment, staring deeper at me. "You love him, don't you?"

My cheeks flushed. I had never felt this way before about anyone, except Jeremy and maybe Dad. Everyone in my previous pack loved me, and I loved them, but they always treated me differently. They didn't love who I really was; they didn't see me for me; they didn't feel the pain I went through during each shift. They saw the fake me.

Ares had seen the real Aurora, and he had loved every moment with her.

I just hoped that it would stay that way.

After another sip of his drink, Elijah gazed out the window in the direction of the cave. "When Jeremy told me that he loved me for the first time, he brought me to that cave in the north. It was in the middle of a snowstorm, twelve degrees Fahrenheit. We slept there that night in the freezing fucking cold, had frozen beer, and, Goddess, it was the best night of my life."

"Have you been back?" I asked.

He shook his head. "Not since he died. Heard it was taken over by hounds."

I brushed my thumb against his, hoping that the motion would lighten the mood. "I have a question to ask you."

Glancing back at me through his new black-framed glasses, he nodded. "What is it?"

"When we find that stone, I need your doctor to implant it into Ares's sister," I said.

Taken aback, he pulled his hand out of mine and shook his head.

"Please, she has cancer and is going to die soon. He has tried everything to find it."

"Aurora ..." he said. "I want to find that stone for you, so you can shift and be whole again."

"Then ... you really won't like this request," I started, grasping his hand again and squeezing it tightly. "If one half of the stone doesn't cure her, I need you to remove mine."

"No," he said with finality. "I'm not doing that. I'm not going to risk your life for hers. I don't even know her, and I promised Jeremy that I'd always keep you safe, no matter what happened to him or to him and I."

"Please," I begged. "She means everything to him."

"Did Ares put you up to this?"

"No, he's against it too. He doesn't want me to sacrifice my quality of life for her, but ... she's everything to him. And I want to see her healthy and happy. Promise me that you'll do it. Please. He's just trying to help his sister survive. Don't tell me you wouldn't have done the same for Jeremy."

He paused for a long moment, a grim expression crossing his face. "I don't like this."

"But you'll do it," I said, hopeful.

He tilted his head downward a few inches, and my heart leaped in my chest.

I held out my pinkie. "Promise me that you won't tell Ares. He would hate me for it."

He wrapped his pinkie around mine. "I promise."

CHAPTER 34

MARS

Aurora loved me.

I washed off the last of my plate in the sink and grinned to myself.

She loved me, and maybe she loved Ares too.

Liam walked into the kitchen and placed his plate on the counter.

Charolette followed him with her hands on her hips. "So, you're not going to stay?" she asked him.

He pushed some hair out of her face and smiled down at her. "I have an early morning tomorrow, sweetheart," he said.

I glanced at him and felt myself smile a bit wider. Everything seemed to be as Mom had always wanted it to be.

We were happy.

Charolette had a good man who loved her, someone who had been there with her since she was diagnosed with cancer. They weren't mates, but from what I had seen, he treated her well.

And I had Aurora.

Liam nudged my shoulder. "Later."

After he disappeared into the living room with Charolette, Dad squeezed my shoulder from behind and stared at me through the reflection against the window. "I haven't seen you this happy in years, Mars," he said. "Hell, I haven't seen *you* in a while, only Ares. I can see Aurora's doing something to you, son."

My smile widened even more, and all I could feel was happiness for once in my life. The pain I had held for years since Mom's death seemed to vanish for a while whenever I was with her. She didn't take it all away, but she made my life more bearable.

She was changing my life for the better, and I owed her everything for that.

CHAPTER 35

AURORA

I didn't know exactly where Marcel lived, so I parked his car in front of Mr. Barrett's house to give Charolette his car keys.

Mr. Barrett answered the door with a huge smile. "Aurora!" He nodded back to the pack house down the road. "Mars just left. He seemed worried about you."

"Oh, I just wanted to give these to Charolette." I handed him the keys. "Good night, Mr. Barrett."

"Hey, wait a minute. I have something for you." He stuffed the keys into his pocket, jogged back into the house, and came back with a container filled with the biggest slice of cheesecake I had ever seen. "Whatever you said to Mars before you left, tell him again. I haven't seen that boy smile like that since his mother was around."

My heart warmed in my chest, and I couldn't help the grin that broke out onto my face at the thought of making Mars happy. Butterflies erupted all over my body. So, this was what it was like to feel loved, to love someone and their family all the same.

After saying my good-byes, I walked down the walkway.

Some chatter drifted out from the upstairs window, and I glanced up at it. The light was on in one of the rooms, and Charolette stood in the middle of her bedroom without her wig and with a huge grin on her face.

She spun slightly, and I smiled up at her. She must be so comfortable with Liam. I wondered how—

Marcel sat on the edge of her bed, grinning at her with a smile that I had never seen before. He watched her spin, grabbed her waist, and pulled her toward him, resting his chin against her chest and staring up at her.

Before they could see me snooping, I hurried toward the pack house. Charolette and Marcel seemed like they were mates. I didn't know if Mars knew about them, but I wasn't one to tell secrets. But why did they act so cold to each other? I didn't know that either.

When I opened the door, he was passed out on the leather couch with Ruffles on his chest. They were both sleeping so peacefully that I didn't want to wake them. I grabbed a velvet blanket from our room and draped it over his torso, deciding on taking a shower before I broke the bad news to Ares.

Just after I covered him and Ruffles with the blanket, he snatched my wrist. "Where the hell are you going?" Ares asked, eyes still closed but his grip harsh. "I want my mate to lie with me, right here ..." He patted Ruffles. "Right on my chest."

My lips curled into a smirk, and I sat at the edge of the couch, pushing some thick brown hair off his forehead. Well, I guessed that shower would have to wait. "I need to talk to you, Ares."

"Tell me you love me first." He slowly opened his eyes, body jerking up when he sneezed. Ruffles jumped off of him, and Ares pulled me on top of him, so my chest was against his. "I want to hear you say it again."

When I'd first said it, I hadn't thought I'd be saying it again so soon. Yet here I was, on top of my mate, who was begging me to tell him that I loved him again and again and again, like a sweet melody that he wanted to fall asleep to.

I brushed my fingers against his cheek and watched the moonlight bounce off his golden eyes. "I love you."

He wrapped his arms around me, hugging me tightly to his chest, and rolled us over, so he was on top of me. He pressed his hardness against my core, his biceps flexing next to me, his hazelnut scent such an intoxicating aroma. I breathed him into me, relaxing under his fingers.

"Ares"—I lightly pushed him away—"I have to tell you something about the stone."

He pulled away and then sat up. "What did you find?"

"Tony has been meeting with a hound. Elijah thinks that he knows something."

Ares's jaw twitched, his eyes turning a darker, harsher gold. "Tony, as in the fuckup who came on to you after I told him not to?" He growled under his breath. "I should've killed the fucking pup when I had the chance."

I pressed my hands against his chest to calm him down. "You can't kill him. If he knows something, you have to let me try to get it out of him."

"He's going to try to come *save* you from me again."

My eyes widened. Had Marcel told him about—

"Yes," Ares said, cutting me off. "He told me that stupid fucking prick thought he'd sweep you off your fucking feet when I raided Elijah's pack." He balled his hands into tight fists. "I should've killed him already."

"He will lead us to the stone," I said, trying to calm him down. "Please, let's go to my mother's pack tomorrow … let me talk to him before you think about killing him." I squeezed his hands. "He's our only chance of finding the damn thing."

He growled. "He won't talk to you."

"Yes, he will."

"He wants to fuck you, Aurora. He wants to take what's mine."

He stared down at me, so territorial. And if I said that it didn't turn me all the way on, I'd be lying. It was a hunger to prove his worth, an innate instinct to demonstrate his dominance. It was raw, real, and recklessly ravaging. And I loved the feeling of his arms wrapping harder around me, tugging me to his body, claiming *me*.

"If he even touches me, you can snap his neck," I said, feeling his heart racing beneath my fingers. "But let me talk to him tomorrow."

Ares should've exploded into a fit of anger like usual, but instead, he just growled. "If he touches a single hair on your head, even if it's just his fingers grazing against you, I will rip his throat right out of his body as your whole pack watches, drench myself in his fucking blood, and challenge any of your mother's warriors who tries to take you away from me."

"Deal." I nodded in approval. "But whatever happens tomorrow, promise me that you won't kill my dad. He doesn't deserve death."

Ares stared down at me. "I won't kill him." He grabbed my jaw lightly in his hand, forcing me to look up at him. "But I can't promise the same with Tony or your mother. If they touch you, I will kill them for betraying us and treating you like shit."

I swallowed hard and nodded my head. I didn't expect anything less.

"We run at dawn."

CHAPTER 36

ARES

Aurora didn't just love Mars. She fucking loved me too.

I held her tight to my chest, brought her to our bedroom, and lay down next to her, brushing a strand of her brown hair from her face. Part of me didn't fucking believe it. How could she like me as I was?

All I had was pain. All I felt was heartbreak. All I wanted was to make other people hurt.

"Why do you love me?" I asked her, brows furrowed together.

Hearing those words had made me feel so good on the inside, but after sitting with them, they didn't make sense. Aurora should hate me.

I deserved to be fucking hated.

Moonlight flooded into the room through our window, bouncing off Aurora's big eyes. A look of sadness crossed her face, yet she held eye contact with me and brushed her fingers against my stubble. "Because you're the only person who's ever accepted me as an equal."

My fingers dug into her hips as I remembered how her family had treated her when I showed up. I had known that something was off about them. They hadn't even fucking asked her to fight with them during the attack.

She sighed deeply through her nose. "My old pack accepted me, but they never treated me as an alpha or even as a warrior. They always gave me work to do that didn't matter, barely included me in anything, acted as if I needed all their protection." Tears welled up in her eyes. "I didn't tell you about the stone because I thought … I thought you wouldn't accept me as your mate either."

I pulled her to my chest tightly, showing her that I wouldn't hurt her and that I wouldn't let anyone try to fucking hurt her again because part of me knew how she felt. Growing up with these polar opposite personalities, I found it so fucking hard to get people to accept it.

Sure, I'd had friends and girlfriends and lovers, but most of those fucking assholes hadn't loved me. They all loved the alpha; they didn't see the man behind the title. They didn't know how to deal with both of us. They'd left. They'd fucking left when I needed them the most.

Holding Aurora tighter, I shook my head. It was only when I had taken over for Dad that people started respecting Ares. Mars had hidden away. Mars—my chest tightened—was terrified of them.

"I love you too, Aurora," I whispered into her ear. "For letting me be myself around you."

And for so much fucking more.

CHAPTER 37

AURORA

"It's time to go," I said to Ares, trying to wriggle out of his strong hold.

Light flooded into the room through our sheer black curtains. Ares wrapped his arm around my waist tighter and snuggled closer to me.

Accepting that I wasn't going to be able to push him off that easily, I turned to face him and poked his stomach. "Don't you want the stone?"

Ares growled lowly when I threw the blankets off us. "We run at dawn."

"It is dawn."

Smirking against my mark, he crawled between my legs, hooked two fingers around my underwear strings, and pulled them off me. "We have time."

"Ares," I said, brows furrowed together, "we ..."

He pressed his lips to my core and stared up at me with sinful gold eyes. "We what?" he asked, tongue moving in small, rhythmic circles around my clit.

I swallowed hard, heat warming my core. "We have to—"

He pushed a finger inside of me, slowly pumping it in and out of me. "We have to what?"

My fingers curled into the sheets, and I arched my back. "Ares, we can't."

Pulling my legs onto his shoulders, he wrapped his arms around my waist and pinned my hips to the mattress, so I couldn't squirm out of his hold. "I'm alpha. I say what we can and can't do, Kitten."

My breathing hitched, and I moaned his name. Heat warmed my core and flared out until my entire body was aching for a release. "Ares …" I closed my eyes, never before having felt such satisfaction from his lips.

"You're mine."

The pressure built higher and higher in my core until I could barely hold myself together.

"Mine to take whenever I want." He continued to massage circles around my clit with his tongue. "Mine to pleasure every morning."

I clenched around his fingers.

"Mine to make feel good."

Someone banged on the door, and Liam cleared his throat. "Ares, the warriors are ready."

"I'll be out in a minute, Liam."

I stared down at him with wide eyes and took a deep breath. Moments … I was mere moments away from …

"How long?"

Ares growled, his eyes turning a darker color gold. "When I'm finished fucking my mate."

Ares thrust two fingers deeper into my pussy, pumping them hard and fast into me. I grasped the sheets, the tension too much, and squirmed up the bed.

Pinning me to the bed, Ares didn't stop finger-fucking me until I slapped a hand over my mouth and was coming all over his fingers. Waves of ecstasy rolled through me, and my entire body relaxed against the bed.

When he pulled his fingers out of me, he stuck them into his mouth and sucked off the juices. His eyes softened, and he grabbed my hand, tugging me off of the bed. "Come on. We have to go."

After we threw on some decent clothes for the meeting with my mother, Ares took my hand again and led me to the backyard, where thirty of his best warriors were gathered. They were the same group of blood-loving, slaughtering warriors that Ares took on every raid.

Charolette and Marcel stood near the front of the group, glaring at each other and ... fighting? Charolette had her arms crossed over her chest and was quietly yelling something at him.

What the hell had happened? Last night, they had been all lovey-dovey, and now ...

When Marcel saw us, he walked up to Ares and grabbed his shoulder. "I don't care what you fucking say. I'm not watching Charolette today. I'm going with you. I'm the best fucking fighter you have. I'm not babysitting."

Charolette's cheeks flushed, and she glared harder at him. "I'm not a baby. You're just too fucking annoying to—"

"You're staying here with her," Ares said to Marcel.

"You should stay with Charolette," Liam said, curling an arm around Charolette's petite waist and pissing off Marcel even more. "Like you said, you're the best fighter here. You can protect—"

"Don't give me that fucking bullshit, Liam. You fucking stay back and protect her then." Marcel stormed toward the other warriors, his silver locks covering his face. "If you fucking love her so much, you'd do that for your pretty fucking *princess*."

Though I was secretly rooting for Marcel and Charolette—even though he was a complete ass sometimes—I glanced between Liam and Charolette. "Liam should stay," I said. "If things go bad at my mom's pack, we'll need Marcel."

And if Tony somehow escaped from our grip today—which

he wouldn't—I wouldn't put it past him to try to take Charolette. She needed to stay here, not come with us.

Charolette peeked over at Marcel, who was talking—flirting—with one of the prettier warriors. Charolette pressed her glossy lips together, clenched her jaw, and looked at the ground, pulling her arms even tighter around herself, as if she was guilty of something.

My heart ached for her. I didn't know what had happened, but I knew she was hurting.

"Liam, stay here. We don't need you bringing Charolette today, like Marcel usually does. This isn't a raid. Just"—he glanced at his sister and frowned—"watch her."

Charolette's blonde hair blew in the breeze. "You shouldn't even be going, Ares. How many times do I have to tell you that the stone isn't going to fix me? Nothing will."

Ares growled, and Charolette huffed at him and stomped into the pack house, slamming the door behind her. My wolf pulled me toward her, but I held myself back. If I didn't go with Ares, Tony would taunt him until all hell broke loose.

After Liam exchanged a few words with Ares, he followed Charolette inside the house. Ares addressed the warriors briefly and then watched them run in the direction of my mother's pack.

Instead of running with them, he led me to one of the pack's cars out front and told me to get in. "If we're bringing Tony back, I'm not letting him run with us. We need a car," he said, but I knew that it was secretly because of my shifting abilities.

And for the first time, I didn't mind it. I didn't mind him going out of the way to make sure I was comfortable. Sure, many people in Mom's pack had done it before I met him ... but Ares just ... he made me feel like a person and not someone that needed to be taken care of.

It took a good few hours to drive to Mom's pack. Thick fog lay heavily through the eerie forest. I stared out the window and looked through my text messages to Mom last night about visiting her with Ares today. I had sent three of them, and unlike the other messages I'd sent her, none of these ones had been delivered yet.

My heart ached. She'd blocked me. My own damn mother had blocked me.

Dad hadn't, but he hadn't responded.

When the fog cleared slightly, I finally started to recognize Mom's property. I smiled at all the little hideouts where Jeremy and I used to go after sneaking out at night. But … that was all gone. All the past.

Ares parked the car in front of Mom's pack house, and I sucked in a breath. His warriors were already scattered throughout the forest in case something went wrong. A handful of Mom's warriors were in the backyard to the pack house, trying to gather as quickly as possible.

I hopped out of the car, followed Ares to the backyard, and prayed to the Goddess that everything went smoothly. All we wanted to do was talk, and she would've known that if she hadn't blocked my number.

Tony, Mom, and some of her strongest warriors stood, guarded and ready for us.

"What is the meaning of this, Ares?" Mom asked, giving him that goddess-awful glare and refusing to even look at me. "You've broken our agreement."

He stepped forward, his gaze fixed on Tony, who stared at me, not caring for a single moment that Ares was about to pounce on him if he wasn't careful.

"Agreement is off," Ares said through clenched teeth.

"Are you bringing her back?" Tony asked, finally looking at him. "Because I'd be happy to take her."

Face contorted into one of pride, Tony pissed me the fuck off. This was all because of him. He had to be the alpha. He'd had to hide the stone from me. He'd had to talk to hounds behind my pack's back.

I seized Ares's wrist, stopping him from leaping at the stupid idiot who I'd once called lover.

Tony smiled at me and held out his hand. "Come on, Aurora. You don't need to spend another day with an alpha who slaughters people for fun."

Ares growled again, his canines lengthening. My heart pounded in my chest, and I grasped harder on to him, digging my heels into the dirt and hoping I was strong enough to stop him from shifting.

Knowing that he was getting Ares angry, Tony smirked and stepped toward me. "Don't worry. I'll take care of you, *Kitten*."

Before I could stop him, Ares lunged at Tony, wrapped his entire hand around Tony's neck, and lifted him off the ground as if he weighed nothing. Tony grabbed his wrist, trying to pull his arm away but not trying as hard as I knew he could. Something about him seemed off. He was acting too arrogant in front of Ares, especially after what Ares had done to him last time.

"Mars," I said softly, grabbing Ares's hand. "Think about Mars, Ares. Think about what we talked about. You can't kill him. We need him."

Ares's grip loosened around Tony's neck, his eyes fading into a lighter shade of gold. When I rubbed my fingers over his back, he tossed Tony to the ground, and I thanked the Goddess that he'd listened to me for once.

"You've let him change you, Aurora." Tony rubbed his neck and shuffled to his feet. "He's changed you so much. That spark in your eyes is gone. You look … tired even. Tired of keeping up this act of liking a man who could never love you."

I had spent years trying to understand people, years when Mom wouldn't let me train with the warriors because of my condition. I should've been able to figure out such a simple man … but I couldn't.

"You should come back," Tony said. "With your pack."

"Ares's pack is my pack," I said to Tony. "More of a pack than you all ever were."

"More of a pack ..." Tony scoffed, shook his head, and looked around at all of Ares's warriors surrounding us. Then, he turned to me, and I saw hell itself in his eyes— cruel, dark, and black. "They don't know, do they?"

I rubbed my neck and swallowed hard, knowing exactly what he was talking about.

He took a threatening step toward me. "You think they'll treat you the same? You think they'll still protect you when you can't even do the same for them? When you can't even shift into your wolf?"

My heart dropped when he said the words out loud, and murmurs erupted over the thirty warriors behind me. All eyes were on me, and I wanted to deny the fact that I couldn't shift ... but ... but it was true, and now, Tony was using it against me.

Ares ripped himself out of my grip and lunged for him again, but I firmly placed both my hands on his chest and pushed him back. My disability couldn't get in the way anymore.

Tony took another threatening step toward Ares this time. "And you ... you know you're fucking screwing with her head. You're lying to her too, acting as if nothing is fucking wrong with you, like you won't crumble when your mother's secret is out to the world."

There was a glint of mischief in Tony's eyes, and I was terrified that he was about to break Ares.

I pleaded with my eyes, begging Tony not to hurt him more. Once the god of war was truly unleashed, I wouldn't be able to stop him from killing Tony and everyone who tried to talk him down.

"If you keep lying to her, you're going to drive her fucking insane," Tony said. "You're going to find her just like you found your mom. Lying in bed, blood gushing from both of her wrists, sheets stained red."

CHAPTER 38

AURORA

Ares growled, the sound rumbling through the forest like thunder on this foggy day. It came out vicious and jarring, but all I heard was the pain and heartbreak behind it. This must've been what had stolen that boyish smile from him. His mother must've committed suicide, and he must've found her.

Before I could settle my racing thoughts, the yard before me turned into a battlefield. Ares's warriors pounced on Mom's warriors, all of them clawing at each other's underbellies, ripping fur from their enemies' flesh, blood spilling everywhere.

Wolves leaped into the air around me, latching their teeth into each other's neck. I gazed around at everyone who moved too quickly for me to keep up with and locked eyes with my furious mother. She howled to the dawn sky, her voice cutting through my mind link, like it had done hundreds of times before.

"What have you done?" she asked, shifting into her wolf. *"We will die because of you."*

I clenched my jaw. *"This isn't my fault. We came here peacefully."*

She killed one of Ares's warriors, her canines digging into his flesh. With bloodied teeth, she looked over at me. *"You brought him here, knowing he'd kill us."* She turned away from me and ran through the pack, finding other warriors to fight.

But she was wrong.

Since I had been with Ares, he hadn't killed anyone, except hounds. And I didn't think he would willingly kill unless provoked so much that his wolf took total control of Ares *and* Mars.

In the distance, my father howled. Marcel stood over him in his large silver-furred wolf with teeth dripping with blood.

I sprinted as fast as I could and threw my body in front of my father's, holding out a hand. "No," I said up at Marcel, feeling his wolf's thick saliva fall onto my thighs. I pointed at him, hoping to the Moon Goddess that he wouldn't attack him or me. "Not my father. Anyone but my father."

Marcel stared at me with rage, and I stared back just as strongly.

"An order from your luna."

After growling under his breath, he ran back through the crowd.

Dad pushed his head against my forehead. *"Aurora, you need to get out of here."*

I shook my head. *"You need to get out of here. Find somewhere to hide once this is all over. Get the rest of this pack to safety. We will talk when I get back to Ares's pack."*

"I can't leave your mother," he said through the mind link. A flash of lightning cut through the fog. *"She's my mate. I need to protect her with everything I have."*

I frowned at him, my heart hurting. Mom was cruel to me, and he sometimes fought her because of it ... but he loved her like all mates did. No matter what, how could I think he'd leave her? But I wanted someone in my family to survive this.

"Just, please, don't get hurt."

"Tell Ares to stand down," he said, brushing his snout into my hair.

The touch was so soft, and I remembered how he used to do that when Jeremy and I were both pups. We'd run around the backyard, and Dad would chase us. We had been happy. So fucking happy.

I pushed my face into his, feeling torn. *"I can't."*

"You're his mate. You can tame him."

"I could." I definitely could. *"But I don't want to."*

The words made Dad recoil and stare at me with such confusion. *"Aurora ..."* His voice sounded so fragile in my mind, like he didn't recognize the name or who I was anymore. *"He's changing you."*

My chin trembled slightly, and I shook my head. *"No, he's not, Dad. He's giving me a backbone. He's making me strong."*

"He's killing your pack members. He's turning you against us. For no good reason at all."

Dad slowly backed away from me, and I reached out to touch his fur one last time. Yet he recoiled again. And I felt that common feeling of loneliness and rejection that I had always felt in this pack ... just not ever this much from him.

"Dad, he's a good man. I promise."

After staring at me for another few long moments, Dad turned away from me and ran toward Mom. I sat there on my knees and tried hard to hold back my cries. Every single time I was here, I just hurt and hurt and hurt, and I didn't know what was wrong with me.

Why had the Moon Goddess given me this life? Why couldn't my family just love me for me? Was that too much to ask of her?

Ares growled harshly, and I broke my gaze with Dad's departing figure. The stench of blood was unsettling, and I screamed at the top of my lungs for everyone to stop, but nobody heard me. I hadn't wanted this to happen. I hadn't wanted there to be a fight.

Blood dripped from my mate's mouth, off of every single tooth. His eyes were so black that I couldn't see any trace of his browns or golds. Those claws dug viciously into anyone that got in his way. I watched two, three, four of Mom's warriors die by his hand.

He was darkness. He was war. All he wanted was for everyone to hurt.

My heart clenched, and I stared around at everyone. Everything seemed as if it were moving in slow motion. Men. Women. Wolves. Everyone was fighting, and nobody knew the reasons why. They were fighting to fight. They were fighting because they had been born into war, born with these innate feelings to kill to protect. They were fighting because they didn't know any better.

And I could do nothing about it.

I reached behind me into my pocket, wanting to grasp my silver knife for protection because I didn't know if Mom would command her warriors to capture and kill me too. I wouldn't put it past her to try to break Ares. But when I went to grab for it, it wasn't there. I must've dropped it somewhere.

After scanning the bloody battlefield, the knife shimmered under another flash of lightning just at the edge of the field before the woods. I sprinted to it, weaving through the wolves attacking from every direction. And just as I was about to grab it, someone latched their teeth into my shoulder and shoved me to my back.

Tony landed on top of me, paws on each of my shoulders, his soft eyes staring down. *"We have to go."* He looked toward the forest, as if searching for something, and then turned back to me.

I shoved my hands into his chest and pushed him off of me. "What is your fucking problem?" I clutched my shoulder to stop the bleeding. "I'm not going anywhere with you. How do you know so much about Ares? Why have you been meeting with the hounds? What are you planning, you stupid piece of—"

Something growled deep in the woods, and my heart stopped.

Oh Goddess, no. Please don't let that be what I think that is. Please don't let it be hounds. Anything but hounds.

"Please, Aurora. If you come with me, they won't hurt you." Tony grabbed my hand between his teeth and pulled me through the crowd of wolves, away from this side of the forest.

He'd said the words with too much certainty that I knew something wasn't right.

I yanked my hand out of his mouth and watched the first hound run from the forest and toward the packs. And then it hit me.

Tony was a fucking traitor. A traitor that I couldn't fucking kill.

"Stop!" I screamed at everyone around me. "This is a setup! A setup!"

Everyone continued to fight, not listening to a single word I'd said.

I stared at Ares, hoping that he'd hear me. "Ares! Please, stop! Please!"

My heart pounded in my ears when he didn't turn around. I tried the mind link, but he must've been too overcome with bloodlust that he couldn't hear me.

Tony growled and tugged on my hand again.

I kicked him right in the underbelly. "Leave, you fucking piece of shit." I seethed at him, and then I kicked him right in his tiny little balls and watched him scurry away and off the property like the fucking coward he was.

Hounds emerged from the forest, their black eyes piercing right through the thick fog.

I grasped on to someone, not caring who it was, and tugged hard on their fur, pointing to the forest. "Hounds! The hounds are coming!"

Mom's warrior growled harshly at me and turned away. I shook my head, tears filling my eyes. Why wasn't anyone listening to me? Why couldn't they see that they were all about to die?

My mind became fuzzy, my arms heavy. I screamed again, but it seemed like I was mute. Nobody could hear me. Maybe I wasn't even making any noise.

More hounds continued to emerge from the forest until we were surrounded. All I could imagine was Jeremy across the field, the hounds attacking him, killing him, slaughtering him. Ripping him to pieces, his blood splattering onto my face, him reaching out his hand for me, me never seeing him again.

We had been set up that day, just like we had been set up today. Because of that, Jeremy's death had been especially heartbreaking, and today wouldn't be any different ... I could feel it already. People I loved were going to be slaughtered.

I shook my head at the thought of him. I couldn't run from this again. I would stay and fight, and if I died, then I would die while protecting the people I cared about. Ares. Mars. Ruffles. Charolette. Dad. And stupid fucking Marcel.

One ran toward Marcel, who had his back turned. I sprinted toward him, shoving him out of the way just in time. The hound fastened his canines into my leg, ripping a chunk of my muscle from my thigh. I cried out in pain, clutching my leg, and scurried away.

Ares turned toward us, dropped a warrior from his teeth, jolted to us, and killed the hound within a moment. The blood from his enemies dripped from his mouth and stained my clothes. I brushed my hand over his fur and let the tears fall.

More hounds ran into the chaos, foam dripping from their lips, beady black eyes on their prey. Ares stood in front of me and lunged at anyone who tried to get close. I put as much pressure on my wound as I could, hoping they'd go away. But they were closing in on him from all directions.

I prayed to the Moon Goddess that Ares wouldn't die because

I fucking loved him more than I loved anyone in the entire world right now.

Totally surrounded by hounds, Ares disappeared from my view.

My heart raced. No. *No!*

"Ares!" I screamed. Tears … so many tears. "Ares, please come back."

I placed my hand on the ground behind me, trying to stand up, but someone snatched my hand in their teeth, latching their canines so deeply inside of me that I couldn't break free.

Thrashing and flailing in his hold, I fought the wolf as hard as I could. Instead of fighting back, he dragged me through the woods—opposite to where the hounds had come from. Twigs dug into my back, leaves gathered in my hair, the fog became thicker and thicker until I couldn't see my pack anymore.

I screamed and I punched and I kicked, and the more I fought, the harder it was to see straight. I grasped my leg, trying to stop the blood from gushing out of it. My arms felt heavier than they had before, so heavy I could barely hold them up.

"Ares," I said through the mind link, succumbing to the pain and lying flat in the dirt, letting this wolf drag me wherever he wanted. My body couldn't physically handle it anymore. Every part of me felt so heavy.

He didn't respond, and I cried fat, ugly tears. I would never see him again. The hounds would rip him piece by piece, like they'd done to Jeremy. I would be brotherless and mateless, all because of Tony.

I gathered all the strength I had left and tried to connect with him one last time through the mind link. *"I love you, mate. All of you, every single bit. I hope you remember that forever and always. You have become my only strength."* My lips quivered. *"I wanted to have pups with you, to watch you play with them, to see you as happy as you were in that picture with your mother. You deserve to be happy."*

CHAPTER 39

AURORA

The sky above faded from a foggy white to black. I didn't know if this wolf had just been dragging me for so long that it was already nighttime, if I had lost too much blood and was hallucinating, or if I had been drifting in and out of consciousness.

Twigs dug into my backside, cutting right through my clothing. My leg had gone numb some time ago. My bloodied fingers lay lifelessly at my sides. Yet all I could think about was seeing Ares again.

Please, Moon Goddess, give me something. A memory. A flashback. A fucking hallucination for all I care.

I wanted to see his smile in the stars and his twinkling brown eyes. I wanted to run my hands through his hair and tell him I loved him over and over and over, like I had last night. I wanted to mark him … something that I would never get a chance to do.

Because if I didn't die with this hound, Ares would in that attack.

The hound dragged me up a steep hill, and I gazed down at the trees below, able to see the Pink Moon Tavern sign glowing between them. The forest seemed eerily familiar, yet my mind was so fuzzy that I wasn't sure if those pink neon letters were actually real or if they were just a figment of my imagination.

When the wolf reached the top of the hill, he pulled me inside a cave. I blinked the blurriness away and opened my eyes wider. This cave was the same one Jeremy and I used to go to, the one where Jeremy had told Elijah he loved him, the one Elijah had said had been taken over by hounds.

Was this all some sick joke? Maybe Tony had told him to take me here to torture me with good memories.

After he leaned me against a rock in the back, I stared around the hideout to see how different it was now that hounds had taken it over. To my right, there was a pile of dirt for wolves to sleep on and a rotting carcass to eat, and to my left, there was a heap of shit and piss that made me gag.

The tears had stopped long ago, and I could finally see who had taken me. A wolf with matted and ratty fur, dead eyes, and dulled canines. Though he had scars lining his brown-furred torso, some of his body parts weren't brown at all and didn't seem as if they belonged. He had a white hind leg that looked to be sewn onto him, a black tail, and an ear that was half-bitten off and sewn back together with a fox hide.

A monster made of innocent animals.

He gazed at the puncture wounds in my wrist and then at my leg, inching closer to me.

I pulled my knees to my chest, my eyes widening in realization. He was the same wolf that had saved me the other day from Jeremy's killer.

What was going on? Was he *saving* me?

After whimpering softly, he nudged my leg. I swallowed hard, having just an ounce of trust in him, and slowly let my leg down to the ground. Blood gushed out of the wound, all the raw muscle exposed. The wolf dipped his head and licked my wound.

Almost instinctively, I jerked my leg back into the air, and a stinging sensation shot through my entire body. He growled at me, and I hesitantly placed my leg back onto the ground, watching a thin layer of skin heal over my gash. My eyes widened in amazement, and I held out my wrist for him to do the same.

"Why are you helping me?" I asked, rubbing my healing wrist. I didn't know if he could understand me.

He lowered his head, almost in submission, and that was when I saw it. Under his fur, just where his C7 and T1 vertebrae met, something glowed the faintest color white. My eyes widened, and I drew my fingers across the back of my neck, feeling the stone underneath my fingers.

"You … you have the stone …" I breathed. "That's why you're helping me?" I drew my brows together. "Wh-what are … *who* are you?"

Without giving me an answer, he walked to the front of the cave, gazed down the hill, and waited. I pushed myself to a seated position and swallowed hard. If he had the stone … that meant we didn't need Tony anymore.

But who the hell was this guy? Did the stone connect us somehow? Could I trust him not to hurt me more?

"What do you use it for?" I asked, hoping that he'd give me some indication that he could understand me, but instead, he continued to ignore me. I sighed through my nose and rested my head against the cave wall.

Cries from my old and new pack echoed through the forest. Everyone I loved was being slaughtered by his kind. I had to do something about it. I couldn't just wait here until the end of my days.

After grasping on to any part of the rock wall that I could, I stood and hobbled toward the exit. The wolf turned around, baring his teeth at me, foam dripping from his mouth. I swallowed hard but continued forward, needing to help my mate and my pack.

The hound growled again and stood in front of the cave in a menacing manner. While he didn't make eye contact with me, he lowered his head and stared right at my hips, watching my every move.

"I need to go help my friends," I said, stepping forward. My mind became fuzzy, little stars appearing in my vision. I must've lost too much blood.

He stepped toward me, and I stumbled back and fell right onto my ass. I hit the ground with a thud and grasped my wounds, a searing pain shooting up my limbs. I felt helpless. Absolutely helpless ... just like Mom had thought I'd be. I couldn't even make it past a stupid hound, who was locking me in this damn cave. How could I ever lead? Who would even follow me?

CHAPTER 40

ARES

Hounds.

Hounds everywhere.

Saliva dripping from their teeth. Black eyes as dark as a new moon. Claws ready to rip into our fur.

There were so fucking many of them that I didn't know which to kill first. They had emerged from the forest, surrounded us, trapped us in.

A growl ripped from my throat as I killed hound after hound. Aurora's pack had to have set us up. How else would the hounds have known to attack while we were here? But how had they known we were coming? Who had fucking told them?

Pools of blood covered the forest floor. My fur was matted. Bodies of wolves from both our packs lay lifelessly on the ground around me … but the deadly hounds kept coming. They didn't stop. Ever.

All I needed was to protect Aurora behind me. I trusted my pack to kill and to get back home.

A wolf swiped their claws across my chest, and I growled. Instead of another hound, it was Aurora's mother. When she leaped at me, I dug my claws into her underbelly and ripped her into two. She fell at my feet, her eyes glazing over and her body shifting back into her human form.

Turning back to Aurora, I froze.

Where was she? Where the fuck did she go? Why wasn't she here?

"Aurora," I said through the mind link. I ran through the entire pack, desperately trying to find her among the wolves, trying to pick up her scent, anything. *"Aurora, answer me."*

But I couldn't pick up any scent of lemon in the midst of all this chaos and bloodshed. My chest tightened.

No. No. No. No. No. This couldn't be fucking happening. I didn't fucking believe it. My mate couldn't be gone.

Suddenly, her voice drifted through my head like a haunting memory. A memory that I couldn't remember. But it was her soft, scared voice reaching out to me in bits and pieces.

"I love you ..."

"... pups ..."

"... be happy."

Had my mate tried to reach me through the fucking mind link, but I was too damn desperate to kill the hounds for her that ... I couldn't hear her?

I let out a guttural growl and sprinted through the forest to try to catch her scent.

Mate.

My mate couldn't be gone.

Those couldn't be the last words I heard from her.

Running back to her mother's backyard, shuffling through every single body, I tried to find her. I wanted my mate.

Where was she? Was she gone? Had someone taken her?

I shook my head, my heart pounding faster than it had when I found Mom dead. No. No, this couldn't ... this couldn't be happening. First, Mom. Now, Aurora. She was the only good thing in my life besides Charolette. I couldn't lose her. I could not fucking lose her.

After shifting into my human form, I ripped bodies off each other, so I could make sure Aurora wasn't one of them, so I could make sure a hound hadn't killed her like one had killed her brother.

"Ares," Marcel said, grabbing my wrist.

I yanked my hand out of his grasp and growled. "Don't fucking touch me."

He nodded to a group of men and women from Aurora's mother's pack. "We have prisoners from Aurora's pack," he said.

But I couldn't think straight. All I could imagine was Aurora out there in the woods, trying to shift to protect herself but not being fast enough to do it before hounds ripped her to pieces.

One of the prisoners was Aurora's father.

Before my warriors could drag him away, I grabbed his shoulder and pulled him back. "Where the fuck is she?" I asked through clenched teeth. "Where would she have gone?"

Her father struggled in my grasp. "Get your hands off of me."

I growled, sank my claws into the back of his neck, dragged him all the way to the car, and threw him into the backseat. "You're lucky you're alive. If Aurora hadn't told me not to kill you, you would be dead." Before he had the chance to speak, I slammed the door in his face and looked at Marcel. "Drive him back to the property. Get him there safely."

Marcel stood by the driver's seat and looked down at all the open wounds covering my body. Blood spewed from each one, drenching me. "Come with us to heal your wounds before looking for Aurora."

"No."

I wouldn't allow myself to spend a second getting healed when she was out there alone. I needed to find her before something happened, if nothing had happened already.

"Now, leave." I seethed. I stormed back to the battlefield and searched for her in the sea of bodies for another hour.

She wasn't gone.

She couldn't be fucking gone.

Dropping down onto all fours, I doubled over in pain. What would Mars say when he found out? How could I tell him that I hadn't protected our own mate? All we'd wanted to do was keep her safe, and I'd failed.

I'd failed, and she was gone. The next time we saw her, she'd be dead.

Just like Mom.

My chest tightened. She never got to mark me. I never got to feel those little canines break my skin and claim me. Mars never got to connect with her, mark her, or be with her the way he always wanted.

We wouldn't have pups.

We wouldn't have a life together.

I'd be alone.

That was all that I was and would ever be. Alone.

I lifted my nose to the moon shining above and let out a broken howl.

When I gathered enough strength to move again, I sprinted home. I'd find Aurora and bring her home with me, dead or alive. I wouldn't let this haunt me for the rest of my life, like Mom's death did.

Blood gushed from my wounds. My vision blurred. Pain shot through every one of my limbs. But I kept running faster and faster until I made it to my property, where everything was in utter chaos.

Pack doctors scrambled to find hospital beds for wounded warriors. Already-healed wolves gathered for battle in our training field. Mothers and fathers ushered children into their homes to hide them from this madness. I transformed back into my human form, threw on a pair of shorts, and hurried through the disarray, putting together a team of trackers who would be able to pick up Aurora's scent.

Alpha Elijah stood near the pack house with some of his warriors and doctors.

I grabbed him by his collar, ready to fuck up his nerdy fucking face again. "Aurora is gone because of the fucking advice that you gave her last night."

He pushed me back. "This isn't my fault. I didn't know you'd get attacked."

My heart pounded against my rib cage. He might've not known about it, but someone in this pack had to have been working with Tony. Nobody in the Sanguine Wilds knew this pack's secrets, especially not secrets about Mom. Who would betray me? Who would take their luna and try to kill their own people?

I pushed him away.

I would find out later. Right now, I needed to find the only thing that mattered to me—my Aurora.

"Oh my fucking Goddess," Charolette screamed, grasping my wrist from behind. "Ares! What the hell are you doing? You need to let a doctor heal you! Even with your alpha abilities, those wounds won't close on their own."

Placing one of her small hands on the wound in the center of my chest, she tried to stop the blood from gushing out and yelled for a couple healers, but I ripped myself out of her grip and turned toward the pack.

"I'm not in the fucking mood for this right now."

"You need to wrap these wounds in bandages." She followed me. "You need to heal."

"I need to find Aurora!" I growled at her. My canines emerged from under my lips. My vision grew dark. My nails lengthened into claws. I couldn't stop myself. "Don't tell me what I have to do. I'm not losing someone else."

"I'm being serious—"

I snatched her chin in my hand. Everyone around us stopped and looked over. Never in my life had I laid a hand on Charolette.

But then again, I had never lost my mate, and I had never had this much control of Mars.

At least Mars knew when to stop. Mars knew what was right and what was wrong. Mars knew I needed to be healed. But I didn't fucking care. My mate was out there. And I had to find her.

Charolette pulled herself out of my grip. "I told you not to go out to find that stone."

"Leave, right now, Charolette."

She was testing me.

"Leave now."

"Not until you get healed," she said stubbornly. "What would Aurora think?"

When she said her name, I growled lowly and clenched my fists by my sides, everything in me hurting. What would Aurora think about this? I wasn't sure. But I knew what I thought …

I thought that Aurora was dead.

CHAPTER 41

AURORA

A thunderous roar of paws hitting the forest floor echoed throughout the cave. Cries from my old and new pack had stopped hours ago, which meant that these were hounds coming to kill me, and I had no way of getting out of here alive unless I acted now.

The hound who had healed me sat by the entrance with his ears pinned back and his eyes scanning the surrounding woods. I gazed around the cave at anything that I could use for a weapon. Whoever he was had saved me ... but I couldn't stay. Not when Ares was out there.

I wouldn't go down without a fight. If I got to Ares before he died, I might be able to put my stone in his back, so he could live. I'd give my entire life for him to stay alive, for him to be happy even if it was just for a moment. He didn't deserve any more hurt.

"Let me out," I said to the wolf through trembling lips. "Let me out now!"

When he didn't respond, I grasped a medium-sized rock I'd found toward the back of the cave and slowly approached him. Goddess, I didn't know why I was afraid of hurting this hound. Though he had saved me twice, he was part of their vicious group of creatures, and he was holding me hostage until they came back for me.

It should be easy for me to kill him.

After swallowing hard, I took another step toward him and grasped the rock in both of my hands.

His head, Aurora. Go for his head, then sprint out of the cave, and don't stop running. Not until you find Ares's body ... then we can stop. Then, they can kill me for all I care.

With trembling hands, I lifted the rock into the air and aimed. Before I could stop myself, I closed my eyes and hurled the rock straight at his head. It hit with a thud and cracked his skull.

The sound made me recoil. I had hurt people before—broken Marcel's finger, killed hounds with my knife—but this felt so wrong. Something about hurting him—the only hound that had helped me before, the hound with the stone like mine—it felt so fucking wrong.

Growling lowly, he shook his head from side to side as blood gushed out of his wound. I rushed out of the cave, but he followed me and sank his teeth into my calf to stop me from moving.

I gazed down at him, trying to pull my leg away but couldn't. My eyes filled with tears. This was so fucking sad. *I* was so fucking sad. Why did I feel bad for hurting him when ... when ... all his kind did was kill viciously?

The hound made eye contact with me for the first time, and my heart stopped. Familiar eyes stared up at me, and my eyes filled with even more tears.

No. No ... I didn't believe it. I couldn't believe it. It wasn't true.

He pleaded with me to stop moving, begged me with his tiny whimpers. I inhaled deeply and smelled cornfields, endless memories, and better days. Swinging at the playground. Chasing each other through the park. Staring up at the moon and talking about how we'd meet the Moon Goddess one day.

More howls sounded through the woods, and the hound's eyes widened. They were coming for me. He released me almost immediately and nudged me in the direction of Mom's pack, as if to say, *Go.*

"Wh-what about you?" I asked breathlessly. Tears spilled down my cheeks. "You c-can't stay here." I didn't want to lose him, not when I—

Stop, Aurora. He's not real. It's not really him.

He died.

"Go," he said through the mind link. It was faint, and I barely heard it … but he said it. *"Meet again."*

I swallowed hard, gave him one last look, and sprinted toward my Ares. My heart told me to stay with this hound, but my wolf tugged me toward my mate. We needed to see him, dead or alive. And so I ran and I ran and I ran until I could smell the putrid stench of pools of blood.

Wolves littered the woods, their lifeless bodies covered in claw marks and bite wounds. Fur hung from trees. Flies flew over bloody guts. The lush greens had turned a sanguine color.

I gazed at each and every one of the men and women, remembering when I used to train with them, when Mom used to *let me* train. Young men and women, some teenagers, most warriors.

The hounds didn't care who they killed. They'd killed people who hadn't even been on the battlefield earlier. Houses had their doors wide open. Windows were shattered. Blood splattered against the siding.

My lips quivered. I was a bad luna and a bad alpha. This was all my fault. Every single one of these deaths was on my hands. If I hadn't told Ares to run on Mom's pack … things might've been different. Tony might not have betrayed us. All these people might still be alive.

A tear raced down my cheek, but I quickly pushed it away. I couldn't cry. Ares thought I was strong, so I would be strong.

When the pack house came into view, I took a deep breath

and walked toward the backyard. I begged myself to be restrained, but a whimper clawed its way up my throat and out of my mouth.

Ares had come here with thirty wolves, and at least half of them were lying in their own blood. The majority of Mom's wolves had been killed, but I couldn't recognize most of them. With faces torn to pieces and all this gore, it was hard to identify anyone.

"Ares," I said, voice shaky through the quiet forest. "Ares …"

Nobody answered.

I stared up at the moon and wondered why the Moon Goddess had allowed something this horrific to happen again. Why hadn't she helped us? Where was she?

Walking through the bodies, I touched each one and tried to find him. But nobody felt the same as he did. Nobody looked the same as he did. Nobody had the same sweet hazelnut scent as he did. Or maybe I just couldn't spot him with bones jutting out of his ripped flesh.

After walking through everyone, the last person I found was Mom. I doubled over, tears falling from my eyes. With her highlighted hair and that scar running down her ear, she was still distinguishable … but I felt like the shittiest daughter to have ever lived.

Though she had made me feel like shit, I knew that all she'd wanted was for this pack to survive. She had given me book after book to study to become a smarter alpha, had tried to train me to be strong, and I really believed that she'd loved me at some point —even if it was just a bit.

And now, I would never see her again.

After closing her dull eyes, I stood up, determined to find my mate. Maybe he was still alive.

A twig snapped, and I whipped my head toward it.

My old neighbor's four-year old child, Yara, stared at me from behind a big oak tree. Dressed in a pink polka-dot onesie, she sprinted toward me with tears streaming down her face. "Alpha Aurora!" When she reached me, she jumped into my arms. "Alpha Aurora, my daddy is missing. I-I can't find anyone."

My heart shattered, and I held her tightly in my arms. "I …" What could I even say to her? "I … don't know where your father is. Let's try to go find any others," I whispered, hoping to keep my voice steady.

Since the last hound attack, I'd created underground shelters for pups to hide and to stay safe in while the warriors fought outside. They were all connected by a series of tunnels that led to a larger underground shelter under the pack house.

Covering Yara's eyes so she wouldn't see any more of this terror, I walked toward the pack house. I set her down, shut the sliding door, and locked it. She sniffled and wiped her snot with the back of her hand.

We walked down the stairs to the basement. After over a decade of not using these shelters, Mom had decided to turn off all the electricity down here despite me telling her not to. I lit a torch and grabbed Yara's hand.

We hurried through room after room, finding no pups inside any of them. My chest tightened as we approached the last three rooms. If there were no pups, that would mean that they were all dead.

First room … nobody.

Second room … nobody.

I opened the third room and peered into the darkness. Five sets of eyes stared up at me from the corner.

I crouched down to their level. "It's okay," I said, reaching out my arms. "You're safe. Everything is going to be okay. It's Aurora."

The pups ran into my arms, clung on to my legs, and grasped my fingers as we walked back to the pack house. I didn't know if everything was going to really be okay, and I definitely didn't know if we were safe, but I knew that I would protect them with my life.

I ushered the pups up the steps and instructed them to sit on the couch as I searched the house for all the silver knives I could find. I stuffed them into a backpack, grabbed a pair of car keys from the counter, handed each pup a bag of chips I'd kept for Ruffles in the pantry, and hurried to put them into Mom's old SUV—hoping the damn thing had enough gas to get us the hell off this property.

After plunging the key into the slot, I thanked the Moon Goddess that the gas tank was full. I threw the car in reverse and sped toward Ares's pack.

When I pulled onto Ares's property, the early morning sun was rising just over the horizon. The kids had only fallen asleep for a couple hours last night and had woken up, hungry and full of questions about their parents that I didn't have the strength to answer, but I hadn't stopped driving. If we'd stopped and the hounds spotted us, I had known that I wouldn't be able to protect them.

I glanced at them through the rearview mirror. "This is where we'll be staying from now on. We'll be safe here."

Some of Ares's warriors watched the car through the woods. I made eye contact with one of them, and he immediately sprinted toward the pack house. All I wanted was to find Ares, alive and well.

I parked in the driveway and tugged each and every one of the six pups out of the car. They grasped each other's hands and followed me in a line, like ducklings following their mother.

Mr. Barrett jogged up to me from his house. "Aurora." He sighed deeply through his nose. "I'm so glad you're safe. Ares is flipping out. He won't listen to any—"

My brows furrowed, eyes widening. "Ares is alive?" I asked in disbelief. He nodded his head, and I gave Yara's hand to Mr. Barrett. "Please, watch them for a bit."

"Of course." He grabbed Yara's hand, smiled down at the kids, and nudged me toward the training field. "Hurry, before he leaves. Ares is preparing to hunt with his warriors."

I hurried through the forest, following my mate's hazelnut scent.

"Mate. Mate. Mate. Mate."

My wolf paced around restlessly inside of me. There was a trail of blood leading me toward the field. Ares's blood. My chest tightened, throat closing up, and I started sprinting. I needed to get to my mate, needed to make sure he was okay.

And when I turned the corner, I saw him standing in the middle of a group of warriors. There were open and untreated wounds all over his tense and bloodied back.

"Ares," I whispered ever so softly.

He turned his head and gazed at me, eyes a raging gold. *"Kitten."*

CHAPTER 42

AURORA

Ares wrapped his arms around me, pulled me to his chest, and spun me. "I thought I'd lost you. I thought I'd fucking lost you," he whispered against my neck, his breath warming my mark and making it tingle.

I pulled him closer to me and breathed in his hazelnut scent that always seemed to help me relax. Ares was safe and not another victim of the hounds. I could sleep well tonight.

"Call all the trackers you have after me home. They're not safe out there." I pulled away from him slightly and stared down at all the open wounds he hadn't healed yet.

Shredded red chunks of flesh jutted out from a gash in his thigh as a thick layer of blood ran down his leg. My eyes widened slightly, and I shook my head. It had been hours since I last heard his howl … and he hadn't had anyone treat him yet?

"We killed all the hounds, Aurora." He brushed his fingers against my cheek as if he didn't even feel the pain. "We're safe."

"We're not safe." I pressed my lips together. "There are still more of them out there. Tony is out there too."

And I was going to kill that piece of shit when I found him.

Ares grasped my hands and ran his index finger over my

knuckles. "Then, we'll go find them. Right now. Get rid of them for good, for everything that they've done to us."

"We can't, Ares," I said.

But I didn't think leaving was his intention at all. If it were, he would've been storming toward the property edges, shouting at his warriors to prepare. Instead, everything in him seemed to soften.

He just stared at me with wavering human-brown to wolf-gold eyes, searching my face, as if he couldn't believe that I was standing right in front of him. "Goddess, Aurora," he whispered, pushing a strand of hair from my face. "I-I thought I'd lost you. I thought I'd never see you again. I thought you were dead."

I tried my hardest to smile, but I couldn't get myself to do it.

Ares had refused to heal his wounds, just so he could spend more time trying to find me. I appreciated the commitment he had to me, but I didn't like how he had refused to help himself. It hurt to know that my mate would rather bleed to death than to heal himself and be strong. What would've happened to him if I had died out there?

After grabbing his hand in mine to show him that I was really here, I gazed at all the other warriors. "No more fighting today. Call everyone back home. Nobody leaves the property, and nobody enters it without permission."

The warriors glanced at Ares and waited for orders. I expected Ares to say something, but he just continued to stare at me in disbelief, as if he didn't even know there were others around.

Ares and Mars had always been in control and led with such power and authority. Seeing him lost for words and so scared didn't sit right with me.

Marcel cleared his throat and stepped forward. "You heard our luna. Don't make her say it again."

When the warriors started to disperse, I nodded to Marcel and reminded myself to thank him later. I pulled Ares toward the hospital, where I would make sure the doctors healed him this time. But on our entire way there, I could hear his thoughts racing through his mind, his wolf begging him to tell me that he was okay and that all he wanted was to spend time with me.

Despite his silent pleas to take me home, I continued through the woods until Ares and I sat in a cold, bleak hospital room. He lay back in the bed and held my hand tightly, refusing to let go, even when a woman knocked on the wooden door.

Dressed in a long white coat, the doctor walked into the room with utensils and a bottle of clear gel. "We have been trying to get him to come in all morning," she said, pulling up a chair next to his bed.

"All morning?" I asked, more to myself than to her.

It was true. Ares didn't take care of himself when someone he loved was hurting. Charolette had mentioned it before, but we had been in the middle of something, and I hadn't had a chance to really think about it. But now, it was right here, smacking me in the damn face.

My gaze drifted from his face tensed in pain to his deep thigh wounds, and my heart ached. Ares had hurt himself before, and this was another form of self-harm.

After the doctor cleaned the wounds, she put some gel right on his raw flesh. "This will help him heal. It's a special gel for werewolves." She stitched every one of his wounds until they were closed. "Time to get you cleaned off, Alpha, so you're not dirty for your mate."

Ares went to stand to wash all the blood and dirt off his body, but I grabbed his hand before he could leave the room.

"I'll do it," I said, intertwining my fingers with his. "Thank you for everything, Dr. ..."

She gave me a warm smile. "Dr. Anand."

After I thanked her again, we walked out of the hospital and toward our pack house. The entire way, Ares held my hand tighter than usual to his chest and stayed quiet while I battled with all the dark thoughts running through my mind. All I could feel was hurt at the thought of my mate not caring about himself.

Why hadn't I taken this more seriously earlier? Why couldn't I see that the man who dealt pain also felt pain? Why hadn't I tried to talk about this with him? Charolette had told me about his self-harm. She'd told me, and I hadn't done a thing about it.

When we got home, I drew him a warm bath. "Get in."

He stared at the tub and then at me. "Only if you get in with me."

"No," I said, voice coming out more stern than I'd intended. "Get in the tub." He parted his lips to protest, but I didn't want to fight with him about this. "Now, Ares. Don't make me say it again."

After a few moments, he pulled his shirt over his head, pushed down his shorts, and stepped into the water. "Can I take a shower?"

"Sit."

When he finally submerged himself in the water, I knelt outside the tub, grabbed a soapy washcloth, and started to wash the blood off him. And when the water turned a musty red shade, I opened the drain and let more fresh water fill the tub. Dipping my feet into the bath with him, I sat on the edge and grabbed his arm, running the cloth against his forearm and seeing all those tiny little scars that I hadn't noticed before.

They weren't scars from a physical battle but a mental one.

I pressed my lips together, an overwhelming sadness washing over me, and tried not to burst out into tears. Ares was broken, more broken than I'd originally thought. He'd hurt himself willingly.

He followed my gaze and then pulled his arm away from me. "I'll do it."

"No," I said. I pulled his arm back to me, brushed the rag against it more gently, and washed away the blood from the battle yesterday morning. And then I pressed my lips to his scars. "I love you."

I knew that it wouldn't make everything better. I knew I alone couldn't heal him. But I could let him know that I would always be there for him, through the thick and the thin and through everything that might happen. I would always try to make him happy and make him smile, wash the hurt off of him when I could, and love him with everything that I had.

Suddenly, his eyes widened and filled with tears. He grabbed my arm, his fingertips digging into my wrist until they turned white. "I-I'm sorry I couldn't protect you, Aurora." Almost as if he was too weak, his fingers slipped from my arm, and his body started to tremble in the water. "I'm sorry I couldn't protect you."

"Oh, Ares," I whispered, stroking his hair to try to calm him down.

But he didn't stop shaking. Beads of sweat formed on the back of his neck, and I could hear just how quickly his heart was racing.

I stripped my clothes and sat behind him in the tub, pulling him into my lap, holding his head to my chest, running my hands through his hair. "Ares, it's okay. I'm here."

"I couldn't protect you," he repeated shakily.

"I'm here with you, Ares."

"I couldn't protect Mom either."

After ten heartbreaking minutes of listening to Ares's broken cries, he slowly stopped shaking. I held him tighter to my chest and let him play with my fingers.

"I could have protected her," he finally said, tensing. "I could have, but I didn't."

I didn't speak a word. I didn't know what to say, and I wanted him to continue.

"She … she was raped. Nineteen years ago, she was raped by a hound," he said, voice cracking. "Our pack was raided by a herd of them. She told me to hide in the closet and not to come out, no matter what I heard or what I saw. I didn't know what was happening. I heard her screaming and crying and …" His chest heaved up and down, the water rippling violently around us. "I watched it happen through the closet door." He parted his lips to speak, but no words came out. "I …" His voice was quiet. "I was five."

My chest tightened. Ares's mother had been raped by a hound, and Ares had watched.

"She had Charolette nine months later, but she wasn't happy. Not truly happy, like she had always been. She tried to be happy with us." He forced a small smile, teary eyes gazing off into the distance. "That picture at my dad's house was taken four days before she killed herself."

"Ares …"

"I found her … she was clutching the picture and the teddy bear that we keep in the toy room. I—" He let out a loud cry. "I hadn't known she wanted to kill herself. I … I should've stopped it. I should've stopped it, but I didn't. I didn't. It's all my fault."

He shook uncontrollably again. Tears streamed down his face. Water sloshed over the side of the tub. I just held him tighter.

My heart ached for him. Ares wasn't the man behind the spear and the shield. He was the spear and the shield, protecting Mars from whatever anguish and hurt he could possibly face. But no matter how strong his armor was … even Ares felt pain.

"Some days, I can't handle it. I think about hurting myself again. I can't help it," he said, lips trembling. "Dealing with both sides of me … is really hard. I don't want to lose anyone that close to me again." He clutched my hand tighter. "I don't want to lose you. You're the best thing that's ever happened to me."

"You're not going to lose me," I said into his ear.

"You keep me strong." He interlocked our fingers and said those three little words that made my heart tingle all over, "Mark me, Aurora." He tilted his head and closed his eyes. "Please," he said so softly that I could barely hear him. "Please be mine forever."

My breath caught in my throat, and my canines lengthened under my lips. I gently grazed my teeth against his neck. *"Ares,"* I said through the mind link, *"you're mine. And I'd do anything to protect you."*

And then I sank my teeth into his neck and claimed him.

CHAPTER 43

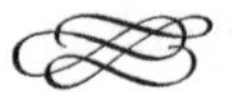

AURORA

Ares shuddered in delight against me, his body relaxing into mine. I sank my teeth deeper and deeper into his neck until I couldn't anymore. Every single insecurity, every single harrowing memory, every single ounce of fear from him exploded through my body.

My poor Ares had been holding the entire world on his shoulders all this time.

When I was about to pull my teeth out of him and lick his wound, he gently grasped my head and held me against him. "Please, just a little bit longer," he whispered. "I just want to feel you."

I plunged my teeth back into him, inhaled his hazelnut aroma, and closed my eyes. I'd meant everything I had said to him. I would protect him from his enemies even if his fiercest foe was himself. And if I couldn't protect him, then I would stand by his side during his darkest battles. I would pull out every sword, spear, and arrow from his armor. I would give him love because even a god like him needed it.

When he released his grip on my head, I pulled my teeth out of his neck and swiped my tongue across his large puncture wounds. With a big smile on his face, he turned in the water, making it splash everywhere, wrapped his arms around my waist, and picked me up. Stuffing his face into the crook of my neck, he pulled me closer to him and walked into our bedroom.

"Ares, we're both wet," I whispered, tugging on the ends of his damp hair.

He pressed his lips against my neck, moving them up the column, under my ear, against my jaw, leaving sloppy kisses all over my body. "I don't care."

I wrapped my legs around his waist and pulled him closer. Cradling my head, he laid me down onto the bed and rested his forehead against mine. He trailed his lips back down my body and then up my thighs, kissing like he had been starved for so long.

He lay between my legs, rested my thighs on his shoulders, interlocked my fingers with his, and pressed his hot mouth against my core. My back arched, and I grasped his fingers tighter. Pleasure rolled through my body, my legs slowly starting to shake. He sucked my clit between his lips, tugging on it gently, and then flicked it with his tongue.

I moaned out and felt Ares groan in response against my pussy. His thumbs brushed against my knuckles, and he continued to eat me, his face dropping even lower to my entrance, his tongue lapping up my juices.

"Ares, please, I need you," I said in a breathy whisper, my pussy tightening. I needed him inside of me more than I needed anything in my entire life. "Please."

He continued to massage my clit with his tongue. Closing his eyes, he inhaled the scent of my arousal and groaned again. "I'm not going to make love to you until you come for me, Kitten."

I swallowed hard, my pussy tightening even more. For the mere week I had been here, I had never heard those words come out of Ares's mouth. Ares didn't *make love*. He fucked, and he fucked hard. But something about the big, bad alpha, the god of war, the strongest and most terrifying wolf in the entire world being soft for me … that was an unexplainable feeling.

He grasped my jaw and made me gaze down at him. "Watch me, Kitten. I want to see your eyes when you come." He trailed his fingertips across my breast, took my nipple between his fingers, and tugged on it.

I dug my heels into the bed. A surge of ecstasy coursed through me, and I curled my fingers into his hair, staring down at his warm golden eyes. He continued to eat my pussy, his free hand splayed open across my stomach to hold me against the mattress.

"Come for me," he murmured.

Almost as if on cue, I grasped the bedsheets in my fists and tugged harshly on them, my whole body quivering. Wave after wave of pleasure pumped through my entire body, making it tingle. I squeezed my eyes closed, the intensity almost too much.

"Open your eyes for me, Kitten."

"Ares," I moaned, staring back down at him. "I need you. Please."

He crawled between my legs, the head of his cock brushing against my aching pussy, and pressed his lips to mine in one lingering kiss.

Please, I mouthed when he pulled away.

Resting his forehead against mine, he steadily pushed himself inside of me, stroked his thumb against my cheekbone, and stared down into my eyes. Unable to hold back, I wrapped my hand around the back of his neck and pulled his lips onto mine.

As our lips collided, he began to thrust into me. Pumping in and out slowly. His tongue slipping into my mouth. His lips devouring mine. With every moment that passed, he thrust harder and faster.

After he broke our kiss, he pulled me to his chest and rolled us over, so I straddled his waist. I placed my hands on his abdomen and moved my hips back and forth to ride him.

Taming an alpha might've been hard, but it had all been worth it.

This moment was more than I could ever ask for.

He continued to stare up at me, his eyes glazed over with lust, his swollen lips parted slightly. "Aurora," he whispered, snaking a hand around my throat and pulling me down to him. He wrapped his arms around my body and locked his hands behind my back. He grazed his nose against his mark. "I love you."

And then he started to fuck me hard. His hips bucking against mine, his cock pounding deep inside of me, my walls clenching hard around him. The pressure built in my core, higher and higher and higher.

"I love feeling your body tremble right before you're about to come," he whispered in my ear. "I love listening to your little whimpers while you're sleeping." He pushed some hair behind my ear, so I could gaze at him. "I love that fire in your eyes."

I furrowed my brows and clenched harder. "Please, come inside of me."

"Will that make you feel good?" he asked. "Feeling my cum filling your tight little pussy?"

I whimpered in his ear and nodded. "Yes, Ares. Please."

Stuffing his face back into the crook of my neck, he sucked on his mark. His body tensed, and I could feel his cock pulsing inside of me and filling me with his cum. I moaned, my body shuddering against his.

A rush of pleasure washed over me. Everything was so much more intense than the last time we'd had sex, all our emotions bare and unguarded this time.

He sat up on the bed, keeping his arms around my body, his cock still buried inside of me. "Goddess, I love you," he said.

My lips quivered as I stared at Ares, eyes filling with tears from the pure intensity of everything that had just happened. I clung on to him, terrified that I would lose him if I let go. Earlier today, I'd thought I'd lost him for good, and I didn't ever want to feel like that again. He pulled me closer to his chest, and we embraced each other in silence for a good fifteen minutes.

Moonlight streamed into the room through the window and bounced off all the muscles in his back. Under the light, I could see every single one of his scars. Some were small and nearly invisible; others were large, swollen, and jagged. I brushed my fingers against them, feeling the rugged texture.

Every one of them made up the man I called my mate.

He touched his fingers to my mark on his neck and looked me right in the eye. "My body is covered in scars from wars that I've won and from battles that I've lost." He glanced down at his forearms and then back at me. "So many memories etched into my skin forever, but yours, Kitten, is my favorite."

CHAPTER 44

AURORA

"Let me take you out on a real date," Mars said with a smile. He had shifted from Ares to Mars a few moments ago as we sat together on our bed, still completely naked and soaked in bath water and sweat. "You haven't really met this pack yet. And I want to take you out."

"And?" I asked, poking his cheek.

"And"—his cheeks flushed—"I want to show everyone my mark."

A grin broke out onto my lips, and I pulled him into a tight hug. I'd never thought that when he took me, he'd be so … loving. I'd thought I was going to have to endure a life of war and pain and violence. But he was just a boy trapped in this big, brooding body. All Ares and Mars needed was some love.

"Go get ready," he said, smacking my ass. "I have some business to take care of before we go."

I crawled off him and rummaged through the closet for my clothes. Ruffles waltzed into the room a few moments after Mars disappeared into the hallway. With a bag of chips between her teeth and suds on her nose, she hopped onto the bed and swayed her tail back and forth.

"Did you get into the bath?" I asked, opening the chips for her.

She purred in response and watched me choose my outfit for tonight, meowing when she didn't like a skirt or shirt or dress. I threw on my last outfit—a simple little black dress with silver earrings—and arched a brow at Ruffles for approval. She squinted her eyes at me and purred loudly.

I placed a kiss on her head, told her not to leave her fur all over Mars's clothes when we were gone, and walked out of the room to meet Mars, who was dressed in a short-sleeved maroon button-up, which hugged his biceps.

He brought me to The Flaming Chariot, located in the heart of the Ironmane Pack. Bustling with people, the restaurant had a stone statue of a chariot led by horses with flames shooting out like wings from their sides. Mars said it had been created over two hundred years ago during the War of the Lycans.

For a restaurant run by werewolves, the place was surprisingly chic with a white-accented wraparound bar. We sat at a table, ordered a bottle of Bacchus white wine, and started in on our dinner.

Some people glanced over at us, and for once, they smiled at me. Before, everyone had seemed so cold and distant, but now that we both had marks on our necks, people were a bit friendlier.

I stared across the table at him and leaned forward. "Did you happen to see my father before you left the pack?" I asked.

While I had saved all those pups, I still wanted to know if the hounds had killed my dad. I couldn't recognize him among the people who were torn up in the raid.

"Your father is in my prison," Mars said. "I would let him out, but he'd end up going back to your pack and getting himself killed."

"He's here?" I asked with wide eyes. "You brought him back with you?"

The light of a candle flickered against his brown eyes, giving them a golden hue. "Yes, he has been treated for his injuries. All the warriors from your pack that survived have been. Some are in the prison as captives; others have been released and are adjusting to life as members in our pack."

Our pack.

The words made me smile even wider.

Though I hadn't seen Dad for so long—besides our little chat in the woods—I missed him. I just hoped that he would forgive me for bringing Ares to Mom's pack and for Mom's death. All I had ever wanted was for my mate and my family to get along, but now that Mom was dead, I didn't know if that'd ever happen.

Dad probably blamed my mate for the hound attack.

Maybe, after dinner, we could go see him and talk.

"Elijah?" I asked, remembering I had seen him here earlier when I was bringing Ares home. I scolded myself for not telling him about the wolf who had saved me in the woods, but at that time, I had been too focused on getting Ares help.

"He's back at his pack. Safe."

I sent a quick text to Elijah to meet me at the prison in an hour, and I leaned toward Mars again. "What about the pups that I brought home? Most, if not all, of their parents are dead. We need to find them homes here. Would families in your pack … consider taking them in?" I parted my lips and awkwardly waited for him to answer. "I mean, we could do it. I just don't think that we're the best-suited people at the moment. We have so much going on and—"

"I love you." Mars grabbed my hands from across the table. "You're going to make a great luna. I can't wait to have our Luna Ceremony." He smiled and nodded at me. "And, yes, there are plenty of people who'd take them in. And if there's nobody, my dad would probably take them all. He loves pups."

My heart warmed, and I felt so loved for once in my life. "Can we send a group of warriors back to my mom's pack? Just to make sure that there isn't anyone else that I missed."

"Already done. I sent them when you were getting ready."

I interlocked my fingers with his and squeezed them tightly. It felt like nothing could ruin these little moments I had with him and that nothing could ruin us. We were good. So damn good. As a team. As partners. As mates.

My gaze drifted from Mars to Marcel, who sat at the bar, alone. Well, he had been here the entire time we had, glancing every now and then at Liam and Charolette, who were out on a date too.

A woman approached him, dragging her nails across his back, and said something into his ear, to which he replied with, "Leave me the fuck alone," before downing a shot of tequila.

The Marcel I knew loved women. He loved fucking them. He loved thinking about them. He loved using them. He wouldn't turn down a good time just to sit around in a bar and drink until his cold, dark heart was numb.

I glanced from Marcel to Mars and then back. "I'll be right back." I squeezed Mars's forearm, placed my napkin on the table, and slid onto a stool next to Marcel.

He barely glanced my way and sipped another drink. "What?"

"Two, please," I asked the bartender. I glanced at Marcel and lightly bumped my shoulder against his. "I want to thank you for what you did earlier today."

"What'd I do?" Marcel asked through clenched teeth, his silver hair falling into his face.

"You didn't attack my dad. You stood up for me in front of all the other warriors. You called me Luna," I said.

For once, he had shown me respect and hadn't been a blatant asshole, like he usually was.

The bartender placed two shots in front of us. Marcel went to grab one, but I snatched them both before he could.

He exhaled deeply through his nose. "What do you want me to say? You're welcome? I would've done that shit anyway. Don't think I did it just for you."

"I don't think that."

"Then, why the fuck are you sitting up here with me?"

"You like Charolette, don't you?" I asked. Marcel growled under his breath and reached for one of the shots again, but I pulled my hand away. "You should go ask her out on a date—on a real date."

"And how the fuck am I supposed to do that, Aurora? She's dating the fuckin' beta."

"But she likes you too, doesn't she?"

He clenched his jaw and slammed his fist down on the bar. Some people looked over, including Charolette. Her blue eyes lingered on Marcel, and she frowned.

He shook his head and lowered his voice. "She doesn't fuckin' like me."

I paused for a moment, unsure how to get him to see it. "I saw you guys together in her bedroom the other night. It was the first time I'd really seen you smile."

My heart warmed at the memory. They had both looked so happy together, and now ... what had changed?

For a split moment, there was a deep sorrow in his eyes. But almost as quickly as it had appeared, it disappeared. Then, he snatched the shot glass from me. "Nothing happened between us, and nothing will ever happen between us. She has Liam. He's good for her." He downed the shot and stood up. "I'm not." And then he walked right out of the bar.

After sighing, I left the drink and walked back to the table.

"What'd he say to you?" Mars asked me, watching Marcel's departing figure with that thirst-to-kill look on his face. "I'm tired of his damn disrespect for you."

I pulled Mars to his feet, ready to talk to Dad. I didn't mind Marcel's attitude toward me today because I'd found out everything I needed to know about him. Marcel *liked* Charolette. And Charolette liked Marcel.

Nobody could tell me otherwise.

But I couldn't tell Mars that because he would flip out. I would keep their little secret until one of them made a move on the other because Charolette was one of the only friends I had here, and Marcel ... well, Marcel reminded me of Ares. Rough on the outside and soft on the inside.

"We're going to go see my dad," I said to him, hoping that it was okay and that it'd take his mind off Marcel for a bit.

Mars grabbed my hand and walked out of the restaurant with me, silently agreeing.

Outside, the horse statue was still burning, brightening the forest around us. Bursts of flames flailed out from the horses' manes, yet the stone wasn't charred. I gazed at it in amazement, feeling drawn to the chariot, but I continued walking through the forest and toward the prison.

We walked past the pack house, and I saw Ruffles sitting on her windowsill, gazing out at the lightning bugs.

"One sec," I said to Mars. I left him in the woods, ran to the pack house, and called for Ruffles. "You wanna come with us?"

She hopped down from the window and met me at the front door. "*Meow.*"

"Mars and I are going to the prison."

"*Meow.*"

"Girl, he's not your man." I opened the door for her and let her hop onto the cement sidewalk. She rubbed herself against my leg and started walking toward Mars.

My stomach fluttered with butterflies as I thought about telling Elijah and Dad the good news. I wanted to go back to the cave now to see that hound again, but I knew it wasn't the right time. Something was telling me that I should just wait for him to come to me.

Ruffles swayed her little butt back and forth, chip dust all over her long gray fur. "*Meow.*" She rubbed up against Mars, and I cut my eyes to her. She gazed up at me with an evil *I'm going to take your man* expression.

We walked farther through the woods until we reached the small cement building with a single light on and three guards posted around it.

My phone buzzed in my back pocket, and I pulled it out. "Are you here?"

There was some chatting in the background, and then Elijah finally spoke, "I'm about to start a meeting with my warriors. We've spotted hounds at our southern borders. I won't be able to make it over until this is taken care of."

I stopped dead in my tracks. "More hounds? Do you need Ares to come help?"

"No," Elijah said. "I'm not planning to attack. Something doesn't feel right. What did you need? Is it important?"

"I'd rather tell you in person. It isn't … just anything. It's important."

"All right. I'll be there as soon as I can," he said.

Ruffles ran ahead to the guards, who all stared curiously down at her and blocked her passage. She meowed up at them, and they moved out of her way, as if she were a queen. She walked into the prison and disappeared down the steps.

Before Elijah hung up the phone, I warned him to be careful. Tony was still out there, and he was dangerous. If he'd betrayed our pack and let the hounds kill everyone, I wouldn't put it past him to try to kill other packs too. He wanted to instill fear in everyone, wanted to be just like Ares.

But he was nothing like Ares.

Tony ran from battle. Ares ran toward it.

After pushing my phone into my purse, Mars and I walked past the guards and into the prison. Ruffles stood in front of Dad's cell, staring at him through the silver bars. I had let her come as a kind of welcoming gift for Dad—a piece of home.

Dad used to love Ruffles up, but now, he just stared emptily at her and sat against the concrete wall in the same cell Ares had beaten up Elijah in. He glanced up at me when I walked into the room.

I furrowed my brows at him. "Hey, Dad … I had Ares bring you her—"

"You should've let him kill me," Dad said.

I stopped in complete shock. Never in my life had I heard him sound so utterly furious yet so lifeless. Dad wanted to be dead? He'd rather have death than have me?

"He doesn't mean it, Kitten. He's just angry," Mars said through the mind link.

But I didn't believe it. All I had tried to be was a good daughter for him and Mom, yet time and time again, they had continued to disappoint me. It was never-ending. It was vicious. It hurt.

I gazed at my father, at the man who had once loved me but who was now looking at me with so much hatred. My heart shattered, and my chest tightened. Ruffles stood between my legs and hissed at Dad, baring her little teeth.

"All your mother wanted was to keep you safe." Dad shook his head at me. "And you betrayed her. You brought your mate back to our pack, and everyone died because of it." He walked closer to the silver bars and stared down at me. "Everyone's dead because of you."

My eyes filled to the brim with tears at his harsh words, but I refused to let them fall. He was just angry and sad that his mate was dead. That was why he was saying this. He didn't mean it … did he?

"Dad, I didn't … I didn't cause—"

"Your mother. Your packmates. Your friends from high school. All of them are fucking dead." He grasped the silver bars in his palms, letting the metal sear his skin, and stepped even closer to me.

Mars let out a vicious growl—and I knew it was Ares here now instead—and stepped in front of me. "Don't try to intimidate her. You disrespect her one more time, and I'll have your fucking head."

"She's my fucking daughter, Ares," Dad said. "I can talk to her any way that I please."

Ares grabbed Dad by his throat and pulled his whole body against the silver bars. "She is your daughter, and she's a fucking alpha. You out of all people should know to respect her, but you've never respected her, have you?" The silver against Dad's skin sizzled, and I winced at the sound, but Ares didn't back down. "You and her mother put her down for years and acted as if you did nothing wrong. But you're in my pack now. You don't get to talk to her like that."

I grasped Ares's arm and pulled him back. "Ares, stop."

"He deserves to die, Aurora."

"No," I said softly. "He doesn't."

Maybe he did, but I didn't want him to die. I hoped that, one day, we could be a happy family again even if it was just him, Ruffles, and me. But I wasn't sure if that would ever happen.

After a few more moments of tugging on Ares's shoulder, I finally brushed my fingers against his mark and felt him relax. Ares threw Dad to the ground, and Dad smacked against the concrete, hitting it with a loud thud. There were red lines on his skin from where the silver bars had burned him.

I grasped Ares's wrist. "Come on. Let's go."

This was a mistake. My mistake. I had come here to tell him one thing, and all I had gotten was yelled at and put down by him. Maybe trading me to Ares was the best decision of his life too. Maybe I was and had always been a burden.

"You're just going to leave me here, A?"

I turned on my heel, anger running through my veins. "You don't get to call me that anymore. When you decide you want to be civil with me and actually have a conversation about what happened, then we can talk, but until then"—I paused and swallowed hard—"all I wanted to tell you was that your son is alive."

Dad stared at me with wide eyes. "Jeremy …" he whispered. He took a shaky, deep breath, his eyes filling with tears. "Why didn't you tell me? How long have you known this? He could've saved us all."

It was stupid and dumb and so damn weak of me, but I couldn't stop my heart from breaking into a million tiny, jagged pieces. I loved Jeremy with all my heart, but Mom and Dad had always loved him just a little bit more than they loved me. They'd always looked to him first, always compared me to him.

Jeremy could've saved us.

Jeremy could've been our protector.

Why're you so selfish to keep this to yourself?

Why can't you be strong like him?

All their words—and their unspoken words—filled my mind until it felt like I was suffocating. Why did I care so much about Dad? Why had I ever even cried for Mom when she died? They hadn't cared about me. It was so fucking obvious. During the hound attack, he had run off to protect her and left me there to fend for myself, knowing that I couldn't shift.

Instead of responding to him, I walked up the stairs and out the doors with tears in my eyes. I'd be back to talk to him. I just needed time to process how unwanted he had made me feel.

The guards shut the prison doors behind us, but I could still hear the disgust in Dad's voice, woven into every sentence, every word, every fucking syllable.

Ruffles walked beside me like my little sidekick, shaking her little booty back and forth in front of Ares and trying to get his attention.

When Ares finally caught up to me, he grabbed my hand and held it to his chest. "What do you mean, your brother is alive?"

I grasped his hand tighter. "I'm almost certain that he is."

"How? I thought you said he was killed."

Ares opened the pack house door for me and waited for

Ruffles to hop into the house. But she just stared up at him, waving her tail back and forth.

"Move your ass, Ruffles," Ares said, pushing her along.

She jumped into the house, looked up at him, and meowed.

"I'll come lie down with you later."

She purred and ran up the stairs, disappearing into the hallway.

I smiled weakly at her departing figure. Even when I was a mess and on the verge of tears, she could always bring a smile to my face.

Ares wrapped his arms around me from behind and placed a kiss on my neck. "She takes after you."

"I'm not that sassy."

Ares chuckled against me, and my stomach filled with butterflies. The chuckle sounded like home, like my future, like a promise that everything would get better with time even though I knew it wouldn't.

"You're both needy," he said, walking up the stairs and guiding me into the kitchen. "For me."

I playfully rolled my eyes and stared out the kitchen window at the dark forest. Jeremy was out there somewhere, and one day —even if it wasn't anytime soon—I'd have to find him. It had been over ten years since I had seen him, and I wasn't about to let him disappear from my life again.

Ares placed two frozen pretzels and a container of dipping cheese from the fridge into the microwave for us, and then he leaned against the counter, brushing his fingers against my chin and giving me that infamous smirk. "So, are you going to tell me, Kitten?"

I rested my forearms on the counter and frowned. "My brother is alive. The other day, when those two hounds were fighting each other, when that one stood in front of me and protected me … that was him …" I smiled, my heart clenching. "I just … I didn't know it was him at the time. He smells different and he looks different and he …"

I wanted to tell him that Jeremy had the other half of the Malavite Stone—which must've been keeping him alive all these years—but I knew that as soon as Ares found out that Jeremy had it, he'd have every tracker in his pack trying to find him, so he could get it for Charolette.

So, I slumped against the counter and stalled, hoping that if I told Ares his life story, he wouldn't chase after him like he had with me.

"He was an alpha," I said quietly. "A damn good alpha. One day, we were attacked by hounds, and he was torn into tiny pieces. I saw them shred every piece of his flesh, saw all his blood nearly drained. Mom pulled me away before I had the chance to say good-bye, but there was no doubt in my mind that he was dead."

Ares leaned closer to me and squeezed my shoulder, his hazelnut aroma calming me. I pursed my lips together, thinking of the only solution that would save my brother from Ares's wrath.

Me.

There was no way that I could or would lose Jeremy again. If I had to trek to the ends of the earth to find him one last time, I would. If I had to live every single day in pain and in terror, I would. I was the only solution to all of our problems.

"Ares," I said quietly, placing my hands on his chest and gazing up into his brown eyes, "the only way that Jeremy survived that attack was because someone put the other half of the stone inside of him." My voice was nearly a whisper toward the end.

As soon as the words left my mouth, I wished they hadn't.

Ares's eyes turned a light shade of gold—his wolf—and then a darker shade, his nostrils flaring. "Your brother has the fucking stone?"

His body tensed, and I thought he was going to rip himself

out of my grasp. There was a darkness lurking deep within him, ready to come out, aching to kill. When he reached for my hands, I almost flinched.

But instead of hurting me, he closed his eyes and took a deep breath.

My eyes widened slightly at his surprising response, and I grasped his face in my hands. "Listen to me, Ares. And listen to me good. I will not let you kill him for it."

"I've been looking for that stone for years, Aurora," he said, voice taut. "Charolette doesn't have much time left."

"I know"—*Please don't hate me for this*—"which is why Charolette will use my stone. Jeremy is my only brother, just like Charolette is your only sister. I love them both, and I don't want either of them to die."

He shook his head. "No. I've already told you before, that will not happen."

"But, Ares—"

"No." He growled down at me, his canines emerging from under his lips. "You will not trade your life for Charolette's."

"It's not trading my life," I pleaded. "It's keeping people alive. I won't die from removing the stone. I'll just ..."

"You'll just what?" He stepped toward me, and I moved back, tears filling my eyes again. "You just won't be able to shift? You just won't be able to move? What if the procedure doesn't work? What if the doctor fucks it up and you die?" I opened my mouth to speak, but Ares held his finger to my lips. And while I wanted to protest, something about that subtle action made me comply. "No," he said in his alpha tone this time. "That's final."

I stared at him and grasped his hands. "Please, Ares. I don't want your sister or my brother dead. I've already lost him once. Do this for Charolette. She deserves it."

Playing the sick-sister card on him was shitty, but I needed to do it. He might not agree to use my stone at the moment, but hopefully, he'd consider it in the future. Because if worse came to worse and Charolette didn't get better, I'd already made Elijah promise to take the stone from me and put it in her.

I didn't need Ares's permission to do what I wanted with my body.

I just hoped that he'd forgive me for it.

The microwave behind us beeped, startling me.

Ares stared down at me, lips pressed together, eyes as golden as the sun. "I said, no." Then, he pulled out the pretzels, handed me one, and walked to our bedroom.

CHAPTER 45

MARS

Curled up next to me, Aurora drew soothing circles across my chest. A slight early morning breeze blew the sheer gray curtains open and against the bed. Last night, I had to wrestle my wolf into submission, so I could try to get some sleep ... but all I could think about was Aurora's proposition.

Ares, our wolf, and I didn't like it at all.

Aurora hadn't slept either. She had tossed and turned all night in my arms. Sitting up and lying back down. Glancing out the window and staring up at the bland ceiling. Back and forth until she finally laid her head on my chest and shut her eyes for a few moments. She must've been thinking about the stone too.

I loved Charolette, but I didn't want Aurora to use the stone to save her. There had to be another way. If Aurora took out her stone, she wouldn't be able to walk, never mind shift. And while I'd make sure she had the best life possible, I didn't want her to be bound to a wheelchair or to a bed for the rest of her life.

My wolf could barely handle seeing our mate not able to shift. He really wouldn't be able to handle her not able to walk.

She tilted her head toward me and placed a lingering kiss on my neck, right over the mark she'd left on me last night. I moved my head to the side and pulled her closer to me, letting her suck it softly.

Last night had been perfect—before she asked me to use her stone. She had marked me, I had gotten a chance to show it off to everyone, she'd finally stood up to her dad, and I'd found out that her brother was alive. Hell, I was still in shock at everything that had happened, especially—she drew her tongue against my mark —that.

"Kitten," I mumbled.

She climbed on top of me, her breasts grazing against my bare chest. Ruffles meowed at her and hopped off the bed, annoyed. Aurora ignored her and sat up taller, grinding her hips back and forth against mine.

"Alpha," she whispered.

I placed my hands on her waist, loving the way she touched me like she owned me.

"Let's go for a run."

"It's barely even morning."

She kissed me again. "Guess that means we'll have the whole forest to ourselves." She hopped off me and pulled on a thin white crop top from the closet. Her breasts bounced against it, nipples hard. "None of your warriors will interrupt you."

I sat back on my elbows and cocked a brow at her. "Interrupt me from doing what?"

"From stopping by the lake, ripping off my clothes, and *getting wet*," she said.

But I wanted to do more than that to her, especially with how she was dressed.

She smirked back at me. "That's *if* you can catch me, Alpha."

My lips curled into a smirk, and a chuckle made its way to my mouth. She slammed the door and sprinted down the hallway. I tugged on a pair of shorts and let her get a good distance into the woods before I chased her out.

The forest was silent this morning, only birds chirping in the distance. I growled lowly, so she knew I was coming and then followed her lovely lemony scent.

There was no *if* I could catch her.

There was only *when* I caught her and *what* I'd do with her when I did.

Though the woods were relatively clear by the pack house, the farther we ran, the foggier it got. Perfect to sneak up on my mate. Her footsteps came to a halt, and I crept around her, careful not to make noise.

"*Mars?*" she whispered through the mind link. "*I think I'm—*"

I sneaked up behind her and pushed her against the nearest tree, pressing my hips against hers. "Think you could outrun me, Kitten?" I asked, fingers trailing dangerously up the column of her fragile neck. "Did you think I'd let you run away from me after you marked me last night?"

She pressed her thighs together, and I could just about taste the juices running down them. I harshly brushed my thumb against her jaw, my teeth grazing against her ear.

"You should've run faster," I said. "I like chasing you."

"Yeah?" she asked breathlessly. "Why's that?"

"Because when I finally catch you, I get to hear you purr for me."

I trailed my fingers down the center of her chest and slipped them into her shorts, touching her clit. Digging her claws into the tree bark, she tensed and tried to breathe steadily.

"Come on, Kitten," I murmured against her ear, rubbing my fingers harder against her clit. "Purr." I strummed my fingers against her bare neck, right where *I'd* claim her soon. "Do it for me."

One finger slipped inside of her, then another, and another. She arched her back ever so slightly and moaned for me.

I ground my hips against hers and smirked against her neck. "That wasn't hard, was it?"

She reached behind and grasped my cock through my shorts. "Please."

I pushed down her shorts, placed my hand on her lower back, and made her arch harder. "What was that?" I asked, pulling out my cock and rubbing the head against her wetness.

"Please."

"Please what?"

"Please, Alpha."

As soon as the words left her mouth, I drove myself into her. Her whole body shuddered against mine, her pussy tightening. I growled lowly to hold back my groan and let her move her hips back and forth against me.

"This doesn't change my mind," I said, turning her around so she was facing me, grasping her hips, and thrusting my cock back into her. "I won't let you risk your life for my sister." I pumped deeper inside of her, groping her breasts. "Because there are only two times I want to see you unable to move, unable to stand, and unable to fight me, Kitten." I wrapped my hand around her neck and brushed my thumb against Ares's mark. "After I fuck you," I said into her ear. "And when your stomach is swollen with my pups."

Lips parted slightly, eyes a hazy blue, she curled her fingers into my chest and clenched hard on my cock.

"You like that, don't you?" I asked, brushing two fingers against her clit. "You want to carry my pups?"

She moaned quietly and sucked her bottom lip between her teeth.

"Louder," I said, feeling the pressure in my dick.

She buried her face into my chest, her pussy tightening even harder on my cock, and moaned louder.

I pounded into her faster and faster until I was about to come. "Do you want me to come down this pretty throat of yours? Or do you want me to come deep in your pussy?" I asked, edging myself.

She furrowed her brows. "Come inside of me."

"Then, beg for it," I growled against her ear, not knowing if I could wait that long. "I want to hear my luna begging to be filled with my cum. I want your claws digging into my chest. I want you to call me Alpha."

"Please, Alpha ..." she breathed, her body trembling. "Please, come inside of me. I'll come with you. Just"—another pant—"please, come."

Groaning against her, I stilled and felt my cock pulsing inside her tight little hole. She cried out and dug her fingers into my chest. I could feel my cum starting to coat the folds of her pussy.

After slowly pulling out of her and letting her watch every inch of my cock slide out, I pulled one of her legs into the air. "Watch my cum leak out of you," I said.

She gazed down at her pussy creamed with my cum. The cum dripped from her mound onto the ground, and her pussy quivered even more as she watched.

"Look how much of my cum you've taken today." I brushed two fingers against her inner thigh, catching my cum on them. I wanted to stuff my fingers into her mouth and tell her to suck them, but I pressed them against her entrance. "While I love to see my cum run down your thighs, Kitten"—I plunged my fingers deeper inside of her and curled them against her G-spot—"I like rubbing it into your wet little cunt better."

CHAPTER 46

ARES

After we returned to the pack house, Aurora and I showered together. I grabbed a towel, wrapped it around my waist, and stepped out of the steamy shower. Ruffles sat on the counter, licking the condensation off the mirror.

"We still need to find the person who betrayed us," I said, my thoughts lost in the limited possibilities of how Tony had found out about Mom.

Nobody in my pack talked to outsiders about Mom's death. Nobody in my pack talked to many outsiders, period. We stayed together, bonded together, hunted together. That was how we remained strong.

But someone had betrayed us, and I had to find out who.

Aurora shut the water off, hopping out after me and arching her brow at the one and only towel wrapped around my waist. Her hair was wet and plastered to her tits. "What'd you do with the other towel?"

I smirked at her. "Looks like you're going to have to walk around the house, naked."

"And have one of your warriors come in and see me?" she asked. "Fine by me."

I growled and tossed her my towel. "Go get dressed before I tear the damn towel off you and fuck you again. And this time, I won't be gentle," I warned.

She wiped the beads of water off her body and then wrapped it around her hair. "That wouldn't be a bad thing, would it?" After winking at me, she walked into the bedroom, leaving her lemony scent all over.

My wolf growled lowly, watching her hips sway from side to side. I grabbed another towel from the closet and dried myself off. Ever since she had marked me, I had this insatiable urge to fuck her whenever, wherever.

Mars might've wanted to take it somewhat slow with her, but I wanted her carrying my pups soon. I didn't want to wait. We had no reason to ... except that fucking traitorous prick who had sold us out to Aurora's old pack and Tony.

Tony could rot with the hounds for all I cared, but I needed to figure out who the fuck had told him about Mom. Only someone in this pack had that kind of information, and I'd made sure of that, so nobody could use it against me.

When I finished drying off, I walked back into the bedroom to find Aurora standing at our door in a skimpy tank-top and a pair of shorts in front of Elijah.

I growled and curled my arm around my mate to pull her out of sight from him. "What the fuck are you doing in my pack house?"

Aurora pulled a shirt over her head and placed a hand on my shoulder. "Ares, it's okay. I asked him to come over. I need to tell him about"—she paused, her eyes glistening like they had last night—"about Jeremy."

Elijah's eyes widened. "About Jeremy? What about him?"

She stepped between us and grabbed Elijah's hands. "Jeremy is ... alive."

Elijah tensed and stepped back. "Don't fuck with me like that, Aurora. It's not fucking funny. I watched him die." He shook his head and tugged on his dark facial hair. "He's not alive. He can't be."

Aurora grabbed his hands back. "I saw him. He saved me during the attack."

"Why didn't he come see me or you?" Elijah whispered.

I eyed their contact, getting agitated at how close he was to her. All my wolf wanted to do was rip them apart, take Aurora back to bed, and fuck her senseless yet again, just to make sure she knew that she was mine, but I held myself back.

"The ston—"

"Ares!" someone yelled from down the hall.

I blew a breath out of my nose and pulled on a pair of jeans.

Marcel appeared behind Elijah with his jaw clenched and his arms crossed over his chest. "I found the fucking rat."

I stepped beside Aurora and out of the room, adrenaline pumping through me. It was about time someone had found his fucking ass. I was ready to beat whoever it was to a pulp and demand to know why they had done it.

"Marcel!" Charolette shouted, stomping up the stairs. "Why did you leave—" She turned the corner, saw me, and pressed her lips together.

It was almost seven in the morning. What were Marcel and Charolette doing together?

Marcel flared his nostrils and clenched his jaw harder, not sparing her a glance.

"Who's the rat?" Aurora asked, breaking the silence.

Marcel clenched his fists. "That fuckin' rogue the warriors escorted home from Hound Territory when we brought Aurora back."

"Oh my Goddess," Aurora said quietly, her eyes widening. "That rogue is still here?" I could hear her heart racing and could feel her *hurting*. She wrapped her arms around herself, as if she was in pain. "This *is* all my fault. I can't believe it. I … this …" She stared up at me in tears. "Ares, I'm so sorry. I should've told you sooner." Her hands trembled slightly. "She's working with Tony ... or at least, she's in contact with him."

Aurora knew that this rogue was working with Tony? When? How?

"I'm sorry. It slipped my mind. So much has happened, and I ... I'm sorry. It's my fault."

I shook my head. "Still, it shouldn't matter. Liam has been watching over her since we got here. Even if she was working with Tony, she couldn't have known what had happened with my mom. Nobody in this pack tells outsiders shit."

Charolette stepped forward. "Wait, Liam is watching her?" she asked, brows furrowed together in confusion. She stood oddly close to Marcel, her shoulder brushing against his. "We went over to visit her the other day to welcome her to the pack, and he acted like he had never seen her."

It wasn't a secret that Liam had been checking up on the rogue almost every night, so why had he kept it from Charolette? He usually shared everything with her.

"That fuckin' son-of-a-bitch," Marcel said, storming down the hall.

Liam was my second-in-command and had all my trust, but he'd kept something this big from Charolette? I didn't know what it was, but it didn't feel right. Whatever the reason for Liam hiding something this big from her ... I needed to find out myself. And if he had betrayed us and told the rogue about my family, then we'd have bigger problems than him lying to my sister.

CHAPTER 47

AURORA

Marcel flung the front door open, nearly taking it off its hinges, and sprinted out into the forest.

Charolette still stood in the hallway, rocking back and forth on her heels. "No … no, this can't be happening. Why would Liam do this? He's a good guy. He's our beta."

By the mere look on her face, I could tell that she was thinking the worst. But if Ares had lied about knowing another woman and had been *checking up* on her without my knowledge, I would be thinking the worst too.

I grabbed Charolette's hand and hurried through the woods, following the hazelnut trail.

"I want more information on Jeremy." Elijah hurried right by my side. "But we have more pressing matters. The hounds didn't attack last night. They just camped out by my property. I didn't engage … but something isn't right," he said, his voice heavy with concern. "They're planning something, something terrible, and I can't figure out what it is."

Deeper into the forest, someone growled.

"Marcel," Charolette whispered and sprinted away from me.

And though she might love Liam, her heart belonged to Marcel. It always had, and it always would.

Grabbing Elijah's hand, I pulled him as fast as I could run in human form. "Did you see Tony?" I asked, brows drawn together.

There must be something more going on because it was unusual for the hounds to camp out near a pack and not attack it.

"I haven't seen him, but I heard that he was spotted with hounds."

I cursed under my breath and clenched my free hand into a fist.

What was Tony's damn problem? Why had he betrayed his own people? Had the hounds promised him something? My stomach tightened. Maybe they had promised him the Malavite Stone—the one Jeremy had.

But it still didn't make sense. Tony had always lusted over my place as alpha, but he knew about the stone in my back. If he'd wanted just the stone, he could've killed me for half of it.

What'd Tony want?

Power? The hounds were some of the most feared creatures in Sanguine Wilds.

Reputation? He had blown that the moment he ran from the hound attack.

Me? I blew a breath from my nose. Well, he had tried to protect me from the hound attack, had tried to get me back from Ares by pinning the stone on Elijah even though he knew I had it, had purposefully tried to get Ares to lose control just to show me how unstable he was.

Maybe the hounds had promised him the other half of the stone for me.

It might be the craziest thing I had come up with, but it was the only damn thing that made sense at the moment.

Charolette disappeared into a house that had its door wide open, and suddenly, Liam was thrown through the front window.

He landed with a thud on the grass, glass raining down around him, completely naked and ... hard. Elijah grabbed my hand and stopped me in the middle of the street, watching the drama unfold.

Marcel leaped through the window in his human form, stalking around Liam, who had stumbled to his feet.

"Do you know how fucking much she loves you?" Marcel shouted, the vein in his neck pulsing violently.

Charolette appeared at the front door again with Ares behind her. He had a look on his face that told me he wanted to kill, slaughter, and take Liam's head for something.

The woman rogue stepped past him, trying to button up her shirt, and Charolette lunged at her, but Ares held her back.

Oh my Goddess. Liam had been doing more than just telling pack secrets. He was cheating.

Marcel threw Liam to the ground, straddled his waist, and rained down fists on his face. Blood spewed everywhere. Bones cracked. Teeth broke. Liam tried helplessly to get Marcel off him, but Marcel refused to budge.

"Do you know how fuckin' much she does for you? And you repay her by fucking the woman you were supposed to be watching as the beta? You're a fuckin' "—punch—"no good"—punch—"piece of shit."

Liam lay lifelessly underneath Marcel.

With swollen biceps, a twitching jaw, and golden eyes, Marcel pulled him up by his throat. "You're not getting off the hook that fuckin' easily."

"Alpha Ares," a warrior said through the mind link.

I listened through the pack mind link, as this was one of the first times I could listen through it since our mating bond was complete, and hoped that there was nothing to worry about because we couldn't deal with another problem at the moment.

But I was wrong. So terribly, terribly wrong.

"There is a hound at our border. Not showing signs of aggression, but he wants entry."

My eyes widened, and I pulled Elijah toward the edge of Ares's property, knowing that it wasn't just any hound. It was Jeremy. Jeremy was back to see us, and I couldn't wait another minute to see him again.

Sprinting even faster, Elijah tried hard to keep up with me. There was some yelling behind me, coming from Charolette, Marcel, and Liam, but I ignored it, needing to get to Jeremy after all these years.

"Kitten," Ares said through the link. *"Don't engage with the hound."*

"It's Jeremy, my brother," I said back, inhaling Ares's scent behind me. *"I know it is."*

The guards stood heavily at the border, all staring at the monstrous hound with the stone in his back, who anxiously paced back and forth in the woods a few meters ahead. When Jeremy saw me, he ran over. Upon Ares's orders, guards stood in front of me to protect me, but I shoved them out of the way to get to my brother.

Pushing his snout against my nose, he looked over at Elijah and gave him the weakest smile he could muster.

Elijah stayed quiet for a few moments, brows furrowed together. "This is him?" he whispered, crouching next to me and holding out a hesitant hand.

After Jeremy pushed his snout against Elijah's hand and licked it, Jeremy looked back at me. *"Aurora,"* he said through my mind link.

I stared at him with wide, teary eyes. His voice. Jeremy's voice … it was the same. My lips trembled, and I collapsed to my knees, taking his paw in my hands and leaning my forehead against his. I hadn't heard his voice in years … I'd thought I'd never hear it again.

Out of all the things that had changed, this part of him had stayed the same. And it was my favorite part. I closed my eyes to enjoy the moment with him, remembering all the times I had heard his voice before ... when he used to sing me sweet little melodies about the Moon Goddess every night on the porch; when he helped me howl to the moon for the first time; when he told me one of Dad's family war stories the night before the hound attack.

I'd thought I had lost those memories forever, but now, we could make some more. Whether he was stuck in wolf form or not, I didn't care. I'd love him no matter the consequences or the struggles that came with him.

"How?" I asked through the mind link, brushing my fingers against the wound in his head that hadn't closed yet, guilt washing over me. *"How are you talking to me? Why didn't you talk to me at the cave? I wouldn't have hurt you."*

"The bite ..." He gazed down on the bite mark in my wrist, and then he looked back through the foggy forest again. *"I couldn't talk to you without biting you."*

Ares slowly approached us with brows furrowed together. "Aurora ..." He gazed down at Jeremy and grasped my shoulder. Though he didn't pull me away, I could tell that he was ready to.

"Ares is your mate," Jeremy said weakly, but his voice wasn't filled with disappointment, like Mom's and Dad's had been. *"I'm glad. He can protect you from what's to come."*

My chest tightened, and I had the sudden urge to cry my eyes out. Jeremy approved of Ares. Someone in my family approved of my relationship with the savage, deadly, hurting alpha. And in that moment, the rumors and my parents' approval didn't matter to me anymore. Only Jeremy's.

"You have to listen to me," Jeremy said.

I stared at him in amazement. The feeling of him being with me was something I'd never thought I'd experience again. I brushed my hand over his ratty fur, wanting to help make him look better. I'd wash out all the dirt and the dried blood, making his coat nice and shiny, help heal his wounds.

"Aurora," Jeremy said, more sternly this time, *"they're coming. You have to take the stone out of me. You—"* He looked back through the woods, as if he'd heard something, with fear that hadn't seemed to leave his face the entire time he'd been here. *"You have to hurry, Aurora. Take the stone. Use it to heal yourself. You can't let the hounds have it. You can't let them take it from you either."*

I shook my head at him. *"What are you talking about?"*

Elijah tapped me on the back. "What is he saying?"

"They're coming. There's no stopping them," Jeremy continued. *"I tried."*

"Jeremy, who? What are you talking about?" I asked, scanning the forest for any signs of life other than the birds in the trees.

Elijah started to pace back and forth next to me, rubbing his palms together, probably feeling his mate's anxiety.

"The hounds aren't what you think they are. They're more dangerous, and they're coming for everyone ... especially you." Jeremy glanced over his shoulder and into the forest. *"Aurora, we don't have time. Take the stone out of me. They were following me."*

"No," I said out loud. "It'll kill you."

Jeremy growled at me and bared his blunt teeth.

Ares stepped between us, but I pushed him away.

"Do it, Aurora," Jeremy said, whimpering and submitting to Ares.

The Jeremy I had known never submitted to anyone. He was an alpha himself, not this broken wolf before me. Whatever he had been through this past decade must've been hell.

"Don't let Tony have it or *you. He's betrayed our pack over and over, and ... and he's coming here. They all want you."*

"Let him try," I said. "I'll kill him."

Jeremy growled at me again. *"You'll die. Everyone here will die. He's coming with hounds."* He gazed back into the woods. *"Aurora, you have to do it. You have to take the stone and survive. That is my only wish for you."*

From deep in the forest, I could hear the thunderous roar of paws hitting the ground. I swallowed hard, not wanting to believe it. Why were they coming for me, and why were they coming at all?

"Jeremy, no ... there has to be another way."

Pain was written all over his face. *"I don't want to live this life anymore,"* he said, voice breaking. *"Put me out of my misery and save your new pack. Lead the people who survived the hound attack and make sure they survive the ones to come."*

The ones to come.

He'd made it sound like a war that we couldn't stop was approaching.

Tears welled up into my eyes, my heart aching more than it ever had in my entire life. Jeremy wanted to die. He didn't want this life anymore. It had been taking a toll on him, and the only thing he wanted was for me to put him out of his torture.

More branches snapped in the woods, the rumbling becoming louder. I inhaled deeply and got a whiff of Tony's putrid stench. He was here, just as Jeremy had said.

"Why? Why are they coming for me?" I asked with tears in my eyes. "For my stone?"

"For divine revenge," Jeremy said. *"Now, shift, Aurora."*

Divine revenge? What the hell did he mean, divine revenge?

"Shift!"

I pushed away all my tears and collapsed onto all fours. *Fuck the reasoning.* I would fight whoever tried to hurt Jeremy, my family, and my pack. If I could do anything, it was going to be trying to save us all.

But I needed to shift quickly. Tony was close, and I didn't have much time.

Gathering all my strength, I willed myself to shift. My bones cracked and snapped back together. Every part of my body ached. Pain shot up my legs until I could barely feel them. My arms felt like they were being stabbed over and over from the inside out.

It hurt even worse because I was forcing this shift to be quick.

I let out a piercing scream and then saw Tony sprinting in my direction through the fog. My eyes widened, and I forced myself to shift faster than I ever had. There were four hounds with him, running directly at us. Elijah shifted beside me and started to fend them off, but Tony slipped past him.

The warriors and guards around me shifted, including Ares, who stood in front of me with Jeremy. When I finally finished shifting, I looked around and realized that there weren't just four measly hounds with him. There were hundreds in the woods, surrounding Ares's pack.

Pain shot through my body as I recovered briefly from the shift, but all I could feel was adrenaline, so much fucking adrenaline. Hounds leaped in my direction, but Ares kept as many off of me as he could.

Somehow, Tony made it past Ares and easily pushed Jeremy to the side. Keeping his head low, he stared at the bare side of my neck and leaped at me. I moved my head away just enough for his teeth to sink into my shoulder instead of my neck.

"Don't resist it, Aurora," Tony said through our mind link. *"I want to help you survive."*

I thrashed from side to side, trying to shake him off me, and dug my claws into his underbelly. When he realized I wouldn't give in to him, he ripped out a chunk of my shoulder, spit it out of his mouth, and then lurched at Jeremy, who reacted too late.

Jeremy struggled to stay on all fours, but Tony took him down within moments. Seeing Jeremy so physically and emotionally weak broke my heart. He had always been the strongest person that I looked up to and had always been my rock.

Tony went straight for the back of Jeremy's neck, about to sink his teeth into it to pull out the stone. There was so much I didn't know about why he was doing this or what this divine revenge meant, but deep in my heart, I knew that I couldn't let the hounds have the stone.

So, milliseconds before Tony could rip Jeremy's spine open to get the stone, I pushed my snout under Tony's teeth and sank my canines into the back of Jeremy's neck. My wolf whimpered as Jeremy instantly relaxed under me.

My body heaved back and forth, but I didn't pull out my teeth from his neck. This was what I had to do. I couldn't let Tony take the stone, couldn't give him that kind of power.

Tony sank his teeth into the back of my neck—right where my stone was—yet he only pricked the first few layers of skin before he was ripped off me and thrown across the forest by Ares.

And even then, I didn't let go of my brother. I stayed on top of Jeremy, knowing that once I pulled my canines from his flesh—whether he had the stone still in him or not—he'd be dead.

"I'm so sorry, Jeremy," I said through the mind link, my voice cracking. My whole body felt so weak, yet I stayed strong. *"I'm so sorry for this. I'm sorry I couldn't save you all those years ago. I'm sorry that you couldn't have a good life."*

"Go back to ... cave, Aurora. Dig. Don't go alone."

"I love you with all my heart. I'll never forget you, Jeremy. Ever."

"I love you too."

And those were the last words I heard from him.

I pulled the stone out of Jeremy's neck, blood dripping from my mouth, and turned on my heel toward Ares and Tony, who were trying to rip each other apart.

That man had taken too much from me, and I was determined to take everything from him. I growled viciously at the two men, pulled Ares off him, and lurched at Tony myself. Ares had weakened him, but he was my kill.

Before he could even react, I latched my teeth into his neck and ripped out his throat. His throat fell from my mouth onto the ground, and a couple moments later, he fell with it. I collapsed next to him and crawled over to Jeremy, resting my head on his back.

It was over. It was all over.

For now.

CHAPTER 48

ARES

Aurora lay in a puddle of blood, her body struggling to shift back into her human. When she shifted back, she collapsed onto her brother's lifeless body with tears streaming down her face. The Malavite Stone lay in her open hand.

I stared at her in shock, not knowing what to do. She had just killed her own brother after years of not seeing him to keep the stone away from the hounds. It was something that even I wouldn't have had the courage or strength to do.

Elijah shifted next to Aurora, eyes glazing over to mind-link with someone. He nodded at me, as if to say that he'd protect her with his life as more hounds ran out through the forest.

They were coming.

They were coming, and again, we weren't prepared.

But unlike last time, I wouldn't let Aurora out of my sight. I'd protect her with my life because these hounds wanted the stone, and for some reason, they wanted her too.

Hundreds of beasts sprinted out from the forest, all running directly toward Aurora. I licked my lips, thirsty for blood and ready to kill. Not only were we fighting on my property now, but we were also at my home—the battlefield. I knew every tree, every hill, and every cave in this part of Sanguine Wilds. They wouldn't win.

But even without the element of surprise, the hounds were stronger than they had been last time. And I couldn't make sense of it. They were rogues. They were mayhem. They should never be this strong.

Something wasn't right with them … it never had been.

I sank my teeth and claws into as many of them as I could, trying to get rid of them before even more showed up. But they kept closing in on us.

Wolves were howling to the sky with their final breath. My pack was falling, my people dying.

Marcel let out a piercing howl and shifted almost immediately back into his human form. A hound ran right at him to kill him, but Elijah sprinted at the beast and knocked him down. Marcel swiped his claws across the hound's neck and killed him instantly.

In the distance, I heard more paws hitting the forest floor.

Fuck … fuck, there couldn't be more. We couldn't fucking die here today to these things, not before I healed Charolette and got my revenge for Mom. And Aurora … I couldn't let Aurora die either. She had been through so much … and for what? To die here and now? No. Fuck no.

Elijah's pack showed up in the woods, ready to fight these savage, ruthless beasts with us. A wall of warriors formed around me and my mate. My pack pushed the hounds deeper into the woods until they were on the outskirts of my property.

From across the forest, I locked eyes with one of the many men I had hunted for my entire life. Two scars ran diagonally across his face like an X, dragon-like tattoos covered one side of his head, and those hollow black eyes that I'd stared at when Mom was raped seemed to cut right through me.

He had almost killed Aurora the other day after I chased her into Hound Territory, but I'd refused to chase after him then and leave her alone. I couldn't lose her to the hounds too. But now that he was here ...

My Goddess had given me a second chance to kill his ass.

I growled viciously and bared my teeth at the man. The only thing I could feel was rage, rattling my insides, begging me to end his life and my misery right now. All I wanted to do was chase after him, rip out his throat, and finally feel closure for everything he had taken from me—Mom's sanity, Mom's happiness, Mom's life. She deserved to be avenged for her rape. She deserved more than fourteen years of misery in the ground. I had to kill him, to shred him to pieces with my teeth, to let rogues feast on his rotting flesh.

I wouldn't have another chance.

He wouldn't get to terrorize me anymore.

"Aurora," I said through the mind link, hoping that she'd be okay with me chasing after him.

There was pain in my heart. I was torn between chasing our life's passion and staying with our entire life. I glanced over at my mate, who was doubled over her brother. Her naked body was heaving back and forth, her head was on his chest, and tears streamed down her cheeks.

If I stayed, I might never see him again. But if I chased after him, then I might never see Aurora again. The hounds would try to kill her to get the stone. They would try to take her from me.

And nobody would take away my Aurora again.

I let out another warning growl, standing in front of my pack and killing any and all of the hounds who got past my wall of warriors. My claws dug into fur like it was fabric. My teeth latched into throat after throat, tearing them out like it was nothing. All while I watched that hound run deeper into the forest like the coward he was.

When our pack had either killed the hounds or chased them off the property, I gazed at my mate, trying so damn hard to ignore the betrayal Mom must've felt because I'd chosen my mate over revenge for her.

Completely lost in all her grief, Aurora clutched on to Jeremy's dead body. The strong and unyielding expression that she had given me the first night I met her was gone, and I could feel every ounce of her pain. I prayed to the Moon Goddess that this wouldn't break her. I didn't want her to feel the way I felt every day, and I didn't want her to feel bad about what she'd had to do.

I slowly approached her with my head down and brushed my forehead against hers, wanting her to know that I was here for her. She lifted a trembling hand and pushed me away, trying to hold back her cries.

Both Mars *and* I felt hurt, but she was the one hurting right now. It couldn't be about us. She had killed her own brother to save him from the hounds.

The stone glistened in her hand, falling from her open palm to the grass beside her. I backed away from her and stared at the Malavite Stone, the thing that had caused this whole mess. And in that moment, I made the second hardest decision of my entire life.

After what Aurora had done, if she wanted to use that stone on herself, I would let her.

I knew I could save Charolette with it, but Aurora had made a sacrifice that I would never have been able to make. She was stronger than I ever hoped to be, and she deserved to be able to shift without pain.

So, I lay on my stomach, rested my head on the bloody ground, and stared at my mate. Marcel walked up next to me and bowed his head to his luna, sitting and waiting with me. And then, one by one, the rest of the pack followed suit, bowing their heads and showing their respect.

CHAPTER 49

AURORA

Sitting around me in the fog, the pack watched me cling on to my brother and cry my damn eyes out … and I felt so weak. I'd let them fight without me. I'd let them protect me without trying to protect them. I was supposed to be their luna. I was supposed to care for them. I didn't want to be like Mom *or* Dad and let other wolves protect me, so I could lead. I wasn't better than any of these warriors.

After letting out my last few tears, I grabbed the stone, feeling its power swell in my hand, and stood on shaky legs. Instead of taking the stone back to the pack house to keep as a memory of Jeremy, I placed it at Ares's feet, unable to look him in his eyes.

When I turned around to get Jeremy, Ares shifted behind me. "Aurora, let me help you," Ares said.

"No." I scooped Jeremy's dead body into my arms, held him tightly to my chest, and walked through my pack members to Elijah and his pack, who waited on the outskirts of the forest to show their respect. Tears still streamed down my face, but I bit back my cries.

"I'm sorry," I said to Elijah, handing him Jeremy. "He was

hurting. He couldn't go on any longer." My lips trembled. "Please don't hate me like my family does. I'm sorry, Elijah."

Elijah took Jeremy in his arms, a tear falling down his cheek, but he quickly pushed it away. He took a deep breath, inhaling Jeremy's unfamiliar scent, and closed his eyes. "I could never hate you, Aurora."

My chest tightened. At least someone I had known before this whole mess didn't hate me for everything I wasn't … or was.

I grasped Elijah's elbow in my hand and leaned my forehead against his shoulder, staring down at Jeremy. "Please," I said quietly, "when you're finished mourning, take him to my father. He deserves to see Jeremy one last time."

I couldn't face Dad right now. It was too painful to even think about him. Last night, I'd told him that Jeremy was alive, but now, he was dead, and *I* had been the one to kill him.

Without looking back at the pack, I walked through the eerie forest to the pack house. Everything was silent, not even the birds chirped in the trees above. I wiped some tears from my face, walked into the house, and collapsed in bed with Ruffles. She walked around on my stomach for a few moments and then settled on my chest, rubbing her face against my cheek.

All I felt was pain. What had I done? Why had I done it? Dad was right. Maybe Ares had changed me into a cold-blooded monster. Was this who I had always been? Had I just really killed my brother?

The front door opened, and Ares shuffled through the house. He didn't call my name. He didn't make much noise. And he didn't barge into the room like I'd thought he would.

Instead, he knocked quietly on the door and said, "Aurora, can I come in?"

I pet Ruffles and gave my weakest, "Mmhmm," as a response.

The door opened, and Ares walked into the room with that stupid stone in his hand. Eyes an *unusual* delicate brown, he crouched by the bed. I sat up and kicked my feet over the edge.

Instead of meowing at me like she usually did, Ruffles hopped off me and lay by my side, her tail brushing against my back.

Ares took my hands and placed the stone in them. "This is yours," he said.

I shook my head and pushed it back to him. "No, it's Charolette's. Give it to her."

He unfolded my fingers and laid the stone on my palm. "If you want her to have it, you give it to her," he said with such finality. There was no room for argument in his voice or on his face. This wasn't a rash decision he had made … he meant this.

The stone emitted a slight white glow, its power radiating through me. I wanted to be able to shift more than anything, but I wanted Ares to be happy, and I wanted Charolette to have a chance at a long life.

My fingers curled around the stone, and eventually, I placed it on the nightstand. Ares squeezed my knees lightly and brushed his fingers across my lower lip. I stared down at him, wanting to feel something other than this pain, so I grasped his face in my hands and pressed my lips to his.

Ares tensed and pulled away. "Aurora," he said breathlessly before I kissed him again. All I wanted was to feel like myself, to be happy and to feel good. He pushed me away. "Stop, Aurora. You're hurting."

"Please, Ares …"

Desperate. I was desperate to feel good, to feel something.

When he didn't say anything, I pushed my lips back against his. The pain didn't subside like I'd hoped it would, but Ares dulled it. I pulled him onto the bed with me and wrapped my legs around his waist, tugging his hips closer to mine. He was sweaty and bloody and dirty, but I didn't care.

After one long kiss, he pulled away from me again. "Aurora, let me hold you."

"I don't want to be held." I grasped his hand and held it against my core. "I want to forget."

Forget about everything that had happened in my family.

He closed his eyes, blowing out a low, steady breath. "Kitten ..."

"Please, Ares."

After sighing one more time, he laid light yet passionate kisses down my neck, his mouth lingering by his mark. Then, his lips traveled lower and lower, down my chest and abdomen, up my thighs, right to my core.

My body stayed tense the entire time as I tried to keep everything bottled up inside of me. I clutched on to the yellow bed sheets and let my tears fall when he kissed my folds. I bit my lip to hold back the cries, knowing that if I even let out one whimper, he'd stop.

I wanted to scream. I wanted to cry out in pain. I wanted Jeremy back.

Ares maneuvered himself between my legs, letting my thighs rest on his shoulders. He peeled my folds apart with his fingers, his tongue moving back and forth against my clit. I let out another breath, this time a shaky one.

All I had left was Ares. Dad would hate me. Elijah would go back to his pack. Ares was my only family left, and he accepted me ... he always did, even when I thought I was weak. More tears slid down my cheeks, and I sucked in a breath, trying so hard not to make a sound.

When my abdomen tightened and I couldn't hold it in any longer, I let out a quiet whimper. Ares gazed up at me, but I gripped his hair to hold him down.

"Please, don't stop, Ares. Please." There was so much desperation in my voice. Hell, there was so much desperation inside of me. All I wanted to do was feel loved for a few moments. I didn't want to think. I didn't want to feel. I just wanted this.

"You're crying, Kitten," he said, words soft and almost inviting.

"Please …" My voice was quiet, and I stared down at him with tears in my eyes. "Please, Ares. You're all I want right now."

He gazed at me, brows furrowed together, and dipped his head between my legs again, reaching up to wipe the tears from my cheeks.

I curled my fingers into his hair, unable to stop the cries. "Goddess, I love you, Ares."

Alpha Ares, the infamous god of war, was the most loving man I had ever known. From standing over Jeremy and me during the fight to letting me decide what to do with the stone … he was more than those rumors. He was mine, and I was his.

To care for.

To love.

To protect.

Ares kissed back up my body, his lips pressing hard to my skin. When he reached my lips, he placed a lingering kiss on them and then rolled onto his side, cradling my head in his arms and holding my body tightly to him. "Come here, Kitten."

CHAPTER 50

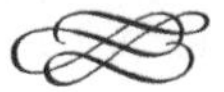

AURORA

One week had passed since I'd killed Jeremy. There hadn't been another hound attack, and the Malavite Stone had stayed where I put it—locked in my nightstand. Everything had returned back to as normal as it could get.

But I needed to do a couple things, including talk to Dad, before I could say anything was *normal*. To say that I was nervous to see him was the understatement of the damn century. Nightmares filled with Jeremy's dull and dead eyes had haunted my dreams and kept me up every night.

And since last night hadn't been any different, I hopped out of bed at five a.m., kissed Ares on the forehead, and decided that I would get it out of the way and talk to Dad. He hadn't asked to see me or to be let out of the cage either. But Ares went down there every day to make sure he was being fed well and had everything he needed.

When I reached the prison doors, the guards nodded to me and parted. I took a deep breath, walked down the creaky wooden stairs, and watched sunlight flood in from above.

Dad slept against the stone wall instead of on the mattress I'd made some of the guards bring down earlier this week. I stood there for a good ten minutes, just staring at him and wondering what the hell I was going to say to my father.

"Dad," I whispered, stepping away from the silver bars.

He grumbled to himself and moved around to get into a more comfortable position.

"Dad, it's me, Aurora."

After blinking his eyes open, he clenched his jaw. "What are you doing here?"

"I wanted to see you," I said.

"After a week, you finally want to see me?" He leaned against the wall and shook his head at me. "You should've come see me right after you killed your brother." His words sounded so vile, so hateful, so full of grief.

I pressed my lips together. I had taken everything away from him … his mate *and* his son.

"I didn't mean to kill him," I said, trying so hard to keep my voice steady. "He'd begged me to do it, so the hounds couldn't."

"Elijah had the damn courage to come down here, and you didn't." His jaw twitched. "And *that*, Aurora, is the reason your mother didn't want you to be alpha. You don't have the strength to deal with half the shit it takes to lead a pack."

I wrapped my arms around myself, feeling the tears well up in my eyes. Had I done this to him? Had I made him so hateful and so angry with me that he thought I didn't deserve to lead?

He stood to his feet and snatched some fresh bread from the only table inside the cell with him. "At first, I thought that Ares wasn't a good fit for you. But now, I see that you two are perfect for each other. You don't care who you hurt or what you take from people. You just do it without a single care in the world."

Something inside of me snapped. He could talk about me all he wanted, but he couldn't continue to disrespect Ares when he didn't have the first clue as to who he truly was.

I stepped closer to the silver bars, jaw clenched. "You want to know what?"

Dad looked over, surprised I had raised my voice to him, but I didn't care anymore.

My whole life, I had grown up in fear of Ares's pack and of Ares himself ... but I shouldn't have been. I should've been afraid of believing in these lies that people made up to *make* me fear him. I should've been terrified of Mom and Dad for believing them too.

"I'm done with everyone judging Ares based on those rumors. The whole fucking time I've been here, the only people he has killed were hounds because they attacked us," I said, feeling the anger pump through my veins. "Yes, we went to Elijah's. And, yes, Ares hurt him ... but he didn't kill any wolves. Not until Tony hurt him."

"He's ruthless," Dad said, taking a threatening step toward me.

"Did you ever think that the rumors were *just* rumors because people have seen him fight in battle, because he's relentless and he stops at nothing to make sure his pack is happy and healthy and protected?"

Dad suddenly became quiet, turned back around, and picked at the bread again. Dull light shone in through one of the small windows up above, hitting the dirty concrete below his feet.

I took a deep breath, hoping to calm myself down before I broke even more. "I'm the monster, not him. If you're going to blame anyone for all your misery, blame me because he doesn't deserve it, and I'm not going to let him feel any more hurt." The world had been too harsh to him already. "I'm the one who brought Ares and a few of his warriors to your pack, but all I wanted was to try to do some good. Hell, all I ever wanted was to help people, and that's why I wanted to be alpha."

"And who the fuck were you helping when you brought them to slaughter everyone in your mother's pack?" Dad asked, knocking the bread off the table and glaring over his shoulder at me. "Were you helping yourself?"

"I didn't think he'd kill anyone because he hadn't. Tony

provoked him," I clarified. "We didn't go there to slaughter anyone … but I was helping Charolette, Ares's sister. She has cancer. And Tony—the man *who betrayed you*—knew the hounds had the other half of the stone, which could help her." I shook my head. "The stone heals people. It healed me. It healed Jeremy."

If only I could've kept him alive …

"Your mother wanted to help her people too," Dad said. "That's why she traded you."

"That's a fucking excuse, Dad, and you know it," I snapped. "She'd groomed Tony for years. She thought I was too weak. She gave me book after book after book to get out of her hair." The pain inside of me festered until I could barely hold myself together. "She wasn't a good person. She didn't even try to protect us. Ever." I took a deep breath and finally came to terms with what had happened all those years ago. "She let Jeremy die."

Dad stormed up to the silver bars, grabbed them in his hands, and shook them. "Don't you say that about your mother."

"All I'm speaking is the truth." I stepped closer to him and stared him right in the eye to show him that I wasn't afraid or intimidated by him anymore. "She let him die, and then she did nothing to protect her pack."

"She made the underground tunnels to save the pups if there ever was another attack, Aurora. Did you forget about that?"

"That was my idea, Dad. While she was recovering from the loss of her son—*my* brother—I'm the one who came up with that idea. *I* was the one who assumed the alpha position when she was too overcome with grief. It was never her, no matter what she told everyone else." My jaw twitched. "I deserved to be alpha more than she did, more than Tony did, more than anyone in that fucking pack did."

I turned away from him, tears welling up in my eyes again. "And now, I deserve all this pain from seeing my friends and family gone." It was hard to admit, but I was strong enough to acknowledge my faults, to accept that I wasn't the best person … but damn, did I try to be.

After taking a deep breath, I decided that I was done talking to him for now. I walked to the stairs. "Don't think that your mate was an angel because she wasn't, and neither are you." And with that, I walked right out of the prison and slammed the door behind me.

I didn't know what I could've done to be a better daughter or a better alpha in their eyes. To them, I had been and I always would be weak. But I knew that I wasn't weak. I was stronger than they gave me credit for.

And if I hadn't had Ares, I never would've realized it.

CHAPTER 51

AURORA

Standing at the top of the stairs for me, Mars smiled down at me with two pretzels in his hands. I closed the front door behind me and walked up the stairs, grabbing the saltiest one from him.

"Do you have a minute?" he asked, sucking in his cheek as if he was nervous.

Mars was rarely nervous.

Something must be wrong, and, Goddess, I didn't know if I was ready for more drama. I already had so much shit to deal with; anything else might tip me right over the edge.

There was a bowl of hot cheese in the center of the table, which Ruffles was staring at from one of the kitchen chairs. Ares opened a bag of Ruffles chips for her and placed a couple at the edge of the table, so she could easily bat them off and munch on them.

He pulled out a chair for me, and I hesitantly sat, my heart racing fast. He sat next to me and stared between the table and the cheese.

"Mars?" I asked softly, needing him to just come out with it. All this silence made me feel uneasy. "What's wrong?"

"There's nothing wrong …" He paused for a long time. "I've just been thinking."

I broke the pretzel into two pieces, dipped one into the bowl, and gazed over into his soft brown eyes. "What've you been thinking about?"

"About those pups that you rescued from your mother's pack." He swallowed hard. "Finding my mom dead in the bed screwed me up, and I don't want those kids to end up like me."

My eyes widened, and I grasped his cheek from across the table, brushing my thumb over his slight stubble. "Mars, you're not screwed up. Having both you and Ares makes you … you."

"I know," he said quietly. "But it took me a long time to accept that Ares and I wouldn't ever be one again, that I'll always be like this …" He swallowed hard. "I … didn't have much of a support system after my mom died. Dad was … off in his own world. The only person I really could rely on was June, a family friend who's also a therapist in this pack."

I smiled at him. "You have me now."

He grasped my wrist and rubbed his thumb in small circles on it. "I know. But those kids don't know anyone here. I was thinking about having them over once a week to talk about what happened or … to help them adjust to their lives here. Have June come over too. Do you … think that's a good idea?"

"You want to have a support group for the pups?" I asked, running my fingers over his knuckles. My heart swelled with an abundant amount of love for this man.

The god of war cared, for not only the people he loved, but also for people he barely even knew. Those rumors didn't do him justice. He commanded the strongest pack, had the most land, and did so many things for himself … but he loved. Hard. And anyone who tried to get to know him would understand that, behind that violent man, there wasn't only hurt and damage, but also so much love.

Mars scratched the back of his head, the mere idea looking as if it was making him uncomfortable when I had said it out loud. "If you don't think it's a good idea, then we don't have to do it. I just thought—"

I placed my lips on his and pulled him into a kiss. "Of course I think it's a good idea. It just surprised me, coming from you." I cupped his chin in my hand and leaned my forehead against his. "And once I see how good you are with the pups"—I bit my lip softly and smiled—"maybe I'll give you some."

He growled and snatched my jaw. "Oh, Kitten, don't tease me like that."

"Or what?" I asked. "What is my big, bad alpha going to do about it?"

"I didn't get a chance to eat my breakfast this morning." He inched closer, grazing his nose against mine. "I'll have to take you right here on our kitchen table."

"That's *if*..."

"If what?" he asked, eyes shifting from brown to gold.

"If you can catch me, Alpha." I slipped under his arm, ran down the hallway, and was caught by the wrist, thrust against the wall, and pinned to it.

Mars stared down at me, lips curled into a smirk. "Trying to run away from me again, Kitten?" he asked. "Remember what happened last time you tried that." He stepped closer to me and ground his hips against the front of my pants. "You had my cum being pushed back up into your tight little pussy."

"I don't remember," I said with a teasing smile on my face. "Maybe you can help me remember."

He chuckled deeply in my ear, picked me up, and walked with me to our bedroom. "I'd be more than happy to do that again."

Burying his face into my neck, he bit down softly on Ares's mark, sucked the skin into his mouth, and drew his tongue over each of the tiny scars.

"Do you like when I toy with our mark?" he asked me, his stubble brushing against it.

I wrapped my legs tighter around his waist and nodded against his muscular shoulder.

With his breath warming my neck, he grabbed a fistful of my hair and pulled it back, so I looked him right in the eye. "Use your words."

"Yes, Alpha."

After growling under his breath, he tossed me onto the bed. I landed with a thump and sank into the blankets. He snatched my ankle in one of his hands, pulled me to the edge of the bed, undid my jeans, and tugged them off me.

"Spread your legs for me, Kitten, like you did the first night we met."

Heat warmed my core, and my cheeks flushed as I thought back to the first night I'd met him and the orgasm after orgasm after orgasm he had given me. I spread my legs and watched him dip his head between them, mouth immediately finding my clit.

"Do you remember how many times I made you come?" he asked, parting my folds with his fingers to give himself better access. After sliding them down my slit to my entrance, he pressed his fingers against it, making the pressure in my core rise. "Seventeen times, Kitten, and I'm ready to do it again."

He pushed his fingers inside of me, and I clenched hard on him, my back arching. Pleasure rolled through me. I grasped the bedsheets in my fists and moaned to the Moon Goddess, feeling like I could tip over the edge any minute.

"Think you still have it in you?" I asked between raspy breaths.

He curled his fingers right over my G-spot, and I came almost instantly.

"Don't sass me, Kitten. I can stay here all day and listen to those pretty moans of yours."

~

Light flooded in through the curtains, hitting every angle of Mars's face and making those godlike features come alive. The man, the myth, the wolf that the Goddess had blessed.

"This isn't over," Mars said, looking over at me from the other side of the bed with those wolfish-golden eyes of his. "The hounds will stay away for a bit longer, but we need to find a way to keep this pack safe from their attacks. They're only getting stronger."

I brushed a strand of brown hair from his face. "We should build underground tunnels to keep pups safe during attacks," I said, remembering the exact system I had come up with a decade ago. It needed improvements, but I was sure I could figure it out with the help of Elijah's pack and their intelligence. "And we need to understand the hounds. They're smarter than I thought."

"We could capture one and torture him."

My lips curled into a smirk, and I rolled onto my stomach, poking his abdomen with my finger. "No." I took a deep breath, knowing that this would sound so crazy. "We should capture him, study him, and ... pick him apart if we need to."

Mars raised a brow. "Your father was right," he said. "Ares is rubbing off on you."

"Sometimes, it's good to be a bit crazy." I hopped off the bed and tugged on his hand. "Now, get up. We have one more thing to do before we even think about preparing this pack for a hound war."

After throwing on Mars's T-shirt and tucking it into my jeans, I opened Ruffles's bedroom door. "Do you want to come with us?" I asked.

She looked at me and then toward the window, as if she was ignoring me.

"Ruffles," Mars said behind me, placing his hands on my waist.

Her head snapped in his direction, and she stood to her feet and purred. I stared at him with one brow arched. Damn, my cat loved him more than she loved me.

Mars smiled at her. "Get your hat. It's sunny outside."

"Her hat?"

Ruffles jumped off the mattress, disappeared under the bed, and came out with a tiny navy-blue hat between her teeth. She pulled it by its string all the way over to Mars, who leaned down and fastened the cap on her head.

I crossed my arms and stared at him.

"What?" he asked. "I brought her to the store yesterday, and she picked it out."

"Ruffles has you whipped." I curled my arm around his and let Ruffles lead the way to the front door.

We decided not to take the car and just walk through the forest to the cave, letting the warm sun hit our faces.

It took less than an hour, but I retraced my steps to it quite easily. The forest was quiet this morning, no signs of rogues or hounds anywhere, which didn't make me feel any safer. I knew that the worst of the hounds was yet to come.

"Jeremy told me to come here," I said when we reached the cave.

It still had that putrid stench of feces and flies flying around in the corner, but the sun was shining brightly through the trees and into the cave this morning.

I stepped inside of it and frowned. "This is where he dragged me away from the hound attack at my mom's property."

Dressed in her little sun hat, Ruffles immediately began sniffing around the perimeter of the cave and stopped in the back.

I crouched by her side and dug my claws into the dirt underneath her paws. "Do you smell something?"

Ruffles continued to sniff, and I looked back at Mars. "Like I said, before he died, Jeremy told me to come here and dig," I said.

I wasn't sure what I was digging for, but I wanted to honor his last wish. Maybe he'd had some old toy or memory here that I could dig up.

With my hands, I tossed dirt behind me into a small pile. Every inch I dug, the stench of rotting shit became more intense. I held my breath, sat on my knees, and continued, creating a larger and wider hole and hoping to find something.

Suddenly, Ruffles widened her eyes and puffed out her tail. She hissed down at the hole and hurried over to Mars, standing behind him in fear. I furrowed my brows at her, my heart rate starting to quicken.

Ruffles wasn't afraid of just anything …

Mars walked closer to me and sat on his knees, helping me, while Ruffles stayed right by the cave's exit, just to make a quick dash if anything happened. I didn't know why she was making such a big deal out of it. It seemed quiet here.

We continued to dig, our hole becoming deeper.

Sweat dripped down Mars's forehead, and he wiped it away with the back of his hand. "We should get a shovel or something." He looked over at me. "You sure your brother told you to dig in the cave?"

"I'm positive," I said, leaning over the edge of the hole.

Ruffles grabbed the back of my shirt with her teeth and tugged on it, trying to pull me back. When she realized that I wasn't going with her, she latched her teeth into Mars's forearm and pulled. He swiftly shook her off and told her that he'd play with her later.

We must've dug four feet into the ground, the hole at least three feet wide. I was just about to give up when I heard Mars's claws scratch on something. He tensed and leaned over, kicking back dirt faster than he had before.

I squinted down into the darkness, and that was when I saw it. My eyes widened. Heart-pounding, sweat forming on my neck, all my arm hairs sticking right up, I scrambled back on my hands and heels. What … what was that?. It … it couldn't be.

Mars suddenly stopped digging and stumbled back.

"Oh my Goddess …" I breathed out.

Mars stood up taller, his entire demeanor changing into Ares. Though Ares had always been so strong and so fierce, I could only see terror on his face.

"We need to leave," Ares said, grabbing my wrist in one hand and Ruffles in the other. "We need to leave right now."

And that was when I realized that Jeremy was right. The hounds weren't who we'd thought they were. They were worse. They were coming alive, and they were coming for us.

To be continued in *Catch Me, Alpha.*

Preorder the next book in the series now > https://books2read.com/u/3RKq6v

ALSO BY EMILIA ROSE

Submitting to the Alpha

Isabella is in trouble. Big trouble. She knows that opening her curtains and touching herself while her alpha watches from the woods is wrong, but she does it anyway. And she plans on doing it again. Every night, in fact, until her alpha teaches her otherwise.

Roman, alpha of the Silverclaw Pack, is tired of Isabella teasing him. Even more, he's tired of her disobeying his every command. And he knows exactly how to fix both problems. Devour every inch of her until she's begging for him at his feet.

Will Isabella succumb to Roman's advances? Or will she toy with him to the very end?

Read Submitting to the Alpha, an erotic werewolf romance, written by Emilia Rose.

Read now > https://books2read.com/u/4N9Bd6

ABOUT THE AUTHOR

Emilia Rose is a steamy paranormal romance author who lives in Pittsburgh, PA. With over 3,500 monthly subscribers on Patreon, Emilia loves creating the newest and sexiest paranormal and contemporary romances for her fans.

Join Emilia's email list for exclusive news and updates: https://www.subscribepage.com/emiliarosewriting1

Follow Emilia Rose on Patreon to read seven complete romance novels and more now: www.patreon.com/emiliarosewriting

CPSIA information can be obtained
at www.ICGtesting.com
Printed in the USA
BVHW091918240222
630016BV00004B/281